PRAISE FOR AMANDA PROWSE

'Amanda Prowse is the queen of family drama'

Daily Mail

'A deeply emotional, unputdownable read'

Red

'Heartbreaking and heartwarming in equal measure'

The Lady

'Amanda Prowse is the queen of heartbreak fiction'

The Mail Online

'Captivating, heartbreaking and superbly written'

Closer

'Uplifting and positive but you may still need a box of tissues'

Cosmopolitan

'You'll fall in love with this'

Cosmopolitan

'Powerful and emotional drama that packs a real punch'

Heat

'Warmly accessible but subtle . . . moving and inspiring'

Daily Mail

'Magical'

Now

The Day She Came Back

ALSO BY AMANDA PROWSE

Novels

Novellas

The Game
Something Quite Beautiful
A Christmas Wish
Ten Pound Ticket
Imogen's Baby
Miss Potterton's Birthday Tea

The
Day She
Came Back

AMANDA PROWSE

LAKE UNION
PUBLISHING

Text copyright © 2020 by Lionhead Media Ltd

Published by Lake Union Publishing, Seattle

www.apub.com

ISBN-13: 9781542014496
ISBN-10: 1542014492

Cover design by Ghost Design

Printed and bound by CPI Group (UK) Ltd, Croydon, CR0 4YY

This book is for everyone and everything I love in Norway – a country I adore. It is for all the incredible cities I have visited: Trondheim, Stavanger, Kristiansand, Tromsø, Bergen, and my beloved Oslo. It's for all my friends, my readers and my colleagues. Each time I visit I leave a little bit of my heart with you. With love, Mandy Xx

ONE

It was late August, and had been one of those long, lazy hazy days of summer when the sun rose slowly and lingered late into the evening. Victoria had moaned about the fierce heat, knowing full well that on chilly winter days she would give anything for a glimpse of the sun. It took all of her strength to lift a hand and swat the darned fly away from the front of her face. In this balmy clime, Rosebank, their large square red-bricked Edwardian home on the outskirts of Epsom, with its rolling Downs and only a short train ride from the hubbub of the capital, felt closer to an African savannah than the suburbs. Especially if that savannah had a Pizza Express, a Waitrose and a roaring social scene based around the horse-racing calendar. Not that Victoria's social life was roaring. The truth was it didn't even mewl.

She and her gran, Prim, had mostly spent the day lying on the wide wooden veranda that ran along the back of the house, with buttons undone, shorts rolled or skirts lifted, and with wide-brimmed hats askew on their heads in the hope of shielding their pale, freckled skin from the harsh sun. Victoria, in a familiar pose, held a book close to her face, squinting behind her sunglasses. Her long curly chestnut hair, shot through with gold, was tied loosely at the nape of her narrow neck. While Prim prayed aloud to the 'Good lord above' for a breeze.

'Does he ever actually answer your prayers, Prim?' Victoria asked, lifting her eyes briefly from the pages of her novel.

The older woman looked wistfully out over the wide bowl of the lake, which her grandparents had, by all accounts, dug out by hand, wielding shovels and two rickety wheelbarrows for a whole summer, long before the days of regulated planning permission.

'Yes, sometimes. But not always.' Prim took a slow intake of breath and pulled a handkerchief from her sleeve, as she was wont to do from time to time when her grief bubbled to the surface and caused ripples of sadness, even on a glorious day like this. 'I do miss him.'

'I know.' Victoria reached out and laid her palm over the crêpey back of Prim's hand. The old lady nodded and sniffed. Victoria now abandoned her book entirely. 'I always think how unfair it is that you lost my mum and then Grandpa.'

'Well, life isn't fair, is it? And besides, I got you, so it wasn't all bad. And now, my darling, you have finished school and are, I believe, almost fully formed, no longer precocious, but mature; an industrious coper, the very best kind of person!' Prim smiled and returned the slightly moistened handkerchief to the depths of her sleeve. 'But yes, you are right. It is monstrously unfair.' She removed her hand and flattened the double string of pearls at her neck, before adjusting the brim of her hat so it covered more of her face.

It made Victoria smile, how her gran, despite her advancing years, still wore pearls on an ordinary day and shielded her skin from the sun's glare. With her hair coiffed, her teeth sparkling and her lipstick always within reach, Prim was glamorous and beautiful – age had nothing to do with it.

Discussions about her mother were rare, and this, too, Victoria understood. If her own measurable pain was for a woman she had never known and a life she could only imagine, then how bad

2

must it be for Prim, who had had Sarah in her life for so long? *Her daughter. Her only child.* It was beyond sad that Sarah had had so little time on Earth, when her potential had been so huge. She had died during her second year at Durham, where she was studying law, shortly after meeting Marcus Jackson, who had, according to the story Victoria had been told, introduced her to the drug that would prove to be her downfall. If Sarah was rarely mentioned, then Marcus was never so, and Victoria's questioning about the pair had waned over the years, mainly because the one source of information she had was the reluctant, tight-lipped Prim. Victoria was certain that had Marcus not taken his own life before she even came into the world, Prim, after the loss of Sarah, and no doubt aided by Grandpa, would have hunted him down.

Sarah: a name, which was of course familiar to Victoria and yet was without substance, no more than an idea, a dream. Her pretty mum, whose photographs sat inside a variety of silver frames dotted around the house. There she was each night as Victoria climbed the stairs to bed, sitting on the windowsill of the half landing, smiling, captured for eternity in her glorious youth. It was one of Victoria's favourite places to sit, with the summer sun streaming in through the square bay window set high in the wall, the stained-glass panels of which cast purple, blue and yellow squares on to the honey-coloured carpet. She liked to sit there in the corner and chat to the Sarah in the photographs, hoping her mother might understand. They were of a similar age, after all.

'So there's this boy I'm quite keen on, not that he likes me, probably doesn't even know my name. He's in my chemistry set . . . in fact, I more than quite like him, I really, really like him . . .'

'It must be time for a cup of tea, darling, surely?' Prim drew her from her thoughts. Victoria stood and shook the creases from the cream linen shirt that had been doubling up as a pillow on the sun lounger, before slipping her narrow arms into it.

3

'Daks is on her way. I think we're going out, but I'll make you one before we go.' Victoria bent down and kissed her gran's forehead. 'And where you are concerned, I think we both know it's "always the right time for a cup of tea!"' She repeated her gran's favourite saying.

'Earl Grey.' Prim raised her finger.

'Gran, I have made you a million cups of tea – you think I don't know it's Earl Grey by now? I know everything about you.'

'Well, you say that and yet still you have not learned, apparently, how much I detest the word "Gran" – makes me sound ancient.'

'You only don't like it when I call you Gran in front of Gerald!' she teased. Gerald was her gran's dapper toy boy, who at seventy-four was ten years younger than her and who accompanied Prim on regular trips to the theatre and out to dinner and was a dab hand with a hoe when the need arose.

Prim wrinkled her eyes in amusement. 'Well, that might be true . . .'

'There's no "might" about it. And by the way, I hate to break it to you, but you *are* ancient.'

'Only compared to you. Good lord, eighteen! What wouldn't I give to be eighteen again!'

Victoria liked the small spread of a smile on Prim's face, as if a memory had hooked itself to the outer extremities of her eyes and mouth and lifted them up. She loved spending time like this; she'd miss her gran when she and Daksha went travelling, which was the plan for six months' time, give or take.

'What was so great about being eighteen?' Victoria asked dismissively. Based on her own rather mundane existence, eighteen was nothing special. Once, when she had complained about her rather bland, mannish face as she looked in the mirror, her gran had informed her reliably and without sentiment that all Cutter

4

women looked like potatoes until they blossomed, and suddenly one day they would look in the mirror and realise they had evolved into a chip.

In fairness, it offered little solace.

Victoria, aware of her low ranking in the Instagram-worthy world of her peers, did very little other than study and spend time with her one good friend, Daksha. In truth, life scared her – or rather, making the same mistakes as her mum scared her. Not that she voiced this, and certainly not to Prim. But it bothered her nonetheless. What *was* the thing that turned Sarah from a bookish scholar into an out-of-control junkie? And if it was something in her mother's DNA, what was to say Victoria didn't possess it too? It was a frightening thought, and as a result she had up until this point lived a rather solitary, buttoned-up existence in the shadow of the popular set. The ones who cluttered up the corridors of school, seemingly more concerned with perfecting the swing of their hair extensions and capturing the best selfie than actually getting an education. All that, however, was about to change, as she and Daksha were off to see the world! The plan was to take twelve months, but the reality was they would be away until their funds ran out, which could happen a lot sooner.

'So come on.' Victoria refashioned her hair into a bun, capturing the long tendrils that had in their usual manner worked their way loose from her hairband. 'What did you do that made eighteen so great?'

'What did I *do*?' Prim fixed her eyes on the middle distance. 'What didn't I do? I flirted with inappropriate boys, swam braless in my underslip – very daring at the time – and then danced in front of a bonfire until I dried off with a very large mimosa in one hand and a cigarette in the other. I was quite magnificent.'

It was Victoria's turn to smile. She loved the woman's lack of modesty, in every sense. Staring at her gran's profile, she took in the sharp edges of her cheekbones, which always seemed dotted with the apple-red hue of health; the thick wave of grey hair that still, despite her age, sat alluringly over one eye, giving her an almost starlet quality; the large, baguette-cut emerald that was never from her finger; and her good teeth. Yes, Victoria could imagine that Mrs Primrose Cutter-Rotherstone had indeed been magnificent.

Once she had gone full chip.

'How inappropriate, exactly?' Victoria was curious. Boys had to her always been an enigma. An alluring enigma, but an enigma nonetheless. Shaking her head, she erased the face of Flynn, the boy in her chemistry set who filled her daydreams and on occasion her night-time musings too. The chances of anything actually happening with him were slim. They had been in the same class for the best part of five years and had exchanged only six sentences, which were indelibly etched in her mind.

> Flynn: 'What did he say?'
> 'I think he said three parts water.'
>
> Flynn: 'Can I borrow your ruler?'
> 'Yes, it's in my pencil case – help yourself, I've got another one.'
>
> Flynn: 'I forgot to time it, how much longer?'
> 'Fourteen minutes.'

'Well,' Prim began, but was quickly interrupted by the front doorbell.

'Daksha!' they chimed.

'You put the kettle on, I'll get the door,' Prim instructed as she lumbered from her chair. This was how they did most things, as a team.

You wash the dishes . . . I'll dry.
You strip the bed . . . I'll pop the sheets in the machine.
You make the toast . . . I'll fetch the tea.
It was a nice way to live.

Victoria filled the kettle and popped it on to boil before rush-ing into the hallway; the cool interior of the old house was a won-derful relief for her sweat-covered skin and her eyes were glad of a break from the sun's glare.

'Come in, Daksha dear, how are you?' Her gran opened the solid oak front door wide and stood back in the square hallway, where anaglypta paper bearing an ornate fleur-de-lys pattern inside raised squares had covered the ceiling for as long as Victoria could remember. When needed, Bernard-the-handyman, as Prim referred to him, climbed up on the stepladder and pasted any edges or corners that had lifted. It was currently painted the palest shade of Indian gold.

'Good, thanks, Prim. How's Gerald?'

She knew her friend was fascinated by the blossoming love between these two very elderly people, finding it a little hard to fathom. Victoria had explained to her that they might be old, but probably felt the same on the inside as they had when they were young.

'Oh, Gerald is an absolute poppet; we are planning a trip to Wales to go on the fastest zip wire in the world – should be fun! The only thing I am dreading is having to wear a standard issue jumpsuit, so very unflattering, but I'm thinking if I go double on the pearls and put on an extra coat of red lipstick, I can counteract the horror somewhat.'

'Can you stop talking about it, please, Prim!' Victoria held up her palm, feeling a little queasy at the thought of the height and speed; conquering her fear was something she thought she might try during her trip away, maybe.

Victoria watched her friend as she stepped over the threshold and, as she always did, cast her eye over the walls crowded with paintings, samplers, decorated plates and various artworks that Prim favoured, some of which she knew had been around since Victoria's great-grandparents first bought Rosebank in 1907. She and Daksha had joked that the house and its particular fussy décor had been in and out of fashion at least ten times, proving the old adage that everything came back around eventually.

With the abundance of space and the special lake in which she often took a dip when the mood took her and the air temperature allowed, she had loved growing up here. However, the older she got, the more concerned she was about what might lurk beneath the murky surface, and she lamented the complete abandonment with which she used to jump in and swim to the middle while Prim and Grandpa clapped her on, encouraging her adventure.

She also heard the way Daksha enunciated her greeting, as if keen to revel in the privilege of being allowed to call this elderly lady by her first name, like they were mates. It made her laugh, but then Daksha did that, made her laugh, a lot; just the sight of her was enough to brighten the dullest of days.

'Are you excited about your travels? I know Victoria is, but a little worried about the money side of it, I'd say.'

'I'm not, actually,' she called from the middle of the stairs, where she now perched and buckled up the straps of her rather bulky brown leather sandals. 'I've planned really well. I even have a spreadsheet!'

'Now why doesn't that surprise me?' Daksha offered the aside to Prim, who laughed.

Victoria ignored them. 'And as long as I don't lose my job, I will be fine to leave for the great adventure in March, as planned.'

'You are disgustingly disciplined.' Daksha fired her a look from behind her heavy-framed glasses, part hidden by her blunt-cut fringe. 'I'm doing my best to save, but then shoes and shiny things seem to call to me and I can't resist. I have the willpower of a gnat.' She patted her podgy tum, as if proof were needed.

'Don't worry, dear, there's still plenty of time to save, plus I am sure that Dr Joshi wouldn't let you travel without adequate funds. He really is a wonder.'

Both girls suppressed a giggle. The high regard in which Prim held Daksha's father, who also happened to be her GP, was no secret.

'Hope so.' Daksha pulled a face at her mate. 'Although my parents aren't nearly as cool as you, Prim. There's no way they would have let me reject going to university.'

'Oh darling, I don't think I have ever been cool!' Prim's face flushed with obvious joy, despite her denial.

Victoria felt a flash of sympathy for her friend, who she knew struggled to keep her mum and dad happy; wonderful as they were, their standards were high. And notwithstanding the sometimes unattainable demands placed upon her, there was much Victoria envied about Daksha's life. She might have the upper hand academically and live with the very cool Prim, but Victoria knew she would have swapped it in a heartbeat – not Prim, of course, but the situation. How she would have loved to have the large family around her that Daksha enjoyed: a mum, a dad, two brothers, one sister and, of course, Nani, who spoke little but seemed to notice much.

It was one of her regular fantasies, to see Prim, Grandpa, Sarah and Marcus all seated at the table for Sunday lunch, swapping stories they had read in the weekend papers and laughing, laughing and laughing some more because life was so damn good! Victoria swallowed the bloom of guilt at the acknowledgement that maybe Prim was not always enough. She knew her gran was a rare being, encouraging her to use her brain and make her own way, agreeing that a fancy scroll and three years' worth of debt would not help her achieve her goals. Although what those goals were exactly was yet to be determined. But that, Prim assured her, was all part of the adventure, and she was confident that a year of travelling and stepping outside of the postcode would help Victoria find something she wanted to pursue.

'Plus,' Daksha continued, 'it's a known fact that ninety-five per cent of all CEOs of Fortune 500 companies did not go to university.'

'Is that true?' Prim queried.

'Well, it might be true.' Daksha pushed her glasses up on to the bridge of her nose, from where they had slipped.

'Ignore her, Prim; Daks does this all the time, makes stuff up and I fall for it. She says I am the most gullible person on the planet.'

'You actually are.' Daksha nodded.

'Well, I don't happen to think you are gullible, I think you are whip-smart and fair. Don't ever change, Victoria. Always be a good judge.' Prim smiled at her.

'I will try.'

'But you're going to need your wits about you for this travelling malarkey. Not everywhere is like Surrey, you know,' Prim offered grimly.

'Thank God for that, or there'd be no point in going!' Victoria let herself picture the tree-covered islands that dotted the wide Ha Long Bay in Vietnam, and the way the sun glinted from the gold-domed temple at dusk in Lucknow, India. All within reach if she continued to save every penny from her job in the coffee shop in Epsom town centre and added it to the travel fund she had been accruing since the idea was first mentioned over eighteen months ago. Prim, who had been gifted her splendid house and had been left comfortably off after the death of her husband, had offered to buy her ticket, but Victoria had noted the old lady's obvious pride when she'd declined the kind offer, preferring to save up and really earn the trip. This was her chance to spread her wings, shake off her reputation as a rather bookish introvert and to grow a new skin. Never had she felt so fired up at the prospect of anything, ever. She was determined not to fear the world beyond the walls of Rosebank, and the thought of wandering the world without time constraint or agenda was not only appealing, but also hugely romantic – and romance was something Victoria was yet to experience in any form. Was it any wonder when she was so plain?

'Where are you girls off to this afternoon? I do hope somewhere nice?' Prim tried, as ever, to keep the enquiry casual as she plucked a pear from her pocket and bit the top from the fruit, stalk and all.

'I know, Daks,' Victoria said when she saw her friend wince. 'She does that – eats the whole apple or the whole pear. It's gross!'

'It's not gross!' Prim took another mouthful. 'It's prudent and economic.'

'It's still gross.' Victoria pulled a face. 'And in answer to your question, we are off to the Ashley Centre and we might grab an iced coffee from work; I need to go and see about my hours for next week.'

'Well, have a wonderful time!' Prim spoke with a flourish of her hand, her large emerald ring glinting in the sunlight and her mouth full of pear as she headed towards the garden room and no doubt the comfort of the wicker steamer chair, which was nearly as old as Prim herself.

'Do we need anything while I'm out?' Victoria rubbed sunscreen into her pale, bare arms and popped her sunglasses on her head.

'Actually, yes.' Prim paused and rested her elegant hand on the doorframe, calling back over her shoulder. 'We need marmalade, and not the sort with the spindly orange peel I find so irritating. I like my peel to be chunky and visible, not hidden and apologetic. Oh, and if you see any, grab some of those glorious little Greek filo things that I should not be eating. The ones with honey and walnuts; what are they called, balaclavas?'

This time Victoria and Daksha both laughed loudly.

'Yes, Prim, balaclavas.'

'Well, grab me a balaclava or two.' She smiled.

'We shall do our best.' Daksha nodded.

The girls closed the gate of the front path and made their way along the lane.

'I am so glad your gran doesn't shop online. Can you imagine? She'd think she was ordering pastries and ten balaclavas would turn up!'

'She's not bad for eighty-four.' Victoria pointed out, feeling mean that they'd laughed.

'God, no! Not bad at all. I hope when I'm eighty-four I'm as switched on as she is. In fact, I want to be like Jane Fonda, all gorgeous and still sexy. I bet she's still having sex.'

'Daks, I love the way you say *still* sexy, as though we are sexy now. I think we both know that our appeal might lie elsewhere.'

'Oh, you mean like if a boy wants someone who can handle his tax return, he might call on you, Miss Maths Brain.'

'Yes, and if he is struggling with an ache or pain, he might look up your number, Dr Daksha.'

Daksha sighed. 'Well, he might have to wait a few years before I can diagnose him, particularly as I'm delaying even starting my training by coming travelling with you.'

'What's that tone? *Delaying your training?* You're desperate to travel! But it sounds like you don't want to come!' Even the thought hurt.

'Of course I do! God, you know that! It's just that sometimes I feel I have to convince Mum and Dad every single day why it's a good idea. They say yes, agree it'll be life-enhancing and then, moments later, quietly drop into the conversation something about commitment, and it feels like we're back to square one.'

'Well, luckily, you are a grown-up and can do what you want.'

Daksha snorted. 'Have you *met* my parents?'

'You know what I mean.'

Daksha ignored her. 'You know, I sometimes think I would like, just for one day, to walk in the shoes of those girls who are so sexy, so shiny, neat and perfect. The ones who just have to look at a boy and his pants fall off.'

Victoria threw her head back and laughed loudly. 'Does that actually happen?'

'You know what I mean. The way Courtney Mulholland stares at the boys and they go a bit gaga. Many's the time I have been chatting to Roscoe or Nilesh' – she mentioned two of the less shy boys in their maths set – 'waiting to go into class, and Courtney walks past, does no more than glance at them, and just like that I'm invisible! It's like she has a magic power, a superpower!'

Victoria laughed again. How she loved being with her friend. Encouraged now by her laughter, Daksha elaborated.

'I mean it, Vic. Roscoe once asked me which module I had chosen out of four we'd been given, and just as I was about to reply "Quadratic equations", Courtney appeared around the corner and his mouth fell open and so I said, "I've chosen the one on cat farts. Why is it my sister can eat a whole jarful, but I literally have one mouthful of cat fart and I shit myself?" And he just nodded and watched Courtney walk past before turning back to me and saying, "Yep, good choice . . . good choice . . ."'

Victoria sprayed her laughter. 'I am Courtney Woman!' She raised her fist over her head and placed the other hand on her narrow waist as she tried to look sultry. 'I have huge tits and I can make a man's pants fall off just by looking at him like this!' She directed a hard stare at Daksha.

'You actually look more constipated than sexy.' Her friend sighed. 'Might need to dip into that jar of cat fart – works for me.'

Victoria dropped her pose. 'As I said, I think our appeal lies elsewhere.'

'Do you think boobs help?' Daksha cupped her own blossoming bust, which rested on her equally blossoming stomach, and stared at Victoria's rather flat chest.

'I don't think they do any harm.' She pulled her shoulders forward inside her cotton vest, trying and failing to achieve a cleavage of any note. 'I think that if the situation should ever occur where we are liaising with a guy of our choice—'

'Ooh, good use of "liaising"!' Daksha interrupted, batting her lashes and feigning coy.

'Yes, if we are *liaising* with a guy, we need to do our very best to summon our inner Courtney. I mean, how hard can it be?' Victoria pictured pulling a Courtneyesque face that was both vacant yet sexy and realised it might actually be harder than she thought.

'Not hard at all! The secret is in the giggle.'

'The giggle?'

'Yes.' Daksha tutted at her friend's ignorance. 'Have you not seen the way they flick their hair and do that kind of high-pitched, silly little giggle that is doll-like and dumb?' Daksha gave a less than convincing example.

'Doll-like and dumb. I can do that. Probably.' She logged this instruction away for future reference.

'Anyway, forget that.' Daksha flapped her hand the way she did to indicate a change in topic. 'My sister is in Maisie McNamara's class.'

'So?' Victoria was missing the point.

'Flynn's sister!'

14

'Yes, I know who she is, but I told you, don't meddle!' She felt conflicted; in part she wanted to glean, if not access to the beautiful Flynn, then any information that might further fuel her fantasy of spending time with him. This boy who seemed to take life in his stride, who whistled as he walked, looking teachers in the eye and giving all manner of excuses about late work or absent assignments, which they fell for! As if they, too, were unable to resist his easy manner and unwavering gaze. It was like Flynn had life figured out. But sadly, she also greatly mistrusted Daks's sister Ananya's ability to act as go-between. Ananya, she knew, would not have to try so hard to achieve doll-like and dumb.

'I'm not meddling! As if I would!' Daksha rolled her eyes theatrically. 'But I just might have some information that you may find useful. And anyway, as I seem to recall, you said, "*Don't meddle*" as it would be too embarrassing "*while we were at school*". But in case you hadn't noticed, we have finished school. Case in point, it's the end of August and I haven't had a panic attack about the start of term.'

'Okay. Just give me the information already.' Victoria cut to the chase and stood in the lane with her hands on her waist.

'Flynn has got himself a job.'

'Is that it? So what? How is that good information?'

'I haven't finished. Jeez! He's got a job in the sports shop in town.'

'Well, we are hardly sporty!' She sniffed, while simultaneously trying to swallow the leap of joy in her throat at the prospect of sauntering casually by.

'Yes, but *he* doesn't know that!' Daksha beamed.

'I think he might. Seeing as we were in the same academic year for the whole of secondary school and neither of us made any sports team, ever.'

'How dare you!' Daksha laid her palm on her chest. 'Do I need to remind you that I was selected to throw the discus in that athletics match against Therfield! They even gave me an orange segment at half time!'

'Selected?' Victoria laughed. 'You were only there because the *actual* athletics team were competing in Leeds and they had to trawl the year looking for anyone willing. I believe you were one of the only people with your PE kit in school that day!'

'You are cruel. But this is good intelligence, Vic. It means we can swoop by whenever you need a Flynn fix. You just need to brush up on Chelsea FC – his team, apparently. Ananya thought it might be useful to know who he supports.'

'God, is this what I'm reduced to?' Victoria hid her eyes with her hands. 'I refuse to learn about a football team just to impress a boy. I don't want to be one of those girls!'

'Well, firstly, I don't believe you, and secondly, you don't have to do a thing.' Daksha beamed. 'I googled Chelsea for you. You can thank me later. They play in blue and are managed by José Mourinho.'

Victoria shook her head as the two continued their amble into town.

◆ ◆ ◆

With an iced coffee sunk, her work hours for the following week sorted and amid much laughter, the two window-shopped, idling around the clock tower and further planning their grand tour, bickering playfully over the minutiae of whether to travel by bus or boat and what to pack, both confident that the bigger issues of travelling would take care of themselves.

An hour or so later and with a jar of marmalade and a box of 'balaclava' nestling in the bottom of her book bag, Victoria stood on the high street and kissed her friend goodbye, watching as Daksha climbed into the passenger seat of her mum's navy-blue Mercedes.

'Are you sure you don't want a lift, Victoria?' Mrs Joshi called across the seats through the open window. 'I'm more than happy to swing by your house.'

Victoria was glad she was out of reach; Mrs Joshi had a habit of pinching her skin. It was, Daksha assured her, how she showed affection. This was good to know, but no matter how well intentioned, it still hurt a little.

'No, I'm fine, thank you. It's the only exercise I get at the moment and it's such a lovely evening,' she lied, the soles of her feet itching to head in the direction of a certain sports shop.

'Well, take care, don't talk to strangers and we will see you soon!' Mrs Joshi waved as she roared away from the kerb. Daksha pulled a face through the window, which of course made Victoria laugh.

Victoria made the slightest detour and found herself outside the sports shop where Flynn McNamara worked, according to Ananya. Her plan was to peek in casually, just to see if she could catch sight of his dark, dark hair or his lopsided, imperfect smile, which for some reason she could not quite fathom made her heart flip. But as she adjusted the sunglasses on her head and tucked wisps of her unruly hair behind her ears she saw him.

Oh no! Oh my God! Oh no!

She hadn't banked on actual interaction and yet there he was! Flynn was outside the shop, shifting a large 'Open' sign from the pavement nearer to the store.

Shit! Shit! Shit!

As Victoria saw it, she had two choices. She could either click her fingers, as though she had forgotten something, turn on her heel and walk back in the opposite direction, or she could take out her phone and pretend to be absorbed in something fascinating on the screen and march straight past. It was in the split second, as she was deciding which course of action might be the least embarrassing, that Flynn looked up and raised his hand in a wave. She captured the moment in her mind, knowing Prim would want every single detail.

'Hi, Victoria!'

He knows my name! I am not invisible! He actually knows my name!

'Oh,' she said, with as much surprise as she could muster, the delight she felt at hearing him speak the word 'Victoria' entirely out of proportion with the act. 'Hi, Flynn, what are you doing?'

Why did you say that, you idiot? Isn't it obvious what he's doing? Moving a great big sign from the pavement to the store. You sound like a moron!

'I work here.' He pointed at the store.

'Oh, right! I didn't know that, no one told me that at all. I had no idea. I was just walking this way home anyway, and there you were, are, were, whatever.' Again she cursed her unnatural speech, spiked through with nerves, and the feeling of her cheeks and chest flushing red.

He looked at her quizzically. 'How's your summer going?' he asked. And there it was, that fantastic, heart-flippingly glorious lopsided smile.

'Good, yes, you know, hot!' She fanned her face. 'And yours?'

'Good, yeah. Been working here, playing football, getting ready for uni.'

'Cool – oh, you're off to uni? Where are you going?'

Newcastle. Business Studies. This I know because I stalk you anonymously on Facebook. I know your mum is called Stella and works in Waitrose and your dad is Michael and works on oil rigs. I also know your birthday is the day before mine, 11 October.

'Newcastle.'

'Oh, really, Newcastle? Cool.' *For the love of God, stop saying, 'cool'! It's a word you literally never use, never!* 'And what are you studying?'

'Business Studies.'

'Oh wow! Business Studies. Brilliant. And they've got quite a football team. I mean, they're no Chelsea, but . . .' She swallowed, feeling her face flush further at the utter absurdity of the conversation and how far out of her depth she was paddling. If the shore was reason, she was already drifting towards a rip tide. She felt equally a little light-headed and thrilled by the prospect.

'I didn't know you liked football?' He cocked his head to one side as if seeing her in a different light.

'Yeah, I do. I do. I like lots of football.' She nodded in an exaggerated fashion, kicking the toe of her sandal against the hot pavement. 'I like the blues, Chelsea, who are blue, and I think Josie Macarena is doing a good job, don't you?' She swallowed.

'Mourinho?'

'Yeah, Mourinho.' She cringed, having got the name so very wrong.

'Well' – Flynn ran his fingers through his hair – 'he hasn't been at Chelsea for a while. More recently he was at Man U and now Spurs.'

'Oh! Spurs!' She raised a finger as a memory stirred. 'And Man U! They are the red ones?'

'Yep.' He nodded. 'The red ones.'

I am going to kill you, Daksha Joshi. I am actually going to kill you!

'Well, I'd better go.' Flynn lifted the sign. 'I think a few of us are going to the Derby Arms later.'

'Oh! Cool!' She wasn't sure if this was an invitation or polite conversation, but her pulse raced either way. She recognised the importance of the moment, knowing that she was either being given the chance to make all her dreams come true and spend time in the company of this gorgeous boy who had fuelled her secret fantasies for the last couple of years, or it was an opportunity to make a monumental dick of herself. It still felt surreal that he was chatting politely to her, a girl in his year. A girl who didn't even know the name of the current manager of Chelsea FC, for goodness' sake, and a girl who could not stop saying 'cool', even though she was anything but. Victoria considered what to say, how to couch it. As she opened her mouth to speak, trusting her words to be appropriate and not garbled, a voice called from behind her:

'Flynn!'

She turned to see none other than Courtney Mulholland walking at pace. She was deeply tanned, and her long legs and swingy blonde hair shone in the sun. Her teeth gleamed whiter than white, almost blue in tone, and her impressive chest was hoisted and partly exposed behind a keyhole crop top. Victoria looked down at her clunky brown sandals on the end of her pale, string-bean legs and swallowed the disappointment that nestled on her tongue.

Looking up at Flynn, she saw that his mouth had indeed fallen open a little and yes, his pants had fallen off. Well, not quite, but this wouldn't have been a surprise. This was, after all, Courtney's superpower.

Victoria raised her hand in a small wave of hello and goodbye, before taking out her phone, pretending to be absorbed in something fascinating on the screen and marching forward.

With the rocks of disappointment lining her stomach, the walk home seemed to take twice as long.

Why? Why would he look at you when there are girls like Courtney around? Did you really think you might be in with a chance? You lanky, freckly idiot! Her interior monologue sabotaged the sapling of confidence that had threatened to take root, strangling it before it had a chance to bloom.

By the time Victoria reached the lane, she was hot, thirsty and more than a little fed up. The sun had begun to sink behind the trees and she now wished she'd slung a jersey over her shoulders, the skin of which stung a little after being exposed to the sun. As she opened the wrought-iron gate, with the gravel crunching underfoot, she fished for the house key in her book bag. Remembering, as she did so, the burnished sheen to Courtney's skin and cursing her own pale, freckled exterior, wishing, as Daksha had suggested, that she could walk in the shoes of those girls who were so sexy, so shiny, neat and perfect, just for one day. And she would choose today, tonight in fact, when she would stroll into the Derby Arms, order a large mimosa, and she would be quite magnificent.

'I'm home, Prim!' Victoria called, throwing her bag down on to the floor and depositing the delicious Greek delicacies and the jar of marmalade on the countertop in the kitchen before flicking on the kettle. A cup of chamomile tea might be just the thing to help restore her equilibrium. That, or she might actually make that big fat mimosa she now had a fancy for. She gulped down a large glass of water, letting it run over her chin and soak her vest. God, it was hot. Too hot.

Fl-ynnn! She recalled the precise way that Courtney had called his name, and it was alarming how much Victoria had managed to glean from the one word. Like a sommelier able to discern a range of tastes and scents from a mere drop of plonk, she had heard much in the single word: a heady bouquet of familiarity, with undertones of assuredness and an almost undetectable hint of ownership in the aftertaste. She paused and rested her outstretched arms on the countertop, cringing at the thought of her two classmates discussing her as she'd tripped away in her chunky sandals and the vest which highlighted her non-existent bust, in sharp contrast to the two envy-inducing balloons that fought for space inside Courtney's lace bra. She knew it was going to take more than a coquettish giggle and a hair flick to make a boy like Flynn interested in a girl like her. He had mentioned the pub . . . Had there been more to that?

Don't be ridiculous, Victoria.

Clamping her eyes shut, she wished she had not taken the detour past his workplace, wished she had never been told he was there. Having quietly liked and fantasised about him for the whole of school, it was a blow to know that she had effectively ruined any chance of him taking notice of her.

Thanks a bunch, Daks. Not that it was Daksha's fault, but it felt good to have someone to blame. Maybe her gran would have top tips on how she too could be magnificent, although dancing braless in a wet slip was, she thought, a step too far!

'Prim! I'm home!' she called out.

The house was quiet, and she suspected her gran had, as was the norm, nodded off in the garden room amid the abundant ferns and the earthy scented tomato plants that grew from plastic bags lined up and stuck with canes in front of the windows. Kicking off her sandals, which had started to rub, Victoria made her way along the wide hallway, enjoying the cool feel of the woodblock flooring on her feet. She sauntered into the glass-roofed room that had been the favourite of her great-grandma, and was now her gran's. And there she was. In her favourite chair with her straw hat in her lap and the double doors open to allow the welcome breeze of dusk to carry in the sweet swell of birdsong.

'Prim . . .' she called gently, as if cooing to a baby, not wanting to wake her up, not really, but knowing that if she dozed for too long then a night's sleep would be a write-off. Victoria stopped to lift a lilac pansy that was sitting in a little blue-glazed pot on the table; its velvety petals tinged with a stunning clash of orange were beautiful. Prim had instilled in her a love of the garden and all its bounty. Some of her earliest memories were of turning the soil with a small wood-handled trowel and planting seeds that she would then watch, fascinated, as they sprouted and bloomed. It was a house full of plants, which meant that no matter how quiet the day or grey the sky, inside, life blossomed.

'Isn't nature clever? I love these little flowers.' She lifted the pot to her nose and inhaled the sweet, subtle perfume, which she always thought seemed strongest at this time of day.

'You have to smell this and then I need to tell you about the most mortifying few minutes of my life so far and yes, before you ask, they do involve a boy . . .'

Victoria turned and looked for the first time into the face of her beloved gran.

She took one, then two sharp intakes of breath, so sharp they cut her chest and threatened to suffocate her, as her breathing lost its natural rhythm and her knees turned to jelly. The potted pansy slid from her fingers and broke on the slate floor. Fragments of china mingled with the dark soil and the pale petals were now crushed, destroyed. She bent over and tried to stay upright, but with the strength gone from her core and her limbs weakened, this was not easy. Her whole body trembled and, despite the fear, the shock and the unbearable stab of loss that punctured her chest, she could not stop staring at Prim's eyes, which were open but vacant. And her mouth, almost grotesque; the good teeth, which Victoria had admired, she now learned were, in fact, dentures, and they had slipped from their anchors and rested over her blue-tinged bottom lip.

'I don't know what to do.' Victoria finally whispered into the ether, her hand clamped over her mouth. 'Please don't go, please, please don't do this to me, I've only got you. Only you . . . please, please, Gran. Please!' Sinking to the floor, she gathered the linen hem of Prim's skirt into her hands and held it to her face, letting her tears fall into its creased confines – but of course it was too late. Prim had gone to a place to which she was denied entry and she had indeed left Victoria all alone.

'I don't know what to do.' She sat back against the wall of the garden room and, as the silence threatened to overwhelm her, she reached into her pocket for her phone. Who to call? Gerald? Daksha? The redial button came to her aid.

'Daks, help me. I . . . I don't know what to do . . .'

'Vic? What's wrong? Are you okay?' Daksha spoke urgently down the line. Victoria, fixated by the sight of Prim slumped in the chair, was almost startled by her friend's voice, as if quite unaware that she had dialled her number.

Two blue lights stuttered their beams into the dusky night sky as the police officer, two paramedics and Dr Joshi filled the house with their soft-soled, slow-handed presence. From her new vantage point on the drawing room floor where she leaned against the sofa, Victoria watched them go back and forth in the hallway, talking in whispers as they gently unfurled instruments and sheets of paper from bags and cases. Their lack of urgency telling her what she already knew: that they had arrived too late. Just like her. Too late to sit with her gran when she might have needed her the most, too late to hold her hand in her final moments and offer a little comfort as she passed from this world to the next, and too late to ask what the plan was.

It can't be true. Please don't leave me! Please don't leave me on my own!

The futile thoughts circled her mind. Dr Joshi placed his hand on her shoulder. 'My wife is on her way, dear. You must come to our house.'

'I think I'll stay here,' she whispered.

Dr Joshi shook his head. 'You need company and a different environment. Plus, there is no need for you to be here for the next hour or so. I can see to things.'

What things? What . . . what does he mean? She pictured coffins and morgues.

Victoria shook her head. 'I feel sick.'

Dr Joshi nodded. 'That's to be expected. You've had a nasty shock. We need to keep you warm.' He pulled the rug from the arm of the chair in front of the fireplace and placed it over her bare legs.

'She's . . . I mean, I know she is, but is she . . .' It was hard for her to explain how, despite having discovered Prim, seen her face, felt her cooled skin beneath her fingertips, she still needed it confirming.

'Your grandmother died. Peacefully.'

'Are you absolutely sure?' she asked with the thinnest gossamer thread of hope still attaching her to the belief that somehow it was a mistake, a rehearsal for the very worst of events, a bad dream . . .

'I am sure.' His voice and gaze were steady. And just like that she saw the thread detach itself and float away, no more than a hair on the breeze: like her, unanchored and at the mercy of the elements to be cast this way and that without control or say. The very thought was terrifying. She closed her eyes and let her head fall forward, her limbs numb, her mind blank save for the thud of a heartbeat in her ears and the sound of blood rushing through her veins and her breath as loud as if she were under water.

'Victoria? Victoria?' Her name louder the second time. She looked up to see Mrs Joshi resting in front of her on her haunches. The gold thread on the sleeves of her salwar kameez seemed to sparkle and her many fine bangles clattered on her wrist as she reached out to stroke Victoria's face.

'Come on, my darling, I have come to take you home.'

'She . . . she's . . .'

'I know.' The woman nodded, stifling her own tears. 'I know.'

TWO

*Just breathe . . . just keep breathing . . . in and out . . . in and out . . .
her face . . . her face was . . .* Victoria was lost in her own interior
monologue, only vaguely aware of Daksha sitting on the wide arm
of the chair holding her hand. *I could have got home quicker if I
hadn't walked . . . If I hadn't been hanging around trying to impress
some stupid boy . . . I could have just . . . I don't remember if I made
her the cup of tea she wanted, did I do it or did I just put the kettle
on? Can't remember. I hope I did. I'm sorry, Prim . . . sorry I wasn't
with you . . .*

'What can I get you, Victoria?'

'Hmm?'

'I said, what can I get you, love?' Daksha's mum asked from the
doorway of the Joshis' neat sitting room.

Victoria jumped, in the way you might when you fall in a
dream and are about to hit the floor or when you think there is one
more step than there actually is. This, coupled with the fact that
recognising the kind lady had taken a fraction of a second longer
than it should. Her brain, fogged with shock, had quite forgotten
where she was and why.

'Nothing, thank you. I'm okay,' she lied, sitting upright in the
chair and looking at the rounded cream leather sofa where Daksha's

brothers and sister sat neatly in a row, all watching her as if she were some kind of spectacle.

'You don't look okay. You have had a very big shock, darling. Can I get you a cup of tea?' the woman coaxed. Victoria realised it was easier to accept and put a stop to the questioning, which irritated, no matter how well intentioned.

Victoria nodded. 'Thank you.'

'You must stay here tonight, love. You must stay here for as long as you need. Don't worry about a thing. Not a thing. Daksha's dad is sorting everything out at the house and you can just stay here and try and get some sleep.'

Sorting what out? What happens now? Where is she? I feel like I should be with her . . .

'I . . . I think I'd rather go home,' she whispered, unable to bear the thought of Prim, or indeed Rosebank, abandoned. This thought was immediately followed by the sinking feeling that there was only her now to protect it and that she would live there alone.

I can't do it! I can't! I don't want to!

Mrs Joshi shook her head, 'No, no, not tonight. Tomorrow maybe, but tonight you need to be here with us, not alone. Let us look after you.'

The woman walked forward and kissed her fingertips, before placing them on Victoria's cheek, something alien to her, not that she cared. She didn't care about much. Numb. Cold. Confused, and only able to see the image of Prim's face, her head tilted to one side, eyes staring . . .

'Shall we go upstairs? You can sleep in with me.' Daksha spoke softly.

Victoria stood and felt the three pairs of eyes follow her progress from the room as she silently trailed behind Daksha up the staircase of the pristine, modern house where ornaments were minimal, gadgetry excessive, art small and all surfaces painted white. It was a lovely family space and yet so very different to the homely clutter of Rosebank. She sat on the edge of the bed while Daksha pulled open a drawer and handed her a pair of pale pink cotton pyjamas. It was then that Victoria realised how cold she was; her teeth chattered and her skin goosebumped, despite the warmth of the summer night.

'It'll be okay, Vic. I promise.' Daksha palmed circles on her back as she put the pyjamas on.

'I don't think it will.' Her voice carried the croak of fatigue and sadness. 'I really don't think it will. Prim was all I had. She was . . . she was my whole family.'

Victoria saw a montage of images in her head, all of them placing her by Prim's side: in the garden planting or in the kitchen cooking supper, nattering as they seasoned a sauce or pausing to listen to something of interest on the radio. 'I love her. I love her so much. I have never had a day in my whole life that I haven't seen her. I can't imagine what that will be like.'

'She was wonderful, your gran. One in a million, but she was old and—'

Victoria fired a look at her friend that stopped her mid-speech.

'Don't tell me how it was to be expected or that she had a good innings. Please don't do that.'

Daksha nodded and pulled back the duvet, guiding her friend between the clean, crisp bed linen as if it were her who was elderly or infirm.

Victoria laid her head on the unfamiliar pillow and took comfort from the feel of her best friend, who spooned in behind her. Grateful for the silence, this was all she needed, the physical closeness, the feel of a heartbeat reassuring her that she was not alone even if she felt it. Even Daksha, who was trying her best, she knew, had no concept of what it might be like to be truly alone. For her friend to find herself in the same situation: six of her immediate

28

family members would have to die, as well as countless cousins, aunts, uncles . . . and that was before she got to great-aunts, great-uncles and second and third cousins. Victoria had only had Prim and Grandpa, and then just Prim and now no one. It was a thought that left her feeling both hollow and afraid.

I don't know what to do . . . I don't know what to think . . . I didn't think about this day, not really . . . I knew it would come, but I didn't expect it, not yet . . .

Without the energy or inclination to engage, it seemed easier to feign sleep than to acknowledge Mrs Joshi, who crept into the room bearing the cup of tea Victoria had no intention of drinking. She listened, as Daksha began to softly cry.

'Mummy! It's so sad!'

'Shh, don't cry, baby. It is sad, but don't cry.'

Victoria felt the mattress sag under Mrs Joshi's weight as she sat by their feet.

'I only saw her this afternoon.' Daksha sniffed. 'And she was the usual Prim: funny and absolutely fine. I can't believe it.'

'I know. I know. And one day, Victoria will take peace from the fact that this was her grandma's end. How wonderful to live a long and happy life without the pain of illness or the slow erosion of disease. How many people would, if they could, choose to sit in their favourite chair on a sunny day and simply go to sleep? I shall tell you, lots of people, everyone!'

'I guess, but she's all the family Vic had. She was everything. She's all alone now.'

'Well, she is not alone. She has you and she has us. And she is strong and smart. She will be fine. Of course she will.'

Victoria closed her eyes tightly as Mrs Joshi left the room. Her words, no matter how well meant and assuredly spoken, provided scant comfort right now. She pictured her wedding day, with no one in the church from her side of the family, and she thought about who might now be her next of kin in an emergency – there was no one, no one. Who would help her make decisions about the future, fill out her new passport form and help pack for her travels? Who would she eat with at Christmas? Who would she call with good news or bad? And the very worst thing, who could she ask about her mum or Marcus? There was no one.

Prim! Her heart broke as again she pictured her slumped in the chair in the garden room. It was hard to feel anything, let alone gratitude for a life well lived. And she certainly didn't feel strong or smart; in fact, she felt weak and stupid. How could she justify the fact that she had taken her time, sauntering home at her leisure and trying to catch the eye of some stupid boy while Prim . . . She again pictured her gran's face, the subtle lilt to her spine and her hands dangling, fingers limp. Why had she not jumped in the car when a lift was offered? She would have been home in less than half the time and then there was the chance that Prim would not have had to face her final moments alone. It also might have given her the opportunity to tell her gran exactly what she meant to her. But instead she had been hovering outside a sports shop talking rubbish! Trying to make Flynn McNamara notice her. And it was this hard fact that sat at the back of her throat like a sharp stick. Daksha continued to cry quietly, and Victoria thought it odd how her own tears were strangely lacking.

Victoria wished she could cry, even screwing her eyes up in a crying pose to see if that might prompt tears. It was as if she knew how she was expected to mourn but was too stunned by the situation to let her emotions flow. This, and the fact that a small part of her ridiculously kept repeating that it didn't seem real and therefore might not be true, there could have been a mistake . . . She was almost unable to think that she would never see her gran again. The facts, no matter what her eyes had witnessed, just would not gel.

The night for her was restless, her sleep fractured, until her eyes opened at dawn: her first day on a planet without Prim and one she did not want to face. The idea was no more palatable to her than it had been when she first considered it the previous day. There was a split second when she blinked at the sight of the morning sun and wondered if the whole thing had been a horrible dream, but no, the fact that she was in Daksha's bed with a twist of sadness in her gut and a feeling like grit behind her lids was proof that her nightmare was real. Plucking her phone from the floor where it lay, she called Gerald, not sure of what to say or even how to begin, but knowing she had to make the call. She cursed as it went straight to answerphone, not knowing what she should say.

'Gerald . . . it's Victoria . . . can you . . . erm . . . I will try again.' She sighed her relief, already dreading calling him later.

'You want breakfast, darling?' Mrs Joshi asked as she made her way down the stairs.

'No, thank you.'

'You need to eat.' Mrs Joshi sighed, as if food might be the answer. Victoria disagreed. The hollow, gnawing feeling in her gut was, she knew, nothing that could be filled with breakfast.

'Maybe a cup of tea.'

The relief on Mrs Joshi's face was instantaneous. It was very different to mornings at Rosebank, where she woke to the sound of Prim pottering in the kitchen, moving to the background hum of Radio 4 and predictably putting teabags into the teapot before placing marmalade on the table and setting two plates opposite each other.

'Good morning, sweetie!'

Never again. Never ever. It was unthinkable. She pictured coming down the stairs to a quiet house where no one had popped the lamps on and no one hummed as they spritzed the potted ferns on the windowsill.

◆ ◆ ◆

To a casual observer it would have looked like any other day as she walked to the front door and inhaled the scent of roses that crowded the flowerbeds. She put her key in the keyhole and looked briefly at her friend.

'It's okay.' Daksha encouraged from eyes that were a little puffy, swollen from having sobbed through the lonely, dark hours until day broke. It would be wrong to say that her friend's distress irritated her, but she certainly swallowed the urge to remind Daksha that she had the support of a large and loving family around her and that it was she, Victoria, who had been left alone. She had managed to drink the cup of tea and, from across the breakfast table, Dr Joshi had told her in hushed tones, which she suspected he reserved for speaking to patients, that it was most likely a heart attack to which Prim had succumbed. She had nodded, thinking in that moment that it didn't really matter why. What mattered was that it had happened at all. And despite overhearing Mrs Joshi's words of support, Victoria felt the new and frightening chill of loneliness wrap itself around her bones.

Her thoughts flew to her mum and she tried to imagine how very different her life might have been if Prim had not been on hand to scoop her up, feed and clothe her in the role of both mother and grandmother – a neat trick that Prim had mastered. And one that had seen Victoria safely arrived at adulthood. Just. Not that the fact that she was now eighteen in any small way alleviated the utter terror she felt at being left by herself. She wasn't ready. She was, in fact, as unprepared for the loss of her gran at eighteen as she had been at four, five, six . . . and in truth she doubted she ever would be prepared for it. The loss of her mother was sad, but the simple truth was that she had never known any different, having been in Prim's care since she was mere weeks old. Her gran had always,

always made her feel safe, but now? Victoria was alone, cut free, floating, and fearful of where she might land.

I need a bath, but first I think I'll make Prim a really good, strong coffee and arrange the baklava on a pretty floral plate, one of Granny Cutter's, and we can sit on the veranda and . . .

It was like a pick to her chest, the realisation that this was not going to happen today. Or any other day, for that matter. It was as if the news simply wouldn't sink in. She felt a strange sensation in her knees, which were suddenly cold and wobbly, her stomach jittery, heart skipping. Daksha reached up and took the key from her friend and, turning it, she pushed the door open.

The two girls stepped inside, as they had done thousands of times before, but today it was a house in a different world, a lesser world, where Prim no longer existed.

The spindle-backed wooden chair that had sat in the corner of the hallway with a needlepoint cushion propped on it for as long as she could remember had been moved to the bottom of the stairs to make way for . . . what? A stretcher? A gurney? She didn't want to know. Yet apart from the odd door that was usually closed left ajar, and the fact that the curtains in the dining room were still drawn, the house looked and smelled just the same as it always had. She didn't know why, but she had expected both to be a little different. What *was* different, however, and markedly so, was the way Rosebank felt. Quiet and still, like a thing hollowed out, scooped free of all that gave it substance. Soulless, an eggshell, a husk, a river run dry. Prim had been the energy of the house, the noise and vivacity, and without her it felt blank, like nothing; no longer a home, just a house. Her house now.

'Would you like me to make you a cup of tea?'

'God, Daks, what is it with your family and tea?'

'I don't know.' Her friend looked into the middle distance, as if reflecting on this very question. 'I think maybe we use the offer and provision of tea as a filler, a way to plug the awkward gaps when we either don't know what to say or are avoiding saying what we know we want to.'

'Which is it right now?'

'I think a combination of the two.'

'Okay then, go make the tea!' Victoria sighed, half in apology and half in exasperation. 'I'll be upstairs; I need to put something warmer on.' She rubbed the tops of her arms. She was still wearing the vest laundered by Prim's hand, the vest she was wearing when her gran had waved her off from the doorway of the garden room, only yesterday. *Yesterday.* It felt like a lifetime ago.

Pausing on the half landing, Victoria let her eyes wander over the photographs of her mother.

'Are you two together now?' She let this thought linger, as her eyes settled on her mum's smiling face, feeling a ridiculous stab of misplaced jealousy, an almost visceral reaction at the possibility that this might be the case. Throughout her life, if Prim had ever reprimanded her, Victoria would take up her favoured spot here on the landing and tell her mum all about it.

'*. . . and Gran said I had to read my book and I told her I only had to do three pages, but she made me do the whole chapter . . . I hate broccoli, Mummy, but she said I had to eat it, they look like little trees and who wants to eat a little tree?*' And later in life: '*I like this boy. Flynn, his name is Flynn . . . how can I make him notice me? What would you do, Mum? How did you attract Marcus?*'

'You've abandoned me,' she whispered. 'You have both abandoned me.' Addressing this to the photograph, thinking most unfairly of Prim, whose only crime had been to get old after dedicating her entire life to her granddaughter's well-being.

Her aim had been to avoid Prim's bedroom, two doors down from hers on the opposite side of the landing. The room in which her gran had slept every night of Victoria's childhood, first with

Grandpa, and then alone. Victoria had taken great comfort in her close proximity. It was one of six rooms on the square landing with a round, turreted bedroom in each corner, and her intention had been to walk straight past, but something told her that whilst it might be hard, leaving the task and letting her nerves simmer at the prospect might just be a darn sight harder.

She pushed the door, which opened with a creak. The small gold tassel on the key that sat in the lock swayed back and forth. The room smelled of her gran, or rather her scent – the lingering waft of Chanel No5 that had been her signature fragrance, and which Prim had applied liberally every time she walked past her dressing table; morning, noon and night.

'Darling, I can honestly say I can't smell it any more! My nose is completely blind to it!'

'Trust me, Prim, I can smell it. And so can the Maitlands at the end of the lane!'

As the story went, her beau, Victoria's grandpa – a dashing, upright, naval officer – had presented Miss Primrose Cutter with a beribboned bottle on his first trip home from sea after wooing her one summer. And that, as they say, had been that.

'How did you and Grandpa actually meet?' she had asked casually some years ago as they sat side by side in the drawing room.

'It was an introduction via Great-Granny Cutter, if you can believe that!'

'What, like an arranged marriage?' She thought of Daksha's parents, who had had just that.

'Not quite, but he was home on leave and I was invited to the Rotherstones' for tea – I now know at my mother's suggestion. And, oh my goodness, darling! He was dashing and clever. He had the ability to turn any woman all of a dither, even Granny Cutter. It was just his way, so charming. Plus, his parents went to the same church and they all vaguely knew each other – you know, Christmas Eve drinks, cricket teas, that kind of thing . . .'

It had all sounded so simple and she had wondered at the time if Flynn McNamara's parents went to church or played cricket. Not that it would have been much good if they had, as she did neither. She felt a tightening in her chest to think of that chat now, knowing there would be no more. A fact that was still unbelievable to her.

Prim's bed was, as ever, neatly made, with fastidious attention having been paid to the arrangement of the vintage lace cushions that nestled in a pile against the grape-coloured, brocade-covered headboard. They might, to the untrained eye, look haphazardly placed, but they were in fact anything but. Victoria sat on her gran's side of the bed and looked at the artful clutter on her nightstand: a silver cigarette case from back in the day, an onyx-based lamp whose gilded cherubs held up a velvet-fringed lampshade of olive green. A floral box of tissues, a tube of L'Occitane shea butter hand cream, a small leather-bound notebook for lists and suchlike, and a silver-framed photograph of Grandpa in his naval uniform.

She pictured Prim's smile, an instinctive reaction to any mention of the love of her life, the man who had stood by her side for over five decades, until cancer felled him like a sapling. Victoria thought it cruel for a man who had stood proudly on the deck of a ship, doing his bit to keep the nation safe whilst serving with the Royal Navy, figuring her rather quiet, cigar-smoking, woody-scented grandpa deserved a more dramatic, heroic death – like in a swordfight or by falling from a sturdy steed – instead of breathing his last sitting on a plastic-coated chair in the communal lounge of Brecon Lodge hospice with the *Countdown* theme playing in the background. He did, after all, have medals. Victoria was nine when he died, too young to understand how his loss depleted her little family, and yet old enough to feel the pang of grief in her gut at the absence of him. But compared to the roaring grief she felt at losing Prim, it was but a flicker. She stared at her grandpa's grainy face, recalling the way Prim spoke about the first time they met and how they had fallen in love . . .

'Well, as clichéd as it sounds, once I had met George Rotherstone, after that afternoon tea and a couple of walks over the Downs, I knew there would not be another person as important or another feeling so all-encompassing. He was all I could see, he was like the sun blocking out everything and everyone else. And handsome' – Prim had drawn breath sharply and spoken as if Victoria had asked – 'he was so very handsome, especially in his uniform. A big, noble nose and eyes that twinkled no matter what the topic under discussion, suggesting mischief was never far away. But essentially, he liked me for me: all of me, warts and all, and that kind of universal acceptance was the greatest comfort. I stopped worrying about the future. I stopped worrying about most things, actually, because I knew that with George Rotherstone by my side everything would be just fine.'

Victoria realised in that second that she was now the sole custodian of the family history, the keeper of all these memories. A responsibility she felt ill prepared for, knowing she was lacking in both detail and accuracy. She lifted the picture to study the smiling, tanned face of the young officer, and yes, if she looked closely, there might have been a certain twinkle in his eye.

'There you are. Can I come in?' Daksha hovered reverentially in the doorway, clutching two Emma Bridgewater hellebore mugs full of tea.

Victoria nodded and returned the photograph to the nightstand.

'This is such a beautiful room.' Daksha walked forward and handed her a mug of tea.

She was glad her friend appreciated her gran's taste and also how she spoke with a softened edge, aware of the fragility of her mood and the circumstances.

'I was just looking at her things. I can't begin to think she won't come in here again. I can't imagine that I won't see her. My brain won't let me understand it.'

'It doesn't seem real,' Daksha concurred. 'I keep expecting her to walk in.'

'Me too.' She looked at the door, as if expecting just that. 'It's funny, isn't it, how you get up every morning and shower and get dressed and make your bed. Then one day you do it and it's the last time ever, you just don't know it. The last time you do everything. Yesterday, Prim ate her last slice of toast, it was the last time she watered her plants, the last time she sat in her favourite spot in the garden room.'

'You were so lucky to have her, Vic.'

'I know. I think I should feel more, but I just feel empty and cold, as if everything is tamped down in my gut and there's this layer, a weight keeping it there and it muffles everything inside me, even sound.'

'I'll go and get your dressing gown.' Daksha disappeared and returned with her old grey fleece dressing gown, which had seen better days, with its baggy, misshapen pockets and bald patches on the arms where they rested on the old pine kitchen table when she read.

'Thank you.' She slipped into it and pulled it tightly around her. It helped a little. Victoria sipped her tea; it was hot and perfect. 'What was it you were thinking about saying to me when we arrived, but instead opted for the tea filler?'

Daksha sat on the small pink, button-backed boudoir chair and faced her friend. She took her time.

'I wanted to say that Prim was fine when we left yesterday. She was happy, talkative and mischievous as ever. Chatting about Gerald and eating her pear. There was nothing you could have done and nothing you should have done. But I know you, and I don't want you to worry or beat yourself up over things you might have done differently.'

Victoria took a deep breath. 'I was thinking that I should have been here with her. I could have held her hand or . . .' She didn't really know what she would have done. But the guilt sat like a fine dust on her shoulders nonetheless. 'And I can't remember if I made her the cup of Earl Grey she wanted or whether I left and she had to do it herself, and that's bothering me.'

Daksha spoke firmly, calmly. 'I don't think she would have wanted to know that everything was her last. Knowing Prim, she would have wanted a happy day in the sunshine with you, and that's exactly what she got. My mum said it was a blessing, really, to fall asleep in her chair and not to have suffered with an illness, like some.'

Victoria nodded again, not letting on that she had heard the whole exchange.

'I did think one thing, though.' Daksha bit the inside of her cheek as if unsure whether to share the thought or not.

'What?' Victoria sat up on the bed and leaned back against the pillows, resting her bare feet on the bedding.

'I don't know if I should say.' Her friend looked at her lap.

'Say it!' She clucked her impatience, wanting to feel something, and anger seemed easiest to reach.

'It's just that Prim was such a classy lady, charming and cultured.'

'Yes, she was.' Victoria ran her fingers over the exquisite ivory counterpane.

'And I bet she would be mortified over her last words.'

'Her last words?' Victoria wrinkled her brow.

'Yes, I think Prim might have imagined a refined exit – you know the way she used to wave her hand or adjust her beads or pat her hair, I think she might have liked to have done something like that and said simply, "Adieu, darlings!"'

'I guess . . .' Victoria felt a small smile play on her lips as she pictured just this.

'But instead . . .' Daksha paused. 'The last thing she said to you was, "*Grab me a balaclava or two!*"' The laughter bubbled from her friend's mouth, and Victoria followed suit. It was quite hilarious, Daksha was right. Her glamorous, elegant grandma had shouted, '*Grab me a balaclava or two!*' Hardly the most delicate of phrases or topics. Victoria placed her hand over her mouth to stifle the giggle, which felt illicit. Her laughter found a way to squeeze past the weight that filled her gut, burbling from deep inside until she was bent double, and it was only when rendered quite weak with something close to hysteria that her tears came. Finally. And once she started crying, it felt like she might never stop.

Daksha rushed forward and took the mug of tea from her hand before placing it on the nightstand. She then wrapped her friend in a hug, and there they sat on Prim's bed, enveloped in the smell of her perfume, with chins resting on each other's shoulders, as Victoria sobbed until she could barely take a breath and Daksha whispered, 'Shh . . .' in the way a mother might do. Although this Victoria could only guess at, as her mother had injected heroin into her veins and left the Earth without so much as an 'adieu!' before Victoria had even got the chance to know her. And yet, strangely, today she missed her more than ever.

The sound of the front doorbell jolted them apart.

'I'll go.' Daksha jumped up and thundered down the stairs. Victoria blew her nose and wiped her eyes, before her friend hollered up the stairs, 'Vic! Gerald is here!'

Of course.

She hadn't considered what this meeting with Prim's boyfriend would be like, hadn't really thought about how others might be grieving, and she had never seen Gerald without Prim in touching distance. She didn't like the thought of it; more proof, as if that were needed, of how her world had changed. Painting on the best smile she could manage, Victoria gripped the bannister, wary of her wobbly knees and shaky legs as she trod the stairs. There was something about the sight of the impeccably groomed Gerald, the side part to his grey hair and the stiff crease to the front of his slacks, that tore at her heart. At first glance, he looked as he always did, dressed to impress the woman he wooed, but there was something slightly altered about him: he looked a little stooped, a little gaunt. And in truth she found his grief a comfort, to know that someone shared her loss, the thing that united them. Victoria knew she needed all the allies she could find.

'Oh, Victoria!' He attempted a tight-lipped smile, in defiance of the sadness that misted his eyes. 'How are you?'

She shrugged. 'I'm not sure. I feel like the world is spinning.'

He looked at her knowingly 'I don't want to keep you or intrude, but I heard the terrible news from Joan at the Over Sixties Club. And then I saw I had a missed call from you and heard your message. I guess that's why you were calling?'

She nodded.

'I can't believe it.' He paused. 'I just wanted to come and say . . .' He paused, and his sadness was hard to witness. 'That the world – my world certainly – is less bright today, less fun.'

'Thank you, Gerald.' She barely knew what to say, but understood completely, as her world too was going to be less bright, quieter.

'I got a card.' He handed her a small, pale blue envelope. 'None of them were appropriate, they were all maudlin and embossed in gold; Prim would have hated them all. I settled on a scene of the Lake District, which was left blank for my own message – I thought it was the least worst.'

'Thank you,' she repeated.

Daksha looked on. 'Would you like a cup of tea or something, Gerald?'

'No, no dear.' He shook his head and raised his hand. 'I need to get on, and I am sure you two need nothing less than visitors right now.'

Victoria did nothing to correct him, watching as he made for the door.

'I am so very sad. I was extremely fond of her.' He spoke over his shoulder.

'I know she was very fond of you too.' Victoria wasn't sure if it was her place to speak this way to the older man but thought it important to say so. She felt his beaming smile more than justified her forwardness.

He closed his eyes briefly. 'She made me laugh, always coming up with some rather bonkers scheme or idea; I never knew what she was going to suggest next,' he smiled.

'Like your zip-wire trip?' she remembered.

'Like our zip-wire trip,' he confirmed. 'Not that we would have actually done it, but part of the fun was talking about zip wires or shark diving in South Africa or going to a full-moon party in Thailand – those discussions kept us young! We lived the adventures through our chat and I shall miss them very, very much.' He bowed his head.

'See you soon, Gerald. And thank you.' She held the envelope to her chest, knowing that she too was going to miss Prim's wonderful ability to plant a picture in her mind, whilst encouraging her to go and see the world!

'Let me know if there is anything I can do, and when the funeral is, of course.' He spoke matter-of-factly as he left. His words were like bolts, fired casually yet pinning her to the reality of the situation.

A funeral! I have to organise a funeral! And not just any funeral, but Prim's . . . I need to call her solicitor too. Who is it? I know she told me . . . I don't know what to do, as the person I would usually ask for the details is Prim . . .

'I need to organise the funeral. Can you help me?'

Daksha squeezed her arm. 'Of course I will. Don't worry about that right now. Would you like a cup of—'

'Don't. Even.' Victoria held up her hand, cutting her off mid-question.

In the rather grand drawing room she sat back on the pale green dupioni-covered sofa, pulling the pink, cobweb-wool blanket from the arm and placing it over her legs. She thought of all the incredible and extraordinary things that Gerald would miss about Prim, but for her it was quite the opposite: she was already missing the very ordinary things. The bustle as she dusted, her scent lingering in the hallway and the sound of her warbling alto shattering the peace of any day. This recollection alone was enough to invite a fresh batch of hot tears.

Having wiped her fingers down the front of her dressing gown, she peeled the sticky flap of the envelope, pulled out the rather dull card and read:

> Victoria,
> What a rotten gap there now is in the world.
>   Gerald

It made her smile, the utterly perfect summary of the situation. Victoria read it twice before letting out an almost primal yell. She wasn't fully aware of how loudly she had shouted, but Daksha came running in.

'What's the matter? Are you okay?' She dropped to the floor at the side of the sofa and placed her hands on Victoria's knees.

'I can't stand it! I miss her, Daks! I need her here. I don't have anyone else. I'm all on my own!'

'I know. I know.' Her friend patted her back and kissed her head. 'It will get easier, I promise.'

'I have never done anything without her; she has been there every day of my life when I wake up and when I go to sleep, and I don't know what I'm supposed to do without her!'

'You've got me. And right now you should come to the kitchen. I am eating all the ice cream.'

Victoria managed a small laugh, grateful as ever for the presence of her friend.

'I can't stand it. I can't stand the thought of not seeing her again.' She howled again, until her voice fell silent. 'Sorry, Daks, not quite sure where that came from.'

'It's good to let it out.'

Victoria laughed a little at the banality of her condolence. 'Will you come to see the solicitor with me and help me organise the funeral?'

'Yes, you already asked me that, honey.'

'I did?' Victoria's thoughts were foggy.

'You did, and you know I will, and Mum said she'd help too – whatever you need. You know that. Anything.'

'I could do with a cup of tea.' She smiled at her friend, who leapt up to go and pop the kettle on.

THREE

Mr Dobson's name was engraved on a brass plaque outside the solicitor's office, which Victoria entered with caution. Their meeting was calm and business-like and an entirely new experience for the teen. Typically, Prim had set out her wishes for her funeral and left the monies in a separate fund. The solicitor was kind and respectful when delivering her gran's instructions and pointing Victoria in the right direction. She was grateful at least that, with Mr Dobson in her corner, she knew she wouldn't have to worry about the paperwork, small print and all the other horrible and complex aspects of life's administration to which she was less than accustomed yet which had now been thrust upon her.

He had been explicit and formal when informing her of the contents of her gran's will, confirming what Prim had told her on several occasions in passing, that Rosebank, all of its contents, all money and investments et cetera were to go to her. She nodded, knowing his voice was going into detail, but try as she might, she drifted in and out of concentration. *I can't believe this is happening to me . . .* Not that she could even think about money right now, but when she did, strangely, the strongest feeling was not one of joy or even relief but instead worry at the weight of the responsibility that came from being in such a position. How would she manage a house the size of Rosebank all alone? It was an odd feeling, knowing she could sell the house or paint it purple or fill it with fairy lights – anything. She had been saving like crazy to enable her travels, but now? She supposed that ample funds were just sitting in an account, not that it meant anything; the desire to travel and have fun had left her on the day Prim passed away.

Victoria lay in the bath and let the now tepid water lap her skin. She had washed her hair and scrubbed her face, and that had taken all her energy. There was even a fleeting thought that she might just stay hiding here and let the day take its natural course; after all, who would care? It wasn't as if she needed to be there to support anyone else; she was the only one who needed supporting and the deep water in the safety of the bathroom was doing that just fine. She sat up, knowing how disapproving Gerald would be if she hid the day away and in turn how much that would bother Prim. The glass shelf above the wide pedestal sink groaned under the weight of her gran's jars and bottles. Chanel No5, of course, but also Guerlain body lotion, lily-of-the-valley- scented talcum powder and a glass-lidded jar that at first glance looked like it might contain sweets but was in fact stuffed with cotton wool balls in the colours of sugared almonds. She thought now that she had never seen the contents depleted or restored.

'When am I supposed to throw your things away? Do I *have* to? Is it weird to live with them from now on? I don't know the rules, and I don't know who to ask. I don't even know what to wear today.' She spoke aloud, thinking of her mum's old bedroom, that was such in name only and no longer contained any of her things. Victoria had spent a little bit of time in there, more so when she was younger, hoping to glean a sense of the woman. Prim would always snap at her to get out, which would be followed by an inevitable bout of tears; this Victoria more than understood – not only did Prim not like snapping at her, but she supposed that, like her, her gran pretended Sarah was behind the door and to have the door opened only confirmed her very worst fears.

It was a solitary room with an unmade bed and old curtains, and it felt sad, as if it carried the knowledge of loss in its very fabric. The thought of removing the everyday objects that made this house their home was horrible. 'I don't want to go today, Prim. I don't want to walk into that church and I don't want to see your coffin. I don't want to say goodbye to you. I'm not ready. I miss you and I miss my mum and I miss my dad and I miss Grandpa – I miss you all, so, so much.' Lying back in the water once more, she closed her eyes and let her tears fall, hoping that they might run out before she got to the church; the prospect of crying like this in public was not one she relished.

◆　◆　◆

Victoria sniffed and smiled as she climbed from the back seat of the Joshis' blue Mercedes.

'Okay, love?' Mrs Joshi placed a hand in the small of her back as they walked up the path to the wide church door.

Victoria nodded.

The church was half empty. Daksha had reminded her when they studied the rather frugal invitation list, scribbled at the kitchen table, that when you got to Prim's age, many of the people who would happily have graced your funeral – family, friends, colleagues and acquaintances – had themselves died. This fact offered some small solace that, whilst her gran's funeral might be sparsely attended, she had beaten a lot of them by surviving longer.

Victoria knew without a doubt that Prim would rather have had those extra years than crowded pews. But this too made her think about her own situation. She was not old, and yet, were she to die, apart from Daksha, who would mourn her? There were no parents, no grandparents, no siblings or cousins. It felt as if she were alone in the universe. Looking up at the ornate ceiling of the church, she wished things were different and tried to swallow the sob that had built in her chest, this time not for her loss, but for all that was missing in her life. It felt indulgent and misplaced and she bit the inside of her cheek to suppress it.

Gerald looked bereft, poor thing, but still dapper in his navy suit and waistcoat. Mr Maitland, who lived at the end of their lane, supported him physically. He had cried when he saw Victoria and it pulled at her heart.

A silver urn sat centrally on the altar and held the most stunning display of flowers. Her request had been simple: to include all the colours she knew Prim would adore. The arrangement was a credit to Sandie's florist, and everyone commented on the variety of pinks and pale blues, the pastel shades of sweet pea and the dark purples and violets, all run through with frothy greenery and gypsophila. The flowers were, if anything, celebratory and not in the least bit maudlin, perfect for a woman who had so loved her garden and perfect for this blue-sky day, which even if she hadn't known it, Victoria had been dreading her whole life.

It was comforting to have Daksha, Dr and Mrs Joshi in the pew next to her; she was aware that, without them, she would have been entirely alone. Victoria couldn't help but mentally fast-forward and wonder how her life would be now. *What happens tomorrow? Where do I fit? How do I live?*

Mrs Joshi blotted at her eyes and nose with a handkerchief and, every so often, when able, she would reach over and squeeze Victoria's arm, one time with quite a pinch, which in any other circumstances would have resulted in a yelp. But as Victoria reminded herself, these gestures were offered in affection.

Daksha, aware of her mother's antics, rolled her eyes and sucked in her cheeks, able to lift Victoria's spirits a little even on this, the very worst of days. Victoria listened to Jim Melrose, the vicar, with his bald head and abundance of facial hair, which stuck out like little grey brush heads, tufting from his ears, nose and resting above his eyes like giant caterpillars, as he gave his dawdling speech on the wonderful life of Mrs Primrose Cutter-Rotherstone, and, in truth, she more than struggled to connect Prim with the woman he described.

'A wonderful woman! A pillar of the community!'

Victoria smiled inwardly, knowing that whilst her gran had indeed been a wonderful woman, she had never had time for the petty politics and antics of the various committees that sought her patronage. Everyone from Neighbourhood Watch to the Epsom in Bloom Society coveted her intelligent, frank and fearless input. Prim, however, politely declined them all and did so with such grace and that practised flourish of her hand that offence was never taken.

Gerald spoke beautifully, offering a more recognisable version of her gran.

'Prim was a person for whom age wasn't even a number – it was an inconvenience. She loved gin and dancing and staying up late to play cards and talk rubbish, keen to sit in the garden in all weathers and greet the first light.' He paused to smile, as if recalling these exact moments with the woman he had been so fond of . . .

Victoria let her gaze wander over the congregation, trying to remember the saying that was something to do with how you could judge a person by the company they kept. Well, whoever came up with that had clearly never met Prim! With the exception of the Joshi family, there wasn't a head present that wasn't grey. The men were jowly and slack-jawed, a little crooked, and they walked slowly, leaning on whatever they could grab en route to remain

49

upright, whether it be a pew or the arm of the person closest. The women uniformly had bloated ankles, gripped sticks and were clad in polyester – black mostly, apart from one older lady who was resplendent, head to toe, in lemon. All wore flat, sensible shoes that Prim would have deemed so ugly she would not have worn them to tend the garden. These people were old! So old! Victoria wondered what they might possibly have had in common with her gran. Prim was nothing like them; she was, in fact, the opposite of them: young and active, busy and fast!

Her eyes fell upon the glossy, blonde-wood coffin with the brass handles and a lump formed in her throat as a fresh batch of tears sprang.

Maybe you were like these people, Prim. Maybe you were a little bowed, a little frail, and I just couldn't see it, or maybe I didn't want to see it . . . To me you were and always will be magnificent! I hope that if there is a heaven, you and Sarah and Marcus have made up, maybe you will all sit around a dinner table together with Grandpa . . . and I have to admit that I envy you and I wonder if I might prefer to be with all of you than here, by myself. I am scared. I am so scared. And I love you and right now I don't know how I am going to put one foot in front of the other and make it out of this church. I feel lonely, even here among all of these people.

The congregation made a slow procession along the path to the church gates, where the vicar stood and gave each person a two-handed clasp in lieu of a shake. When it was her turn, Victoria thought it felt a little possessive for a stranger and it did nothing to ease her discomfort.

'Primrose was a wonderful woman. I met her quite a few times over the years at various concerts, Christmas services and so on, and of course when we laid your grandpa to rest. She was a real tour de force. I was a little terrified of her, truth be told!' He whispered the last from the side of his mouth. 'But mostly I found her to be terrific fun!'

'She was.' It still felt alien to be talking about her in the past tense. 'And thank you for today.'

'My absolute pleasure, and you know where we are if you want a chat or need an ear. My wife makes a passable lemon drizzle and it goes very well with a cup of tea; just the ticket when the world can feel a bit too big.'

'Thank you.' *There we are again with the tea . . .* She eased her hand from his, genuinely touched by his offer.

As she climbed into the back seat of Dr Joshi's car she noticed for the first time a woman with short, dark hair hovering to the side of the path. She was wearing a long, black coat, despite the warmth of the day, a coat more suited to winter, she thought. Bernard-the-handyman was standing to the side of her and he reached out and touched the woman's arm tenderly. Victoria wondered if it was his wife or daughter, neither of whom she had met. She smiled at them in a way that she hoped conveyed her gratitude for making the effort. Bernard raised his hand and then looked to the floor. She was touched at how affected he was and knew Prim would have been too.

Mrs Joshi reached back between the front seats of the plush car and squeezed her leg, hard.

'You are doing your grandma proud, Victoria. You really are. I think that is the hardest bit over.'

Victoria wasn't sure this was true, fearing that actually the hardest bit was yet to come. The bit where everyone's lives got back to normal – Prim *was* her everyday, her normal, so where did that leave her? She felt a shiver along her limbs at the prospect, but smiled at Daksha's mum, and rubbed her thigh where she could still feel the throb of her grip.

Despite the house having so many visitors, it was oddly quiet, quieter than the church had been. She considered putting some music on but was unsure of the right thing to do. Plus, she didn't think the mourners would necessarily appreciate her playlist and she didn't want to hear Prim's music; her gran's taste had been eclectic – everything from Sarah Vaughan to Simply Red – but today, to surround herself with the sounds she could only associate with the woman she had lost would, she knew, be too much. She wished at some level that a party *had* broken out, giving her licence to drink too much and dance and cry until her feet ached and her body collapsed in the kind of sleep that had proved elusive in the two weeks since Prim's death. No such luck. The elderly guests gathered in huddles, ate slowly and sparingly, and spoke at an irritatingly low volume that sounded like the collective hum of pensioner bees.

She spied Gerald sitting alone in the garden room in the very chair where Prim had taken her last breath. Try as she might, her gran's empty face was all she could see when she looked into the room, and since that horrible day she had avoided coming in here unless it was absolutely necessary. And to comfort Gerald, who cut a lonely figure, did indeed seem absolutely necessary. He was, after all, the only other person on the planet who might be mourning her gran in the way she was; the irony wasn't lost on her that he was no more than Prim's acquaintance and could easily disappear from her life altogether. She truly hoped not, knowing she would need as many people in her corner as she could garner. The cloak of loneliness was only ever a heartbeat away and, it seemed, was always ready to wrap itself around her slender shoulders.

'How are you, Gerald? Are you doing okay?' she asked softly, bending down and resting on her haunches by the side of the chair. She looked at his liver-spotted hand lying casually along the rounded cane arm and realised it would be on top of where Prim had rested hers. Very much like they were holding hands across the great divide. It brought a lump to her throat.

'Not really, dear.' He acknowledged her, his gaze far off. 'You know, it doesn't matter how many people you lose, it never, ever gets any easier. It's not something you can condition yourself against. You'd think it might be, wouldn't you? But no. Each loss is unique and each has a new and distinct level of pain, like a layer of paint coming off that leaves you feeling a little raw, exposed.'

'Yes.' Not that she could relate, not really, having never known her mum and having lost her grandpa when she was too little to fully understand the impact.

'I shouldn't be so selfish; yes, I will miss her, but I know that my loss pales in comparison to your own.' He looked up at her. 'She did a good job of raising you to be strong and independent, despite your start in life, and this, I suppose, is when it will be tested. So my question is: how are *you*, Victoria?'

She tried her best to phrase it. 'I'm a bit lost, really. I've been busy planning today and sorting stuff out, and that's kept me occupied, but honestly? None of it feels real.'

He nodded. 'I know that feeling. I keep checking my phone to see if I have a text from her. She used to keep me informed on everything from the weather to what birds she'd seen in the garden or what show was coming to the Playhouse. I shall miss that. But most of all I shall miss her noise.'

'Her noise?'

'Yes, she was so very loud! So full of life – listen to that lot in the drawing room and hallway.' He cast his eyes in their direction. 'At least twenty of them, but no one making a peep! That's what old people do, they go quiet, apologising for their presence, as if they have outstayed their welcome on the planet, aware of the inconvenience of their existence. But not Primrose – she was loud, vivacious and wonderful!'

'She was. I was thinking, Gerald . . .' She drew breath. 'You will still come and visit, won't you?' Victoria realised in that instant that, should he stop, she would miss not only his visits but also one of the last links to Prim. 'I would . . . I would like to still see you. I'd like it very much,' she whispered, unable to stop the latest trickle of tears.

I don't have anyone else, Gerald! I don't have anyone that loved Prim, only me!

'You try stopping me.' He winked at her. 'I think someone is going to have to take these tomato plants in hand.'

'I think that person is you, Gerald.' She smiled fondly at him and wiped her eyes.

'Yes, yes of course!' He beamed.

Victoria wandered towards the kitchen, nodding at the group on the sofa, who offered tight-lipped smiles of condolence. Gerald was right: apologetic. It all felt completely different from the last wake she had attended in this very house. She recalled summer at the age of nine, when her grandpa had passed away, an event that Prim did her best to shield her from, dressing her in a pink pinafore, white lace tights and her silver ballroom shoes; no sombre colours for her. And when everyone had left, rather than set about clearing the plates of sandwich crusts and quiche crumbs or ferrying the glassware into the kitchen to swill the contents down the sink, Prim had instead put The Supremes on the stereo and they had danced and twirled to 'You Can't Hurry Love'. Victoria had gone to bed feeling like she had had an adventure or been to a party, and not remotely sad. The sound of Prim's crying later had therefore shocked her, the dull moan of a sound floating along the landing and under her bedroom door. This was what Prim did: no matter her own thoughts, she always made Victoria feel safe and secure.

What am I going to do without you?

Mrs Joshi kindly handed around food, refreshed drinks and stopped only to squeeze Victoria's arm or run her hand over her hair. She felt lucky to have the Joshis on hand. Daksha was quiet, unconfident, she knew, in being able to strike the right balance between consolatory and comical, with a tendency to make inappropriate comments that at anyone else's wake would have been funny. Not that Victoria was complaining. Daksha had stayed with her at the house every night for the past two weeks, making the obligatory cups of tea when needed and pulling tissues from a family-sized box like a magician pulls scarves from his sleeve, as and when her tears just wouldn't stop. The thought of Daksha returning home and leaving her in this big old house all alone was enough to make the breath catch in her throat. She found it easier not to think about it.

It was odd but unsurprising that all the things that usually occupied their conversations, topics as diverse as Flynn McNamara, the best way to island-hop in Greece, and Brexit, were pushed to the background, irrelevancies now in the wake of the loss that consumed Victoria. But in recent days, as night closed in, they had spoken of Prim, sharing memories of her, and yesterday, as dawn raised its golden head over the rooftops of this leafy corner of Surrey, Daksha asked what she might do with this big house and all the stuff in it.

'Live in it,' she'd replied, barely able to disguise her astonishment at the question. *What else would I do? Where else would I live?* Still unwilling to admit that, whilst she loved the place, the thought of living here all alone was a little terrifying. Not because she feared crime or even the running of the house and all that it required, but because she knew that, with all those empty rooms echoing to the tune of lives long gone, there was a very real risk that loneliness and the ghosts which lurked might swallow her whole.

Victoria had naively envisaged a future where she would work and hopefully fall in love but would always, always live under the roof of her family home, knowing that the older Prim got, the more care she would require, and it was care she was more than willing to give. In some ways it would be payback, but a joyous payback for how Prim had loved her unconditionally when there were no other takers.

Victoria wandered into the kitchen, thinking she may drink some wine to see if that might make the afternoon pass a little quicker. As she reached into the fridge where the chilled bottles hid, she saw a tall, slender figure in the garden, standing by the edge of the lake. It was the woman in the dark coat. The woman from the church. But Bernard, she knew, had already left.

'How very odd.'

She watched her from the window, wondering why she had not come inside with the rest of the mourners. The woman stood still and stared into the murky depths of the water, her hands pushed deep into her coat pockets.

Victoria opened the back door and walked slowly across the grass, calling as she did so, wary of disturbing the woman, and also more than curious as to why she was standing in the garden. Who was she if not a relative of Bernard's? A cousin on Granny Cutter's side? Someone from the library? Or maybe she was the carer of one of the infirm currently sipping sherry and nibbling on smoked-salmon sandwiches in the drawing room.

'Hello?' Victoria called as she approached, lifting her hand in greeting when the woman turned towards her. There was something about her that was familiar, something that she couldn't place, but she supposed that they must have met before. Maybe it *was* the library, this being one of the places she and Prim ventured together.

The woman turned and opened her mouth. Her lips moved, but no words came. Victoria was mortified to see the big, fat tears trickle down her cheeks and was equally moved by her sadness.

'Oh! Please don't cry. I understand, I do. Prim really was amazing. In truth, I'm just waiting for everyone to leave so I can sit in the bath and have a good cry myself. I don't think it's quite sunk in yet. I keep expecting her to walk in through the door. I don't know if that feeling ever really goes away.' She reached into her pocket and pulled out two squares of kitchen roll, which she divided, handing one to the woman, who took it into her hands like it was a precious thing and nodded as she wiped her red nose and leaky eyes.

'Thank you so much for coming. I'm Victoria.' She touched her fingertips to her chest. 'I saw you in the churchyard and I wanted to say hello.'

'Victoria.' The woman breathed the word, her face crumpled and her tears fell harder.

'Please don't cry,' Victoria repeated, placing a hand on the woman's forearm. Rather awkwardly, the woman put her hand over hers, holding it tightly. It was not only an odd sensation to see someone, a stranger, so affected by the death of her beloved grandma, but also this physical contact was odd, embarrassing even. She carefully extricated her hand and curled her fingers against her thigh, cringing more than a little.

'Victoria,' the woman repeated, again with a quiver to her mouth and yet more tears.

'Yes, I'm Prim's granddaughter.'

The woman nodded and looked at the floor, trying and failing to catch her breath. Victoria followed her eyeline, and both stared at the rounded toes of the woman's black patent Mary Janes, which now stood firmly planted in the hard-baked mud at the side of the lake.

The woman mumbled something too quiet for her to discern. Victoria had to lean in closer.

'I'm sorry, I missed that.' She cupped her ear. 'What did you say?'

'I said . . .' The woman straightened, swallowed and looked her in the eye. 'I said, "Your name isn't Victoria."'

'Oh!' She let out a small, embarrassed laugh. 'It is. Yes, I'm Victoria.' She smiled nervously. It was a strange thing for this person to say to her. Was the woman nuts, just some random interloper who had found her way into their home? Was she grief-stricken? Confused? Victoria glanced towards the back of the house and was both happy and relieved to see Gerald still in the chair of the garden room and, further along in the kitchen, Mrs Joshi and Daksha pottering around the sink. She took great comfort from knowing they were only a yell away.

The woman shook her head. 'No, your name isn't Victoria.'

'Okaaay.' Victoria raised her eyebrows, thinking she would get this conversation over as quickly as possible and make her way back into the house. Even the maudlin, quiet gathering of the pensioner bees was better than this. 'What is it then?' she challenged, intrigued. 'What's my name?'

'Victory.' She smiled. 'Your name is Victory.'

The woman searched her face and Victoria saw a brief reflection of something so familiar it made her heart jump.

'Victory?' She bit her lip. 'Is that right?'

'Yes, a strong name, a name that I thought would see you through anything.'

Victoria took a step backward.

Her heart beat loudly in her ears and her stomach flipped with nausea. Whatever this was, whatever joke, prank or deception, she was not enjoying it and wanted to be anywhere else. It was as if her feet had grown roots in the mud and, as much as she wanted to run, she felt stuck.

'I don't know why you would say that to me. Who are you? Who did you come with? Because I will see if they are ready to leave.' Still she was torn between wanting to throw the woman out and being polite: it was a funeral, after all. She was aware she had raised her voice slightly.

'Who am I?' The woman's tone suggested the question almost pained her.

'Yes, who are you?' Victoria asked, more forcefully now, as fear caused the blood to rush in her ears and her heart clattered out an unnatural beat.

'This . . . this is even more beautiful than I remembered it.' The woman ignored the question and looked out over the water. 'My dad used to spend hours and hours tending the plants while my mum sat here shouting instructions from under the brim of her hat, usually eating a pear.' She smiled and wiped at her eyes, which had misted. '"*To eat the whole thing, core, stalk and all, is both prudent and economic.*" That's what she used to say to me; I don't know where she got that. She had lots of funny little sayings and ways.'

How the hell? Victoria couldn't speak, her leaden limbs meant she couldn't move and she was aware of her breathing, which was unnaturally loud in her ears.

'I want to tell you who I am, but this will be hard for you to hear . . .'

Then I don't want to hear it . . . I don't want to hear it . . . I don't . . . Victoria's sixth sense told her that whatever the woman was about to say was far more than she was able to cope with today.

There was a beat or two of silence while the woman prepared to speak and Victoria braced herself to listen. They looked at each other and Victoria felt an uncomfortable current of recognition. *No! No! No! No! You are mad, Victoria. You are going mad!*

The woman took a deep breath and raised her chin.

'I'm your mum.'

Victoria shook her head vigorously and felt a bolt of sickness fire through her gut.

'No, you're not! And that is not funny. Not remotely funny, today of all days. I would like you to leave. Leave right now! Go on! Get out!' All consideration of politeness now gone, she pointed towards the path that led to the driveway at the front of the house. Shaking her head, she walked to the kitchen without looking back, trying to reach the safety of the house as quickly as possible, ignoring the bunching in her gut and the scary feeling that sat on her shoulders like a weight as her limbs trembled. It was odd, a hoax, a cruel joke, whatever. The woman had clearly been snooping around. Victoria pictured the private correspondence that Prim kept in the top of the bureau in the drawing room. *Oh my God! Supposing she stole something!* Of one thing she was certain: whatever it was, and whoever the weird woman was, she was a liar. She buried the recognition she had felt under a pile of facts and reality – that reality being that her mother had died a long, long time ago.

◆ ◆ ◆

'Are you okay, Vic? You don't look so good.' Daksha noted her agitated state as she came in from the kitchen and shut the back door forcefully.

She nodded and went to the fridge, this time determined to have a glass of wine.

'Who was that you were you chatting to?' Daksha nodded her head towards the lake.

'Some woman. A bloody nutcase.' Victoria's hands trembled. *Why would someone do that to me? Why?*

'Bit weird!' her friend summarised.

'Daks, you have no idea!' She pulled the cork from a half-empty bottle and was about to pour when she noticed the faintest tell-tale of red lipstick around the rim of the bottle. It made her laugh.

Prim! Swigging out of the bottle? Really!

This, her gran's last ever bottle of wine, and she had left the other half for her. As was often the case of late, her laughter turned quickly to tears, and again she folded, resting her head on the countertop until Mrs Joshi swept forward and wrapped her in her arms.

'Come on, dear. You are going to bed.'

With exhaustion washing over her, Victoria didn't have the strength to fight the suggestion. Mrs Joshi almost pushed her up the staircase and past the pictures of her mother on the windowsill. The sight of them only made her tears fall harder.

You died! You are dead and I have wished my whole life that it was not the case, but it is!

'Don't cry, dear. Don't cry. You need to sleep. Daksha will stay with you and you will feel better in the morning, I promise. Everything feels better after sleep. Trust me.'

Victoria slipped off her shoes and cotton cardigan and climbed between the sheets. Mrs Joshi drew the bedroom curtains to block out the last of the day's sun, leaving her room bathed in the muted yellow glow of evening-tide with birds wittering and sunlight filtering through the trees, forming dappled shapes on the ceiling.

'Go to sleep,' Daksha's mum cooed as she stroked her forehead. 'Go to sleep.'

As Victoria's eyes closed, summer colours danced behind her eyelids and she pictured the woman's tear-streaked face as they stood by the lake. It had unnerved her more than she cared to admit.

'Victory . . .' she whispered. 'It's not even a name . . .'

FOUR

Mrs Joshi was right; she did feel better after sleep, although the first thing she thought about upon waking and the last thing before sleep finally claimed her was what the woman by the lake had said to her the day before. It was such a very odd thing and it played on her mind, which was already overstuffed with worry and sadness. There had been a familiarity in her face, but, as if aware of her own fragility, Victoria knew that to jump down that particular rabbit hole of believing the loony story would lead to nothing good.

'Don't be so bloody stupid!' she reprimanded herself as she stepped out of the cotton dress she'd slept in. A shower restored some of her well-being, the hot water running over her face and eyes, which were puffy from grief, reading by lamplight and a deep sleep. Choosing jeans, a short-sleeved linen T-shirt and going barefoot, Victoria walked into the kitchen.

She decided not to mention to Daksha that at 3 a.m. she had kicked off the covers and made her way down the stairs. The roll-top bureau had creaked as she lowered the shutter-like lid and rummaged through her gran's things, which felt far from comfortable. As far as she could tell, everything was just as she had left it. Nothing missing.

Victoria had, however, discovered a coupon for half-price Botox and laughed out loud while crying tears of joy and sadness.

It was such a Prim thing to consider. How she missed her! How she wished she could talk to her about the weird woman, about everything. When she thought about it logically, the woman must have snooped somehow, found out about her family – maybe she had grilled some of the elderly mourners who were more concerned with refreshing their cups of tea and eating the sandwiches. With the topic on her mind, she had fired off a text to Bernard, figuring he was the only person who might be able to throw some light on the odd situation. It was unsurprising to her that he didn't instantly reply. He, like most people at that ungodly hour, was most likely asleep. Before turning off her bedside lamp and retiring for the second time, she lay back on the soft pillow nest.

What if she is my mum? She let the thought permeate and placed her hand on her stomach to quell the visceral leap of joy at the very possibility. *But she's not, Victoria, she can't be . . .*

Instead, she pictured her mum and gran reunited in heaven, wondering what that might be like and how long it would take for them to catch up: years and years and years, if she had to guess . . . The very thought made her smile.

And now it was a brand new day, one where the dreaded funeral was behind her. All she wanted right now was a cup of tea. She checked her phone; frustratingly, there was still no reply from Bernard.

'Morning, sleepyhead, how are you feeling?' Daksha greeted her from the kitchen table, where she sat with an array of desserts in front of her. It felt good to have her noise, her company.

'Bit better, I think. I'm certainly cleaner – just stood in the shower for an age.'

'Good. I think it went well yesterday. The old people seemed to have a nice time and all were very grateful when they left. One or two took sandwiches and a slice of Battenberg wrapped in a napkin for their tea.'

They both smiled at the idea of the elderly equivalent of a party bag.

'Thank you for seeing everyone out, Daks. I just crashed. It was like someone pulled my plug out.'

'I did notice. Anyway, don't thank me. Mum went into overdrive; you know how she loves a drama *and* mass catering. This was two of her very favourite things combined.'

Again she managed to raise a smile.

Daksha began spooning large mouthfuls of pavlova into her mouth with a serving spoon.

'Didn't want it to go to waste!' She grinned by way of explanation as she swallowed and reloaded the spoon.

'You are all heart.' Victoria filled the kettle and reached for a mug from the hooks on the underside of the shelf on the dresser.

'I *am* all heart, and in my quest to reduce waste, last night I polished off a wheel of Brie along with half a jar of chutney and this morning I have already consumed a Portuguese custard tart, washed down with three cups of coffee.'

'I thought we were on a healthy eating plan so we could be in the best shape for our travels?'

Daksha put the spoon down and swallowed her mouthful. 'Are we still going? I mean, I want to! I just didn't know whether it was appropriate to mention it or ask. I completely understand if you've had a change of heart – no pressure from me, none at all. Only you know how you feel. Of course I still want us to go. I really, really want us to go, but it's got to be what's right for you and I will understand either way. You know that.'

Victoria stared at her rambling friend, who had a blob of cream and a tiny puff of meringue on her chin. She poured the hot water into the mug. It felt somehow easier to go with the flow and not disappoint her mate than voice her utter paralysis when it came to thinking about going travelling, or even next month, next week or tomorrow . . . in fact, such was her sadness it was hard to see beyond the now.

'I will need to organise something for the house – I can't just abandon it for however long we are away – but I do still want to go, I think, and it's not like we leave next week. We have nearly six months.' She noticed the smile that split Daksha's face, remembering how the trip had meant as much to her only a week or so ago. 'Can you imagine Prim's reaction if she thought she might be the reason for us cancelling our big trip?'

Daksha extended her arms and lifted her pudding-smeared chin. '*Darlings! Don't be so utterly ridiculous, go and have fun! Dance in the moonlight. Meet boys! Swim in every ocean and eat lobster whenever you have the chance!*' Daksha stopped talking and looked at her friend, seemingly unsure now, when it was too little too late, if her impression was a comfort or something insensitive.

'Exactly.' It was bittersweet for Victoria, touched by the sentiment she knew Prim might well express but still too grief-stricken to hear her name, let alone a muted version of her voice, without feeling swamped by sadness. She sloshed milk into her drink. 'That is exactly what she would say. We should go.' She hoped that by making a decision it might help her move forward, a plan of sorts.

Daksha leapt from the chair. 'Yes! Yes! Yes! We are back on track and we're going to have the best adventure ever!'

'I hope so.' Victoria chose not to share her fear that, weighed down by sadness, it was hard right now for her to see herself feeling happy or enjoying an adventure ever again. She noticed the pristine surfaces, shiny floor and sparkling sink. 'The place looks great.'

'Mummy and I did it after everyone had left.'

'Thank you. Your mum's wonderful. She has been so amazing to me; your dad too.'

'I'm lucky,' Daksha agreed, and reached again for the spoon. Seemingly, the confirmation that their travels were actually happening was not enough to encourage her to lay off the pudding. 'So come on, tell me about "weird woman" yesterday. What on earth was all that about? You seemed a bit freaked out!'

Victoria took the seat opposite her friend at the table, widening her eyes at the understatement and wondering what to say. 'I was. I'm still a bit freaked out, actually; the whole thing was so weird and it's really bothered me. I don't know where to start: everything about it was odd. Ridiculous and odd, but it's upset me a bit too,' she whispered.

'Upset you how? What did she say?' Daksha jutted her lower jaw, enabling her to speak without losing any of her mouth's precious pavlova cargo.

Victoria sipped the drink she held in her palms and rested her elbows on the table. 'Well, the first thing she told me was that my name is not Victoria.'

'Ah, marvellous! A loon of the psychic variety, I bet – my favourite kind. Let me guess, you were actually christened Nefertiti! I shall be happy to call you this, of course. But you'll have to get your passport and railcard altered.' Daksha grimaced. 'Have you noticed that if anyone talks about a previous life, they never say, "Oooh, you were a car mechanic called Roy from Loughborough. You died in the 1970s by choking on a cheese sandwich!" It's always someone from medieval times or Joan of Arc or one of Henry VI's eight wives!'

Victoria knew this was her friend at her finest, trying to lighten the mood. 'I think you'll find it was Henry VIII who had six wives.' It was one of the few historical facts she knew. *Divorced, beheaded, died* . . . and whatever came next.

Daksha reloaded her spoon. 'I'm a scientist, not a historian, so shoot me! You get my point, though.'

'Actually, you are not as wide of the mark as it might seem. She told me my name is Victory.'

'Victory? I *like* it! And how, pray, did she know your name was Victory?' Her friend stared at her wide-eyed, waiting for the punchline. When it came, it didn't disappoint.

'She knew because she said she had named me.' Victoria shook her head, knowing it really was as ridiculous as it sounded and yet was no less upsetting for that. 'She said . . . she said she was my mum.'

Daksha stopped laughing and the smile slipped from her face. She placed the spoon on the table and stared at Victoria with her hands in her lap.

'That's not even funny.'

'I know. It was a horrible thing to say, and it's made me feel out of sorts. I can't get it out of my head.'

Daksha took a slow breath and it was a while before she spoke. 'You need to not think about it. She obviously got wind of Prim's funeral and gatecrashed; there are some bloody strange people out there. She probably does it all over the county, like a wedding-crasher. Just ignore it. You have enough going on.'

'Believe me, I'd like to not think about it, but . . .'

'But what?'

'I don't know. There was something, Daks . . .'

'What?'

'Just something. I felt like we might have met before. I thought maybe she was someone from the library or someone I've seen in town. She looked, I don't know . . .' Even she was too embarrassed to say the words, because the words, and indeed the very thought, was absurd.

'She looked what?'

'Familiar. She looked familiar,' was the best she could manage, unwilling to share how she had spent more minutes than she could count trying to match the face of the woman to the eyes that had smiled at her from the windowsill on the half landing all her life.

'Well, she might well be someone you've met, but you still have to forget about it. You don't need people like that near you right now.'

Victoria nodded, knowing this might be easier said than done. The two sat in silence for a second or two, each digesting the exchange.

'I wish Prim was here.' Victoria uttered the words that were enough to break the dam on the next surge of emotion that flooded her. 'I miss her! I really miss her! I just want her to come home! And I can't believe that she won't, not ever.' Abandoning the mug, she placed her head on her arms on the tabletop as she sobbed. 'I miss her so much!'

Daksha leaned across and stroked her hair. 'I know you do, honey. I know you do. And it's going to hurt, but the thing is, if Prim were here, she'd—'

The doorbell rang, interrupting her.

'Damn. You stay put. I'll go.' Daksha tucked her hair behind her ears and made her way to the front door.

Victoria sat up straight and sniffed, wiped her eyes and face on her palm and dried her damp, snotty hand on her jeans. It was still the case that these mini breakdowns, the release of tears, actually made her feel a little better for a short while, almost like draining the sad system of its woe before it refilled and she would once again sob. It was a wearying cycle. She heard Daksha on the doorstep and guessed that after the funeral there would be a slew of thank-you cards or notes from all of Prim's acquaintances who had attended. She half wondered if it might be Gerald at the door, sweet Gerald, making good on his promise to visit and get cracking on those tomato plants. She looked forward to seeing him and thought that, if it wasn't him, she'd better check how he was doing.

She heard the front door close and Daksha walked slowly back into the room.

'Who was it?' She wiped the residual tears with her fingers.

'It was no one.'

'No one?'

Daksha nodded. 'No one, but I found this.' She slid the pale envelope across the table and picked up her pavlova spoon.

'Ah, so it begins: the thank-you notes.'

'Do you then have to thank them for thanking you, and do they then have to—'

'I get the idea, Daks.' Victoria cut her short.

She opened the envelope and withdrew the single sheet. The script was neat, ordered and not dissimilar to her handwriting. The note, short.

September 2019

Hello Victory,

I know this is a lot for you to take in. I understand.

And the truth is I don't really know where to start.

I return to Oslo tomorrow and would dearly, dearly love to see you before I leave.

I am staying at the Holiday Inn up on the Downs.

My cell number is at the top of the page.

It would mean the world for you to get in touch.

I have waited eighteen years for the opportunity.

With love,
With so much love!
Sarah Hansen.

Victoria read it twice more and stared at Daksha. Her heart thudded in her chest and she felt the light-headed sickness of a swoon.

'Are you okay? You look a bit pale.'

Victoria didn't answer but stared at the writing. *It looks similar to yours, or maybe you are imagining that, looking for things . . .*

'Vic? What is it?' Daksha probed again. 'What does it say?'

Jumping up from the table, Victoria crashed out through the hallway and on to the driveway, ignoring the bite of small stones on the soles of her feet as she frantically looked up and down the lane. There was no car and no sign of Sarah Hansen. With weak legs and a racing heart, she closed the front door and walked back into the kitchen. Daksha was sitting in uncharacteristic silence.

Victoria looked at her in disbelief. 'I can't believe she came here again! I can't believe it! She actually came back to the house!'

'Who did? Weird woman?'

'Yes!' She waved the paper towards her friend.

'Shit!'

'What should I do? Do you think I should call the police?' Victoria bit her lip and fingered the note before flinging it at her friend, aware of the rising panic in her voice and not sure of quite what she should do or say; this was an entirely new and frightening situation.

Daksha tilted her head and read the words Sarah had written. 'No, Vic. No, I don't think you should call the police.'

'Okay, maybe not the police, but I have to do something! Who the hell is she?' She opened up the paper and re-read the note, twice. 'I am so freaked out right now!' She knotted her fingers in her hair.

'Do you think . . .' Daksha began, her voice quiet.

'Do I think what?' Victoria pushed as she went to the sink and ran a long glass of water, sipping it, trying to calm down.

'Do you think she might be telling the truth?'

Victoria laughed loudly and spun around, slamming the glass on the countertop. Her laughter stopped when she saw her friend's expression. 'Really, Daks? Really? What, you think she actually *is* my dead mother, come back from the grave on the day of her own mother's funeral to give me a new name and drag me to Oslo? What the fuck is wrong with you?' The tone and language she used rarely enough, and this was the first time ever towards her very best friend. The exchange bruised the air around them, which now hung heavy with the echo. But the truth was, despite her best efforts to the contrary, Victoria half believed it too.

'I do. I think she . . .' Daksha swallowed. 'I think she could be your mum.' She held her ground, her voice steady.

Victoria knotted her hair loosely and fastened it on the top of her head with a band, then folded her arms across her chest in the hope it might stop them shaking, curling her fingers tightly until she felt them cramp in response.

'I don't know what to say to you. I swear to God, I actually do not know what to say to you right now! Why? Why do you think that?' There was a tremor to her voice.

'Because . . .'

'Because what?' She was almost shouting now.

When Daksha spoke, her voice was steady and Victoria envied her the apparent calm with which she viewed the situation. 'Because thinking about when I saw her yesterday – her posture, her manner, the way she kept out of the way – and this note, quietly dropped and putting you in control.' She shrugged. 'And the way it's affected you – like you might have seen something that makes *you* believe it's true but are not saying. I don't know, I guess it's just a gut instinct. You know how you can be told something and you either believe it or you don't for no other reason than how it feels inside? That almost inexplicable sense of a lie or the truth? Well, it feels like it might be the truth to me.' Daksha held her gaze.

Victoria walked backwards until her legs found a chair and slumped down, shaking her head. It was one thing to have contact from a nutcase, but quite another for Daksha, one of the few people in the whole wide world she relied on – the person who had her back – to be adding credence to the mad, mad suggestion. For mad it must be, because the alternative was . . . the alternative was . . . unthinkable.

'But my mum *died*,' she managed. 'My mum died when I was a baby and I have missed her every single day of my life!' It felt cruel and wearing to have to be repeating this to her friend. 'I missed having a mum. They say you don't miss what you never had, but I know that's not true because I have missed her. I've missed her so much.'

'But what if she didn't die? What if Sarah Hansen *is* your mum?'

Victoria let her thoughts race.

'It's just not possible, Daks! It's not! It's completely ridiculous! It wouldn't make any sense! Because if she wasn't dead, why would Prim tell me she was? Why would Prim not want to see her in all that time? And if she were my mum, why would she stay away from me? Why would Grandpa and Prim lie to me? Why would everyone lie to me?' She returned to this, the most hurtful premise of them all.

'I don't know. I don't know!' Daksha stood and wrapped her friend in a hug. 'I don't know, Vic, but I don't think you should let this woman go back to Oslo without seeing her, even if it's just for five minutes, to try to get to the bottom of it.'

'I don't like it. I'm scared, Daks,' Victoria whispered, gripping her friend around the waist.

'Because it's scary, that's why. Really scary.' Daksha kissed her scalp and once again the dam broke its banks and Victoria's tears flowed. It seemed her sad system of woe was filling almost faster than she could cope with today.

She didn't confess to her friend that buried beneath the total confusion that the woman's arrival had brought her there was a sliver of happiness at the prospect that this woman just might be telling the truth.

How? How would it even be possible? A mum! My mum! But it's not possible! Don't be so bloody stupid! It's not possible!

'Prim . . . Prim, please, please tell me you didn't lie to me. I can't even begin to . . . Oh, Daks, what if . . .' The air felt very thin and her chest heaved.

'It's okay, Vic. Take deep breaths. That's it, keep breathing.'

She did as Daksha instructed.

FIVE

Victoria straightened the collar of her blouse and knocked on the door. She wiped the thin peppering of sweat from her top lip and coughed.

'Victoria!' Jim Melrose stood back to allow her entry. 'I was very glad to get your message. I must say I didn't think you would take me up on the offer quite so soon. But do come in! Come in! I thought it was a wonderful service yesterday. Really wonderful.'

'Yes, yes, it was, thank you.' Her mind raced. Was that only yesterday? It could have been weeks ago . . . Her head was swimming with the facts that were still crystallising in her mind, and the person she thought might help her make sense of the whole thing was the jolly, hairy vicar who now beamed at her.

'Although I do have a confession to make: the lemon drizzle I promised is in short supply today, but we do have some fancy biscuits Mrs Melrose won in a raffle – they should keep us going! Come in! Come in!' he repeated.

She stepped past him into the narrow hallway, noting the rather austere peachy-coloured woodchip and a single wooden cross hanging by the door. She followed him into a cluttered study that smelled of dog and where piles of paper on various surfaces teetered and threatened to fall as she skirted them.

'Sit down!' He pointed at a rather saggy-based wingback chair where several flattened cushions were stacked, as if they could compensate for the dip in the upholstery. She sat down and yes, the chair was as uncomfortable as she had suspected and she was certain that a spring was digging into her thigh.

'Now, first things first, can I get you a cup of tea?' He clapped loudly from the other side of the imposing desk.

'No, thank you.' She was nervous, and the last thing she wanted to do was juggle a cup and saucer in her agitated state.

'Okay, well, let's get right to it. What is it you would like to talk about, Victoria? And no need to hurry. I can imagine that this is a very difficult time for you. Grief is debilitating and it affects no two people in the same way. But I do have some experience; it's not unusual for people to sit in that very chair, trying to make sense of their loss.' He smiled and sat back with his fingertips joined to form a pyramid against his chest.

She exhaled. 'I don't know where to start, really.'

'I think the beginning is always the best spot.' He stared at her.

Victoria took a deep breath and looked into her lap; getting started was a lot harder than she had thought. 'It is partly about losing my gran, but it's more than that.' She smiled at him as anxiety tied her tongue. 'It's an odd one, but . . . a woman came to Prim's funeral who I didn't recognise and she came to the house afterwards, not inside, but she was in the garden.' She paused, remembering how she had walked over to her at the lake. 'And I know how crazy this sounds, but she told me . . . she told me she was my mum.'

'Forgive me.' He lowered his hands. 'But I thought your mother passed away?'

'I know.' She looked up briefly. 'Yes, she did. Or at least I thought she did. She *did*, I mean, I don't know. I don't know anything . . .' She ran her fingers through her hair.

'Take your time.' He spoke kindly, and it helped.

'There was something the woman said yesterday – about my name, my real name, and her handwriting, and the way she looked . . .'

'I don't really understand what you are saying to me.' The vicar too was clearly struggling with the inference. 'You think this woman *is* your mother?'

'I'm not sure!' Victoria bit her lip. 'I don't really understand it either, but the woman who turned up at the funeral came to the house again this morning and left a note. She has asked me to make contact with her, as she is only here for a short time, and I don't know what to do and I wondered if you might know anything about it. I left a message for a man she was chatting to in the churchyard, but he hasn't got back to me. I know Prim wasn't a churchgoer, not really, but I thought if she might have told anyone about this, it would be you. Or her boyfriend, Gerald, but I thought I'd try you first.' She hated the desperate, hopeful longing in her chest, wanting nothing more than answers from him, or anyone else for that matter.

The vicar sat forward in the chair and shook his head, his expression now more solemn than jolly. 'No. I don't know anything about this. I heard from others that your mother had died when you were a baby. I think your grandfather might even have told me about the situation, but Prim and I never discussed it. She was a very private woman.'

'Yes, she was.'

'And you think there might be grounds to what this woman is claiming?' he asked softly, with an unmistakable air of disbelief. And she understood; if she'd heard it, she too would think it implausible. God, she *did* find it implausible! And yet here she was.

'I honestly don't know what to make of it. I guess I felt there was something familiar about her when I met her and then, this morning, my best friend, Daksha, who's really good at this type of thing, said she thought there might be something in it.'

Jim Melrose drew breath and took his time forming his response. 'In my job I see a lot of people, Victoria, who are grieving the loss of someone they loved. Your situation is even more poignant, as your grandma was effectively your whole family and you are very young. I think that there might be a tendency for *some* people in your situation to want to believe that this might be a possibility, because it would be the fairy-tale ending, wouldn't it? To have your mother come back from the dead when you need her most. I'm sorry to say there are charlatans out there who are more than aware of this. I have had some . . .' He paused. '*Heartbreaking* conversations with people who have paid huge sums to so-called "psychics" to receive messages from those who have died. Of course, it all comes to nothing, it's a con. I think if anyone did have a real gift, a vocation like that, then they would not be making money from it. They can take advantage of vulnerable people in the worst way. Because they give false hope.' He looked wistful. 'And I don't want to presume or pry, but I think the assumption is that you are now a young woman of means.'

She swallowed the inappropriate desire to laugh as nerves bit, glad Daksha was not within sight. The very phrase *a woman of means* made her feel like something out of a Jane Austen novel.

The vicar continued. 'I guess what I am saying is that there are a number of very obvious explanations and sometimes the most likely answers are not the most pleasing ones, not the ones we hope for. I am concerned that your grief and your understandable desire for this to be true might cloud the reality and I would hate to see you get hurt in any way, Victoria. I think you have enough going on right now.'

'I'm not sure I *do* have a desire for it to be true!' She shook her head defiantly, if not convincingly. 'I think I hope it's not true, but then if there's the smallest chance that I could get to meet my mum . . .' She held her head in her hands briefly. 'I would hate to see me get hurt too, but what if the hurt comes because I find out that Prim has been lying to me my whole life? What then?' The thought was enough to make her tears bloom.

Jim Melrose held her eyeline. 'And why would she have done that? Surely she, more than anyone, would have wanted nothing more than to be reunited with the daughter she mourned?'

'I guess.' She looked away, knowing she was more or less going to dismiss his advice. 'But I think I need to find out.'

'Well' – he smiled a little stiffly now – 'if you are going to meet her, make sure you do it in a public place and not alone. Take all sensible precautions and do not give her any personal information.'

'I won't. Thank you for seeing me today at such short notice.'

'My door is always open.' He stood to indicate the meeting was over.

'Thank you.'

'Any time. And Victoria?'

'Yes?' She looked directly at him.

'Prim was a good woman. She really was. And if anything should come to light, remember that.'

'I will.'

Victoria walked home with the vicar's parting words playing on her mind, suggesting that even he didn't discount the possibility entirely. She looked around and dawdled, partly to use the quiet commute as thinking time, hoping to order her maelstrom of thoughts, and also because, despite a deep sleep, she was bone tired.

As she walked along the pavement, thinking also of the vicar's note of caution, she thought she heard someone call her name. She ignored it in case she had imagined it or misheard. Today she found it hard to trust both her instinct and her hearing. Then she heard it again.

'Victoria!'

This time it was unmistakable. She turned in time to see Flynn McNamara as he caught up with her.

'Thought it was you.' He was panting a little after the run and, on another day, she would have felt ridiculously flattered that he might have put in this much effort just to walk with her. But the extreme excitement and flurry of joy in her gut that she had felt the last time she had seen him was muted. Unsurprising when she considered what had happened that very evening, and every day since . . .

'How are you, Flynn? Getting ready for uni?' She looked down, not caring about her frumpy brown sandals. Gone was the nervous, unnatural speech pattern and the desire to pepper her conversation with words that might make her seem a little more relevant. And the state of her hair and the possible allure of what she was wearing didn't occur to her. She was calm because she could now see that this boy and her preoccupation with him over the last few years did not matter. Nothing mattered as much as the more pressing issues that dogged her: like recovering from the loss of Prim, trying to figure out whether Sarah Hansen could conceivably be her mother and concentrating on breathing, because with so much going on in her brain, with thoughts and doubts coming at her quicker and faster than she could swallow, she thought she might actually drown . . . her head was working at lightning speed and she wished it would all just – slow down.

'Yeah, kind of. I go in a month. There's not that much to do, really. Just pack a bag, buy some posters and try to figure out how to stop my little sister taking over my room the moment I shut the front door.'

'I'd go for padlocks and a big, snarling dog.'

He laughed, and the old Victoria would have used his laughter as a fuse to spark her self-confidence, but not today.

'I like that. Padlocks and a big, snarling dog.' He held her eyeline. 'You didn't come to the pub that night?'

'Oh. No. I didn't realise you were asking me, plus' – she took a deep breath – 'things have been a bit rubbish. My gran died.' She detested saying it out loud, making it real, and she then cursed the tears that inevitably followed.

'Oh shit! And she was like . . .' He paused. 'You don't have a big family.' He phrased it cautiously.

'That's right. The tiniest family imaginable. Just me now, actually.'

'Shit!' he said again, shaking his head as if this were beyond his comprehension. She was tempted to point out the plus side: no little sister waiting to steal her room meant no need of the investment in padlocks and snarling dogs.

'That's messed up.'

'You don't know the half of it.' She pictured Sarah Hansen's note, and in her head saw a clock counting down. *I leave tomorrow* . . .

'Well, look, I need to get the bus.' He pointed along the street. 'But come to the pub, or I could message you . . .'

'Sure.' She nodded, not sure what exactly she was agreeing to and genuinely cool in her response. 'Flynn?' she called as he balanced on the kerb, waiting for a break in the traffic.

'What?'

'Are you and Courtney, are you guys, like . . .' She didn't know what she was asking or why, but pictured the girl calling his name with such purpose.

'No! No way!' He laughed and curled his top lip, as if the very idea were distasteful. This gave her food for thought; maybe Courtney's superpowers were not as strong as they had suspected.

◆　◆　◆

Victoria kicked off her sandals and slumped down into the vacant chair on the veranda next to Daksha, grateful as ever for her presence, knowing that she was the only thing that stood between her and an existence of total isolation. A thought that was unbearable. The two watched the lake, over which a cool breeze drifted, lifting the hair from their faces.

This place . . . my place now . . . and yet I don't even know if I want it, not without you. Oh, Prim – I wish we could talk and you could tell me what to do about Sarah Hansen! And if it is her, if she is my mum, I don't think you can have known. You can't have. I know you wouldn't have lied to me about something like that . . . I know it!

'So how did you get on with Mr Vicar?' Her friend yawned.

'Okay.'

'Please stop with all the detail!' Daksha held up a hand.

It might only have been ten days or so since they had waved goodbye to August, but already the days had lost the heat of summer and were now pleasant – warm still, but with the gift of a cold snap at night to aid sleep – should a whirring brain ever calm long enough to allow it. She thought of Gerald and how Prim was his weather girl as well as his theatre partner and felt a stab of sadness at his loss. Prim was, after all, more than just hers. She picked up her phone and fired off a text.

Bit cloudy today, Gerald. I would say summer definitely on the way out and autumn is around the corner.

Hope you are okay today.

Pop in any time.

Victoria X

'So come on! What did the vicar say?' Daksha urged.

'I suppose nothing very helpful and everything I expected. How the whole Sarah Hansen thing might be a ruse, a con by someone interested now I am a "woman of means".'

'He did not say that!' Daksha sat up.

'He did. And he has a point. He said it might be what I *want* to believe, the fairy-tale ending and all that.'

'And what do you think?'

'I think I just don't know.' She clicked her tongue against the roof of her mouth, as irritated by her response as she knew her friend would be. 'And that's the truth.'

'I don't want to influence you either way.' Daksha sighed. 'It's such a personal thing. I don't want you to have regrets, but I also don't want you to get hurt.'

'God, Daks, I think I am going to have regrets either way.'

'Possibly, but I know that if it was me, I couldn't stand not to know. It would eat away at me. But then, I get the whole self-protection thing. And at the end of the day, I keep asking this question: would Prim have lied that your mum had died?' She shook her head. 'Of course she wouldn't. It was her daughter, after all.'

'That's what I think. Which doesn't help me make a decision on what to do – call her, don't call her? See her, don't see her?' She rolled her eyes.

'Well, I was thinking.' Daksha's considered, calm response showed a certainty that Victoria could only envy. 'I would ask her for proof that she is who she says she is, and then, based on that proof or lack of, I would make my decision on what to do next.'

'Yes.' Victoria nodded. 'Of course! If she was my mum, she would have proof, right? She would know stuff.'

'Yep, she'd definitely know stuff,' Daksha confirmed.

The two friends watched the remaining swallows of the season, agile and elegant as they dipped low over the lake, no doubt to feast on the bugs and airborne grubs lurking over its green-tinged surface.

'I think this lake must be like a bird service station, the equivalent of stocking up on snacks before they fly off up the motorway,' Victoria said.

'Definitely! They'll pick up two different types of sweet, an out-of-date chicken salad sandwich and a compilation CD of crappy cover songs, which they'll listen to all the way to Africa!' Daksha chuckled.

'Do you think we'll ever get to Africa?' Victoria turned to face her.

'I hope so. I really hope so. Although the way you look today, I can't see us making it to the clock tower on the high street.'

'Why? How do I look?' Victoria tucked the stray wisps of hair behind her ears, suddenly aware that this 'look', whatever it was, had greeted Flynn McNamara.

'Like you want to sleep for a thousand years,' Daksha whispered, before reaching out and joining her hand with her friend's. Victoria took comfort from the contact, and there they sat, hands swinging between the chairs and watching the birds that twittered and chattered as they fed and drank.

Victoria's phone beeped with a text from Gerald and the two let their hands drop.

Victoria, how lovely to hear from you. Made my day.

Yes. I've put an extra jersey on.

Thinking of tackling the crossword.

Gerald X

She smiled.

'Now that's a smile I have missed. Who was that from? Flynn?' Daksha joked.

'No, Gerald, actually. But I did see Flynn and he kind of asked me to go to the pub with him.'

Daksha scrabbled forward with her palms in the air. 'So hang on a minute, we sit here chit-chatting about the vicar and bird motorways, and all the time you have this juicy bit of gossip nestling in your pocket! What is wrong with you? This is huge! Flynn McNamara! *The* Flynn McNamara!'

Victoria breathed slowly, trying and failing to feel her friend's level of enthusiasm. 'In answer to your question, the matter with me is that I just don't care about anything, really. I am too sad.' She made no attempt to swipe at her tears that fell. 'I can't imagine ever getting over this feeling, I just wish Prim was here to tell me what to do. And now this whole thing with this Sarah, it feels like too much.'

Daksha covered her eyes. 'God, I'm the worst friend in the world. Of course you are too sad. I got carried away.'

'So what's new?' Victoria sniffed. 'And, for your information, you are not the worst friend in the world, you are the very, very best. Thank you for being here with me.'

It was Daksha's turn to let her tears fall and, at the sound of the two girls crying, the birds fell silent and took flight, no doubt off to seek a happier place, or at least one where the listening to their covers CD wasn't going to be interrupted. Victoria more than understood, envying them their wings and wishing she could do the same.

'I think you're right. I'm going to go and see her, Daks, but only to tell her that I want proof.'

'You are?'

'Yes. I mean, I kind of have to, don't I? Just to confirm that she is either a total scam artist, a nutcase or to find out that my whole bloody life has been a lie . . .' The words were easily spoken, but they sat in her mouth like glass. 'Either way, I am not looking forward to it.' She felt the jitter of nerves simply at the prospect of going to see the woman.

'Do you want me to come with you?'

'I think this is something I have to do alone, but I'd like you to be close by.'

'I think you're very brave.'

She looked at her friend. 'Brave or bonkers, Daks?'

'Truthfully?'

'Yep, truthfully.'

'Bit of both.'

◆ ◆ ◆

It felt surreal that after one anxious, stuttered phone call she was walking into the foyer of the Holiday Inn Express on Epsom Downs. Having driven her there, Mrs Joshi was now parked and had told her to take as long as she needed, and to keep her phone within reach, as she could be inside within seconds. All Victoria had to do was call. Daksha was in the back seat, peering towards the building, having squeezed her shoulder in support for most of the journey.

And it was a familiar journey, one she had made countless times, driving in Prim's Volkswagen Beetle over the open road of the racecourse with a clear view of the grandstand and the track, but today it had felt anything other than familiar. It felt like a drive into the unknown and her stomach was in knots. She was glad of Mrs Joshi and Daksha sitting in readiness close by and knew that, if the need arose, her friend's mother could give one hell of a pinch.

Victoria walked towards the doors, which opened instantly, not allowing time for the nerves that bubbled in her gut to evolve into the nausea that threatened. She looked into the building and there was Sarah Hansen, standing on the striped carpet in the middle of the foyer. Waiting. She was make-up free, her short dark hair blow-dried and her hands clasped. She was neatly dressed in slim-fitting jeans with a navy belt, a pale-blue shirt, the collar of which was undone to reveal a slender silver chain, and white trainers on her feet. Her expression, Victoria noted, was anxious, as if she might have doubted Victoria's arrival, or perhaps it was because she knew time was of the essence and was keen to get on with things; possibly both.

The woman stepped forward and reached out her hands before clasping them again and knitting her fingers, clearly, like Victoria, unsure of the convention. Sarah smiled at her hesitantly and she saw it now. She saw it plainly. And her gut folded over.

What the hell . . .

In the light of this new day, with her head not full of a church service and the sermon of Jim Melrose ringing in her thoughts, and without the awful, awful tiredness pawing at her senses, she saw that the eyes of the woman in the photographs around the house and the eyes of the woman standing in front of her were, indeed, if not the same, then very similar. She felt herself sway.

Mum! Mummy! My mum! This was immediately followed by the questions, pushed forward by anger. *Why? How? How and why would you and Prim and Grandpa do this to me? They can't have known, they missed you too! It can't be real. It can't be! Get a grip, Victoria, it can't be real.*

'This is harder than I thought,' Sarah whispered.

Victoria nodded. It was.

'I have thought about this moment so many times, and now it's here I can't quite believe it. I want to take you in my arms, but

I know I can't. I want to hold you because you have lost Prim and I want you to hold me because my mum has died, but I know that's too much to ask. Too soon.'

Victoria held her gaze and listened to the accent – British, but with a hint of Scandi around the vowels. 'I . . . I don't even know who you are.'

'I am your mum,' she mouthed. 'And I feel adrift right now. This is surreal and wonderful and sad and a whole host of other emotions. I know I won't ever forget this day, or yesterday, seeing you for the first time in all these years.'

'How you feel is how I have *always* felt. Because my mum died. I felt it every day.' Victoria too whispered, as if both were aware that the exchange was too important, too personal, to share. It was a strange thing; Victoria knew no different, had never had a mum, and yet had keenly felt the Sarah-shaped hole in her life . . .

Sarah closed her eyes as if the very thought of this was more than she could stand. 'I am so glad you came, Victory.'

'Don't call me that! How did you know that Prim had died?' Her bottom lip quivered. She tried her best to keep her tone level, still undecided on how to act, hesitant, and all of her thoughts were bookended by understandable fury at the fact that *if* this were true, she had been abandoned by this woman.

'Bernard. He was my friend – *is* my friend.'

'I saw you with him at the church.'

Sarah nodded. 'It was the first time I'd seen him in a very long time. He has fed me bits of information for years, secretly of course. I don't think I would have been able to get through without that.'

This news another gut punch of betrayal that left her feeling sick – even Bernard was in on the secret! She felt her legs sway a little.

'He was always very chatty and nice to me. And to think all the time he knew you were alive! Bernard-the-bloody-handyman knew, and *I* didn't!'

'I am so sorry. It's an inadequate word, but it's—'

'It's the worst kind of conspiracy, Sarah.' Victoria cut her short, her voice trembling as her anger rose.

'I can see how it would feel like that,' Sarah answered drily. 'I shouldn't say it, but to hear you call me Sarah is odd, it hurts. When I chat to you in my daydreams, you always call me Mum.'

'Well, this is not a daydream,' Victoria reminded her through gritted teeth.

'It is a dream for me, Victory-ia, sorry. I never imagined I would see the day . . .'

Victoria's mouth felt dry and her tongue stuck to the roof of her mouth. She felt weak and light-headed, and a lot like she was dreaming. Maybe she was, but it was a nightmare.

'I'm sorry!' Sarah was flustered, flexing her fingers. 'I'm not really sure what I am supposed to say or do. And I have spoken to you every day in my mind since the day you were born and I always use your name and it will take a bit of getting used to, calling you something different.'

'Did—' Victoria drew breath, steeling herself to ask the question. 'Did Prim know you are alive?'

'Yes.'

And there it was, the killer word that was a dagger to her chest. *Oh my God, no, no, no, no, no . . .* 'Can you . . . can you tell me who it was that decided to lie to me? How it happened? How you all agreed on something so . . .' She took another deep breath. 'So fucking awful!'

Sarah looked at the floor, her eyes brimming. 'There was no plan as such. No conspiracy, as you see it. I was broken. The one thing Mum and I agreed on was that we couldn't allow you to get broken too.'

'So you gave me away.'

'I gave you to Prim.'

'When is my birthday?' she fired.

'October the twelfth, and you will be nineteen this year,' the woman answered quickly, and Victoria thought of all the birthdays where Prim had dressed her in a frothy frock and watched as she sent wishes up to heaven, chatting to the woman above the clouds who had missed out on eighteen birthday cakes, eighteen cards, eighteen rounds of exaggerated applause when she blew out the candles . . . She gave a dry laugh. Ridiculous, really; there she was, sending thoughts and prayers up to heaven when this woman was suggesting that, in reality, all she had to do was pop them in an envelope, lick a stamp and send them to Oslo. She thought she might throw up and placed her hand on her stomach.

'Shall we sit down?' Sarah pointed to a vacant table with two tub chairs either side and took a step towards it.

'No.' Victoria shook her head and stood resolutely with her arms folded, largely to stop them from trembling. 'I'm not staying. I only came to get a look at you and to tell you that it all feels very convenient, you turning up when you did, but actually, you haven't told me anything that anyone couldn't find out with a bit of digging.' Victoria did not believe this, her instinct told her differently, but she knew that if she didn't stick to the planned speech in her head, there was no telling what she might say or do.

'I see.'

'Do you? Have you the first idea what I am going through right now?' She heard the anger on which her words coasted, the only emotion she felt able to express. Refraining, just, from breaking down and shrieking that this was her whole life they were talking about – the very fabric of who she was was now in question. The entire exchange was formal and awkward. The way the woman stared at her, as if drinking her in, monitoring her every move, was more than a little disconcerting. 'I also came to tell you that I need to see some proof. Proof that you are who you say you are and, if you can provide that, then we *might* have something to talk about, but if you can't, then I suggest you stay the hell away from me.' She was shaking now.

Sarah looked at the floor.

'I have, erm . . . I have photographs and letters and—'

'Fine. It should be easy then.' Victoria cut her short. 'But until I see something concrete . . .' She breathed out through pursed lips. 'You could be anyone.' She cursed the crack to her voice and the gathering of her tears, indicating she didn't believe this for a second.

'Do I seem like *anyone* to you?' Sarah asked.

Victoria chose her words carefully, looking skyward and then back at the woman who looked at her with a pleading expression. 'I am so freaked out right now. I don't know *what's* going on. I feel very confused.'

'I can imagine, I really can.' Again she reached out, but seemed to think better of it and folded her fingers away. Victoria felt a pull in her chest, almost willing the woman to place her hand on her. Sarah tried to gather herself.

'I hated to put time pressure on you, but I have to be back in Oslo and I was so very desperate to see you.' And just like that, her voice was reed thin, spoken from a throat raw with emotion. 'Can I have your email address?'

Victoria gave it to her, watching as Sarah tucked in her lips and tried to stem her tears. 'I am so sorry. I can't stop crying.'

'Because Prim died or because you've seen me?'

'Both,' Sarah managed, her voice no more than a squeak. 'Both.'

'I have to go.' Victoria turned on her heel, suddenly keen to put distance between herself and the woman, needing to be alone to try and order the complex range of thoughts and ideas that questioned the only truth she had ever known. She stopped and faced Sarah.

'You know, I always thought that if it was ever possible to meet my mum, in heaven or whatever, I would run to her and fall into her arms and she would hold me tight and we'd never let each other go. And it would feel like coming home—'

Sarah's noisy sob interrupted her.

'Me too . . .' she muttered between stilted breaths.

'But here we are.' She let her palms fall open. 'In the Holiday Inn Express on Epsom Downs, and I feel . . . blank. Confused. Angry. I feel nothing like I should! And so that makes me doubt what you're saying. It's like I'm in a waiting room to see a dentist or a doctor with that same churn of nerves, but magnified. You are a stranger, and the thought of falling into your arms or even calling you my mother is—' She stopped and her face contorted, trying to think of how to phrase it. 'Is the last thing I would be able to do.'

Sarah nodded vigorously with her eyes tightly shut, as if this was all to be expected, but no less painful for it. It pulled at Victoria's heartstrings.

'I want to see some proof. I think that's what I need,' Victoria spoke as she swept from the foyer and didn't look back.

Mrs Joshi leaned over and opened the door, and Victoria jumped in and fastened the seat belt, in a hurry to be gone from the place.

'You okay, sweetie?' Mrs Joshi asked as she started the engine.

Victoria could only nod, her speech impaired by a desire to vomit that was almost overwhelming. She felt Daksha's hand on her shoulder and was thankful for it.

◆　◆　◆

'Here you go.' Daksha handed her a cup of tea and Victoria took it without question. She lifted her knees on the mattress and sat back against the pillows. Daksha jumped into the other end of the bed, and this was how they chatted, top to toe in the way only good friends can.

'How are you feeling?'

Victoria sighed. 'I don't know. I don't know how I'm supposed to feel.'

'But you're glad you went? Happy you saw her?'

'I don't know about happy, but I think it's the only way for me to figure out what's going on. She said she had photographs and letters, the proof I asked for.'

'Is she going to send them?'

'I gave her my email; I don't know.' She took a sip of the restorative tea. 'Thank you for coming with me today. I don't think I would have been half so brave if you and your mum hadn't been in the car park.'

'Yes, you would. You can do anything, Vic.'

'I wish I believed that.'

'It's true, you're amazing.'

'Thank you, Daks. I don't remember much about it; it was over in a blink. I feel like I ran in and ran out. I was so scared.'

'It was longer than a blink. I was watching you both.'

'So what did you think?' Victoria necked a mouthful of tea, keen to hear her friend's appraisal.

'From what I could see, she looked a lot like you. And yours is a face I stare at every single day and have done for the last five years. It's a face I love, and I probably know it better than you because I look at it more.' She swallowed. 'And because her mouth went up at the edges like yours does when you are trying to convince someone of something. She had the same expression. She looked like your mum, I would say.'

'God, Daks.' Victoria's chest felt tight and her breathing constricted. 'I need not to get ahead; I need to wait and see proof. I can't let myself think that she . . . that she is . . . because what does that mean for me? What does that mean for my whole life?' *I need proof . . . I need to wait for that . . . because it's too huge to get wrong . . . too important to mess up . . . but I know . . . I know it in my heart . . . I do . . .*

But yes, even she could see it: Sarah Hansen looked a lot like her. With this thought came a tidal wave of emotion that threatened to knock her sideways. She held on to the mattress and closed her eyes, and even though she was stationary, she felt it entirely possible that she might fall over.

'Half of me wants it to be true and the other half can't bear to think about it. She's a stranger, but she might be my mum . . .' She shook her head. *How, Prim? How?*

'Shall we google her?' Daksha sat upright, as the idea occurred to her.

'I . . . I guess.'

'I mean, you've not googled her before, have you?'

'No, Daks. Firstly, there was no point in googling my dead mother and, secondly, I didn't know the name Hansen until yesterday!'

'Good point.' Daksha scrabbled from the bed and reached for the laptop on the floor, handing it to Victoria. 'You do it.'

With her mug of tea now on the nightstand, she slowly opened up the machine and typed: 'Sarah Hansen'. There were many, but one thumbnail picture stood out. Her Sarah Hansen, a partner in a law firm in Oslo – *a lawyer!* She clicked on the bio and read the woman's credentials and her expertise of working in family law, before handing the machine to Daksha.

'That's her. A lawyer.' She thought of the conversations over the years where Prim had lamented the waste of her daughter's life.

'She had the whole world at her feet, reading law at Durham! Set for life, until that man came along and got her in his clutches!' It was invariably at this point that her gran would reach for her

handkerchief, as usual secreted up her sleeve. Even the thought of Prim sharing confidences with her was more than Victoria could stand tonight.

'What are you going to do now, Vic?'

Slipping down under the duvet, she closed her eyes, wanting to hide from the world. If her thoughts were usually anchored, tonight they were in free fall, floating in her brain and recoiling as they collided.

'I am going to sleep and will wait for the proof.' *I want to disappear, shut down . . . just for a while . . .*

'You go ahead, honey. I'll guard you,' Daksha cooed, and just her kindness, the fact that she was not going to leave her alone, was enough to make Victoria's tears fall, travelling over her nose to form a damp patch on the pillowslip.

She was quite unable to settle and turned over on the mattress, crying quietly at the wonder and horror of the news. Flipping her hot pillow to the cold side, she kicked off her cover, only to reach for it minutes later.

Victoria woke the next morning glad of the chance to get up and face the day, knowing that, at least in the daylight hours, she might be able to occupy her thoughts with chores or the distraction of chatting to Daksha, blocking out the tsunami of intrusive questions that were coming at her thick and fast. She carried the same feeling of anticipation tinged with nerves. A movie played in her mind over and over of the way Sarah had tried to hold her, reaching out as if desperate to make skin-to-skin contact, and her own confusing revulsion whilst half wanting, no, *craving* that contact. Of one thing she was certain: if the woman was a con, then she was a bloody good one. The truth was, Victoria expected to have their relationship confirmed, anticipated that proof would be forthcoming and was putting off the moment she had to face that particular reality: that her whole life up until this point had been a sham. The thought was enough to make her catch her breath. Daksha had fallen asleep at the other end of the bed and was snoring.

Victoria reached for her laptop, deciding to google Sarah again and read some more about her career, keen to glean any little detail she could. She flipped open the screen and there were no less than sixteen new emails waiting for her. Sitting up straight, she stared at her inbox – they were all from Sarah.

Hello Victoria,

I have only just got home and am scanning these so you get them sooner rather than later. Having to send them separately as I only know how to load one at a time.

I can't imagine what the last few hours have been like for you, but expect, like me, you are doing a lot of reflecting. My thoughts are all over the place and my emotions high.

I am still replaying every word you said to me and each moment I got to see your face. This is tough for you, tough for us, but I hope these give you at least some of the answers you are looking for.

I am sending you a copy of my most precious photograph, taken when you were born. In fact, the only one I have of us together. And also letters sent between Mum and me when I was at Henbury House, the rehabilitation centre where I was staying when I was pregnant and when I lost Marcus. They are uncensored and quite raw, but I think it's best I don't censor them – they are honest and I think the proof you are looking for. And I understand that need to see evidence, I do.

Contact me any time, day or night, if you want to talk about anything, anything at all! Any time.

I shall wait for that contact.

I wish I knew how to sign off, so for now I will just end with –

Sarah X

With her thoughts and heart racing, Victoria felt the need for privacy. Creeping from the bed with her laptop under her arm, she quietly closed the bedroom door behind her and made her way to the drawing room, where she sank down on to the sofa. The morning light filtered in through the side window and lit everything it touched; she saw dust particles floating in its rays and thought for the first time about housekeeping, knowing she wanted to keep the place as nice as Prim had, but that could wait for now.

Is this it, Prim? Is this the moment I find out why you lied to me? I am scared, so scared . . .

Victoria opened the second email and there it was: a photograph, which filled the screen.

'Oh my God!' she cried, lifting the screen until it was close to her face, enabling her to better study the detail. She stared at the young, thin Sarah – painfully thin, in fact, with long, lank hair hanging over her sallow cheeks, pale lips and huge, haunted eyes, holding a tiny baby swaddled in a pale lemon blanket – but that wasn't what drew her attention. She stared at the side of the image and the arm of a woman standing behind Sarah. A woman who had almost been cropped from the picture, save her hand, supporting the child's head and the light almost glinting from the unmistakable large baguette-cut emerald that graced her finger.

With a shaky touch, she opened the next email and devoured it, word for word:

February 2001
Rosebank
Epsom
Surrey

Dear Sarah,

How are you feeling? Is there anything you need? Daddy and I think about you each and every day. I hope Henbury House is everything we hoped it would be. It sounded like the perfect place and they promised results, which is all that matters, so I would say no matter what, stick with it! This is a bump in the road, but doesn't have to be your path.

I say that with a heavy heart because I have a terrible feeling in the pit of my stomach that this might be our last chance. I feel like we are running out of options and, though it is hard to say, running out of energy too.

I have to believe that in the controlled environment with counsellors and good doctors on hand, you stand your best chance of coming off that terrible drug. A drug I hate with as much passion as I have ever loved anything, and you know how fiercely I love!

Nothing else has worked, has it? Empty promises and half-hearted efforts will always come to nothing if you are within sight and sound of a temptation that is stronger than your resolve.

And to see you looking so . . . hollow, so broken,
is almost more than any mother can stand . . .

Victoria paused in her reading – it was odd to see her gran's handwriting on the screen, and jarring to know that Sarah was in pos-
session of these letters – sent to her as proof. *Oh my God, Prim . . .
you might have written these words on this very sofa . . .* She ran her
hand over the seat cushion, swallowing the bitter tang of betrayal,
before she carried on reading.

> Daddy read a book about an approach where it
> suggests you almost have to abandon your loved
> one, change the locks, unplug the phone and look
> the other way in a bid to make them understand
> that this is the absolute last time, rock bottom. I
> cannot conceive of doing that. Cannot conceive
> of not being your safety net. Not ever. That's the
> deal: to always catch you if you fall.
>
> And I know that even mentioning his name
> in a negative way will cause your anger to flare
> because you are so very blinkered, but can you
> imagine what it has been like for us? We are the
> people who have loved you your whole life long,
> have steered you through school, held your hand
> when you cried and have done our very best to
> give you the skills with which to navigate the
> choppy waters of life. For what? This? And I know
> you think you are grown up, and indeed you are
> in law, but you are twenty-one, a mere chick,
> really, and our little chick at that.
>
> When you won your place at Durham! Oh
> my! I couldn't sleep! I was so full of excitement for

all the wonderful things that lay ahead for you. I pictured your marvellous, marvellous life – our little girl, a lawyer – I thought you had it made. I thought you would live the life I always dreamed for you. Because I love you and, to me, you only deserve the very best life. You say this man loves you – but I am unable to imagine a kind of love where you give the person you love a drug so foul it robs them of everything that made them wonderful . . . how is that love, Sarah, how?

Think about it!

Think about everything.

Keep working hard and know that we love you. We might not like your choices, we might not understand, but we always, always love you.

Mum X

Victoria paused again to wipe her eyes on the sleeve of her pyjama top and to catch her breath. *Proof . . . this is my proof . . . but how . . . how is this even possible? I feel sick, so sick.*

March 2001
Sarah Jackson
Henbury House
West Sussex

I'm feeling better, thanks for asking. I'm doing really well.

And for your information, this place is more like a prison. I am locked in. LOCKED IN! It may come with a glossy brochure but be under no illusion the place is a jail. A jail you pay for. You knew that, though, right?

Of course you did.

I don't need anything from you.

Nothing!

So do your worst, change the locks, unplug the phone, bag up the stuff in my room and bin it – or whatever else you are threatening – I really don't care!

Marcus is everything. I love him! I don't know what part of that is so hard for you and Dad to get. But I'm sick of trying to make you understand. Bloody sick of it!

The way you want to hem me in, control me, I can't stand it. I'm twenty-one, a grown adult, and it's not fair. I won't let you do it any more.

You always said you wanted me to find someone to love who loved me back. Well, I have, but now that's not good enough because what you meant was you wanted to pick someone for me, someone you and Dad approve of, someone from the bloody tennis club.

Here's the thing, like it or not, Marcus and I come as a package.

And when I get out of here we will start afresh.

The plan is to get a nice little place and maybe have a garden, grow some vegetables. I'd like a dog – you know I've always wanted a dog . . .

Life will be good, but I can't see you being part of it, not with how you hate the man I love. And I know you hate him so don't try and deny it! Can you imagine your precious Sunday lunches at Rosebank with Marcus and me on one side and you and Dad on the other, scowling at him over Granny C's best china?

No, me either.

Marcus says: *Hate and recrimination are big things and if you let them fill you up it brings you the opposite of peace because if you hate it takes all of your energy – and that's such a waste; how can you live life weighed down like that?*

But that's something for you to figure out, not me.

Oh, and I guess you should know; I'm pregnant.

It's the incentive I need to finish what I've started here.

As I said, I am doing really well.

I think it's wonderful news, a baby, but as I sit here at this desk in the corner of the recreation room, I can see your face as clearly as if you are standing in front of me and you look upset, shocked, angry – in the way you always do because nothing, nothing I ever do is quite good enough for you.

But you know what? I don't care. I DON'T CARE!

S

Pregnant . . . pregnant with me . . .

Reaching for her phone and with her fingers shaking, Victoria dialled the number at the bottom of the email.

She read the numbers aloud: '0047 22 . . .'

'Hello?'

The sound of Sarah's voice threw her, and the words stuck in Victoria's throat. It took all of her effort to get sound out.

'You . . . you *are* my mum, aren't you? You're really her!' she croaked, holding the computer screen to her face, again studying the minute detail of the photograph, wishing she could remember some of it, anything.

'I am.' Sarah spoke slowly, clearly, as if overcome with emotion. 'I am your mum. I am.'

'You didn't die. Even though everyone told me you did, you didn't die!'

'No, darling, I didn't die.'

Victoria gripped the phone as a sob left her throat with a sound that was close to a whimper.

'Prim *lied* to me! She lied to me! *You* lied to me! You all did! Everyone! Everyone I loved, everyone I have lost.' Her voice was clear, despite being distorted by her sobs. 'What am I supposed to think? What am I supposed to do now? And who am I supposed to trust?'

Sarah took her time in replying. 'I have always hoped – believed – that one day I'd get the chance to explain to you what my life was like, what *our* life was like.' She took a slow breath. 'It was a mess of a time, chaotic, and it was only when we all came out the other side, years later, that we were able to analyse the decisions we made. Did we get it right? Probably not, but we did the best we could, Victory. We did the best we could.' Sarah started crying so hard she could barely catch her breath.

'And, and you are sure Prim knew you were alive?' Victoria sniffed and asked the question, still hoping at some level that there was a reasonable excuse that would keep Prim from being implicated, meaning her gran had not lied. Meaning their relationship could remain intact.

'Yes. Yes, she knew,' Sarah levelled.

Victoria felt like she'd been punched in the chest. She let her head fall to her chest and lowered the phone for a second. What was it Prim used to say?

That's the things with lies, darling; they are like wounds that never quite heal, the hurt goes too deep. It's not only the thing that is said or done that rankles, it's also the fact that the person lying to you thinks you are stupid enough to fall for it.'

Victoria knew she must be very stupid, because she had fallen for it hook, line and sinker. Again she put the phone to her face.

'And . . . and Grandpa too?' Her bottom lip quivered.

Again, Sarah's voice was steady. 'Yes, he knew.'

'I don't know what to say.' She breathed deeply. 'I . . . My whole life! The people I trusted, the people I *loved*. They lied to me. It's like grieving – this feels like grieving, but no one has died, the opposite, someone has come back to life, but I am still grieving – no one told me the truth!'

'I know,' Sarah whispered, as if shamed.

'I don't know what to think. I don't know how to feel. What about my dad? Did he really die? Or is he living in a different European city with a new wife, just waiting to pop up out of the woodwork at another low point in my life?' She regretted the flippant, almost callous nature of her comment, fuelled by distress and embarrassment. The noise Sarah made was one of deep sorrow, almost torment, and Victoria knew it would stay with her.

'Your dad . . .' Sarah coughed to clear her throat. 'Your dad died while I was pregnant with you. He never got to meet you, but he did hear your heartbeat and it was the most wonderful day we had ever had.'

The picture she painted was so beautiful that for a short while Victoria forgot her pain and, despite her tears, smiled briefly at the image.

'My head is such a mess.' She spoke aloud.

'I can only imagine. Please try to forgive me. I know your hurt is raw, new. But you have to know that not a single day has gone by that I haven't thought about you, loved you, ached for you . . .'

'But you never got in contact, never came to see me or Prim or Grandpa! How could you *do* that? You say it has hurt for all these years, but if that's true, how could you stand it?'

'Because, Victory, my beautiful girl. That was the deal . . .'

'The deal? You made a fucking deal? I am a person! I am a *person*, Sarah! Not a thing, a deal! How could you? How could you?' She only realised she was yelling when Daksha rushed into the room.

'What's going on?' She placed her hand on her chest, like she was ready to face an emergency.

'I gotta go.'

'No, Vi—'

Victoria ended the call and slammed her laptop shut. She jumped up with her fists balled and punched the cushion on the chair by the fireplace.

'What's the matter?' Daksha took a cautious step into the room.

'Everything! Is the matter! Everything!' Victoria yelled.

SIX

Victoria spent much of the morning in contemplation, with a shiver to her bones, despite the warmth of the day. Dozing for moments on the sofa before waking with a feeling of confusion so profound she thought she might be dreaming. Mentally prodded by the facts that would not sink in.

Sarah Hansen is my mum.

My mum did not die.

Prim lied to me. She lied!

My mother is Sarah Hansen . . .

Sarah Hansen. A lawyer.

A lawyer from Oslo.

I still don't think it's true! It can't be true, can it?

It was a surprise when Gerald poked his head around the door of the drawing room. 'Hello, dear.' He pointed towards the front door. 'Your friend let me in.'

'Hi, Gerald.' She sat up on the sofa and swung her legs around to make space. He sat next to her. The kind man who still believed that Prim was a good person, but she knew differently.

'No need to ask how you are doing. I can see not great, and I mean that in no way disrespectfully.' He folded his hands into his lap.

'And you'd be right, but not necessarily for the reasons you might think.'

He twisted to face her, his eyes bright, and she felt a shot of something like malice in her veins; it felt appropriate to shatter the regard in which he held her gran, the woman who had lied to her, made a mockery of her life. The woman who had held her hand while she cried for her mum and who had helped her draw pictures of her mother in heaven, which she would store under her pillow, when all the time she knew that Victoria's mother was in bloody Oslo! It was the worst betrayal, and Victoria was angry.

'Is life getting you down?'

'Just a bit.' She laughed at the understatement.

'Well, if there's anything I can do, or if you just want a good listening ear, I—'

'Actually, Gerald.' She cut him short. 'There is something I would like to tell you. Not a secret exactly, not any more, but a strange thing, that's for sure.'

'Oh?' He looked at her as if what came next might require his full attention.

She took a deep breath, aware that she might be stripping away some of Prim's veneer for him too, having to inform him that she had lied for all these years . . . but that was just too bad.

'You know about my mum, that she, erm . . .' It felt weird saying that she had died, the most definitive of human actions, when she was about to immediately disprove it.

'Yes, dear, I do. A sad, sad business for you all. I know what happened and that you were very small, I believe.'

'Well' – Victoria made a clicking noise at the side of her mouth – 'here's the thing. My mum turned up at Prim's funeral. She even came back here to Rosebank, but stayed in the garden, and then I met her briefly to talk before she had to leave again.'

Gerald held her eyeline, his mouth moving silently in confusion as he knitted his brows. 'I don't understand. What do you mean, your mum "turned up" at the funeral? Do you mean in spirit form?' he asked quietly. 'I personally am not a believer, but if it brings you comfort, dear, to think you met with your mother, then I think that is a fine thing.'

Victoria actually threw her head back and let out a snort, shaking her head. 'No, Gerald. It's even stranger than that. My actual mum, who it turns out did not die, pitched up after all this time to inform me that she is very much alive.'

'But I don't understand!' He looked a little ashen.

'That makes two of us.'

'She's not dead?'

'Not even a little bit.'

'And she came here?' He was clearly trying to fathom what was going on.

'She came here and stood by the lake.'

'Are you *sure* she is your mother?' He asked the most obvious question.

Victoria nodded. 'Absolutely positive.' She found his expression of complete and utter disbelief comforting. It proved to her that she was right to be outraged, upset and defiant because it was the worst bloody thing imaginable!

'But, I don't . . . why did . . . how does . . .?' he floundered.

'Trust me, all the questions that are whizzing around your head right now have been whizzing around mine since I found out.'

'Why would Prim say she had died if she hadn't, and why would your mother agree to it?'

She shrugged. 'Who knows, Gerald? That's the big question.'

'Well, I never did.' Gerald shook his head and gave a long sigh. 'As if you don't have enough to deal with right now, Miss Victoria.'

'Tell me about it.' Victoria stared at the fireplace and thought about Christmas when she was six.

'I wish I had my mummy here with me . . .'

'I know, darling, but she's like that angel on top of the tree, watching over you . . .'

'I must say, I don't know what to think,' Gerald sighed. 'I don't know where to start with this. It's . . . it's wonderful terrible.'

'I guess it is.' *Wonderful terrible.* 'My head is swirling constantly.' She rubbed her temples.

'I bet. Where does your mother live? Locally?'

'No. Oslo.'

'Oslo!' He gasped loudly, as if this revelation was worse than the first. 'Goodness me!'

'Prim used to say that lies rankle, because the person lying to you thinks you are stupid enough to fall for it. I always thought I was smart, turns out I wasn't.'

He whipped his head towards her. 'You *are* smart, Victoria, and you will find a way to figure it out. Life has thrown you a curve ball and it's knocked you off your feet, but you'll get back up again. You will.'

She hated that she cried, wanting to rage, wanting to get mad, but tears hauled her back to square one, leaving her lost and bereft and with the weight of loneliness crushing the breath out of her. Gerald patted her arm.

'Don't cry, dear. Don't cry. Prim would not want you to cry.'

'You don't know that! You don't know what Prim would or would not want because you didn't know her – how could you? I lived with her every day of my life and even I didn't know her!'

'I know she loved you. I know she loved you very much.'

'How?' she fired. 'Because she *told* you that? Because, let's face it, she told me lots of things that weren't true – like the fact that my mum had died but she hadn't!'

'No, she was living in Oslo,' he mused, and for some reason this made Victoria laugh while her tears continued to fall.

'Yes, she was living in Oslo.'

'I'm going to leave you to it.' He stood. 'I think you need to be alone with your thoughts, but you know where I am if you need me. On the end of the phone. Day or night.'

'Day or night,' she acknowledged through her tears.

◆ ◆ ◆

'I'm not sure we need a fire, Daks. It's not that cold.' Victoria watched from the corner of the sofa as her friend took great care in twisting rips of newspaper into spills and placing them under small shards of firewood that Bernard-the-traitor-spy-handyman had some time ago prepared and piled into the log baskets on either side of the fire in the drawing room.

'It's not about cold.' Daksha drew her from her thoughts. 'It's about cosy. Plus, I can't tell you how much I love a real fire. In our house, if we want a fire my dad presses a button on a remote control and a flame whooshes along a glass panel and hey presto! But this' – she now ran her fingers over the gnarled bunch of dried twigs in her hands – 'this is old school.'

'I guess.' Victoria curled her feet under her legs and pulled her favourite soft, pink blanket from the arm of the chair, placing it over her legs. It seemed she lived in her denim cut-offs right now, as if aware that the warm days would be ending soon. Daksha was right; it was a night for cosy. Mrs Joshi had dropped off a chicken dish that was simmering in the bottom oven. The subtle smell from coconut and spices wafted from the kitchen, enough to make her mouth water – quite a feat, considering her recent lack of appetite. Her ribs, she noted, were a little more pronounced than she was used to, her jaw sharper. Being slim meant there was no spare

109

weight for when illness or the lack of desire to eat struck. She had never been a girl who strived for skinny.

'You've been quiet today. I'm worried about you,' her friend levelled.

This she knew, both that her friend was worried – the give-away being the frequent petting of her hair and the making of cups of tea, which she delivered with a small smile of concern – and that she had been quiet, unable to settle.

She had spent more minutes than she cared to admit poring over the photograph of her as a baby lying in her mother's emaci-ated arms with her gran standing to one side, complicit. She toyed with the idea of devouring the remaining letters and then calling Sarah to rage at her, her mind fraught with conflict. Part of her wanted to delete the woman's number and punish her in the way she felt she had been punished – banished with silence for so many years. And the other part wanted to jump on a plane and rush into her mother's arms, where she would lay her head on her chest and never, ever leave . . .

But it wasn't Sarah who bore the brunt of her anger – it was Prim. Her thoughts were vignettes of all the platitudes offered by her gran in her moments of distress, many when she was a small child and her sadness was more honestly expressed:

'But I don't want to make a Mother's Day card for you, Gran – I want to give one to my mum!'

'Oh, I know, darling! I know! But it would be wonderful for me. Don't forget I don't get a Mother's Day card now either . . . your mummy was my little girl . . .'

You liar! How could you? You liar!

Daksha arranged a final bundle of twigs and looked more than a little chuffed with her handiwork.

'Eat your heart out, Bear Grylls! So, come on, it's not like you to be so quiet, Vic. Talk to me!'

'I just *feel* like being quiet.' She spoke softly, a little irritated by her friend's line of questioning, no matter how well intentioned. 'I think everything that's happened is percolating. I can't stop thinking about all that I've read in the letters: replaying them in my mind.'

'Of course.' Daksha struck a match from the large box of Cook's Matches and knelt low, carefully touching the little flame to several points on the paper spills. She then sat back and watched closely with a fixed look of determination. 'How are you feeling about it all?'

Victoria stared into the grate as small flames flickered and the fire began to cradle the kindling.

'It changes. I think about the fact that Prim lied to me for all this time and I go nuts, even swear at her in my head.' She winced with the shame of this admission, knowing she would not have conceived of such a thing when Prim was here. Her tears were, as ever, not that far from the surface. 'I can't stop crying! I'm sad because she died, and I love and miss her so much. And that feeling of missing her is mostly greater than my anger, but not always. Like, right now, I also wish she were here so I could yell at her!'

Victoria bit her fingernail, a new and pleasing habit.

Daksha blew into the fireplace and the flames flickered and flared, starting to take hold before she carefully placed a cut log on to the fire, watching as they licked up the sides of the dried bark.

'Do you understand what happened that made Prim lie to you?'

Victoria took her time in responding, liking the crackle of the fire. 'Not really. But in some ways, it's like they are two different people. There's my Prim, who baked me cookies when I got in from school and who made my costume for the summer play, and the other Prim, who took me from my mum and lied to me; lied to me about the very worst thing I could imagine. I think I need to let everything settle and try not to think about it all so much. I need to calm down and try to make sense of it when I'm not freaking out.'

'I like the sound of her.' Daksha turned in the hearth to look her friend squarely in the face.

'Who?' Victoria knew who she meant but wanted to give the impression that Sarah was not the first and last thing she thought about each day and night and every minute in between.

'Sarah!' Daksha tutted.

Victoria nodded. 'You do?'

'Yes, the way she's handled things since making contact, like sending everything through to you immediately and the way she was at the hotel – I mean, what's not to like, right? She's very elegant, attractive, a lawyer, lives in Norway, which is always voted one of the happiest places to live.'

'Yes, Daks, she's a regular Wonder Woman. You've not met her properly; she could be a total cow when she's got her guard down. She abandoned me, don't forget!' There it was again, the anger that bubbled in her throat.

'She doesn't seem like a total cow,' Daksha offered quietly.

'That's right, because only a total cow would choose drugs over her baby, would still mourn a bloke she knew for the equivalent of five minutes, would choose to have no contact with her elderly parents, have the bloody nerve to pitch up on the day of her mother's funeral and tell her long-lost daughter, who believed her dead, that her name is in fact Victory! A fucking stupid name if ever I've heard one!'

'I just . . . I just thought she seemed nice.'

'It's bullshit, all of it! What if the vicar's right? What if she is after the house?'

She didn't believe this, not for a single second, but was running out of verbal ammunition to fling in the direction of Sarah Hansen's reputation.

'Did she mention the house?' Daksha asked almost sheepishly.

'Well, no, not yet! But she wouldn't, would she, if she was clever; she'd bide her time!'

Daksha lay two chunky logs on the flames, which had now truly taken hold, and took up her place in the opposite corner of the sofa. The two sat awkwardly.

'I'm worried about you.'

'So you've said, Daks! God! Give it up! What do you want me to do? Jump up and down? Make out to be happy? Sing? What are you, my *mother*? Wouldn't that be absolutely brilliant? No mum for eighteen years and then suddenly I've got *Mrs* Joshi cooking my food and cleaning the kitchen, Sarah, and now you! Mother figures crawling out of the woodwork! Oh, lucky me!' It frightened her a little how close to the surface her anger lurked, revealed by the most minor verbal scratch of irritation.

Daksha stared at her.

There was a beat or two of uncomfortable, unbearable silence, which rang loudly, cocooning them. And suddenly, in that beautiful room with floral paintings on the walls, vintage cushions nestling into the crooks of the arms of the sofas and chairs and a glorious orange fire roaring in the grate, it felt like the least cosy place she could imagine.

'Do you want me to stay here tonight? Or would you rather I went home?' Daksha asked calmly.

'I don't care! I don't care right now!' Victoria rammed her fingers into her fringe, hating the words that left her mouth, hating the bitter tang of regret on which they coasted from her tongue and hating more than anything the fact that everyone had lied to her! But she didn't know how to stop, how to calm down, and she certainly didn't know how to apologise. Her emotions were a whirling tornado, stoppered inside a bottle, and try as she might, she couldn't smash it. Everything felt like too much, even having to be nice to her friend. Her very, very best friend in the whole wide world. She despised the moment, knowing she would hate it for as long as it lived in her memory.

Daksha calmly stood and smoothed her jeans. 'In that case, I think I'll go and pack my stuff and get my mum to collect me.'

'Whatever you want.' Victoria pulled the blanket up to her chin and slid down on the sofa.

'What I want is to go home,' Daksha spoke directly, if quietly, as she left the room.

Victoria felt the sharp pang of regret at the thought of her friend leaving her alone, but misplaced pride and confusion prevented her from speaking up and trying to make things good. It was self-punishing and felt appropriate for her state of mind, in which she kept reminding herself that she was the victim in all of this. She heard Daksha clatter down the stairs and stayed put.

When the car beeped on the drive, Victoria sat up. She felt torn between running to the hallway, throwing her arms around her friend and crying out her apology, and wanting nothing more than to be by herself, alone with her thoughts and the photograph and letters that offered such a horrible insight. It was still surreal to her that Prim had let her down in this way and that even Grandpa had known, Bernard too, but not her. Daksha stood in the doorway to the drawing room with her overnight bag in her hands and resting against her shins.

'I took the chicken out of the oven.'

'You haven't eaten.' Victoria felt bad that Mrs Joshi had cooked for them both.

'I'm not hungry.' Daksha wrinkled her nose, as if even the thought of food was more than she could stand. 'You know where I am if you need me.'

'Yep.'

Victoria watched her go and heard the clunk of the front door, followed by the sound of the car crunching its way across the gravel to the lane, and then it was quiet. It was the first time she had been on her own, properly on her own, since Prim's death. She felt odd, tired, sad and already lonely.

Is this what it will be like now?

Slipping down further on the sofa with her knees curled to her chest and her head sinking into a silk cushion as the fire crackled in the grate, she fell into a deep and restful sleep, claimed by exhaustion . . .

The beep of her phone woke her with a start.

There was a split second when she didn't know where she was. Her neck ached, as she had slept with it at an odd angle, and she felt the chill of the early hours in her bones. It was unusual for her to wake and find herself downstairs and not in her bed. And again, a recurring theme in recent weeks, her first thought was *where's Prim?* Before the sharp bite of reality clamped her throat, making breathing momentarily tricky. And not only this, but the Prim she had relied on, Prim her friend, her mentor, her mother figure – well, she didn't even exist. This thought was enough to plunge her into an icy pool of loneliness where it was all she could do to stay afloat.

The room was now in darkness, the fire long ago dwindled. And of course no Daksha. Jumping up, she switched on the table lamp at the back of the sofa and was glad of the soft light that helped calm her racing pulse. Pulling the patchwork eiderdown from the back of one of the chairs, she wrapped it around herself. Finally, sitting in her quilted wigwam, her breathing settled and her chill subsided.

Victoria reached for her phone and was surprised to see the beep had come from a Facebook alert and not, as she had assumed, a text from Daksha. It was a message request from Flynn McNamara.

Her gut leapt with expectation. She accepted it immediately and read the words with more than a pinch of curiosity.

What you doing?

The message was as uninformative as it was random and surprising. It made her laugh, a welcome distraction that lifted her momentarily from the emotional tempest in which she was mired. She considered her response before replying with:

Well it's 2.45 in the morning! I should be sleeping . . .

She fired it off with a sense of nervous anticipation, unsure of the convention when it came to chatting like this.

But your not sleeping – your chatting to me.

Victoria cringed at his grammatical error. She might not have been au fait with the rules of flirtation, but she knew enough to stay shtum on this.

You got me!

Have I?

Came his immediate response.

It would have been hard to describe how this brief exchange, his words curt and unimaginative, made such a difference to her state of mind. It was the finest distraction, and also, at some subtle level, she wanted to talk to someone who had no part in the whole sordid lie that was her life. Her first thought, with a ball of excitement gathering in her gut, was to shout for Daksha and show her

116

the messages, picturing how they would hug each other and squeal with childish excitement, but Daksha was no doubt sleeping deeply in her loving home with her mum and dad keeping watch and her siblings within earshot along the corridor. Unlike her, who was all alone, having more or less sent her one friend and ally packing. It was this thought that sent a wobble of fear through her very core. Looking out of the side window towards the path, which snaked its way around the house, she wished she had had the forethought to draw the curtains. She listened hard now, in case there might be footsteps on the gravel, alerting her to . . . what? An intruder? Now she gathered the quilt around her shoulders a little tighter and curled her toes beneath the fabric.

I honestly don't know what to say to that.

She wrote the absolute truth.

Ill take it as a yes.

What was it with him and apostrophes?

A yes to what? I don't know what the question was?

Victoria felt bold and liked the rush of confidence that swelled in her veins.

The question was, would you like some company?

Now?!

Her panicked response.

Her thoughts were so frantic they collided with each other, making it almost impossible to think straight and come up with a coherent plan.

I haven't washed my hair for days! How can I see Flynn! I've got a spot on my chin. He wants to come here, to this house, right now? It's late! I'm wearing dirty shorts! Do I like him? Do I know him? What would Prim think? What would Daks say? This boy who I have thought about for years wants to come here and see me!!!

Sure.

Felt like the best response.

On my way. We can talk about Chelsea's latest performance!
Ha ha! (they are blue ones by the way!)

This final message sent Victoria into something of a tailspin. Letting the quilt drop to the floor, she ran around the sofa for no good reason, before rushing up the stairs and into the bathroom, where she thoroughly cleaned her teeth and rinsed with mouthwash twice for good measure. She stared at her reflection and pulled her hair back into a loose knot before letting it down again and then putting it up again. There was no disguising the dark circles of grief that sat beneath her eyes or the lack of polish to her skin, which she had neglected in recent times. But this was who she was and this was how she was. She remembered what Prim had said about when she met Grandpa and he had liked her for being her, 'warts and all'. Her tears gathered and she cursed the memory, which like all memories of her gran right now were bittersweet, tinged with the pain of recent loss and betrayal. She bit the inside of her cheek until she tasted the irony seep of her blood.

'Why the fuck did you do it to me?' she asked the mirror, picturing her gran standing behind her at a time when she might stop by to chat while Victoria got ready for bed, in the time before – when she was in the dark; before she felt like her whole life had been compromised.

The wardrobe doors were propped open with bundles of dirty laundry. Prim had been fastidious about gathering up anything on the floor and shoving it into the washing machine. Victoria rummaged through the rail stuffed with overloaded hangers. To her dismay, she discovered that many of the items in there were no more than jumble fodder. Old sweatshirts with transfers of ponies on the front, dresses that were at least three sizes too small and a whole range of school uniform for the school she had left a few months ago now. She chose her linen shirt from the laundry pile, giving it a quick sniff before spraying it with her perfume and slipping it over her vest. It was as she stood back and pondered what to do about the bottom half that the front doorbell rang. Too late; her denim cut-offs showing off her chicken legs would have to do.

Despite having known that Flynn was en route, it still shocked her. It was rare, if not unheard of, for the doorbell of Rosebank to ring any time after dusk.

Supposing it wasn't Flynn?

Being alone in the house for the first time in the dead of night, intrusive, fearful thoughts gathered around her. She felt her blood race as she looked at the closed doors along the landing, wondering what might lurk behind them. It wasn't so much that she had relied on Prim to come out wielding a hammer in the event of an emergency, more that she had never considered there *might* be an emergency, not with her gran close by, keeping her safe. Prim, the woman who tamed her wild thoughts when her grief felt a little overwhelming.

'What a joke!'

She gripped the bannister as she crept down the stairs. His dark hair was visible in the small leaded window at the top of the door.

And then, just like that, there he was.

'Hi, Flynn.' She spoke with as much calm as she could muster. Trying desperately to give the impression that it was no big deal, an everyday occurrence. Whereas, in reality, it was the stuff of her daydreams come true. Flynn McNamara was in her house! Standing in the hallway in the middle of the night with his backpack in his hand. She had quite forgotten what the sight of him did to her: warmed her gut, made her smile and sent shivers of longing through her body.

'You live in an old-lady house!' His opening gambit as he looked around and then laughed. Victoria laughed too, because she didn't think it through, overwhelmed by the whole experience, but remembering enough that 'doll-like and dumb' were what she needed to strive for. She took in his unkempt curly hair, scruffy trainers, skinny jeans that sat tantalisingly low to reveal the navy-blue waistband of his underwear, and his slightly bloodshot eyes, their gaze a little off-centre. As her giggles burbled, however, each one left a dot of shame on her tongue.

This is your home! Prim's home! And you know and love everything in it! Or at least you used to . . . But it was too late; she had slipped into that role. The one some take on when they meet a person they like too much and try to squeeze themselves into the shape of someone they think that person might like. Assuming, sadly, that the *real* them, the 'warts and all' them, would simply not be enough.

'I didn't decorate it, any of it. No way!' She hated the disloyalty and knew deep down this appeasing cowardice paved the way to a destination she did not want to visit, but it was too late; she had jumped into a cart and it was hurtling along a track faster than she knew how to steer.

'No shit!' He gave her his beautiful, lopsided smile and walked forward. 'Good morning, Victoria!' He gave an elaborate bow with one arm flat against his stomach, his other outstretched.

'Are you drunk?' She laughed again, like some giggling stupid thing, stating the obvious, as Flynn wobbled on the spot and the air around him thickened with the foul odour of booze. He straightened and teetered towards the wall; his outstretched palm, fixed to break his fall, thankfully found a space between a Victorian framed needlepoint and a black-and-white photograph of Great-Granny Cutter on her wedding day, looking, it was fair to say, less than ecstatic about the whole affair. Victoria felt her heart leap at the mere prospect of something getting broken or damaged, aware almost for the first time that she was now the custodian of Rosebank and everything in it. And then another thought: *if stuff got broken, so what?* Who did she have to answer to? No one.

'Where have you been?' She thought she might be able to help him focus by engaging him in conversation, anything to try to control those flailing hands and unsteady feet.

'What, tonight?'

'Yes, tonight!'

'Oh, pub, and then to Jasper's, and then I was walking home and I thought' – he clicked his fingers loudly – 'Victoria!' The slur of his speech was a little more obvious to her now.

'Would you like some coffee?' She didn't know the right course of action; his state was seemingly something very different from how she felt after sipping a glass of wine with Prim over dinner. Her concern was now in figuring out how to get him to sober up – she wanted to talk to sober Flynn.

She led the way to the kitchen and he walked slowly beside her. This was not how the many fantasies of Flynn McNamara pitching up at her house in the middle of the night had usually played out.

'So you, like, live here all by yourself?'

Even the words were alarming. It was something she was only beginning to consider, living in and caring for this big old house alone. She didn't know if she was up to it and desperately wished Daksha was asleep upstairs.

She watched his eyes rove the painted ceilings and then peep into the open doors of the rooms leading off the hallway and wondered what his house might be like. If she had to guess, it was probably much closer to Daksha's than to this.

'This place is massive!' He sounded impressed, which made her feel more than a little uncomfortable. She revised her mental image. *Like Daksha's, but smaller . . .*

'Uh-huh. I'm on my own *now*, but Daksha has been staying, so I haven't really been alone. But she . . . she's gone home.' She blotted out the image of her friend's face, her look of hurt, not wanting it to blemish this interaction.

'And now you're not alone because I'm here.'

'Yup.' Her hands felt clammy and her gut full of jitters. She knew she was perspiring and hoped she didn't smell, thinking now not only of her sweat but the worn blouse she had hastily retrieved from the bedroom floor. Her stomach jumped with all the possibilities of what might happen. She was as excited as she was petrified.

'It sucks what happened to your nan.' He held her eyeline and she was thankful for his sincere tone.

'Yes, it sucks. I know it's real, but I don't *believe* it's real, if that makes any sense. It's all been really shit.' She decided not to elaborate, not yet.

He nodded. 'Yep. I know that feeling.'

'Have you . . .' She coughed, trying to relax but still feeling over-awed and anxious. 'Have you ever lost anyone?'

'Yes.' He sat at the kitchen table. 'My big brother.'

'Oh no! I didn't know that.' She took the chair opposite him, trying not to think of how she and Prim had sat like this to eat their breakfast every morning.

'Did you have any sweet dreams, darling girl?'

'Grapefruit or muesli?'

'Oh, by the way, a funny thing: you know I told you that your mum was dead, well . . .'

'Well, it's all a bit weird; he *would* have been my big brother,' Flynn explained, running his palm over his face. 'Except he died when he was a toddler, so he is kind of always my little brother too.'

'So you don't remember him?'

'Again, weird.' He yawned, suggesting the night might finally be catching up with him. 'I was born after he died so I don't remember him at all, but my mum and dad always told me I had a big brother watching over me, and they'd kind of point upwards. I thought for years he lived in the loft and wondered why I'd never met him.' He smiled at her and she took this as permission to release the giggle that was brewing behind her lips.

'I thought he might come down when I was at school or while I was sleeping, like we had the job of being my parents' kids on a shift system. And then by the time my little sister, Maisie, was old enough to be told about him, I heard my mum tell her that Michael junior was in heaven, and that's when it clicked for me.'

'How old were you?'

'Seventeen.' He smiled, and again she laughed, liking this ready, easy humour. It put them both at ease.

'Just kidding, I must have been about six.'

'That must be really hard. Your poor mum and dad.'

'It *is* hard, even now. They still mourn him, of course, but I can't because I never really knew him. I'd never tell my parents that, though. They cry on his birthday and the anniversary of the day he died, and I sit with them and they hug us, like we are sad too, and Maisie and I look at each other, a bit embarrassed, but I don't feel much at all – I never knew him, he's just a baby photo on the sideboard.' He rubbed his eyes and exhaled foul breath. 'God, I'm starving!'

Her eyes fell upon the chicken dish prepared by Mrs Joshi. 'Do you want some chicken?'

'Yeah! Chicken!' He sat up, brightening.

She ladled two large helpings of the succulent dish with its aromatic coconut-scented sauce and dug the spoon back in to retrieve the golden, plump rice from the bottom of the pot, which nestled on a bed of onions. A quick whizz in the microwave, and the smell of the steaming-hot fare filled the room with the subtle scent of spice, tantalising enough to make her taste buds sing.

Flynn took the fork she offered and dived straight in, filling his mouth and refilling the fork before he had finished chewing.

'Oh my God! This is so good! Did you make it?'

'No. Daksha's mum made it.' She felt the pang of guilt that here they were, tucking into the food Mrs Joshi had made in good faith before being summoned to come and drive her daughter home from the house where she no longer felt wanted.

'Do you want a glass of wine?'

'A glass of wine?' He let out a loud guffaw and small flecks of rice flew from his mouth and landed on the table. 'What are you, like, sixty?'

She felt the bloom of embarrassment on her neck and chest.

'No, I just . . . My gran always drank wine with her dinner and she used to give me a glass with supper sometimes.' There was much she hated about the situation: the fact that she was having to discuss Prim, as well as trying to justify her habits. She also smarted from his criticism: the fact he thought it was uncool that she drank wine at all, and finally, that she had absolutely no clue as to what the fashionable or right thing was to do.

What would Courtney do?

Picturing the drinks cabinet in the dining room, she mentally worked her way through the shelves: port, brandy and advocaat, which had probably gone off, and a bottle of whisky bought for Grandpa's wake and still, as far as she knew, unopened.

'What do you usually drink?' She hated the timidity to her voice, confirming again that this wasn't the real her but the doll-like and dumb version of her, trying to be the kind of girl that a boy like Flynn McNamara might like.

She continued to summon her inner Courtney, and thought of Daksha, knowing this one aspect would be the thing she remembered for the retelling, where she would embellish and make it funny. That was if they ever reconnected and she got the chance. A thought that, in the company of this boy, didn't distress her as much as it should have.

Flynn paused mid-mouthful and considered what might be his tipple of choice. 'I drink beer or vodka, but mainly beer and then vodka afterwards, and then sometimes I switch back to beer.'

'I don't think we have beer or vodka.'

We . . . we . . . there is no 'we', it's just you now . . . just you in this big old-lady house of lies with your bottles of wine and fine antiques . . .

'Could I have a cup of tea?'

'A cup of tea?' This time, her laughter was the relieved kind. 'Yes. That I can manage.' She abandoned her food and filled and flicked on the kettle. 'Well, this is a strange evening. One I won't forget.' She found it a lot easier to talk freely and be herself when looking away from him. Maybe that was the key, to always avert her eyes . . . 'I didn't think when I sat on the sofa tonight that it'd end here in the kitchen at this time, eating supper with you, Flynn.'

'Me either.'

'What made you decide to message me? You never have before.'
She placed two mugs on the countertop with teabags nestling inside
and retook her place at the kitchen table.

Flynn finished his mouthful, wiped his lips with the back of
his hand and rested his fork on the edge of the bowl.

'It was when I saw you the other week when you walked past
and we talked a bit.'

Yes, that day . . . The guilt she had felt was now replaced by
a frothing anger. *I wish I'd got home earlier, I wish she had told me
herself and given me the chance to ask her why!*

'And I was thinking about you. You're not like the other girls
at school.'

Victoria smirked at the irony, thinking how she had always
figured her life would be that much easier if she were exactly like
the other girls at school.

'You're sensible.' He slurred a little.

'Oh God! Is that code for boring?' She rolled her eyes.

'No, it's code for easy to talk to because you get stuff and you
don't seem to give a shit about the rubbish that Courtney and her
mates harp on about.'

'I didn't think we'd spoken enough over the years to allow you
to have formed an opinion.'

Just the three exchanges in our whole school lives, in fact.

'True, but I used to listen to you chat to other people like
Daksha. I used to watch you in class.'

This she did not know. And it thrilled her.

'And tonight, I didn't feel like going home and I knew you lived
close by and so I messaged you. I think I wanted to talk to you.'

'And here we are.' She swallowed as the kettle boiled.

'Yes, here we are.' He reached around his gums with his tongue,
to free lodged chicken, no doubt. 'I've never told anyone that
before.'

'Told anyone what?' She had lost the thread a little.

'About my brother.'

She felt ridiculously flattered that he had shared something so personal with her. This felt like a sure-fire way to leapfrog the chit-chat and get close quickly, the thought of which she relished right now, as loneliness and confusion lapped at her heels.

Flynn shook his head. 'Yeah, and about me not feeling anything for him. I keep a lot of shit locked in. It's easier, I think.'

'I won't tell another soul.' She meant it.

'I know.' He smiled at her, that glorious, stomach-flipping, lopsided smile. 'You are cool, Victoria.' Not for the first time since his arrival she thought of Prim and the chat they had had before she and Daksha had left for town, on her very last day . . .

'Oh, darling, I don't think I have ever been cool!'

'I don't think I've ever been cool,' she whispered.

'You are. You are really cool and smart. Why didn't you apply for university?'

'Lots of reasons.'

'Tell me four of them.'

She loved the random number. Flynn sat back in the chair and folded his arms as she reached for the sugar bowl and heaped two large teaspoons into her mug.

'Because I want to carve my own path and I don't want that path to be too predictable. I think that's the most exciting way to live.'

'Easy, I guess, when you don't have to worry about where your next meal is coming from. Poor people crave the stability of that predictable path.' He sipped his tea. 'I'm not blaming you, just sayin'.'

She gave a half laugh, embarrassed that he too might recognise she was now 'a woman of means'.

'Come on: three more,' he urged now, holding his tea in his cupped palms. His gaze, she noticed, was now slightly more focused.

'Erm, I couldn't decide what I wanted to study and so I figured that, if nothing was leaping out at me as an obvious choice, did I really want to commit to it for three or four years of my life?'

'Fair enough. Next one.'

'I . . . I didn't want to leave my gran on her own. Prim, her name was Prim, Primrose.' She swallowed. 'She wasn't ill or anything, but I knew she liked having me around and I knew she wasn't getting younger.' She felt her tears pool and widened her eyes, trying in vain to dispel them. 'Although now I might make a different decision. Funny how a few bits of information can change your view on just about everything. Can make you question your loyalty.'

'Okay, and the last one?' he asked softly. Reaching out, he placed his hand over hers, acknowledging her sadness, and in truth she took immeasurable comfort from it.

'My mum went to university and she never came home, and the thought of that happening to me scares me more than I can say.'

He nodded and leaned in. No wisecrack, no quip, no opinion. She felt the damp path her tears had left on her cheeks. 'And I have never told anyone that before.'

'I won't tell a soul.' He smiled. 'Why didn't she come home? Was this when she . . . I mean, I had heard . . .' he whispered.

'Drugs.' It only felt like a half lie.

And without any more words, Flynn stood from the chair and walked around the table to where she sat and went down on his haunches. She placed her hands either side of his head and looked into his eyes as he stretched up to kiss her. It wasn't the frenzied, urgent kissing of her dreams or imaginings, instead it was quiet, contained and almost chaste, and she was grateful for it.

'Don't cry,' he soothed.

'I can't help it. I'm really, really sad.'

Flynn took her hand and led her into the drawing room, where he lay on the sofa. She slipped into the narrow space beside him, glad that she was not alone and quite unable to describe the feeling of utter abandonment as he drew the patchwork quilt over their tired limbs. It was heady and intoxicating to be in such close proximity to this boy, dizzying and wonderful. She inhaled the scent of him and liked the way his very essence caused desire to flare in her gut. His touch was rough and unconsidered, his breathing heavy and his eyes fixed. And it felt . . . it felt glorious. Many were the hours she had lain in her bed, imagining what this might feel like, and here she was! The flames of joy flickered, filling her up until it was a furnace that fuelled her.

Flynn lifted her face to his and kissed her, kissed her properly, with promise. It felt a lot like a beginning. Her skin prickled and every nerve and every fibre in her being yearned to feel his skin against hers. Victoria peeled off her vest and shrugged her bony hips out of her cut-offs before lying on top of him. She liked the way he pushed down on her back muscles, forcing out any gap between them, as close as they could be – well, almost.

It was only tiredness that put a halt to their making out. And with the rare and wonderful comfort of being held and with her head resting on his chest, Victoria felt safe and slept until mid-morning.

SEVEN

Victoria opened her eyes and found she was smiling. This had been rare in recent weeks and the feeling of bunched-up excitement deep in her stomach even rarer. Flynn was no longer on the sofa, but she could hear him pottering in the kitchen as the bang and crash of pots and pans echoed along the hallway. She wasn't sure how she felt about him still being here, about him having been here at all, but turning her head to inhale the cushion that held the scent of his head was enough to send her into a dizzying spin. Plus, it was nice to have company. She kicked her legs against the sofa cushions, child-like. They had enjoyed skin-on-skin fumbling in the dark, which had not only been exciting but also the most glorious distraction imaginable. Who would believe it? And, actually, the question was more: who did she have to tell now that Daksha was not instantly the person she felt she could text/call/speak to? A quick check on her phone confirmed her friend had not composed something comi-cal and cutting by way of reparation, as she usually did after even the smallest tiff. This felt different, like a deeper cut, and she didn't like it at all. It would have hurt a lot more, however, if she were not already feeling a little bruised and let down by life – what was one more loss?

She stood, stretched and raked her fingers through her unwashed hair, strangely caring little just how presentable she was, as if they had quickly got past such things. Her skin still glowed at the memory of his hand resting on the flat of her stomach.

The sight of him in the kitchen was both surprising and thrilling. Her concerns about his presence evaporated, wiped out by the frisson of joy in her gut. Flynn hummed as he whipped eggs in a bowl and took his time over grinding in fat twists of black pepper and then sprinkling salt flakes from a respectable height.

'Eat your heart out, Nigella!' She leaned against the dresser, happy to watch him work.

'What time do you call this?' He flapped the dishcloth towards her. 'I've been slaving over a hot stove all morning and you roll in, expecting to be fed!'

She laughed, a softer, more natural kind of laugh this morning, because she felt the first forgotten flickering of happy, because he had kissed her passionately and she no longer had to fear that first kiss, because Flynn McNamara was the boy she had thought about for more nights than she could count and because he was still here and he was cooking her breakfast. There was also relief, and her interior monologue was very clear as to why:

See, you are not alone. Flynn is here, no need to be scared. Someone is here with you . . .

'I see you found everything you need?' She took a seat at the table and saw for the first time the messy counters, the sink full of dirty implements and the discarded rubbish strewn on the floor.

'Yes!' he shouted. 'Apart from the toaster, and we can't have bacon, egg and hash browns without toast; that would be so wrong.'

'It would, and the toaster lives under the sink.' She pointed.

'*Lives* under the sink,' he repeated. 'Like a naughty or unwanted pet. Tommy the toaster!'

'Tommy the toaster,' she agreed. 'I think he nibbles the trapped crumbs, those dark bits that fall from the bread and become charcoal, lurking in the crevices so you have to turn the machine upside down over the sink and give it a good whack. I always think it's very satisfying to see them all tumble out. And very disappointing if you don't get a rich haul.'

'Poor Tommy, no wonder he hides under the sink if all you do is shove bread in his mouth and whack him on the arse.'

'I think some people pay good money for that.' She grinned.

'True that!' he yelled with a flourish of his whisk as he set the eggs to one side and placed the skillet on the stove. 'What shall we do after breakfast?'

'Oh.' This was unexpected. She had thought that he might leave after eating, and yet here he was, arranging the day ahead. It made her feel a little giddy that he was making a plan and also a little relieved that he was not intending to leave any time soon. 'I'm supposed to be working in the coffee shop today, a late shift.'

'How late?' he asked over his shoulder as he wrestled Tommy from under the sink.

'Start at four, finish at eight.'

'That's not going to happen.'

'It's not?'

'No, Victoria. After we have eaten breakfast we need to watch a movie.'

'Which movie?' She was confused, wondering if she had lost the thread.

'Any movie! And then after that we might watch another.'

'And after that?' she asked playfully, feeling quite ecstatic at the thought of a duvet day in front of the TV with this boy she so liked and who she hoped might be up for more of that kissing. A day where she didn't have to think about anything. The prospect of a mental break from her anguish was a welcome one and she relished the thought of not having to try and figure out who had lied and why.

'I dunno, we'll play it by ear . . .' He stopped what he was doing and stared at her, his expression serious, and she felt the flutter of something deep in her chest as he continued to stare, taking her in. And it was in this moment that Victoria wondered if she had finally, finally, gone full chip.

She was carefully formulating her response when the doorbell rang and they both jumped.

Daksha . . .

Relieved in part that her friend had come back, she decided to go straight in with a big hug that she would hold for a little too long – this, she knew, would speak more than any words – before dragging her straight into the drawing room and giving her the five-second low-down, whispering of course, knowing time was of the essence.

Youarenotgoingtobelievethis, but Flynnisinthekitchnenhespentthenight andnowhesmakingeggsforbreakfast! Ohmygoddaksthisisactuallyhappening!

She bit her lip to stifle a squeal at the raucous delight she was certain would follow this revelation; she and Daksha had been known to squeal in unison over far, far less.

The face that greeted her as she flung the front door open was not, however, that of her friend, but someone rather different.

'Gerald!' She smiled, hoping the disappointment she felt at the sight of him didn't leak through into her expression and then feeling instantly guilty that his presence irritated her a little. Why, oh why had he decided to visit today of all days, when she was . . . preoccupied. Daksha, she knew, would have joined in, pulled up a chair and not diluted the wonderful atmosphere! But Gerald? He was a visitor on a whole different scale.

'Good morning, Victoria. How are you today, dear?' He ducked his silver head to walk forwards, as he had done numerous times before, and she had little choice but to stand aside and allow him entry into the hallway. She turned briefly to look back towards the garden room, half expecting to see Prim drift into view.

Gerald, darling. Good morning! Let's pop the kettle on – I'm assuming it's too early for gin?

'I'm okay. Thank you.'

'Well, that's very good to hear. I must say I have been mulling over the thing we discussed and I can only come up with more questions than answers. It's not something you hear every day and it requires a lot of thought.'

'Yep, that's about the sum of it,' she agreed.

He gave her the smile that made his eyes crinkle up at the sides and, paying no heed to the warmth of the day, he unwound the maroon knitted scarf from his neck with one hand and deftly hooked it over the bannister in a well-practised movement. In his other hand, he gripped a wide, newspaper-wrapped bundle, which he now presented to her with his heels together and his head tilted, giving the act a certain grandeur.

'I was up at the allotment this morning, and these beauties are flourishing. Thought you might like some. Prim used to slice them very thinly, sauté them with a little garlic and pepper and finish with a generous squeeze of lemon. They are perfect with any meat or alone with lumps of crumbly cheese. Feta is best, and a large glass of white!' He tapped the side of his nose as if sharing a confidence, not a recipe.

'Courgettes!' She inhaled the distinct, earthy scent of vegetables freshly picked. 'Thank you, Gerald. I shall do just that.'

She felt torn, wanting to invite the kindly man in and make him a cup of tea, just as Prim would expect her to, but similarly wanting him to skedaddle back out the way he had come, leaving her alone to enjoy her brunch with Flynn. Flynn! Just the thought of him in her kitchen was enough to make her beam and her toes grip the floor. There was also a thin veil of self-consciousness over her – she had, after all, had a boy here for the best part of the night, and she wondered if, in the wake of her new and enlightened physical experience, she looked changed in any way.

'I also wanted to say, and don't think I am interfering, dear, because that is the last thing I would want to do and you must feel free to tell an old fuddy-duddy like me to mind my own beeswax!' He smiled. 'But I noticed on the day of Prim's funeral that it's a lot more than the tomato plants that are in need of some attention. The geraniums need deadheading, and one or two of the orchids need a little spritz. I would hate to see her plants wither, she loved them so, and I was wondering whether it might be appropriate for me to—' He stopped mid-sentence as Flynn appeared in the hallway, holding the skillet of eggs.

'Morning!' He waved the spatula in his hand.

'Good . . . good morning.' Gerald straightened and flattened his shirtfront with the palm of his hand. 'I am sorry, I didn't realise you had company.'

She saw the old man's gaze wander to the open door of the drawing room, where she knew he would spy the patchwork quilt, heaped and abandoned on the floor by the sofa, whose cushions were awry and topped with a discarded bra. The coffee table was littered with empty food bowls, with licks of spicy coconut sauce congealed on the sides, and half-empty mugs of tea, one placed on the novel that she was yet to finish.

'This is Flynn.'

'Flynn. I see.' Gerald nodded. 'How do you do?' He held out his right hand, as if to shake hands with her friend, but as both of Flynn's hands were occupied he instead raised it into a wave.

'Would you like some breakfast? I've made plenty.' Flynn jerked his head towards the kitchen. His offer sounded genuine and she liked how he included Gerald.

'Have you now?' Gerald paused, his smile a little forced. 'Well, thank you for that kind offer, but breakfast was a long time ago for me. I am, in fact, already thinking about lunch!'

'No worries!' Flynn smiled and returned to the kitchen. Gerald's slight and tone were not lost on Victoria, who knew that Gerald, like Prim, would think that lounging around at this time of day with no chores done and only just starting breakfast would indicate that they were lazy. But there was something more. She felt by the stiffening of his spine and the slip of his smile that he was judging her for allowing this boy into her family home. And whilst she reminded herself that it was absolutely nothing to do with Gerald what she did and who she did it with, it didn't feel nice at all, the idea that her gran's beau might in some way think she was being disrespectful or sleazy, and so soon after saying goodbye to Prim. In fact, how dare he? It was an incredibly rude and judgemental way to behave towards Flynn, who had done nothing other than offer Gerald breakfast! Sweet Jesus, did *everyone* think they could comment on her life? Intervene? Take control?

'Thank you for my courgettes, Gerald, and yes, please do whatever you think is best with the plants; I'd hate to see them wither too. It would be the worst. Anyway, this isn't getting breakfast served!' She looked towards the kitchen. 'And I am starving!'

The man rocked on his soft-soled shoes and looked a little lost for words.

'Maybe . . . maybe you could let me know when would be a good time to come and tend to them?' He shot a look towards the kitchen.

'Maybe I will do that.' She was aware of the change in her tone but wanted to get her message across – *bloody Gerald! Bloody Prim!* And just like that, she was right back to her gran's betrayal . . .

'Righto. Well, we'll leave it at that then.' Gerald gave a small, tight-lipped smile and reached for his scarf before letting himself out of the front door.

Victoria laid the bundle of courgettes on a shelf in the fridge and sat at the table, where Flynn had set two places.

'Was he a friend of your nan's?' Flynn asked as he placed a loaded plate in front of her. She laughed at the sheer volume of food: a pile of crispy bacon, a small mountain of soft, buttery scrambled eggs and three golden, crisply fried home-made hash browns. This was accompanied by several slices of bread, all browned to perfection by Tommy and spread generously with butter.

'This looks amazing! Thank you, Flynn, and yes, he was her kind of boyfriend, I suppose, and now, apparently, he thinks that gives him the right to pitch up and tell me what to do.'

'Did he tell you what to do?'

'Not in so many words.' She flicked her hair over her shoulders. 'But you know when someone is having a sly dig at you and you know it? It was like that. And it makes me mad! I mean, God, I'm not a kid!'

'You are definitely not a kid.' He smiled at her and her stomach flipped. 'I didn't think people would bother having boyfriends or girlfriends when they were that ancient.'

'You'd be surprised.' She picked up a rigid strip of bacon and snapped the end off into her mouth. The salty fat melted on her tongue and her hunger surged. She reached for another piece. 'Oh my God! This is *so* good! She picked up her fork and attacked the food mountain in front of her.

'That's another thing I really like about you,' Flynn observed.

'What?' She spoke with her mouth full, suddenly ravenous and ridiculously flattered that he had said 'another thing', suggesting there were many others . . .

'Most girls I know – Courtney and her lot – they never eat. Like, never.'

'Well, maybe they have never had your breakfast experience?' She tried to sound coy and yet knowing, and wondered if she had pulled it off.

'They definitely have not,' he confirmed as he took the seat opposite her. This new, flirtatious exchange was enough to wipe out the memory and associated guilt of Gerald's visit, and in its place sat something that felt a lot like happiness.

Her phone buzzed.

'What?' she answered, yelling, showing off, purely to make Flynn laugh, which it did.

'Victoria, it's Gerald.'

'Oh, I thought it was someone else.' She snickered as Flynn put a square of kitchen roll in each ear and crossed his eyes.

'I wanted to call because I am not in the habit of leaving things unsaid.'

'Right.' She rolled her eyes theatrically.

'I know we are not actually related and that I am not in a position to advise or otherwise, but I wanted to say that Prim and I were very good friends and we spoke about you often, and only ever in the most glowing of terms; you really were the apple of her eye. She adored you. The Prim I knew was a good woman and, whatever she did or said, I am certain she did it with the very best of intentions.'

Victoria cursed the lump in her throat. 'Is that right?' She felt as if she might choke on the woman's betrayal.

'And I know she would not forgive me if I did not speak my mind and say that the young man you have at the house . . . well, his timing is a red flag to me.'

'Oh God, Gerald, I'm not stupid!' She thought of the vicar, who had had similar concerns. Did everyone think she was useless?

'It's not that you are stupid, Victoria, far from it, but more that others are wily and you are still young and you are, like it or not, vulnerable.'

'I like it not,' she spat.

'I can imagine.' There was an awkward and uncomfortable silence on the line. She watched Flynn, who was eating quickly now, shovelling food into his mouth with his head down. Gerald took a sharp breath. 'I know I am not family, dear' – he swallowed – 'but as I have said before, if you ever need anything, anything at all, day or night, just pick up the phone. I am mere minutes away by car. If I can remember where I have put the car keys.' He chuckled at his own joke. She said nothing and heard him swallow again. 'Well, there we have it. I'd better get on, Victoria, but I mean it. Day or night.'

'Goodbye, Gerald.' She ended the call and picked up her cutlery.

It was the first time that Victoria had ever called in sick to work when she had not actually been sick. She avoided looking at the portrait of Granny Cutter, directly in her eyeline, whose expression, she was sure, had changed to one of extreme disapproval. Victoria felt her face flush scarlet, and her mouth was dry as she made the call, explaining to Stanislaw, her boss, that she was not feeling too well, was sick, in fact.

'Erm . . . I was thinking that's it's best . . . erm . . . if I . . . erm . . . don't come in.'

'I hope you feel better soon, Victoria.'

The whole exercise had been excruciating, the man's kindly comments the very worst part, and she was absolutely certain that he knew she was lying. Nothing about it felt good. The moment, however, she ended the call, unburdened not only by the thought of having to *make* the call but the fact that she now didn't have to go to work, her spirits soared.

'I can't believe you looked so scared over a phone call!' Flynn lay on the rug in the hallway, laughing.

'That's because I *was* really scared!'

'It's only like bunking off school.' He sat up.

'I never bunked off school.' She grimaced. 'I never understood why people did. I mean, how hard is it to give a lesson an hour of your time?'

Flynn laughed again. 'I said you were smart, didn't I?'

'You did. Anyway, you make out to be a rebel, Flynn McNamara, but I know you worked hard, and now you're off to Newcastle to do Business Studies!' The thought of him going took the edge off her happy. Ridiculous, she knew, to be feeling this way about a boy who had spent the day at her house, cooked her breakfast and kissed her twelve times yet was still a stranger. He leaned up and pulled her face to meet his.

Thirteen . . .

The plan had been to watch movies, but after the mammoth breakfast came another snooze. And after an hour or so of sitting in sleeping bags in chairs by the lake, a lunch of grilled cheese sandwiches, which they dipped in ketchup, and an episode of *Pointless*, they were now in the garden room, where Victoria had done her best to water any plants that looked a little limp.

'Do you mind if I smoke?' Flynn asked suddenly.

'Sure.' She smiled, burying the thought of how much she hated smoking, not wanting anything to upset Flynn or her time with him.

'I don't do it all the time.' He gave her that lopsided smile.

'I'll open the French doors.' She stood up and did just that, pulling up the ancient metal bar and pushing the glass to allow the early-evening air to rush in. Gerald had indulged in the odd cigar after dinner a couple times, and this was where Prim had made him come and sit. She turned back to see Flynn grab a hard-backed book on bonsai trees from a side table and place it on his crossed legs before reaching into the front pocket of his backpack and pulling out a little green packet of cigarette papers, a carton of cigarettes and a small tin, which he flipped open.

Victoria cursed her stupidity. She had thought he meant smoke a cigarette, but he had of course meant weed. She knew Prim would disapprove – heck, Daksha would disapprove – but what about her? She used to readily agree with her gran and her mate that drugs were for idiots, but right now? She felt nothing but a frisson of excitement, a little intrigued by the whole sordid business. She quite liked the fact that she, straitlaced, potato-faced Victoria, who had never bunked off school and who thought wine was a suitable alternative to vodka, was here in the garden room with a very handsome boy who was about to roll and smoke a joint. It felt illicit. She stared at the boy, who she knew her gran would deem unsuitable, and the words of Prim's letter to Sarah came to her.

> You say this man loves you – but I am unable to
> imagine a kind of love where you give the person
> you love a drug so foul it robs them of everything
> that made them wonderful . . . how is that love,
> Sarah, how?
> Think about it!
> Think about everything.

Oh, I'm thinking, Prim, I can't stop thinking . . . She spoke to her gran in her mind. Sitting back in the chair, she watched, rapt, as Flynn took his time, his concentration absolute, as he went through the steps that were clearly familiar to him. His movements were precise and considered, his fingers nimble as he joined two of the cigarette papers together, having licked along the gluey edge. He then tore a corner of cardboard from the packet of cigarette papers, rolled it into a tiny curl and set it to one side. From a little plastic bag pulled from his tin, he sprinkled the green, dried-herb-like, grassy drug on the laid-out papers, picking out and discarding a couple of minute specks and smiling up at her as if he were making a cup of tea.

Flynn placed the fat paper cone in his mouth, holding it between his teeth. He struck a match and held the flame to the twisted nub on the end. Sitting on the floor next to him with her back resting on the chair, she watched, fascinated and drawn, as the sweet-scented smoke from his mouth spiralled up in delicate, ethereal wisps to curl over his head.

'I've never smoked cigarettes or drugs, but I guess that won't surprise you.' She ran her fingertip over his bare arm, enjoying the moment and liking the Victoria that was emerging from the chrysalis fashioned of lies and betrayal. Flynn took a deep drag and closed his eyes before reaching across to hand the joint to her.

Victoria took her time, her hesitancy not brought about by fear or indecision but a wariness of doing it wrong. She didn't want to show herself up, having had enough humiliation over the last week or so to last her a lifetime.

How could you be the only one not to know?

'You want to try it?' he asked, waggling the offending article in her direction with only a hint of teasing.

My mum smoked weed, she took pills, she did worse and it nearly killed her. In fact, as far as I'm concerned, it did kill her, and so I feel a bit scared, really scared. Suppose I'm like her and can't stop? I guess there's only one way to find out . . .

'Sure.'

◆ ◆ ◆

The afternoon had been an intriguing one, an education for sure. Once she had got over the unpleasant burning sensation in her throat and lungs, she and Flynn had laughed at just about everything, because everything seemed so funny! And time seemed to pass much, much more slowly . . . Then, with locust-like appetites, they polished off the remainder of Mrs Joshi's chicken, along with the rest of a loaf of bread and three packets of biscuits.

It was early evening and, with Flynn in the bathroom, Victoria stood in the kitchen, waiting for the kettle to boil, desperate for tea to slake her thirst. It was in that instant that she heard Prim's voice in her ear, as surely as if she were standing behind her.

What's going on, Victoria, darling?

'I like him. And I like having someone here. Not that it's anything to do with you, not any more,' she whispered. There was no answer forthcoming and she closed her eyes tightly, wishing she could communicate with her gran right now. Not only did she want to discuss the boy in the garden room, but also, she had a list of ever-growing topics she wanted to scream at her. She was desperate for answers.

You looked at me and lied!

You put your arm across my back and told me my mummy was in heaven!

You let me plant a little tree for her and buy cards for her that we put on the fire, hoping the words might fly up and reach her ears!

You held me tight when I sobbed with longing for her!

You told me lying was the worst thing, the very worst thing!

You didn't let me see her and you didn't let her see me!

And then, all of a sudden, it was again one of those moments when everything felt a little overwhelming. Her tears came in a rush, upsetting the natural rhythm of her breathing and making her nose run.

'Hey, hey . . .' Flynn rushed over to where she stood and put his arm around her shoulders. Her nose wrinkled a little at the scent of weed, body odour and the residue of the food he had fried for breakfast. Were it not for the warmth and comfort she took from the feel of his body next to hers, she would undoubtedly have pushed him away.

'I don't know what's happening to me.' She slumped down on to the old linoleum floor and sat with her back against the cupboard, raising her knees, on which she rested her head. Flynn sank with her. Her body shook with the fear that every solid foundation of her life was turning to dust. 'I am on my own, Flynn.'

'You are going to be fine. Even if it doesn't feel like it right now. You are strong; strong and smart, remember?'

She shook her head. 'I was strong because I was on solid ground. I had Prim's backing and support: she was always here. And now she's not and it's like my safety net has disappeared. A safety net that I now know was full of bloody big holes. And I don't feel strong at all. I feel really lonely, and I'm mad, Flynn, angry! So much has happened. I don't know who I am.'

'It's okay, Victoria. Don't cry.'

He placed his head against hers and, in that instant, she felt a little confined. Gently, she eased herself from his grip to stand, making her way back to the garden room, where evidence of their drug use littered the floor and a cool breeze from the open French doors washed over her. She laid her hands on one of the worn potting tables, the surface of which had been scrubbed over the years, so the wood was bare and pale. Dirt, however, still lurked in the deep crevices and cracks, which, if the table could talk, would no doubt have revealed decades of chatter over its knotty surface, as Prim and Granny Cutter strived to better their green-fingered credentials. This particular tabletop was crowded with seedlings in compostable paper cups and plants in various stages of legginess. There was also a small, sharp pair of secateurs resting on a single floral gardening glove, the suede finger panels stained green, their worn shape bent to accommodate the hand of the person they fitted so perfectly. To see Prim's tools and her handiwork close up was the final jolt Victoria's sadness needed to flood her being.

'I just need a minute, Flynn.'

She spoke as she rushed from the room, up the stairs and into Prim's bedroom. She lay face down on the soft selection of vintage pillows, all faintly tinged with the scent of Chanel No5, and sobbed. It was both distressing and cathartic to give in to the desolation that consumed her. She whispered to her gran with her eyes closed.

'How could you do it to me? How could you? You must have known I would find out, and you robbed me of the chance to hear you explain! And to know your reasons . . . it would have helped, but right now you are just a liar. A liar, Prim! You have spoiled the way I love you because each time I think of you I see Sarah at the side of the lake, saying, "This will be hard for you to hear . . ." And when she spoke I thought my heart might explode! It's not fair, Prim. Didn't you think I had enough to deal with?'

When her grief came at her like this, with daggers drawn, a dark thing lurking, took control of her whole being and did so on its terms, she was powerless to resist the charge. Coiled now in the place she felt closest to her gran, she lay in a tight ball with the damp fabric beneath her face stuck to her cheek and her chest heaving. Her tears were hot, drawn fresh from her well of despair. To cry like this was exhausting.

As the storm passed, she sat up against the headboard and wiped her face with a tissue from Prim's box on the nightstand, her breath coming in restorative gulps. Reaching for her phone, she saw she had a message from Sarah.

> Thinking about you today – every day. You know where I am when you want to talk.
> X

She felt torn, wondering if hearing Sarah's voice might help or if it might make her feel worse. Her mother was, after all, as much part of the problem as Prim, and Victoria was unwavering in the thought that it *had* been a conspiracy of the very worst kind.

As she went to close the message her thumb skirted the contact details and a little green phone receiver flashed up on the screen. She had dialled Sarah's number!

'Shit! No!'

She spoke aloud as she ended the call as quickly as she was able, hoping the woman might not notice the missed call and would not have heard it ring. She was, she decided, not ready to talk to Sarah, no matter how strong the pull. She was still wrestling with the thought that she had hidden away for all those years, and furious at the part the woman had played in the cruellest of all pranks.

Victoria's next actions were almost instinctive; she did what came naturally, something she had done hundreds of times before: she fired off a text to Daksha, her beloved best friend.

> Daks – what's going on? I miss you. I'm sorry. Please call me.
> Xx

Daksha's reply was almost instant.

I'm sorry too, should not have run out on you like that. Our first ever fight – what do you think, couples counselling or a night in watching GOT? I'll bring popcorn. Xx

Victoria replied, beaming with an overwhelming sense of relief.

Yes! Daks! Yes please, bring popcorn and we can do just that. I love you so, so much. Xxxxx

I know. I am very lovable.

Victoria laughed loudly at her friend's reply and felt the last of her tears evaporate. How she had missed her best friend; it might only have been one day and one night, but it was one day and one night too long. Plus, she had so much to tell her. She wondered how Daksha would react to the news of her and Flynn and the fact that she had smoked weed. Even the thought of sharing the information made her smile; it was still unbelievable to her. Plain old Victoria was quite unable to believe this new version of herself. Daksha's next message took the edge from her joy a little.

Popcorn visit will have to wait, won't be until the weekend. Mum has taken (kidnapped) Ananya and me to visit Auntie Khushi in Solihull – never heard of her? Me either! Should be a fun visit!! See you soon and I love you tooooooooooooooooo Xxx

'There you are!'

The sound of Flynn's voice at the door made her catch her breath – she had almost forgotten he was still here, and she slammed the phone face down on the counterpane, as if caught out.

'Are you feeling less sad?' He spoke slowly, and again his eyes had that off-centre look going on.

'Yes, a bit, thanks.'

Flynn crawled on all fours on to Prim's bed and laid his head on her chest. It felt nice and, again, desire tumbled in her stomach, albeit tinged with the unease that this boy was on Prim's bed.

'I don't want you to be sad,' he cooed, reaching up his face to kiss the space below her throat. It made her pulse race.

'Trust me, I don't want to be. But it feels a bit like my default state at the moment.' She sighed at this truth.

'Life's not easy when it goes wrong.'

'True.' She thought of Mr and Mrs McNamara, who still cried all these years later for Michael junior, their baby son, and her heart flexed for them. It was her belief – it *had* to be her belief – that her grief would ebb and there would be light at the end of the tunnel. It was how she got through, the thought that somehow this whole horrible mess would unknot itself.

'Do you not need to go home, Flynn? Won't your parents be worried about where you are?' The thought of staying away from Rosebank and not contacting Prim would not have occurred to her. Strange how it was still a concern, even though there was no one to care whether she was home or not, whether she washed her hair, changed her clothes, gathered the laundry from the floor, smoked a joint . . .

'Are you trying to get rid of me?' He laughed.

She shook her head and ran her fingers through his greasy curls. 'No. I'm not trying to get rid of you.'

Quite the opposite, I don't want to be alone . . .

'Good.' Again that kiss, and again she felt her concerns slip from her mind as her body yielded to all the good things this contact promised. To lose herself physically in his embrace was like flicking a switch that dulled her sadness, filling her instead with things she did not associate with grief: lust, happiness and the flood of joy she felt at being desired. It was validation of sorts. Prim had lied to her. Sarah had, to all intents and purposes, abandoned her, but Flynn McNamara wanted her, and he wanted her right now, in the worst state she had ever found herself.

Warts and all . . .

Flynn kissed the base of her throat again, and she was lost to him. The feel of his skin against hers, the way he held her . . . it was as close to intoxication as she could get without drinking or smoking one of Flynn's dodgy cigarettes. Yes, in the midst of the murky waters of grief, this glorious physical experience was not only all-consuming but wonderfully life-affirming. At a time when her world had been mired in death, it felt good to be reminded of something that was so good about being alive!

Flynn reached down and she heard the snap of his waistband and then, in an instant, he was naked. It was at this point, when things were about to go further than she had planned and far more quickly than she had considered, that she decided to take the plunge. After all, who was going to stop her or advise differently? This thought was fleeting, as what happened next came so naturally.

She wriggled low on the mattress and watched him in the half-light, knowing she was setting a course from which there could be no return, but she did so willingly, wanting to be wanted. This was how she would show everyone who had lied to her that she was moving on: a new, adult version of the Victoria they had duped, and one who would care less. With her eyes now closed, she felt the weight of him pinning her. It was both thrilling and reassuring, and she placed her lips on his bony, tanned shoulder. The anticipation made her head swim and her heart beat fast. He held her hair, and the two strangers found a rhythm that united them, briefly taking her away from that place of emptiness where her every thought was wrapped in sadness and doubt . . .

♦ ♦ ♦

Propped up on her elbow, Victoria now watched Flynn snoring, with his arms above his head. The tea-coloured lace edging of Prim's pillow framed his young face. She had, of course, discussed sex with Daksha, seen movie sex and read about it a fair bit too, but actual sex had been nothing like it, nothing like it at all. Turning on to her side, she reached out and carefully laid the photo of her youthful grandpa in all his dashing glory face down. She had expected to feel differently, to feel . . . something, hoping at some level that the act might be a bit like shaking off an old skin, leaving her fresh and new and a whole lot more confident, happier. But, in truth, the overriding sensation was one of disappointment with the gnawing gripe of loss still acute in her gut. It wasn't that she had expected violins, roses, sweet words of sentiment and a moving soundtrack, but she had thought maybe there might be some discussion, a cerebral connection of sorts. Instead, her sex with Flynn was noisy, a bit awkward, slightly painful even. To say it was unpleasant would be a step too far, but there were certainly no fireworks, not even a crappy sparkler, and still the thoughts she'd hoped the act might help erase whirred louder than ever. And now Flynn was in the deepest sleep, snoring, while she stared at the ceiling. No, this had been nothing like movie sex. If movie sex was diving into a deep, warm bubble bath where scented candles flickered on a shelf and a wide, soft towel awaited her when eventually she rose from the depths of the tub, this sex was a quick wipe down with a cold flannel.

Flynn shifted position and his snores roared. She wondered how sleep could be so instant and consuming when, for her, this big thing that had happened needed to come to rest in her thoughts. So that was it, virginity lost on the same day she had smoked a joint. Quietly, she pulled back the duvet and, retrieving them from the floor, she pulled on her T-shirt and pants, thinking how crazy life could be and how you never knew what might happen when you opened your eyes to greet a new day . . . Instantly, she thought of Sarah and saw her standing at the side of the lake.

'This is going to be hard for you to hear . . .'

Fuck you, Sarah! Her imagined response.

Victoria crept to her own room, where she retrieved her laptop and slipped under her covers. She opened the next couple of emails and read two more of the letters.

March 2001
Rosebank
Epsom
Surrey

You are pregnant? Sarah! You are truly? I have read and reread your letter so many times I know it by heart. A baby! A baby, Sarah! Daddy and I are beside ourselves! Life's greatest gift, and one we ourselves had to wait decades to receive. But, oh, the joy when we did! You were and are our whole life – our whole life.

I cannot stop crying.

I never, ever imagined in a million years that the day you told me I was going to be a granny it would be via letter from a rehabilitation centre with your life so wildly off track. I have laughed and cried and paced the rooms into the early hours, trying to order my thoughts and feelings.

Is the baby okay? Are you okay? How does it work, now that you are pregnant? Does your treatment stay the same? I have so many questions. How are you feeling? What do you need? What can we do?

I am hoping that this baby is the incentive you need to see sense and when this is over, come home . . . please, please, please, I am begging you to come home. Just you and the baby. We can make it work. We can make anything work. We have the space. It will be wonderful. Please, please, please, Sarah, think about it, and think about what will be best in the long run.

I noticed in your letter you have started going by the name Sarah Jackson. I haven't told Daddy yet. I think that will hurt him more than I can say. Is it something you have decided to do on the spur of the moment, as some kind of protest, or did you actually get married? I write that with a nervous laugh and a shake to my hand. I pray to God you have not, but in all honesty, Sarah? Nothing would surprise me.

A baby . . . A baby! It is all my hopes and dreams come true, yet because of the situation you are in, my worst nightmare too.

What a terrible mess it all is.

How far pregnant are you, darling?

I ask again, is there anything you need?

Anything we can do?

A baby, Sarah! A little baby . . .

With love, with all the love in the world.

Mum x

Victoria waited a beat before reading Sarah's response. It didn't feel good to learn that Prim thought the whole situation was 'a terrible mess'.

'But you had a plan, didn't you, Prim? You knew how to fix the mess?' She spoke into the ether as her teeth ground together.

April 2001
Sarah Jackson
Henbury House
West Sussex

I got your letter. Thanks.

In answer to your questions: yes, I have started using the name Jackson; I am married to him in the truest sense of the word, I feel married to him, so why not?

And as for your second question: I am four months pregnant.

I know you won't want to hear this, but I was nearly clean when I got pregnant and I am clean right now. I am.

I don't think you will ever have any concept, Mum, of what a big deal this is.

It's not like sticking to a diet or going without for Lent.

It's like going against the thing that every cell in your body is screaming for you to do. And I can't recall how many cells there are in your body, but I do remember it's a lot.

Give each cell a loud voice and that is what I hear in my head every single second of every single day.

It's deafening.

It's a madness.

But I am trying.

I am really, really trying.

Marcus is doing well on methadone and yes, I know you didn't ask, would never ask. But that's too bad because, along with fighting this addiction, the only other thing I think about is him.

I love him. I love him! Like you love Daddy. It really is that simple. You don't seem to get it, Mum, but if I came home, he would come too – can you imagine if I said now you have to live away from Dad? You'd think I was mad. We are no different. We need and want to be together when I get out of here.

Actually, there is something else I think about – my baby.

I have a baby book and look at pictures of how she is developing, yes, she . . . a little girl . . . I saw the scan and they told me it's a girl.

Right now, she is about the size of a small orange.

A miracle.

The thought of her keeps me strong. She keeps me going through the toughest of times. I picture her wonderful life and all the things I can show her, teach her. I love her already. I do. I think she will be the most amazing thing I have ever done or could ever do.

Marcus had a supervised visit and he heard her heartbeat. It was . . . it was wonderful. He was so happy and I am so proud of us all.

We have agreed to give her a strong name, a name that will carry her through the best and worst of times, a name that will define her, a name that she will always know we chose with great care because we love her. We love her as much as we love each other and that is how we will all get through this: with love.

I guess that's all for now.

S

'What are you doing?'

'Jesus, Marcus!' His voice made her jump. She placed her hand on her chest, lost in the letters; having momentarily forgotten Flynn was there. She was glad he had seen fit to put his underwear on before roaming around the house.

'Who the fuck is Marcus?' he asked with mock offence.

Victoria threw her head back and laughed as she sat up straight and closed the laptop.

'No one! Is that what I said? He was my . . . my friend's boyfriend. Old boyfriend. He's dead,' she babbled.

'What's wrong?' He looked more than a little nonplussed, his eyes half closed, as if adjusting to being awake. 'Why are you crying?'

'Oh!' She touched her fingertips to her cheeks. 'I didn't realise I was.'

'Are you feeling upset about . . . about what just happened? That was so not the plan; it's supposed to make you feel good.' He smiled awkwardly. 'I wouldn't ever want to be the reason you cried.' His words were as sweet as they were reassuring and carried the faint echo of promise.

'It did make me happy, Flynn. But my head's a mess. Like, a proper mess. I just . . . I can't . . . I don't . . . I don't know what's happening to me, but I know that it's a lot and sometimes it's more than I can cope with.' She shook her head, aware that she didn't know Flynn well enough to put into words all the reasons that her life was spiralling out of control. It was in this moment that she realised the boy she had given her virginity to was someone she barely knew. Not that there was a darn thing she could do about that. A sob built in her chest.

'S'okay,' he mumbled. 'You can cry, Victoria, just let it out.'

She was grateful that he simply sank down on the mattress, extended his arm across her pillow and patted the space, which she then filled, lying on her side with her head resting on his shoulder. And this was how they slept, comfortably.

EIGHT

The atmosphere in Rosebank the next morning could best be described as charged. Victoria could not deny that to lie with Flynn in a double bed, lost in the moment, had been a glorious awakening. And yet in the cold light of day, the sight of his head on her pillow, his body taking up a lot of mattress space, had been enough to evoke something close to irritation. It was only the second morning that he had been here, but looking at him right then she felt as if he'd been there for an age. It felt intense, too intense, and she wanted a chance to gather her thoughts and ponder the letters without interruption.

'Flynn!' she had shouted, jumping from the bed. 'You have to get up! I've got stuff to do!'

'What stuff?' he had asked, one eye closed, his head half lifted from the pillow and with the faint outline of dried drool on his chin.

'Just stuff!' She wanted nothing more than to take a long, hot bath, alone. He chuckled and laid his head back on the pillow, as if what she wanted was of no consequence.

'Stuff can wait. It'd be a shame to waste the morning.' He reached for her, taking her by the hand. 'Come back to bed, just for a little while.'

The sight of his beautifully formed, semi-naked body was enough to melt her resolve. His skin and the novelty of sexual contact was a magnet. With the pull of her arm, she felt her body slide back on to the mattress. After some intoxicating, hypnotic kissing, the rush of blood to her head and the feel of his hands on her skin – her body overruled her decision to get up and start the day. The question for her was: would sex be any better the second time around? Maybe it was like anything else, only going to improve with practice?

And she supposed it was a little better, but still a whole world away from fireworks.

Flynn showered as she loped around the kitchen, pouring the last of the orange juice into two glasses and rattling the empty carton before lobbing it on the floor next to the bin and filling the kettle with water. She did her best to ignore the rubbish that had accumulated in such a short space of time: egg boxes, empty plastic milk bottles and biscuit wrappers, not to mention the sink piled high with used tea-stained cups, dirty coffee mugs and plates with crumbs and indeterminate smears clinging to their edges.

Flynn filed into the kitchen eventually, his hair flopping over one eye and his lids heavy, but dressed and with his backpack in his hand, seemingly ready to go. The sight of him preparing to leave made her stomach flip with dread. Instantly she regretted her earlier thoughts of wanting to be alone.

'What time is it?' He propped his head on his hand on the table and looked like he might nod off again.

'Latish. More brunchtime than breakfast.'

'Cheers!' He raised a glass of orange juice in her direction, and it made her laugh. She liked the way he did and said things. She liked him.

'So, Victoria, are we, like . . .'

'Are we what?' She spoke over her shoulder as she peered into the empty bread bin, as if staring long and hard enough might make some bread appear. She wanted to feed Tommy, and herself.

'Are we good . . . after last night and this morning?' he asked, with an uncharacteristic hint of nerves, a slight tremor to his voice and a leg that jumped, his foot beating time on the kitchen floor.

She put the lid back on the bread bin before taking up her place opposite him at the table. 'Do we talk about it? I am a bit out of practice at this whole . . .' She struggled to find the appropriate word – *relationship* thing? *No, God no. Hook-up? Yuck!*

He took another sip. 'It was your first time, right?'

'Uh-huh.'

'And I guess a bit weird because we only really started hanging out, like, a few days ago.'

'Mm, I guess.' *Two days ago, to be precise.* She nodded, a little embarrassed by her seemingly rash actions and yet more than a little thrilled by them too.

'I just wanted to check that we're cool?'

'Am I not going to see you again?' His words sounded like a coded goodbye and the thought shocked her. Not only did she want more of him, but the thought of him disappearing now sent a quiver of regret along her spine. Was he too going to abandon her, reject her?

'What?' He laughed. 'Of course you're going to see me again! Like, today and every day till I leave for Newcastle.'

She felt her shoulders relax, thankful for this.

'Good.' She made the tea. 'I like spending time with you, Flynn. It means a lot to me right now, when everything feels a bit . . .' She looked up, again trying to find the word. Her grief had done this, left large holes in her vocabulary and her thought process.

'A bit shit?' he offered.

'Yes.' *That'll do.* 'A bit shit. And, I mean, I know that we're not . . . I understand that . . .' *What exactly are you trying to say?*

159

'It's okay.' He jumped in. 'I get it, and I'm *not* offended if you don't think we have any future. I get that we're casual, if that's what you're worried about. I mean, that makes sense, with me heading off to uni.' His tone was soft and conciliatory.

'Well, no.' She paused, trying to think how best to explain her mindset, that, and how he had no right to be offended or unoffended; it was her body, her life and her decision to make.

The two now locked eyes over the tabletop, sipping at their orange juice.

'It should have been a big deal for me.' She swallowed. 'I always thought it would be, but at the end of the day, it's just sex, isn't it?'

'I think so.' He nodded, as if listening to an unheard beat. 'Just sex.'

It was her turn to nod. 'I really like you, Flynn, always have, really.' She swallowed.

'I really like you.'

'Thanks.' She smiled a little shyly, in part at his admission, but also at the rather pedestrian exchange. 'I guess what I'm trying to say is, I have a lot going on right now. My head really is a mess.'

'Of course it is. Your nan just died.'

'Yes, and I have some other stuff going on.' She paused; did she want to tell him about Sarah? In truth, she knew she would welcome someone to talk to about it in the absence of Daksha.

'What other stuff?' He slurped noisily.

'It's about my mum.'

'It's okay,' he cut in. 'You don't have to tell me. I know she died too; everyone knows it. I'm guessing it was the drug thing you mentioned? We used to talk about it a bit in school, how it must have been rough for you, having to live with your nan.'

Victoria pulled her head back on her shoulders. 'It wasn't rough for me living with my gran.' She was aware of her slightly defensive tone and felt conflicted. 'She was wonderful. Until after she died. Now, I'm not so sure . . .'

'Well, that's good then.' He looked a little perplexed and took another slug of his juice.

'The thing is, my mum . . .' She swallowed, aware of how utterly incredible this was going to sound. It *still* sounded incredible to her, and she had been living with it inside her head for a little while now. 'My mum isn't actually dead. She came to my gran's funeral, turned up out of the blue.'

Flynn placed his glass on the table and blinked.

'So you *lied* about having no mum?' He sat back in the chair. 'That's fucking messed up!'

'No! God, not at all. I was lied to. My gran told me my mum had died, but in fact she hadn't.'

She watched his eyes roam the space above her head, digesting the facts.

'Are you kidding me right now?'

'No. I'm not kidding you. I kind of wish I was.'

He was quiet for a beat or two, his brow furrowed. 'Why would anyone do that?'

The laugh that left her mouth was sharp and incredulous and she lay her hands on the tabletop. 'I don't know, Flynn! I am still trying to piece it all together, but I can tell you it is the worst thing imaginable. I have mourned her all my life, comforted by my gran during the saddest of days, and all the time . . .' She traced a pattern around the rim of her glass with her fingertip.

'So you hadn't seen your mum until the funeral? Not once?'

'No.'

'Was she living close by?'

'No. Oslo.'

'Oslo,' he repeated. 'Did she not want to see you in all that time?'

'I don't know. She says she did, but I don't know . . .' She wished she had better answers.

'Did your nan tell you *when* she died. I mean, did you think about her on the anniversary? Go to church? Light a candle, all that shit?'

She knew he was thinking of his own family, sitting and mourning the passing of Michael junior, and was no doubt, like her, trying to think of this happening when, all the time, her gran would know it was a farce, as Sarah was very much alive.

'Not really, no. There was no specific day mentioned. We used to talk about her, though. Not a lot or in any detail, but it wasn't taboo. I was told she died when I was a baby of a drug overdose.'

'Shit!' he surmised. 'That's seriously, seriously messed up.'

'Yep.' *So you said.* 'And part of that was true. She was a drug user and was in rehab when she had me, but the overdose bit – that was apparently not; at least, if it is true, it wasn't fatal. Obviously.'

'That's a lot for you to take in.'

'As I said' – she took a sip of her juice – 'I have some other stuff going on.'

Flynn bit at the skin around his thumbnail, clearly thinking. 'So what happens now you know she isn't dead? Are you going to see her again? Is she going to come and live here?'

'No, she won't be coming to live here and I'm not sure about seeing her again. She wants us to get to know each other, but . . .'

'But what?'

She ran her hand over her face. 'They lied to me, Flynn, all of them. All the people I trusted and who were looking after me, they all lied, and not just once, and it wasn't a small white lie – it was a big lie! The biggest! And they did it for my *whole* life, and my gran and grandpa died without giving me a chance to hear it from them or ask them about it or . . .' She shook her head at the unpalatable truth; her list of gripes was long. 'And I can't seem to get past that. Do you think you could get past something like that?'

'Hmm . . . I think at first I'd be too angry to feel anything but furious. Maybe that's where you are now?'

'Maybe,' she conceded.

'But then, looking on the positive side, you've got your mum back! And that's got to be pretty cool.'

She nodded. 'The hardest thing is just that . . .'

'What?' he asked softly.

'I was able to cope with not having my mum around because I knew, or *thought* I knew, that she would never have chosen to leave me. I kind of felt sorry for her because she had no choice, because she died. But that's bullshit. She *did* choose to leave me, and I feel more abandoned and alone than I ever thought possible. Even though she is still here.'

'It will all get easier.' The platitude irritated her.

'Here's hoping.'

'And you know, Victoria, people lie for very different reasons.' He finished his drink and stood from the table, balancing his empty glass in the crowded sink, like setting up a game of washing-up Jenga.

'What do you mean?'

'Well' – he picked up his backpack – 'everyone thinks a lie has to be a bad thing, but I lie to my parents every day because, if I told them the truth, it would destroy them, hurt them. Can you imagine? *Actually, Mum and Dad, I couldn't care less that this would have been Michael's twenty-first birthday because I don't remember him, and no, I don't want a piece of the birthday cake made for a person who only existed for a couple of years who I don't even remember!* And so I'll eat the cake and I'll lie.' He shrugged, as if it really was that simple.

'I guess.' She decided not to go into the detail of how she believed her circumstance to be very different.

'You look fed up.'

163

'I *am* fed up!'

'So we need to do something to change that.' He drummed his fingers on his chin. 'How about a party?'

'A party?' She instantly thought of what she might wear to a party; her experience of such things was a little limited. Parties were definitely the domain of Courtney and the hair-extension brigade and, generally, she wouldn't be in favour of going to one, but with Flynn on her arm – it might be worth it just to see the look on the faces of those girls. 'Can Daksha come too?' This was the kind of event she knew she could only get through with her best friend by her side, with whom she could exchange looks of support or understanding.

'Of course she can! Anyone you want to can come because it'll be *your* party.'

'My party?' She didn't try to hide her confusion.

'Yes! You've got this big old house, everyone is about to scatter to the four winds, heading off to uni or whatever. You should have a party!'

'I . . . I've never had a party.' *Barely been to one . . .*

'All the more reason. You've had a rough time. A party would take your mind off things, cheer you up.'

Victoria beamed. 'I have had a rough time and yes, I do need cheering up. But I don't know if a party is the way to do that.'

'The way I see it, you need to feel like this is *your* house, and what better way to do that than hold a gathering here, make it yours!'

'I don't think I know enough people to invite to a party and I think Nilesh, Roscoe and that lot have already left for uni.'

Flynn looked at her as if he had no idea who these people were.

'You don't need a ton of people, just a few, and I know everyone!'

Victoria decided to get Daksha's thoughts on the matter. An image of Prim floated into her mind: strict, judgemental Prim, who had apparently clipped Sarah's wings.

'I flirted with inappropriate boys, swam braless in my underslip, very daring at the time, and then danced in front of a bonfire until I dried off with a very large mimosa in one hand and a cigarette in the other. I was quite magnificent.' And the thought struck her: perhaps it was time *she* learned how to be magnificent . . .

Victoria, now aware of the march of time, stood. 'Let's do it! Let's have a bloody party!'

Flynn gave her his lopsided smile, which felt very much like a reward, and walked over to kiss her on the mouth, the novelty of which hadn't worn off. Her stomach flipped accordingly.

'I think I'm happy.' He beamed.

She squeezed his hand and had to admit that, despite all that was going on, at that very moment, she thought she might be happy too, even if only as much as her complex situation allowed – a small, good thing, like the edge of the sun glimpsed through heavy cloud.

'I'll see you tonight,' he breathed.

'Tonight?' she asked with a giggle of surprise, wondering where he was headed today.

'Yes! I've got people to see and things to sort out. Will you miss me?'

'No,' she lied, laughing. He kissed her again and, in that moment, the thought of more fumbling in the dark beneath the duvet suddenly seemed quite attractive. She couldn't wait for him to return. 'Okay, Flynn, maybe I'll miss you a little bit. I'll see you tonight.'

◆ ◆ ◆

The doorbell rang around midday. It was Bernard, in his standard blue overalls and the checked flat cap he favoured. Victoria steeled herself and opened the door, having rehearsed this encounter in her mind more times than she might care to admit. He smiled at her through the glass pane, as if it was any other day, and his smile, one that indicated all was well, was enough to spark her fury. In fairness, it was fury directed at the whole gang who had deceived her, but neither Grandpa, Prim nor Sarah were in front of her right now and so Bernard became the target.

'I usually use my key to let myself in the back doors of the garden room and get cracking, but thought today I'd better knock,' he explained. The only indicator of any potential nerves was the way he licked his lips.

'Well, I'm glad you did.'

'Oh, oh good.' He spoke with obvious relief, clutching his small stepladder and workbag.

'No, I don't mean I'm glad you came, Bernard, I mean I'm glad you knocked. I wanted to talk to you before you started.'

'Oh right, of course.' He looked at the floor, his face coloured.

'I did send you a text.' She recalled the 3 a.m. attempt at contact to which he still had not replied.

'I saw that . . .'

'You did? Right, I did wonder, as you didn't reply and it was something important: my life, in fact, that I wanted to talk about, needed help with.'

He hesitated. 'My wife said not to reply as you were . . . I think she said, agitated.' He nodded. 'She said you sounded agitated.'

'Did she? She was probably right. I am a *little* agitated.' She gave a dry laugh, *agitated* . . .

'I've got to be honest, it feels very strange coming here and not having your gran answer the door.'

'Well, at least you have decided to be honest. That's something, I guess.' She watched his face colour and his mouth flap. 'How did you see this working, Bernard?' Her tone was clipped.

'Oh! I suppose the way it always has. I do whatever is needed. It's like the Forth Bridge, this house!' He tried out a small laugh, which she ignored. 'I still need to finish repairing the veranda that is proper rotten in some places, and I need to dredge the pond, the garage door needs painting, I have a list . . . Then I get a payment direct into my account every second Friday – and your gran adjusts it – sorry, used to adjust it – depending on my hours. I keep a log in my little book.' He patted his pocket to indicate that this was where his little book lived.

'I see. So I make you a cup of tea the way Prim used to, while we chat about the weather and the state of the wood on the veranda, and we just ignore the fact that you have been at the heart of the deceit that has ripped apart my life? Is that what you thought?' She clenched her fists to stop them trembling.

'I . . . I don't know. I thought—'

'I don't care what you thought!' She cut him off, despite having asked the question. 'But this is what *I* think: I think you have some nerve. You were a spy in this house, watching my every move and reporting back to Sarah—'

'It wasn't like that!' It was his turn to interrupt.

'Wasn't it? Tell me how it was then.'

She thought of all the times she had stumbled across him and Prim laughing over a cup of tea as he leaned on the countertop, or how they would stand admiring a flower bed, deep in conversation. Fury balled in her gut at the thought that she might have arrived home from school, given them a quick wave and made her way to the privacy of her bedroom and all the while there was the very real possibility that they were not discussing the loose linen cupboard door or what to plant around the lake, they were talking about *her*, about Sarah! How could it be that Bernard was in receipt of such important information while she was left out in the cold? It was monstrous, and she vented her anger on him, too blinded by emotion to question whether or not it was justified.

'Prim didn't know.'

'Didn't know what?'

'Didn't know I wrote to Sarah. I never told her.' He hung his head and took a deep breath.

It should have made a little difference to her rage, but she was too deep in the pit of anger to think straight or claw her way up to the calm surface.

'Sarah contacted me not long after you were born and asked me if she might be able to give me the odd call. And she did, once or twice a year, that was all, and then she sent me a new address in Oslo when she got settled, and I started jotting her notes – again, just once or twice a year.'

'Did you ever see or hear about me crying for her? For my mum who died?'

He nodded and kept his eyes averted.

'And all you had to do was tell me, tell me that my mum was still alive and that you knew where she was!' Her voice cracked at the most monstrous thought.

'How could I? You were a little girl and Prim would have been mad, she'd have told me to leave and Sarah would have lost the only contact she had . . .'

'Jesus! So instead you became part of it, part of the conspiracy that has left me feeling like a stranger in my own house, my own family! I don't know what's real any more.' Victoria kicked her toes against the brass lip of the step.

'I couldn't stand it, Victoria. I couldn't stand for her not to be part of your life, that was all. It felt cruel.' He tried and failed, in her eyes, to justify his meddling.

'And what about me? That wasn't cruel? I can't stand that I have mourned my mum for my whole life; I thought she had died, Bernard! I thought my mum *died*! And one word from you and my life would have been so different!' she cried.

'I guess Prim thought—'

'Prim's not here any more, is she?' Frustratingly, this phrase alone was enough to make her tears gather.

'No, no, she's not.' His voice was soft. He rubbed his palm over his face, suggesting the reminder had moved him. 'I don't know how I got mixed up in it all, I just want to fix things.' He looked like he might cry, but that was just too bad; she had cried her own fair share of tears.

'You spied on me and fed information back to Sarah, and to make matters worse, Prim paid you for the privilege.'

'It wasn't like that!' he implored.

'So you said.' She folded her arms, feeling simultaneously a little scared and elated that she was now in charge and in control. 'I don't want you to come here any more. Well, there's no need, is there? Not now I can write my own notes to Sarah telling her to fuck off and leave me alone – should save you some stamps.'

He opened his mouth as if to speak, but clearly thought better of it, before turning slowly, taking one last lingering look at the front of Rosebank, the house and gardens he had been tending for the best part of thirty years, and walking over the gravel towards his van.

Victoria watched him leave with something like satisfaction lining her gut. She looked up towards the brooding sky; it looked like rain might be coming in. She welcomed the idea, the washing away of the summer heat that was thick with lies and deception, which spun webs inside every room.

Her pulse settled. With Flynn out of the house and Daksha away, she felt the tendrils of loneliness reach out and stroke her skin. Grabbing her novel, she sank down on to the sofa in the drawing room and opened it at the place where she had folded a corner of a page as a marker, a habit that used to infuriate her gran. Her eyes swept around the room: cushions were still littered on the floor, and the dirty plates, which had started to give off a rather unpleasant hum, were still on the coffee table. She knew these things would have infuriated her more.

The last time she had read was on the day Prim died. They had lain in the steamer chairs, her reading and Prim watching the lake, commenting on the ferocious heat and the bees that buzzed around the irises, noting their industry and choreographed moves. Their conversation came to mind. This, like every other memory, now tainted with the betrayal of lies.

'I sometimes wonder, Prim, if my mum took too many drugs because Marcus had died, like something Shakespearian, you know: couldn't live without her one true love?'

'I think you've been reading too many books,' Prim had snapped.

'Guilty as charged.' Victoria lifted the novel in her hand.

'I also think, darling' – Prim's tone, softer then – *'that you shouldn't romanticise what was a very painful and unattractive time. A tragic time . . .'*

Victoria ground her teeth and kicked out at the coffee table, making a mug wobble. *Yes, tragic and truly Shakespearian how you plotted and lied to me . . .* It was as she remembered this conversation that her phone rang; she lifted it to her chin and spoke as she settled back in her seat, her novel poised.

'Victory.'

The word and the sound of Sarah's voice was enough to make her jolt. She wondered if she would ever get over the fact that her wish of having a direct line to her mother might come true. This, however, was not how she had envisaged it.

'Victoria. Yes.'

'Sorry, Victoria.' Sarah corrected herself speedily; her voice had an undercurrent of excitement and anticipation. 'I had a missed call from you. I'm so sorry – my phone was off, I've only just seen it. Is everything okay? Are . . . are you okay?'

No, I'm not! I am still mad and confused and scared of being on my own, and Flynn McNamara has been staying here and we have had sex, twice! And I'm worried I didn't feel more – and I smoked a joint and liked it. And what I don't like is being on my own, but then I crave space, confusing right? And I miss Prim, the Prim I thought she was who was always honest with me, the Prim who told me I knew every little thing about her, but I didn't, did I? And I hate the Prim who lied to me – and I just took this out on Bernard and it felt good, but now I feel like shit . . .

'I'm okay.'

'Good, good! I was hoping you would call, there is so much I want to say to you, things I keep thinking about to tell you and that I think might help you to—'

'Sarah.' She drew breath, interrupting the woman's flow. 'I dialled you in error.'

'In . . . in error?' Her voice was thin. 'What do you mean?'

'I mean, it was a *misdial.* I was closing the text you sent me, and . . .'

'I see. So you didn't mean to call me? Didn't want to chat?'

Victoria knew well enough the sound of a voice that was trying to cry in secret as it spoke, as if a little overwhelmed with disappointment. The guilt that bloomed on her tongue was quickly replaced with the sweet taste of vengeance. Victoria was hurting and she wanted to hurt those who had hurt her and, as there was only this woman left, she took the full brunt.

'That's right.' She bit the side of her cheek. 'I didn't mean to call you.'

'Well,' Sarah sniffed, 'now that we are on the phone, however it came about, do you have a minute to talk?'

'I don't, I'm afraid. Bye, Sarah.' Victoria ended the call and went back to the dog-eared page of her novel.

NINE

She liked sharing a house with Flynn; they had a further three days of playing grown-ups, having sex and smoking weed as the sun went down. It was the cosy domesticity of eating and waking together that was enough to keep her loneliness at bay. It was also a taster of a different kind of life, one she had never properly considered, but where she lived with someone she loved and they looked after each other, just like she and Prim had done. She was undoubtedly happiest when naked with Flynn and the thought of him going to Newcastle was one she pushed to the back of her mind.

'Daks? It's me!' She slumped down on to the stairs and smiled into the phone.

'Hey, you. How's life in Surrey?'

'Peachy.'

'You sound it. This is good, my friend, very good!'

'I have been baking!'

'Sorry, Vic, I think the line must have gone a bit dodgy, either that or my hearing has gone; I thought for one terrible moment you said you had been baking!'

'Very funny.' She laughed more than the joke warranted, happy – beyond happy – that things were restored between her and the girl she so loved. 'I have actually found it quite therapeutic.

I've made brownies!' She giggled, deciding not to divulge all of the ingredients.

'Wow! Brownies! Well done, my clever friend.'

'Thanks.'

'I can't wait to come home. I have eaten my body weight in cake and am quite keen to leave before I actually explode!'

'Don't explode.' Victoria laughed, knowing it would not occur to her friend to simply say no to the cake on offer. 'Anyway, I think I might have just the incentive you need to want to be in shape, plus the perfect thing to occupy your thoughts while you are away.'

'Oh God, that sounds ominous. Okay, shoot.'

'I am going to have a party! Or, more specifically, we – *we* – are going to have a party!' She couldn't help the creep of excitement in her voice.

'A party? When?' Daksha sounded more perplexed than thrilled. Parties were not and never had been their thing.

'Saturday night.'

'Oh my God! *This* Saturday?'

'Yes. Why, do you have plans? Because if you do, cancel them!'

'Ha ha! Four days' time? How much weight can I lose in four days?'

'Quite a lot, if you stay off the cake.' Victoria laughed again.

'Not gonna happen. Where's the party?'

'Here, at Rosebank.'

There was a moment of hesitation before Daksha replied. 'Really? You want to have a party at Prim's house?' Her friend's shocked tone put a big dent in Victoria's happiness and irritated her in the way that dissent when an idea was good often did.

'Actually, it's my house now. And yes, right here.' She looked around the hallway and tried to imagine the twinkle of fairy lights and the low hum of conversation over the chink of glasses.

'Who are we going to invite? Do we know enough people to make a party?' Daksha laughed as she voiced the uncomfortable truth.

'Well, maybe not, but Flynn McNamara does.' She screwed her eyes shut and danced her bare feet on the step below, knowing the bombshell she was about to drop.

'Well, yes, I am sure he does, but what makes you think he'll want to come to our party? We're hardly Flynn McNamara-worthy. He's barely spoken a word to us in the last five years, save your outside-the-shop chit-chat the other week.' Her voice dropped an octave, as if she, like Victoria, was aware that this chat had happened on the day that her life was about to change . . .

'Actually, it was his suggestion that we have a party.' Victoria paused. 'He suggested it over breakfast this morning.'

Daksha let out a small giggle. 'Of course he did. In your dreams. Don't tell me: he made you scrambled eggs while naked?'

Victoria bit her lip and grinned. *If only you knew . . .*

'No, Daks, not in my dreams. This is absolutely for real! Oh my God! I've got so much to tell you. He pitched up here the night you and I . . . you know, when your mum came to get you . . . and he has been staying here for the last few days and only left briefly the other morning because I kind of made him because I needed a break, but he came back. He's out now seeing friends, but he's coming back again tonight!' She shoved her knuckles into her mouth, hoping this might take the full force of the excitement that threatened to burst from her. She hadn't realised that the telling about Flynn would be nearly as thrilling as the actual being with Flynn, if not more so.

'You *are* joking me?'

'I am *not* joking. He has been staying here and we shared a bed and slept on the sofa and we have kind of, you know, we have done stuff. *Lots* of stuff,' she whispered, wary of her ancestors' portraits

174

and photographs all around. 'And it's good and he's great and, when I am with him, I can forget all the other shit that's going on. He is exactly what I need right now. I like him, I do. I mean, I don't think it's a long-term thing, or a serious thing, of course not, he's going off to Newcastle, but it's good fun. He's sweet, *and* he makes breakfast!' She laughed. 'So, what do you think?' She sat back on the stairs.

'I . . . I still don't know if you're mucking about.' The laughter had gone from Daksha's voice and this alone was enough to cause a flare of embarrassment.

'No! God! Why is it so hard to believe? Because I'm not Courtney? Because I like books, not boys? Why can't I like both? And why do you think I am so out of Flynn's league? What is so wrong with me, Daks?' Her tone was sharp.

'Nothing! There is absolutely nothing wrong with you!'

'That's not what it sounds like. You sound really pissed off, actually.'

'Because I *am* pissed off. Actually.'

'I can tell. Why can't you just be happy for me?' She hated that those darn tears were still so very close to the surface, and she cursed the catch in her throat.

There was a beat or two of silence while she waited for her best friend to speak. The tension was palpable.

'I have been happy and sad for you your whole life. I have lived all your emotions with you, good and bad. And the fact that I am a little taken aback by your crazy, sudden news is because to have a party in *Prim's* beautiful house that she gifted you is bloody madness! And the Victoria I know and love would not dream of doing anything like that, not because she is boring, but because she knows how absolutely shit it would be if anything happened to any of Prim's lovely things, if her home got destroyed. And for your information, Victoria, I *do not* and *have never* thought that

Flynn McNamara was out of your league, but I have *always, always* thought that you were way out of his.'

The silence across the miles rang out.

Victoria didn't know what to say, but Daksha did.

'I have to go. My mum's calling me.' Her lie was brazen and obvious. 'See you soon, and I hope your party is a great success.'

With that, she ended the call abruptly, the implication being that she had no intention of being part of any event, this Saturday or any other.

The phone call had been draining. Victoria, weakened, crawled up the stairs and along the corridor until she fell on to her bed. This grief business was tiring and it sledgehammered her when she least expected it, adding a layer of exhaustion to anything else negative that happened, like a chaser to knock her out. She folded her pillow into her chest and fell into a deep sleep.

The front doorbell woke her. She wasn't sure how long she had slept, but long enough for the sun to sink and night to pull its inky shade on the day.

Flynn . . .

Victoria pulled on her dressing gown over her clothes to ward off the chill of early evening and trod the stairs.

She had barely opened the front door when Flynn rushed in and lifted her clean off her feet, spinning her around, kissing her neck.

'This is happ-en-ing!' he sang.

'What is?' She laughed, wriggling to be free and giving that girly giggle, desperate to feel wanted, trying to bury the disappointment she felt at Daksha's words, which had cut her fragile stays of confidence. And in truth, much preferring his infectious enthusiasm for the event than her so-called best friend's fun-sucking negativity.

'Party central!' He put her back on firm ground and she noticed he had changed his clothes and showered, glad that he had gone home and that his parents wouldn't now be worried. 'Do you know Sab in the lower sixth?' He spoke quickly, clicking his fingers. 'Hangs out with Jordan and Jay and that lot?'

She shook her head. None of the names were familiar. 'I don't think so, no.'

'Well, he's borrowing decks off his cousin.' He clapped in delight.

'Decks?'

'Decks!' He laughed loudly. 'Music decks, for djing!'

'Yes, Flynn – I know what they are!' Did everyone think she was stupid or had been living in a cave? 'I just didn't realise you were thinking of decks for the party.'

'How else would we get music?' He looked at her quizzically.

'I thought . . .' What had she thought? 'I thought we might put a phone in a speaker with a good playlist.'

He laughed loudly again and, not for the first time that day, she *felt* stupid. 'It can't be a big, big party, Flynn, not like a nightclub thing. Not here.' She was adamant: Daksha was right about one thing, she would absolutely hate for any of Prim's lovely things to get broken.

'No, of course not. Just a nice gathering, some mellow music and a chance to all let our hair down before we jump on trains to uni!'

'Not all of us,' she reminded him, wondering for the first time if she had made the right decision, and feeling a flicker of panic – *everyone is going to leave . . .* She tried to picture the house with no Prim, no Daksha and no Flynn, before rubbing the tops of her arms inside her dressing gown to warm them.

'No, not you, Miss Supercool, intent on paving your own way. Travelling the world!'

She nodded, unwilling to share the fact that the plan was looking a little sketchy with the way things between her and Daksha stood at that very moment.

'I thought we could make noodles for supper?' he asked casually, removing his jacket and tossing it on to the stairs as if he had lived here for years and they were a couple. It calmed her fears a little.

'Noodles sound good.' She smiled, heading to the kitchen, switching lamps on as she went and aware of the deep rumble of hunger in her stomach. She watched him wield the knife against the chopping board like a pro, thinly slicing spring onions, carrots and broccoli with speed.

'I like this.' She smiled from the doorframe against which she leaned.

'You like what?' He looked up.

'I like . . . the two of us being here and kind of looking after each other a bit.' She felt her cheeks bloom with embarrassment, still so wary of saying the thing that might make Flynn McNamara bolt for the door.

'I like it too.' He held her gaze.

'It's . . . unexpected.'

'I think the best things often are, don't you?'

'Yes, yes, I do. Although I'm trying not to get too used to it. I mean, you're heading off to Newcastle in a couple of weeks . . .' She let this trail.

'You can come to Newcastle. Jump on a train and I'll show you the sights.'

'Would you like me to?'

'Yes! Of course I would!' He tutted and waved the knife as if it was a forgone conclusion. It filled her with a bubble of joy – maybe this was more than a holiday fling; she welcomed the thought.

The two sat end to end on the sofa, bowls held to their chests as they fed the long, salty noodles into their mouths, nibbling at the spring onion and spicy prawns that ran through them. Victoria was aware of the illegality of eating in the drawing room. Always a no-no as far as Prim was concerned; she had insisted on them eating at a table. But then there was much Prim would not have approved of: bare feet on the sofa, the washing-up sitting idle in the kitchen sink, Flynn's jacket discarded on the stairs, where someone might trip over it, having sex wherever and whenever the fancy took them, smoking weed in the garden room – oh, and the planning of a party where a DJ was going to take up residence with his decks. But then there was much about how Prim had lived her life that Victoria did not approve of: lying about the fact that her mum had died, watching her pray to her mum in heaven when she was in fact only in Oslo, without saying a word . . .

Fuck you all! This her overriding thought on the matter.

'I'm having a really nice time with you.' He beamed over the rim of his bowl.

She smiled at him. 'Me too.'

'Heard from courgettes guy?' He spoke through a mouthful.

'Gerald? No.' She shook her head, not overly bothered, seeing him as very much in the 'Prim' camp.

'So he's not going to pitch up in the morning with a bundle of rhubarb or some grubby carrots?'

'No.'

'Good, no one to disturb us. I like our morning sex best.'

Her laughter was loud and raucous; it felt simultaneously thrilling and shocking to be having these very open discussions.

'Me too.' She smiled at him. 'Can I ask, Flynn, do your parents not mind that you don't sleep at home?'

'Why would I sleep at home when I can sleep with you?' He stopped eating and held her gaze, as if it were obvious, and it made her heart skip. He grabbed her ankle and ran his free hand up under her jeans and over her calf. 'I like being with you.'

'And I like being with you.'

'This party is going to be kicking.' He removed his hand from her skin and went back to his noodle consumption.

Yep, kicking . . .

◆　◆　◆

Victoria walked home on Friday evening, having finished her shift at the coffee shop. It had felt good to concentrate on the making and serving of hot drinks and sticky buns, almost freeing, in that her grief was relegated for an hour or so. Stanislaw was sweet and asked repeatedly if she was feeling better after her recent sickness bug, which, ironically, made her feel sick. She had worked doubly hard, was extra polite to the customers and gave a greater share of her tips to the kitchen pot-washers than was necessary, trying to appease her guilt. Stanislaw was a good man. And it worked, a little. It felt odd walking the lane home, knowing that Flynn was at Rosebank waiting for her. His presence in the house felt comforting and invasive at the same time and her head swam with all that had happened. She still carried the strangest feeling, as if the sadness and the flurry of emotions were a whirling tornado stoppered inside a bottle and, try as she might, she *still* couldn't smash it. If she let herself think about everything – it all felt like too much.

I lied to Stanislaw, and he deserves better. Prim died. My beautiful gran died! I found her. I can picture her face in that chair. My mum is not dead. She is not dead! Sarah is my mum and she is alive, living in Oslo! They lied to me, all of them, even Grandpa. Flynn likes me; Flynn McNamara, who is right this very minute waiting for me at home, something I have fantasised about for so many years. Flynn and I have had sex, quite a bit of sex, yes, me, me with my potato face! And

Daksha, my sweet, sweet Daks, who doubts me, who isn't here and who I miss so, so much . . . it's all too much, all of it. I can't think. I just need to keep smiling and keep going . . .

The party was the following night and she had left Flynn with a long list of instructions. He had queried some of them.

'Nibbles? What's that?' He looked at her, his expression clueless.

'You know' – she tutted – 'crisps and things for people to eat. In little bowls dotted around? We need to buy stuff.'

He had laughed hard. 'You crack me up, Victoria.' He plucked the red felt-tipped pen from her hand and put a thick line through the word 'nibbles'. 'And this one?' He lifted the used envelope to his face, trying to decipher her writing.

'It says "neighbour notes". I thought maybe we should write little notes explaining to the neighbours either side that we are having a few friends over and so apologising in advance for any noise, and giving them a time we expect everyone to leave so they can see an end to it and know we aren't going to disturb their sleep or anything.'

Flynn shook his head. 'What time were you thinking, ten o'clock?'

The sarcasm wasn't lost on her. 'No, but midnight would be fair.'

'Midnight?' he screeched, as if scolded. 'What party ends at midnight? It probably won't start until gone ten, eleven!'

'Really?' It was her turn to screech.

He crossed through 'neighbour notes' and handed her back the pen.

'Let's just go with the flow, see how things develop and keep chill. Okay?' He had kissed her then; the number of kisses she had lost count of, but she knew it was a lot more than thirteen. In truth, she felt more nervous about the party than excited, but she didn't want to quash Flynn's excitement. Not only did she want to please him but, for one night, she wanted to be the kind of girl who had a party and didn't give a fig what the neighbours thought. Flynn handed her the joint, which she took into her fingers.

'Okay.' She kissed him again.

After sleeping late and eating one of Flynn's gargantuan breakfasts, much of Saturday was spent in preparation. Victoria had run the vacuum over the carpets and swept the flagstones. All precious or valuable items had been locked in the cupboard in Grandpa's old study on the second floor, and shelves and surfaces had been cleared of glassware and ornaments, replaced with coasters, should someone decide to abandon a glass or can on a shiny surface. The door to the garden room was locked. Access to Prim's beautiful plants was strictly forbidden. Victoria carried with her a feeling of intense anxiety, unaware that hosting a party would bring this much pressure. There were a million things to worry about: would people turn up? And if they did, would they have a good time? Did they have enough booze? Would people drink too much? Would the music be too loud? Not loud enough? What if the whole thing was a flop? Should she and Flynn sneak off upstairs? When *could* they sneak off upstairs? What should she wear? How should she do her hair? These last two items would have been a doddle with Daksha on hand to offer advice, but her friend was far from on hand and this thought was constantly at the front of Victoria's mind. Daksha's absence removed a huge chunk of her joy.

'Wowsers! You look fricking amazing!' Flynn grinned at her from the open door of the bathroom across the landing as she took the small gold-tasselled key and locked the door to Prim's bedroom before putting it in the brass plant pot on the landing. She walked slowly towards him in her silver high heels – the first time she had ever worn them, having bought them from a charity shop a few months earlier. Her legs were shaved and slathered in glossy lotion and her perfume spritzed in long bursts. The look on his face was one of appreciation as he took in the oversized shirt she had decided to wear with a large leather belt around the waist, thus turning it into a dress. A very short dress, but a dress nevertheless. Her hair was loose, and she had, for the first time in her life, applied fake tan to her pale, freckled skin. And with a slick of red lipstick purloined from Prim's dressing table, she was all set.

'I mean it – amaaaa-zing!' He whistled, reached out, pulled her to him and, with his hand in the small of her back, kissed her. 'You want some?' He proffered a joint he had rolled earlier and she took a single long, deep draw before heading down the stairs and into the kitchen for a cold glass of wine. She felt euphoric, excited, elated and sexy – the heels certainly helped, but there was no doubt this was shaping up to be quite possibly the best night of her life! She felt *magnificent*!

Victoria hadn't planned on getting drunk, far from it, but nervous anticipation meant she knocked back more than she might usually; in fact, more than she ever had. Her state of inebriation not only helped combat the horrible feeling of isolation without Daksha by her side, it also felt like the only way to handle the terrible lag between getting ready for the party and people actually arriving. She sipped wine quickly and refilled her glass regularly, taking the joint from Flynn's fingers whenever he passed. He was busy, preoccupied, whispering in corners with his mate and queuing up tracks for later. It was a reminder of how new they were that, rather than take his hand as she wished, she felt more comfortable dancing alone in the kitchen, practising a few steps and watching her reflection in the window to check out her moves. She looked good and was at the glorious arc of inebriation where she didn't realise quite how drunk or stoned she was.

She watched Flynn and his friend swallow a pill and grin at each other.

'Boyfriend . . .' She practised the word out loud, and it made her laugh. ''Smyboyfriend . . .' she slurred, raising her glass to him.

Sab and his two mates had set up the decks in the drawing room, where the furniture had been pushed to the sides of the room and the rugs rolled and put in a spare bedroom. The three of them nodded their heads in time to the relentless beat of a track that to her untrained ear sounded exactly like the last one they had played. She knew, however, it was more than her credibility was worth to ask if they had any Ed Sheeran or George Ezra.

Flynn caught her eye and winked; as usual, desire flared in her gut. This was happening: she was hosting a party with Flynn McNamara and, of all the girls he knew, *she* was the one he wanted. For the first time ever, Victoria felt a swell of something in her chest, and it felt a lot like belonging, a lot like popularity, and she liked it. In that moment she wasn't thinking about Prim, she wasn't thinking about Sarah, she wasn't thinking about much, other than getting Flynn alone, upstairs, and the sheer joy of feeling his hands on her skin. The thought in itself was enough to make her throw her head back and laugh! It was like she had a glorious secret.

With a glass of wine in her hand, she heard Flynn and the DJ boys laughing loudly in the drawing room and, just as she was wondering if anyone was ever going to show, and caring little at that point whether they did or not, she heard a different kind of laughter. Guests! By the time the first of the revellers arrived, a little after 10 p.m. she was positively sloshed and viewed proceedings through an alcohol-induced haze.

Victoria made her way out into the hallway and stood on the second stair, enabling her to look out over those arriving. She jiggled on the spot to the beat and let out random shouts of 'Woo-hoo!' for no particular reason. She saw at least ten heads of people she didn't know or recognise crowding through the front door all at once. Girls with poker-straight hair, their faces daubed in glitter paint, wearing faux fur bomber jackets, bikini tops and platform boots, accompanied by boys with slicked-back hair and sharp cheekbones sporting bare chests inside zip-up tracksuit tops – beautiful, beautiful people. And they were at *her* party.

'Hi!' She raised her hand in greeting, which was universally ignored. 'I'm Victoria. This is my house, my party! I'm with Flynn!' she hollered, one arm outstretched, the other fiercely gripping a can of lager, the drink to which she had now switched. One man raised his fingers in a peace sign as acknowledgement and looked at her over the top of his sunglasses but, other than that, no one seemed particularly interested in her name or her announcement. She felt the crushing blow of disappointment and loathed how much she wanted these people, whose opinion she shouldn't care less about, to like her. It was very different to the scenario she had played out in her mind over the last few days, where a gaggle of girls crowded around her in the kitchen, having introduced themselves. Shiny new friends.

So you're with Flynn? Ohmygod, he's gorgeous!

Cute couple, I love your hair!

Your house is so cool!

You should come out with us, come shopping!

Instead, people filed past indifferently as she watched from her vantage point on the stairs. Strangers snaked into the drawing room, as if drawn by the repetitive beat, dancing as they moved forward with their arms raised, elbows up and out. Some, she noted, were holding cans; others carried half bottles of spirits; and a couple were smoking. Taking Flynn's advice, she decided to go with the flow, keep chill and join in. That was the answer.

In a moment of drunken clumsiness, with a lack of coordination and unused to wearing the towering heels, her foot slipped on the bottom stair and she tumbled inelegantly forward, launching her can and its contents in the air and landing in an ungainly heap on the hall floor with her shirt/dress having ridden up over her hips and exposing her underwear. There was a roar of laughter, and no one helped her up. She felt like crying, but instead managed to get on to all fours and lever herself up against the newel post, pulling the shirt down to cover her modesty. Her ankle throbbed and, even though she wasn't crying, her eyes watered and, wiping her cheeks with her fingertips, she saw that her mascara streaked her face. 'Fuck it!' she yelled, and danced her way back into the kitchen, trying to make everything okay and wishing that Flynn was by her side. Grabbing a square of kitchen roll, she wiped her eyes and lifted the bin lid to throw it away.

She was unsure which particular odour caused the bile to rise in her throat. It could have been the old, cold, dead prawn noodles that lined the bin or the gone-off milk that sloshed in the bottom of an open plastic bottle or possibly the cold bacon fat that was inadequately wrapped in tin foil; not that it mattered, the result was the same. As the smells reached her nostrils, Victoria bent her head low into the bin and vomited. And then vomited again. She felt her skin break out in an uncomfortable sweat as the room span. She gripped the countertop as thick dribble hung from her chin in a lacy bib.

'Oh my God! What is that stench?'

She whipped her head around to see two of the bomber-jack-eted, poker-straight-haired girls looking at her like she was . . . like she was disgusting.

''S'okay!' She raised her hand. 'I'mokay!'

The girls wrinkled their noses and shook their heads in a way that was both pitying and dismissive. It was then that she felt the next bout of sickness rising and, rather than let them witness her shame, she ducked into the larder cupboard and vomited into the stash of shopping bags that sat in a box in the darkness. The sound of the girls' laughter was enough to finally encourage her tears to the surface. Pulling the door closed, Victoria removed her ridiculous shoes and sank down until she sat on the floor of the dark, cool cupboard, vomit covering the damp front of her clothing, her hair mussed and her make-up ruined. Her breath, she knew, was foul, and still the room span.

'I want to go home . . .' she murmured, as her sob built. 'I just want to go home . . .' But therein lay the problem. 'I liked things the way they were before. I liked it when I didn't know, when I thought I was happy . . .'

She placed her head on the wall and welcomed the brief respite from the company of strangers. It was hard to say how long she stayed in the dark confines of the larder while the party raged around her, but long enough for her to start feeling the beginnings of sober. With her head in her hands, Victoria cried.

'I am in a bloody cupboard!' she whispered. 'And I am covered in sick.'

When her tears had subsided sufficiently, she crept out and washed her face in the sink. Knowing she certainly did not want any more wine, she made herself a cup of tea and laughed, looking out over the wide sweep of the back lawn, wondering what Daksha would make of it all.

Yes, I swear to God! Everyone was dancing and I was in the kitchen, looking like I'd been dragged through several hedges backwards, all on my own, making a cup of tea. And you know why, Daks? Because it's 'always the right time for a cup of tea!'

She missed her friend. Missed her so much. Nothing, she knew, felt half as much fun when Daksha wasn't involved. She felt for her phone but decided against calling, hating the tears that threatened.

'Not tonight, Victoria. No more crying tonight.' Sniffing, she managed to halt the tears' advance.

Having downed her tea and with the beginning of clarity edging her thoughts, she emerged from the kitchen to find the hallway busy with people. Ignoring the snickering and whispered comments about her appearance, she peered into the drawing room; the ten people dancing had become twenty or possibly nearer thirty, or more . . . the place was rammed. She watched the crowd take up positions in the spaces on the floor as if choreographed, comfortable and familiar with how to move to the pulse of the music. She watched through the open door as Sab placed one earphone over his ear and seamlessly led them like a puppeteer from one tune into another, and still they danced. It was like they were connected, his hands on the decks and the feet of those who now shuffled, slid and jumped en masse.

Her eyes scanned the sea of heads, each and every one of them a stranger and not one of them remotely interested in talking to her. She was invisible. The way heels were dragging across the hardwood floor bothered her; similarly, she noticed a couple who had stretched out top to toe on the sofa with clunky boots resting on the dupioni silk. Another girl flicked ash over her shoulder, careless of where it might land.

It was as if a switch had flipped in her brain. This was not fun. This was not the best night of her life, and this was her house. She wanted everyone to leave, she wanted the party to stop and she wanted nothing more than to lie in Flynn's arms.

Slowly, she made her way through the crowds and across the hallway, which was chock-full of bodies. Here there was less laughter and more shouting, people calling to each other to be heard, lobbing lighters and cigarettes across the heads of others and swilling booze from carelessly held cans. Then came the crash of glass, followed by a clap of derision from those standing close by. She didn't know what had got broken: a wine glass? A painting? Her heart began to race as she sobered enough to feel the full fear of someone who was in a situation that was veering wildly out of their control.

She needed to find Flynn.

'Flynn?' she called out in the kitchen, and again in the hall-way, before making her way into the drawing room and battling through the crowd to Sab and his mates. 'Have you seen Flynn?' she shouted.

'Nah!' came his downturned-mouth response, followed by a shake of his head, before he turned his attention back to the music. Victoria went hunting for the boy who could make this all stop, the person who had invited all these people to the party – his friends, *his* bloody friends! One thing she knew for certain: this was not a nice gathering and there was nothing mellow about it. She felt the very real beginnings of panic as she prowled the rooms and garden, looking for him.

It felt like more people had arrived. Strangers crowded every corner. Some kissed wildly on cushions in the window seats where she and Prim had sat and read books; others lay in dark corners trying not to get trampled; one girl, she noted, was wearing what looked suspiciously like her ratty grey dressing gown. Her heart raced and her breath was coming fast.

'Oh no! Not upstairs!' Her heart continued to thud as she navigated the inebriated, the high and the sexual adventurers who cluttered up the stairs, tripping over the bodies, not caring at that point if they could see right up her short, short dress. The breath caught in her throat at the sight of people up here too, on Prim's landing, where her gran had blown her a kiss goodnight across the soft carpet on more nights than she cared to remember, in this, the home Prim had lived all of her married life with Grandpa.

'Night night, my darling, sweet dreams, see you in the morning . . .'
Her head continued to clear and her anger burbled.

I need to find Flynn . . . this is getting way out of hand! He can send them all home . . .

189

'You need to go downstairs!' she yelled, waving her arms to indicate where the stairs were, thinking this might help speed up the process. 'You all need to go back down the stairs, this is out of bounds!' she called again, trying to make herself heard over the beat of the music, which she was certain had gone up in volume. People ignored her, all apart from one guy, who gripped her arm and whispered, 'Chill out!'

'Fuck off!' she yelled back, and he laughed.

Making her way along the landing, she put her hand on the handle to Prim's bedroom, this special place.

Please, please, no . . . She prayed that no one had done the unthinkable and found the key, taken up residence in this room, this one above all others. Even the thought of someone lying on Prim's bed, near her things, was enough to make her tears gather and her gut bunch with guilt and regret.

I'm sorry, Prim! I'm sorry!

Opening the door quickly, there was a split second where she felt utterly paralysed. The long cascade of blonde hair shivering down the naked back of the girl was the first thing she saw. The same girl now kneeling with her arms raised provocatively over her head as she sat like a queen on a throne. The throne, however, was Prim's mattress.

'What the hell do you think you're doing in here?' she screamed through gritted teeth. 'Get out! Get out of this room! What do you think—' The words ran out as the girl turned around to face her and Victoria's stomach jumped so violently she feared she might throw up again. It was none other than Courtney who pouted at her in the lamplight, pulling off the doll-like and dumb in a way she could never emulate.

'Courtney!' she managed. Her eyes then fell upon the boy wedged beneath the voluptuous Courtney on the mattress. And that's when she did throw up, managing to grab a handbag that had been discarded on the floor by the end of the bed. Lowering her head into it, she deposited the remainder of her wine and lager consumption and much of a large mug of tea.

'That's my bloody bag! My phone's in there! What the actual fuck?' Courtney wailed, as the boy sat up and tried to hide his nakedness. That boy was none other than Flynn McNamara. Of course it was. And by the looks of things, his pants had fallen off.

'Victoria!' he called after her as she ran to the bathroom, locking the door behind her before she finished throwing up into the loo, and running the cold tap to rinse her face and mouth. Standing in front of the mirror above the sink, she stared at the person reflected back at her.

'Who are you?' she whispered. 'And what the hell are you doing?'

Plucking the bottle of Chanel No5 from the glass shelf above the wide pedestal sink, she carefully removed the lid and sprayed it on to her décolletage and wrist, which she brought to her nose and inhaled deeply. It was a sweet scent of remembrance that brought Prim into the room. The tears that followed were different from the angry, thin tears that had dogged her for weeks, they were drawn from a deeper place, a place where the memory of the life she had shared with Prim played like a home movie. A warm place full of love, and in it there was no place for strangers, loud music, drugs and certainly not for shitty boys who lied.

'You are Prim's granddaughter. You are Sarah's daughter. You are Victoria. And you are Victory. And right now, you need to be an industrious coper, the very best kind of person!'

Sitting now on the edge of the bath, she tried to think of the best course of action. With her phone in her hand, her fingers trembling, she scrolled through her limited contacts and, with time against her, dialled the number of the person who had told her they would be there for her day or night, all she had to do was pick up the phone . . . The closest person she had to Prim, almost family.

While she waited for his arrival she reached into the laundry basket, threw on her pyjama bottoms and donned the trainers she had abandoned before her bath only hours earlier. She went into survival mode, steeling herself to face Flynn and wishing again that Daksha were here. To think she had wanted nothing more than sex with Flynn this very night.

'Okay.' Again, she stared at her face in the mirror. 'You are a Cutter-Rotherstone and you've got this!'

Ignoring the quake in her gut, Victoria raced through the upstairs rooms, throwing belongings and clothes out of windows and screaming at the interlopers, 'Get out! Get out now!'

She spied Flynn and Courtney hand in hand as they fled Prim's bedroom, giggling together and in a state of semi-undress. Her gut folded with humiliation and fury. Suddenly she heard screams, and the music came to an abrupt stop. She was glad that it had but also fearful as to why. The bodies on the stairs started to gather themselves and leave via the front door and, with their exit, came the beginnings of relief. Not that it was over quite yet.

She watched from the half landing, the one where she liked to sit and watch the sun cast purple, blue and yellow squares on to the honey-coloured carpet.

Flynn and Courtney reached the bottom stair, still hand in hand, he with his backpack slung over his shoulder. At the same time, her saviour came into view. The screaming in the drawing room had stopped and people were streaming from its confines and heading out of the front door in haste with barely a backward glance.

'Ah, courgettes guy!' Flynn called out.

Gerald stood squarely in front of him. 'My name is Mr Worthington.'

'My apologies, Mr Worthington.'

She watched as Flynn became the charming boy who had drawn her in. All part of the act, no doubt.

'Get out of this house!' Gerald was clearly not quite so easily taken in.

Flynn stepped forward. 'Oh, come on, don't be like that! I'm drunk and maybe a little high.' He snickered. 'But it's all cool here. It's all cool.'

'I said get out of this house!' Gerald stood his ground.

'I need to talk to Victoria . . .' He let go of Courtney's hand and turned, trying to locate her.

'You are not going to talk to Victoria, you are going to leave this minute!'

'Or what? What will you do, throw a courgette at me?'

'No.' Gerald didn't budge. 'I don't need courgettes, son. I've got this.' And from behind his back he pulled a revolver and, with both hands grasping the pistol grip, he aimed it at Flynn.

Victoria gasped. This was insane! Gerald had a gun, a bloody gun! Courtney screamed, loudly, and clutched her vomitty bag to her voluptuous chest, as if this might offer the protection needed, and Flynn lost most of the colour in his face.

'All right, all right!' Flynn held up his hands. 'Take it easy!' he managed, his voice quavering with fear as he sidled past Gerald and out of the front door.

Gerald lowered the gun and swept the rooms, making sure the last of the stragglers had left. Victoria felt a strange mixture of relief that Gerald had come to her rescue, or rather Rosebank's rescue, but also a little afraid that he might be furious. He did, after all, have a gun.

Victoria walked slowly down the stairs and into the now empty drawing room, which carried the odour of too many sweaty bodies that had been squashed into a confined space and the tang of booze, cigarettes and weed. She threw open the windows, inviting the chill night air to whip around the walls, trying not to look at the detritus that littered the parquet flooring: the empty cans trodden flat, vodka bottles, cigarette butts ground underfoot, and discarded hippy crack canisters that had been used and abandoned. Her tears flowed and she did nothing to stop them, taking great gulps of air to fuel her sobs. She shifted a flattened cushion and sank down on to the sofa.

'I've had enough!' she wailed into the silence. 'I have bloody had enough! I don't know what's happened to me, but everything is upside down, Gerald. Everything is broken, everything . . . I don't know what's going on. I don't know what to do.'

'Come on.' Gerald put his arm around her shoulders and planted a kiss on the top of her head. She reached up and held him close, clinging on, thankful not only for his intervention but that, unlike others she had trusted in recent times, he had kept his word and had been there when she needed him.

'I'm sorry I was rude to you, Gerald. All you were doing was being nice, trying to help, and I was horrible to you – all you've done is bring me courgettes and be kind!' she wailed. 'I even shouted at you down the phone – I was showing off in front of Flynn.' She cried harder.

'That is water under the bridge.' He coughed to clear his throat.

'I'm sorry!'

'No need to say it again. You don't have to worry.' He hugged her back and straightened. 'Right, let's lock the place up and come back tomorrow. You need sleep; a cup of hot cocoa and sleep.'

That sounded good.

She watched as he gently closed the windows she had only just opened and switched off the lights.

'You've got a gun, Gerald! A bloody gun!'

'Yes, dear. Yes, I have.'

TEN

It took a monumental effort for Victoria to open her eyes and face the day. Her preference would have been to sink down into the mattress, let her eyelids fall and sleep for a hundred years . . . but if the last few weeks had taught her anything, it was that this life of hers was no fairy tale. It had in fact been the first peaceful night she had had since Prim had died; she had nodded off feeling safe and calm, knowing Gerald was only a shout away. She now nursed her hangover in the florally decorated spare room at Gerald's house, still wearing the oversized shirt with its dubious stains and her pyjama bottoms from the previous night, which, frankly, all needed a good hot cycle in the washing machine. She had been bundled into the car with a tear-streaked face and brought here by her knight in shining armour with the party mess partially contained and the rooms locked up.

An image of the state of the house, thoughts about the way the evening had ended, the horror of the party itself and the way she had caught Flynn in Prim's bed with Courtney, was all more than she could stand. She pushed her face down into the pillow and wished, not for the first time, that she could rewind time.

A gentle but firm knock on the door pulled her from her thoughts.

'Morning, Victoria. Breakfast is on the table.'

'Thank you, Gerald, I'll be right down.' The thought of breakfast made her feel sick.

'I didn't want to say anything last night, figuring you had enough to deal with, but I noticed the French doors to the garden room had been forced open from the outside. No damage done inside, thank goodness, I think it was just someone having a nose around, but the frame needs a bit of attention and the lock has been smashed off and needs changing – should I give Bernard a ring, or can you do that?'

Victoria pictured Bernard sloping off down the garden path, looking hurt and a little lost. She felt like shit. It wasn't his fault; she knew this, had always known it.

'I'll do it.'

'Righto. I'll leave you to it. See you down in five.' She liked his gentle instruction. It was how Prim used to operate – steering, gently guiding.

Victoria sat up, reached for her phone and dialled Bernard's number. Her mouth was dry with nerves. There was no answer. She took a deep breath and left him a message.

'Erm, Bernard . . .' Dammit! These tears seemed to spring at the most inconvenient of moments. 'It's Victoria. I don't really know what to say or how to say it; apart from I'm sorry. I am so sorry for taking my anger out on you. You didn't deserve it. You were right: what were you supposed to do? You were doing a kind thing, a good thing for Sarah, and I can see now that to tell a little girl the truth . . .' She shook her head at the absurdity of the suggestion. 'Well, it was not your story to tell, was it? I am truly very sorry. Please come back to work. I need you. Rosebank needs you. I did something rather stupid . . . had a party, and the house is a wreck. Someone forced the lock on the garden room door and, well' – she closed her eyes, aware that she was probably rambling – 'I am sorry, Bernard.'

Finally, having tied her hair up and washed her face in the tidy bathroom, removing the last remnants of her make-up, she made her way down the narrow stairs of the three-bedroom semi. The little square kitchen was bright, with a table on a supporting leg jutting out from the kitchen wall and a stool placed either side. She sat down. Gerald, she noted, was already immaculately turned out in pressed slacks and a white shirt beneath a cherry-red V-necked jersey as he warmed a teapot over the sink. She did her best to look favourably at the slices of toast in the kind of stainless-steel toast rack she imagined you might get at a seaside bed and breakfast. There was a selection of jams and a jar of Marmite and two small glasses of orange juice. Her appetite was zero, but his actions were dear and his effort so reminiscent of Prim and how she liked to serve breakfast in a particular way. It brought a lump to her throat.

'This looks lovely.'

'Good. Now, I am sure you just want to get back to the house, but you need a good breakfast to set you up for the day and you need to take a moment to make a plan.'

She took a deep breath, knowing he was probably right.

'Did you call Bernard about the door?' he asked casually.

'I did. And I told him how sorry I was. I took my hurt out on him and that wasn't fair. It didn't feel good, not when I thought about it, but I was so mad!'

'Yes, he might have called me.' Gerald turned and smiled at her.

'Thank you for what you did last night, Gerald. I panicked. I didn't know what to do and you had said to call, day or night, if ever . . .' Victoria knew she would forever be grateful to this kindly man who had stepped in when she'd needed him the most and had simply bundled her up and driven her to a safe, warm place without anger and, seemingly, without judgement, and she thanked God he was still in her life.

'And I meant it. I must say, I hadn't banked on quite such an emergency and so soon, but there we go.' He poured hot water on to the tea leaves in the pot and set it aside to steep while he took his place at the table and tucked a napkin into his shirt collar before reaching for a slice of toast. 'Tuck in!' He waved a butter knife in her direction.

She began buttering a triangle of toast, which was cool to the touch. 'I can't believe you turned up with a gun.' She smiled at him and reached for the jam.

'Not just any gun, a standard issue Webley and Scott no less – my father's from the Second World War. An ornament, no more.' He winked at her.

'Does it not work?' she asked with no small measure of relief.

'Oh, it did at one point, and of course my father had many, many tales of derring-do, most, I suspect, fabricated for my benefit, and nearly all involving his faithful sidearm, but it was decommissioned over fifty years ago, doesn't work at all. My mother couldn't bear to part with it.'

'But Flynn didn't know that.'

'No.' Gerald made a disapproving *tsk* sound. 'Flynn did not know that. The little turd.'

She could not contain the bubble of laughter that escaped her lips. 'Did you just call him a little turd?' She had heard perfectly but relished the joy of repeating the unexpected insult. It made her feel a little better.

'I did. I disliked the chap on sight – with good reason, it seems.'

'I trusted him. I liked him. I still do a bit; I can't help it. He made my life feel slightly better, but last night it felt a whole lot worse.' She thought of the things Flynn had said to her: *'I wouldn't ever want to be the reason you cried.'* The little turd. She felt angry at herself, not only for how she had fallen for his shtick, but also how she had let him into Prim's home, into her bed . . . *I'm sorry, Prim.* She bit her toast and licked the strawberry jam from her top lip.

'Then you, my dear, are not half as smart as I thought you were.'

His words caused the crumbs to stick in her throat. 'I think you might be right.' She pictured Courtney's long hair shivering down her back.

'Well, the important thing is that you learn from this. It's one thing to be naïve and trust someone like Flynn, but quite another to be downright stupid and agree to have a party at Rosebank and to let a stranger invite more strangers into Prim's home.'

She hated the shameful self-consciousness that cloaked her. He was right, of course. Not that his words could make her feel any worse than she already did.

'I know, Gerald. I know you're right and I am so mad at myself and sorry to Prim; she'd be horrified, and I know we've been joking, but you're not young and you had to come out in the middle of the night and sort it all out, and you could have got into real trouble for having a gun.' She felt the tears slip down the back of her throat and any appetite she might have had for breakfast faded.

'I'm glad you're sorry. I also know you won't do it again, even though, of course, you are an adult and at liberty to do exactly as you see fit, but to take that route' – he sipped his orange juice – 'to take that route would, I think, be the biggest waste of all your wonderful potential.' He reached across and patted her hand.

'Thank you, Gerald, for caring about me,' she offered sincerely. It felt nice to know that she was not alone, that there was someone like Gerald looking out for her. And someone like Daksha . . . *Oh Daks, I miss you, my lovely friend! I need you to forgive me . . .*

'I do care about you. And I cared about Prim and I know she would have wanted me to say something. Plus,' he said as he went to retrieve the teapot, 'don't tell a soul, but it was one of the best evenings I have had in an age! One minute I am in my pyjamas with an Agatha Christie in my palms, and the next I am toting a pistol at a rave! How many members of the bowls club can say the same thing?'

'Not many, Gerald.' She smiled at the man. 'Not many.'

He brushed his hands over his plate and wiped his mouth with the napkin. Victoria liked the neatness of his house, the calm predictability of his routine; she figured being old wasn't so bad.

'Now, how about you have a soak in the bath while I clear the breakfast things away and then we go tackle whatever awaits us at Rosebank?'

Victoria nodded; that sounded like a plan.

As she watched the bubbles foam and grow under the gurgling hot tap, Victoria picked up her phone and composed a text to Daksha.

> Daks, I don't expect a reply and I have no right to ask for one. I just wanted to say that I am truly sorry. I am so very sorry. I lost my head. I lost control (and my virginity – but that's a whole other story!) but the very worst part of it all is that I may have lost you and that is something I can't bear to think about. I literally can't bear it. V Xx

By the time she stepped out of the bath, there was a reply, and it gladdened her heart.

> How was the party?

Victoria wrapped herself in the big towel from the towel rail and wrote:

Horrific. Every aspect completely horrific. One of the worst
nights of my life and considering recent events – hope
this conveys just how bad. I am such an idiot. An idiot now
knee-deep in carnage – and yes, I know, it's my own stupid
fault. X

Daksha didn't reply and Victoria understood. She had blown it. It
was no more than she deserved. And no matter how much it hurt,
this was, after all, just another loss to thicken the shell encasing her
already broken heart.

As Gerald pulled on to the gravel driveway, Victoria was delighted
to see Bernard's van already *in situ*. She could hear the steady
rhythm of a hammer and knew he was at work.

'Bernard!' She smiled.

'Yep, Bernard.' Gerald killed the engine and they climbed out.

The two looked at the grass of the front lawns and flowerbeds,
where fast-food wrappers ranging from cardboard chicken buck-
ets to brown-paper burger bags nestled among the rosebushes and
behind the ornamental shrubs.

'Oh God.' She felt sick.

'Come on. Chin up! Moping about it isn't going to help with
the clear-up. We get tea when we have progress!' Gerald's words
motivated her as he handed her a black bin bag.

She put her key in the front door and gingerly pushed it open.
The house smelled like a grubby pub. Pulling the front door wide,
she wedged it open with a concrete rabbit that had long ago lost
an ear and had lived by the porch for as many years as she could
remember. Next she marched through to the garden room, where
Bernard, who had gained access via the broken French doors, had

thrown them open to allow a breeze in from the east side of the property. She was glad; it had been her plan to literally blow away the stench and memory of the previous night.

'Thank you, Bernard, for coming over.' She spoke quietly.

The man stopped hammering and looked at her, clearly wary about his reception.

'I got your message.' He nodded.

'I meant every word. I am sorry, for . . . for everything.' She swallowed.

'You know, there have been countless times over the years that I've wanted to write you a note.' He tapped the hammer gently into his palm, as if this helped him concentrate. 'I was in a very difficult position. I'd always got on well with Sarah and her request sounded reasonable, asking me to let her know occasionally how you were doing, nothing more. And I told the wife, who said, "Don't get involved", but I was already involved. And Sarah said something that made me think. She said, "If you couldn't see your little one grow up, what would you give just to know she was doing okay?"' He blinked and looked out towards the garden. 'And I thought about that a lot and I knew that I'd give anything, anything at all, and so to drop her a line once in a while felt like a small thing.'

'It was a big thing to me.' She spoke calmly.

'I can see that now. But I never meant no harm, I was only trying to do good for Sarah.'

'And *I* can see that now.' She held his gaze. 'So, you have known Sarah for a long time?'

'Yes. Thirty-odd years.'

'And is she . . . I mean . . . do I . . .?'

'You are very much like her.' He intercepted her thoughts, and his words sent a bolt of joy through her. 'She was smart and head-strong, and I think that's why she and your gran clashed.'

'Did she suddenly start taking drugs, or was it a gradual thing?' She was curious, feeling her face flush and thinking of how she had smoked weed in this very room.

'Sarah was a free spirit and was very open. I don't think she did anything that most teenagers don't do at first. The difference is, most teenagers hide it, but not her, and Prim found that tough to deal with.'

'Did you ever meet my dad?' Her voice cracked.

Bernard shook his head. 'No.'

'What did you think, Bernard, about the fact that they told me she had died? That they lied to me like that?'

He exhaled slowly. 'I thought it was . . .' She could see that, when it came to it, he too was struggling for words. 'I thought it was bound to come back to them at some point and you'd all have to face the consequences, is what I thought. Bit like having a party and letting people run wild in your house.' He tutted.

'A bit like that.' She rustled the bin bag in her hand. 'Better crack on. We are stopping for tea when Gerald gives the say-so.'

'Tea? Prim would have cake too, or at the very least a biscuit.' He chuckled.

'I'll see what we can do!' She felt a small weight lift from her shoulders; to have things restored with Bernard-the-handyman felt good.

Gerald had already unfurled his own bin liner from a roll and was gingerly stepping among the flowerbeds, popping litter, cigarette ends and at least one condom into its dark confines.

She cringed. 'Thank you, Gerald,' she called from the hallway.

'Less thanking and more doing is, I think, the order of the day. Let's stop in an hour for tea.'

She liked his offer of a reward and looked around the hallway walls; thankfully, everything looked to be intact. There were, however, several scratches and scuffmarks on the parquet flooring, which she knew she could tackle with beeswax polish and a soft cloth. With her own bin bag now at the ready, she bent low to gather the horrible clutter of stuff on the floors and in corners that did not belong there, tutting at the rather grey-looking bra that not only had someone neglected to wash carefully, shoving it in with the dark colours, but had also seemingly neglected to put back on before going home.

Unsurprisingly, the drawing room looked the most forlorn. Partly due to the bare surfaces, from where Prim's precious *objets d'art* had, thankfully, been removed, but also because the memory lurked of the crush of bodies and their squeaky trainers and heels, which had run rampant over the block wood floor. Here too she managed a sizable haul of trash, and she stepped outside to place her third bulging bin bag on the driveway. She looked up at the sound of a car door closing and saw Daksha walk up the driveway wearing rubber gloves and carrying a bucket from which poked various cleaning products.

Victoria couldn't hold back; she ran to her friend and threw her arms around her, holding her tight. It meant more than she could possibly say to have her friend back by her side, and with Bernard in the garden room and Gerald roaming the hallway, for the first time since Prim's death, she realised she was not alone, *she was not alone.*

'I . . . can't . . . breathe . . .' Daksha managed over her shoulder.

Victoria pulled away and looked into the face of her beloved friend. 'I am so sorry, Daks. I was an arsehole.'

'You were an arsehole,' Daksha agreed, restoring her glasses. 'And I have to ask, are you now cured of this arseholeness, do you think?'

Victoria nodded. 'I am. I really am.'

'Well, thank goodness for that. I missed my friend.'

'I missed you too. So much happened.' She looked around the garden and remembered the flare of panic she had felt.

'Give me the highlights or the lowlights, whichever.' Daksha flapped her hand.

'I guess a weird highlight would be there were people I had never met before having sex on the stairs.'

'How on earth do you have sex on the stairs?' Daksha looked perplexed.

'Very carefully.' Victoria nodded. 'And then I struggle to pick a lowlight. It's a toss-up between falling off my heels and then throwing up in the larder or finding Flynn in Prim's bed with Courtney.'

'Let me guess, his pants had fallen off?'

'They had.' She allowed herself the smallest of smiles, even though to recount it hurt. 'And then Gerald turned up with a gun.'

'You *are* kidding me!'

'I'm not. He opened a can of whoop-arse and went all gangster. Everyone ran, taking their decks with them.'

'Decks?'

'Yes, you know record decks, for music.'

'God, Vic, I know what decks are. What, did you think that I live in a cave? I was just wondering what kind of party it was if you needed decks at all?'

'I love you, Daksha Joshi.' Victoria smiled.

'This is all well and good,' Gerald called from the hallway. 'Hello, Daksha dear, but love isn't going to get this house straight. That we can only do with elbow grease and effort!'

'I thought you said we could have a cup of tea?' Victoria called out. Gerald checked his watch. 'Not for another eight minutes.' He winked and disappeared inside.

◆　◆　◆

By mid-evening they'd finally, finally got the house almost fully restored and smelling fresh: the rubbish was gone, the floors cleaned and laundry sat in piles on the floor of the boot room. Bernard had left a little after midday and Gerald had only just headed home, with a huge hug of thanks. Victoria and Daksha now took up their favourite spots on either end of the freshly plumped and cleaned sofa in the drawing room. The three had worked tirelessly and had enjoyed congratulatory fish and chips around the kitchen table not an hour since. Victoria ran her hand over the waistband of her jeans, her stomach full of the food she had devoured at speed.

The drawing room felt wonderful. Having dusted each surface before returning Prim's ornaments, and polishing the floor before replacing the rugs, the place actually shone a little more brightly than it had before the party.

'There, all back to normal.' Daksha yawned.

'Are we all back to normal?' she hardly dared ask.

'Nearly.' Her friend smiled. 'Don't worry; we'll get there. I think you are going through something that most of us can't begin to understand, and so the odd breakdown of normal service, nuts behaviour and pockets of lunacy are probably to be expected.'

Victoria nodded, not proud of the breakdown in normal service and hoping her nuts behaviour was drawing to an end, because, quite frankly, it was exhausting.

'I have been feeling so empty and so angry,' she confessed.

'I can imagine.'

Victoria picked at a thread on her clean pyjama bottoms. 'It's been like my thoughts were on a loop. I've been a bit obsessed with wanting to know exactly what happened, how the deal was struck, who suggested what and who agreed . . .' She let this trail.

'Why do you need that level of detail?'

'Because I thought it would help me understand.'

'I don't think it would help, not really. I'm not saying you shouldn't discuss it – I absolutely think you should – but I bet it was a storm of events that led things to turn out how they did. I worry that if you're like a dog with a bone, then it might just prolong the breakdown of normal service. And I don't want that for you.' Daksha squeezed her toes.

'I just want the truth.'

'You *know* the truth: your mum is still alive. Prim made decisions that you can't challenge her on because she isn't here any more and you have to live with it. That's it!'

Victoria sighed and looked into her lap. 'I guess so, but there are still so many gaps. I'm thinking of going to Oslo to talk to Sarah.' She felt a flash of nerves as the thought left her mouth. 'I'd like answers, and she is one of the only people who might just be able to give them to me.'

'I think that would be a brave thing to do and a brilliant thing to do.'

Victoria smiled at her friend and slid down to rest her head on her end of the sofa. 'I have kind of been avoiding her to punish her a little bit. I wanted her to miss me, like I have always missed her.'

'You think she hasn't missed you? Jesus, Vic, you only have to look at the woman to see that she is utterly broken! The way she looked, standing like that in the foyer waiting for you . . . I think she's been punished enough, and actually by letting strangers smash up Rosebank, ignoring the mother you have longed for, shagging Flynn the dickhead and shutting me out, you are only punishing yourself. Enough already!'

Victoria lifted her head and stared at her friend.

Daksha flapped her hand. 'Sorry. Too much?'

'Too much.' She smiled at her friend.

ELEVEN

Victoria tucked the duvet around her legs, reached for her laptop and opened up Sarah's emails. She took a deep breath and opened the next two letters.

May 2001
Sarah Jackson
Henbury House
West Sussex

Hello Mum,

What to say?

Your letter has provoked every emotion possible.

At first I was furious, raging! How dare you? How dare you assume that because Marcus has an illness – that's right, the illness of addiction – that he could not be the best father to our child?

Would you suggest the same if he had a different illness? Cancer? A missing limb? Of course not, and if you think that either he or I would knowingly put our daughter in danger, then you are deluded! Bloody deluded! She is the good thing that will pull us out of this; she is the one bright light at the end of a very dark tunnel and we will cherish her!

I spoke to one of the counsellors here, who calmed me a little, and you know what, Mum? Now I feel sad for you, sad that you are willing to dismiss him so willingly and that ultimately you don't have more faith in me. You say you do, but words are easy.

And I don't write this to be cruel or calculating, but it is the truth.

I will be out of Henbury House before I give birth to my daughter and I was considering asking you to play a part in the arrival of this child.

But you can forget that.

How many times do I have to say it: Marcus and I come as a package.

It's either us as a couple or neither of us.

That's it.

There's nothing more to say.

Sarah

'Knock knock?' Daksha spoke as she walked into Victoria's bedroom.

'Hey.'

'You okay?' Her concern was sweet, touching.

'Yup.' She touched the screen. 'My heart aches for her, this woman in the letters.' There was a crack to her voice.

'Your mum?'

'Yes. It's hard to think this is me they are talking about, and hard to think it's Prim that she is talking to. I can feel her pain. I can feel *both* of their pain.'

'Well, I call that progress. Have you booked your flight?'

She shook her head. 'No, I'm going to call Sarah first and just check that it's okay for me to go.'

'I bet it will be.' She closed her eyes briefly. 'Heard from Flynn?'

Again, she shook her head.

'Do you *want* to hear from Flynn?' Daksha pushed.

'I don't think so, but it feels weird. We had sex, ate noodles and then he just disappeared.' She threw her palms up. 'It's not what I pictured when I thought about losing my virginity. But then, he's not who I thought he was.' She closed her eyes and sighed. *I'm such an idiot . . . falling for that shit.*

'No, I bet. So what was it like?'

'What, the sex?'

'No, Vic, the noodles! Of course the sex!'

Victoria laughed. 'It was . . . disappointing and brilliant and exciting and flat and intimate and embarrassing and addictive and strangely awkward.'

'Good God! Doesn't sound like I'm missing much.'

'I think it'll be good when it's with the right person.'

'Here's hoping.' Daksha pulled a face and stood. 'Anyway, the spare room is calling and I am turning in. Night night.' She blew a kiss from the doorframe.

'Night.'

May 2001
Rosebank
Epsom
Surrey

Sarah,

I can feel the anger in your written words. Let me try again to explain.

That man might, as you say, be a very nice person, he might have the makings to be the very best father, but all of that pales into insignificance when I consider the welfare of you, the person I love most in the whole wide world! He gives you drugs! If not now, then he has given you drugs in the past! How, how am I supposed to welcome him into my home, into my heart, when he has left a dark hole in both?

I do have faith in you. I always have. But is it a coincidence that you, who had never lied, never stolen, never been anything other than trustworthy and wonderful, met him and then lied to Daddy and me about a trip to Barcelona – using the money instead for drugs? Read that back, Sarah! And trust me that I do have faith in you. The fact that you are at Henbury House at all is the most positive step.

But I have no faith in him, none at all.

And I do not trust him.

I think he brings you into harm's way.

And I do not trust you when you are with him.

That is a hard thing to write and an even harder truth to bear.

And so, if you and he do indeed, as you say, come as a package, then, as heartbreaking as it is, I can only agree. It would be impossible for me to help at the birth, to smile and make out everything is rosy, when I believe the very opposite.

What a desperate state of affairs.

Utterly desperate.

Think this through, Sarah! Think about that little baby girl you are carrying. Think about it! I want you home safely and I want your baby to have the best start.

I am begging you. I am begging you . . .

Mum. X

Victoria closed the laptop and let the words of the letters settle.

Prim knew you so much better than I do, and she didn't trust you, Sarah – so should I? But then, on the other hand, I trusted Prim and she let me down . . .

It was nine o'clock – which made it ten o'clock in Oslo. Victoria turned the phone over in her palms and tentatively dialled Sarah's number. Her stomach churned and she lost her nerve, half hoping the call might go straight to messages. Closing her eyes, she breathed slowly, still in two minds about the wisdom of her actions, but before she had a chance to reconsider, the call was answered.

'Hello! Oh, hello!' And there it was: the note of hope, the undercurrent of joy that was something Sarah evidently felt at no more than seeing her name pop up on a phone screen. It felt nice to know that was the effect she had on her, flattering even.

'Hi, Sarah.'

'Is this a misdial? Or did you want to call me?' Sarah asked with quiet intensity.

How Victoria answered this question would, she knew, set the tone for what came next.

'No, it's not a misdial. I . . . I wanted to call you.'

'Oh! Oh, that's wonderful! Really wonderful!'

Victoria could hear the smile in her words, and it made her smile too.

'It's not too late for you?'

Sarah took a deep breath. 'Too late? I would talk to you any time, any place, all night if I could.'

Her response was reassuring and warm.

'How . . . how are you? I wanted to call . . . so many times . . . but I didn't want to make you feel . . . I don't know, crowded, spied on, pressured.' She sensed Sarah's nerves and knew they matched her own. 'I find it hard to get things right, to strike the balance. It feels like one false move and I might ruin everything. That's *exactly* how I feel. I am so nervous. And riven with guilt, sadness and regret, and I hate feeling like I am out of control, like I might mess up this chance I've been given; this wonderful chance! I have been given the opportunity to get to know you, but there is glass between us that I am scared to lean on, scared to push in case it breaks into a million pieces and takes me with it.'

'Well. I think that might be the first truly open and honest exchange we have had.'

'I think it might, apart from that I have thought about you every single day of your life. That was true, every word . . .'

Victoria heard the crack to Sarah's voice.

'Sarah, you know, if you and I are going to be able to talk, we need to do it without that glass wall between us, and we need to try and do it without one or both of us crying every five minutes!'

'I know. I know.' She sniffed. 'I can try. Where are you? At home?'

'Yes, in my bedroom, it's the one almost opposite Prim's.'

'I know it.'

'How long since you were here last?' Victoria was curious.

'Well, apart from for Prim's funeral, the last time I went inside was during the holidays of my first year at Durham – that's where I went to university.'

'Yes, I know that.'

'Of course you do.' Sarah tutted, and sounded a little flustered. 'I left my course mid second year, and that was the last time I came home. Came there. Went there. Home,' she flapped. 'So, about twenty years ago, give or take.'

'But you grew up here.'

'Yes.'

'I know you had one of the turret bedrooms.'

'Yes, the one on the back-left corner. I loved it. I had the best view of the lake. I used to spend a lot of time sitting on the landing. When the sun hit the window in the right way, the stained glass would make shapes on the carpet. They fascinated me. I used to sit there in a warm spot like a sun-puddling cat and read.'

'I do that too.' It felt nice to have the connection, no matter how weird it was to hear Sarah talking about the house so familiar to them both, and yet they had never lived together. She also loved listening to her voice, a bit similar to Prim's, a bit like her own – strange how a thing like a voice could be inherited, passed down. It wasn't something she had ever considered.

'When I was little, there was a ghastly wallpapered celling in the hallway. And Granny Cutter's plates were all over the walls.'

'It's still like that!' They both laughed a little. It made the breath catch in her throat. To hear Sarah refer to her own great-grandma was a strange and wonderful thing. For the first time, she considered running into her mother's arms and holding her tight. Thought about saying goodnight on the landing each night, but to Sarah, not to Prim:

Night night, Mum.
Night night, darling.

All the things she had missed . . .

'Mum never did like change. Don't tell me the garden room still has the old potting tables in, and the steamer chairs?'

'It actually does!' Victoria beamed.

It was the oddest sensation; despite their estrangement, tiny threads joined them: memories of the same experiences. Prim was unwittingly their glue, and this in itself was tough, as she was also the woman who had kept them apart.

'You know, Mum and Dad didn't think they could have children and I arrived a little late in their life, a surprise, I think – or actually a shock would be more accurate. Mum was in her forties when she had me, which was quite uncommon back then. I have often wondered if that was why she was so strict, as if she was overly keen not to mess up the thing she had to wait for. I spent my whole life feeling like my wings were clipped and I couldn't wait to leave and fly.'

Victoria settled back on to her pillows, quite unable to recognise the woman Sarah described.

'Strict? She was never strict with me. She was . . .' She wondered what the best word might be. 'Really cool.'

Sarah snorted her disbelief. 'Really?'

'Yes.'

'I guess she learned to do things differently with you. Or maybe you were easier to handle.' Sarah let this hang. 'I found her quite hard to live with. We clashed. She wanted to mould me into a specific type of person and I was adamant about not being moulded. She loved me, but could be overbearing and judgemental, and in response I rebelled in just about every way possible. I felt like someone had tied my hands behind my back and all I wanted to do was climb and run. It wasn't great. But my dad' – Sarah made a clicking noise with her mouth – 'oh, he was wonderful. Kind, sporty, funny, and he would always shout, "Yes, dear!" to Mum's many requests

215

and then wink at me as if to say he had no intention of doing what she asked. He was a great joker, smart too, and was always finding new ways to make me laugh.'

Victoria tried to picture her grandpa in this way and failed. As much as she had loved him, he was to her the old man who would slowly tend his roses, come rain or shine, stepping out at dusk if a hard frost was forecast to wrap the delicate, blousy heads in plastic bags tied with nimble fingers. The stooped man who wheezed when he got to the top of the stairs and would mop tears from his eyes if he looked at her in a certain light, as if she reminded him of someone else, someone he loved and missed very much. She now considered how the loss of his daughter, or rather the loss of contact with his daughter, had changed him, and she more than understood, thinking for the first time what it might have been like for him to have to live with that deceit.

'I feel closer to them by being able to talk to you; it's lovely for me.' Sarah sniffed.

Victoria realised in that moment that she was not an orphan, not alone and *not* the last surviving member of the Cutter-Rotherstone family. It was almost overwhelming.

'Dad just wanted me to get my degree, that was all he focused on. Marcus, too, was very keen on me finishing my education.'

'He was an addict too, wasn't he?' she asked softly, aware this time that they were talking about her deceased father. Marcus Jackson was no longer just a name.

'Yes, but oh! He was so much more than that! He was a poet, a musician, a linguist and the kindest, kindest soul on the earth. And very handsome. So very handsome. You have his hair.'

Victoria ran her hand over her springy curls.

'Mum and Dad always blamed him for giving me drugs; they wouldn't believe that I was already using when I met him, but that's the truth, I was. We met in a dealer's flat. It was a horrible, dark world and one we were trapped in. But out of the dark, dark place we found something incredibly beautiful; we found a wonderful love that has shaped my whole life, shaped the way I look at the world. He taught me a lot, and of course we had you!'

Victoria felt tears slip down her cheeks. It was a new and wonderful thought in recent times to feel so wanted and not like a thing abandoned. It was hard to explain how in that moment she missed her daddy, a man whose face she could not picture but who had the same hair as her. These thoughts of Marcus again skewered her with a simmering coldness towards Prim – how, how could she not see that to be with her mum and dad was the very best thing for her?

'You loved him then, my dad?'

'Very much.' She spoke softly. 'It was the kind of love that hits you in the chest and fills you up, and it doesn't ever really go away, not ever.'

'But you didn't actually marry him?' She thought of the letter and had so many questions, all queued up on her tongue.

'No, I have only been married once, to Jens – my husband, Jens. I never married Marcus, but only because we never got the chance.'

'What does Jens do for a living?'

'A lawyer too.'

'Does he know about me?' Victoria wondered where else pockets of dishonesty might lie. She steeled herself for more deceit.

'Oh yes! He knows all about you, every little thing I could think of.'

'And Jens knows all about Marcus?'

'I forget how young you are. Yes, yes, he does.' Sarah paused. 'There are many ways to love many different people, and it's only life that teaches you that.'

Victoria felt her cheeks flame as if admonished and with this came the flicker of anger, as if this woman, in truth a stranger, had no right to make her feel this way.

'I've been reading the letters you sent.'

'I wondered if you had. What's that like? Hard, I bet?'

'Yes, it's so sad and, as you said, raw. I have to remind myself that I am the baby you are discussing. It's weird.' She paused at the understatement. 'I'm about halfway through, and you talk about how much . . . how much you love me, or the idea of me.' It was harder to say than she thought. 'And so I still don't understand why you thought it best to tell me you had died?' She bit the inside of her cheek.

'It was . . . it was . . . Oh God, it was . . .' Sarah paused, as if deciding how to phrase something tricky.

'It was what?' she pressed.

'This is too much to talk about briefly over the phone. I need to give you the background, the full story.'

'I was thinking of coming to Oslo for the weekend—'

'Yes! Yes, oh my goodness, yes, come to Oslo,' Sarah interrupted with childlike gasps of excitement. 'That would be . . . that would be . . .' Emotion trapped her next words in her mouth.

Victoria closed her eyes; this pose somehow made it easier to say. 'I don't . . . I don't want you to be so excited. It makes it feel like a big deal and that brings even more pressure to an already strange situation.' She spoke bluntly, her words coated with the dust of anger, of hurt. But Daksha was right: *enough already.*

'You don't want me to be so excited?' Sarah laughed, 'I have waited my whole life for this call, waited for this chance to—'

'Sarah!' Victoria cut her off again mid-sentence. 'This is exactly what I am talking about. I don't want you to think everything is going to be rosy because it just might not be!' she reminded her.

'I understand.'

'I know you say that, but when you speak to me or hear from me, it's as if you've won a prize and are about to go running off the deep end. I need things to go slowly. I really do.'

'I will go slowly; I promise I will try, but it's *exactly* like I have won a prize. You making contact with me, us chatting like this before bedtime, is the best thing in the whole wide world . . .'

Victoria closed her eyes, and again let her head fall to her chest.

Switching on her phone, she watched as it located a new service provider: Telenor Mobil.

She had a new message, from Daksha of course.

You got this! Enjoy – and don't be an arsehole! See you soon D x

The flight had been a doddle. Just over a couple of hours from Heathrow, and here she was, walking towards the gate where Sarah would, she knew, be waiting on the other side. Her stomach lurched at the thought and her palms felt clammy, although it was possibly now a bit late in the day to be having second thoughts about the trip.

Daksha had agreed to house sit with her sister, Ananya, for the weekend and they were under strict instructions to water Prim's plants, make Gerald a cup of tea if and when he pitched up to look after the tomato plants and orchids, and not, under any circumstances, to have a party. In the days since the whole debacle, she thought occasionally of Flynn, the little turd. She felt flashes of hatred towards him, angry at herself that she had not only offered up her body but also her story: precious facts he had no right to. She was also irritatingly curious as to what he had been trying to talk to her about when he'd been calling out her name before Gerald ushered him from the party. The question nagged at her, but it also bothered her that she cared even a little bit.

'Hurry home!' Her friend had waved her off. 'We have to plan for your birthday – I am thinking a triple-stack chocolate birthday cake, with sprinkles!' Daksha had clapped.

Victoria was, in truth, dreading her birthday, which loomed, her first without Prim. 'I'm not planning on celebrating, not really. Plus, I think there is more to birthdays than cake.'

'There is? Who knew!' Daksha pulled a face.

And now, here she was, with a gut full of nerves and a head full of confusion, walking through the white shiny terminal of Oslo Airport, which seemed to have coffee shops, bookshops and tall and beautiful people in abundance. She pushed her dark, curly hair behind her ears and, not for the first time, wished she weren't so pale. The sliding doors opened and the first person she saw in the crowd was Sarah.

She felt conflicted by the thoughts that bubbled to the surface, still trying to get her head around the basic and yet almost incomprehensible fact that someone she had believed to be dead was in fact alive and that she had been fed this lie by her own family, while a small part of her wanted to rejoice!

My mum . . . that's my mum . . . right there, not dead, not at all. Here she is!

Sarah lifted her joined palms under her chin, as if subconsciously offering thanks, and watched intently as she walked towards her. Victoria stared at her, capturing her profile, the curve of her neck, the shape of her nose, building her in her mind, storing her away piece by piece. *Will I look like you when I'm older? Did Prim look like you when she was younger? You are it, Sarah . . . the missing link.*

'Here you are!'

Victoria watched as Sarah stretched out her hand, placing it lightly on her forearm, as if this was the closest to a hug she figured she was allowed, whilst at the same time confirming she was real. Victoria had on countless occasions wished to feel her mother's touch and had certainly missed the feel of Prim taking her in her arms. Yet, in that moment, she felt unable to react, stifled by all she didn't know, still hungry to understand how her mum could have let her go, and with a throb of loss and longing beating out its rhythm in her chest.

'Here I am,' Victoria confirmed.

'You look absolutely wonderful!' Sarah beamed.

'Thanks.'

'Can I take your bag?' Sarah eyed the large carpetbag on her shoulder. Victoria resisted the desire to point out that the offer of a bag-carry, a pair of warm gloves, a bedtime story or a piggyback across a puddle were almost a couple of decades too late.

'I've got it, thanks, I can manage.'

'Of course.' Sarah fidgeted, smoothing her hair, nervous. 'How was your journey?'

'Easy.' The banality of their conversation as they walked slowly across the concourse gave no clue to the unique and mind-blowing, nerve-shredding situation in which they found themselves.

'I thought we could get the train, if that's okay with you? The terminal is right here in the airport.' Sarah pointed ahead and Victoria could see the up and down escalators in the distance and the sign: *Gardermoen Stasjon*. 'Then we can chat and you can see a bit of the countryside – what do you think? Jens wanted to drive, but I thought this might be nicer.'

Victoria could tell she was nervous too and felt a flicker of understanding. Thinking for the first time how it might be just as hard for Sarah to come back from the dead as it was for her to accept it.

'I think whatever you think. This is your city. Do you live in Oslo itself?'

'Yes, we're very lucky. We have one of the new apartments on the edge of the fjord in Aker Brygge. It's a whole new development of warehouses and restaurants on the waterfront and we are right where the ferries come in and out, taking commuters and tourists out to the inner fjord islands like Hovedøya and Gressholmen. It's beautiful. The apartment is small, but what more do we need? In the warm weather we are out and about and when it's cold it's less to heat.'

Sarah's Norwegian accent was impressive. And Victoria was pleased to note that her extreme excitement, which could at times feel a bit like hysteria, seemed to be a little more under control now: her voice a little calmer, cheeks less flushed and her hands still.

'So, do you speak Norwegian?' she asked, realising in that moment how utterly crazy it was that this woman had given birth to her, was her mother and yet Victoria didn't know the first thing about her now: what languages did she speak? Did she play sport? How did she vote? Did she prefer tea or coffee?

'*Ja, litt.*' Sarah nodded.

Victoria smiled at the brief and easy moment of connection, finding it reassuring. 'It's nice to have a small apartment, cosy. I think Rosebank is too big, really. A lot to heat in all weathers. Prim used to like real fires in the drawing room.'

'She did.' Sarah nodded. 'The fireplace in the dining room never worked. I think someone said Grandpa put a board halfway across the chimney somewhere and no one was sure how to get it out. I don't think anyone was sure how he got it in!' She gave a nervous, dry laugh, reminding Victoria of someone who had been told off and wasn't sure it was appropriate to laugh. It made her feel awkward. She didn't want Sarah to feel that way, preferring the ease of earlier.

'Exactly.' She wasn't sure she would ever get used to this woman, a stranger coming in with snippets and shared facts about *her* home, *her* family, already known to Victoria. It made her feel conflicted; it brought a joyous flare of shared intimacy, but at the same time it was odd. 'But I don't know why we need all that space – don't know why *I* need all that space,' she corrected.

'You think you might sell it?' Sarah asked casually, as if it were of no consequence to her either way. Victoria kept her voice steady, remembering both the vicar and Gerald's warning that she was potentially, as 'a woman of means', a target.

'I literally find it hard to think till the end of a day, let alone any further ahead than that.' She shrugged. 'I think I just need to let everything settle. As Gerald said, I've been through a lot.'

The way Sarah's face fell again suggested this felt like a personal dig. She didn't assuage her.

'Who's Gerald?'

Sarah might know all about the history of Rosebank and their family stories, but on recent events she was a little behind. It was a strange mental juggling act as the past and present collided with huge gaps in the understanding of them both.

'Gerald – he spoke at the funeral?'

'Yes, of course!' Sarah shook her head, as if she was embarrassed to have not made the connection.

'He was Prim's friend, companion – whatever you want to call it; her beau. They went to the theatre together and out for supper. He's been very kind to me.'

Sarah's eyes widened. 'God, that's so weird for me to hear.' She placed her hand over her mouth, as if shocked.

'That Gerald has been kind to me?' She felt a flare of anger – for what, she didn't know, but it seemed any negativity from Sarah was akin to putting a match to the defensive kindling that lay bunched in her stomach and ready to flare.

Sarah shook her head. 'No, no.' She bit her bottom lip. 'I know it's ridiculous, but I can only ever think of my mum with my dad.'

'Bernard didn't mention Gerald?'

Sarah stared at her. 'No, he didn't. It was only ever short cards saying things like you had passed ten GCSEs or how you had got really good at the piano. Snippets, as if he was a bit reluctant to go into detail. He *loved* Mum and was loyal to her. I am grateful to him, still.'

'He loved her?' This was news.

'Yes, I think so. Not in a romantic way, but he's worked for her for decades, as you know, Rosebank is a safe haven for him.'

Victoria felt glad that she had made things right with him.

'I don't think Bernard has had the nicest life. His wife is quite scary. She has a mean mouth, I seem to remember.'

This too: news. Victoria felt the rise of guilt in her chest.

'And without him I would have lost touch with you completely and this would not be happening, so I'm grateful to him and I always will be.'

'I wanted to ask you. I know Bernard would've let you know, so why didn't you come to Grandpa's funeral?'

They stepped in unison on to the escalator that would take them to the platform. Sarah, on the stair below, turned to look at her.

'I wanted to!' Her response deliberate and wide-eyed. 'More than I can tell you – the chance to say goodbye to my lovely dad . . . But that was the rule!' She wiped her face.

'The rule?' Victoria gave a short laugh. 'Who made the rules?'

Sarah bit her lip and looked decidedly uncomfortable. 'I knew getting in touch with you would only be possible when Mum died, and even then I knew it would be going against everything we had agreed.'

'But *what* did you agree and *why*? How was the whole thing concocted?' She knew she was pushing, but her need to know the details had not lessened.

'I want you to read some more of the letters when we get back and then I promise we can talk about it fully.' Sarah looked around, like she was afraid of being overheard. 'I think Prim knew I would get in touch. I sensed that from her.' Sarah held her wedding ring, like it was a thing of comfort. 'Strange how, even after all these years, it never really occurred to me that she might have someone else.' She changed the topic. 'I can't picture her in my mind with another man, someone who replaced my dad.'

The two walked from the escalator and Victoria followed Sarah until they came to a bench and sat down. She placed her carpetbag on the floor by their feet.

'Gerald didn't replace Grandpa.' Her tone was kinder now. 'I don't think anyone could have done that. But Prim was sociable and outgoing until the end, and I think it was nice she had someone to sit on the veranda with or to discuss her plants. Gerald used to do a lot of jobs in the garden and the lake. And there were a lot of jobs to be done.' She smiled, remembering the way they would call to each other through open windows or the French doors and meet in the garden room or on the veranda for tea and shortbread . . . or gin. She thought fondly of his neat house, and liked knowing that if and when she needed him he was on call – to offer toast from his dainty toast rack, a warm bath with the provision of soft towels or to tote a gun to dispel an unruly crowd. It felt good to know he was in her corner.

Sarah put her hands in her jacket pockets and hunched her shoulders. 'I know I have no right to feel odd about Gerald, none at all, but it's a bit like the world I left at twenty is frozen in my mind. I don't imagine it to have moved forward at all. It's good Mum had help in the garden. The house takes a lot of upkeep; I remember that even back in the day. But you will have your inheritance and your money from Granny Cutter too to help with that.'

Victoria felt uncomfortable that it was being mentioned so casually, feeling suddenly protective of not only what was hers, but also her gran's choices.

'Mind you, the question is whether you want to spend that money maintaining a big house when there's a whole wide world waiting to be discovered.'

'Actually, Daks and I are going away in March. At least, that was the plan. We've been thinking about it for a while. I don't always feel like going, not with my head all over the place, but I know it will be good when it comes to it. We're going to the Far East and South America and will stay away until our money runs out.'

A sleek, shiny train pulled in and Victoria watched the commuters pile on and the doors close. It left, leaving them on an almost deserted platform.

Sarah nodded at her. 'That sounds wonderful. And you're not going to university? Bernard *did* tell me that,' she added with a little humour.

'No, I didn't think it was for me.'

'*Didn't* – so you might think it is for you after all? Have you had a change of heart?' Sarah twisted on the seat to face her.

'No, not exactly. I guess I'm just questioning my reasons for deciding not to go . . . and besides, everything is up in the air.' Victoria looked skyward, as if that was where the answers might lie: questioning her choices that had been based on a set of facts that were now no longer relevant.

'What were those reasons?'

She quashed the memory of Flynn asking a similar question.

'I . . . I didn't feel good about leaving Prim alone. I mean, she was fine and not ill or anything, there was nothing she couldn't do if she went at the right pace, but I worried about her and I didn't want to miss out on being with her or have her struggle or be lonely or a million other things.'

'Shit.' Sarah kicked at the floor.

'What?'

'That responsibility – it was mine but you, you took it on.'

'I had no choice, I was all she had – or so I thought. Anyway, I didn't mind – I loved her.' This the truth, despite her battling emotions. 'Plus . . .' Victoria queued up the words on her tongue. 'I was a bit scared of . . .'

'Bit scared of what?' Sarah pushed.

'I was a bit scared of the thing that happened to you happening to me.'

Sarah gave a nervous laugh. 'What do you mean? How . . . what thing . . .?'

'Prim always said you were studious and happy until you started at university, where you went off the rails, started taking heroin and then you died. It sounded like a straightforward progression and it scared me. I didn't want that to be how I ended up and I thought I might be like you.' There, she had said it. Sarah looked aghast as some of the colour drained from her face.

'But . . . but that's not how it was. Not at all.' Sarah shook her head. 'I was already "going off the rails", as you put it, trying to carve a path, *escape* if you like, and I had that kind of personality – I wanted more and more and more. Which is okay if what you crave is spinach, binge-reading or walking outdoors, but for me it was hard drugs; not good.'

'No. Not good,' she agreed.

'You don't need to worry, Victoria. Mine were a unique set of circumstances. I would hate my past mistakes to affect how you live your life.'

'Are you kidding me right now? I am paying a huge price for how you lived your life; I always have!' The words erupted from her without too much thought of how they might land.

Sarah looked crestfallen. Her mouth fell open.

'I shouldn't have said it like that.' Victoria positioned her bag on the floor, feeling horribly uncomfortable. She didn't want to have this conversation in public. 'I didn't mean it how it came out. Can we change the subject?'

'Sure.' Sarah rallied a little and there was a beat of readjustment while the topic was indeed changed. 'I envy you and Daksha; I always planned on travelling with Granny Cutter's money after university.'

'Granny Cutter's money?' *What money?*

'Yes! She set up a trust fund for me, and then Mum and Dad set up one for you, so that when we got to a certain age we would have an income, a very good income. Her father, your great-great-grandpa, was a wealthy industrialist who moved to Surrey to open a paper mill. He gave Granny Cutter the money for Rosebank and she bought it outright, quite a thing for a woman back in the day.'

'I didn't know that. I don't seem to know much, do I?' *Just another secret, another aspect of my life to be kept secret . . .* 'The lawyer, Mr Dobson, was sorting all the paperwork and he gave me the run-down. I think I missed a lot of the detail – I was still very numb when I saw him.'

'I think maybe Mum might have been anxious about talking about family and history and things in case she let slip anything about me. You would only have to look at the paperwork to see that I have received my trust allowance every month since I was twenty-four.'

Victoria felt weakened by the fact that every apparent revelation only served to throw up more questions and, with it, more deceit. She wasn't sure how she felt about a trust fund, having always found the idea of earning her own money and making her way the most exciting, along with a healthy dollop of guilt at having survived financially a little too easily. Flynn's words came to her now, uttered from his beautiful, lying, cheating, lopsided mouth:

'Easy, I guess, when you don't have to worry about where your next meal is coming from . . .'

'You know, Sarah, I thought that maybe part of the reason you gave me up to Prim and disappeared was because you didn't have any money and that you thought you might struggle to care for me financially in the long term, and believe it or not, whilst it didn't excuse the lies, I understood that a little. But the fact that you had an income, a good income, just waiting for you . . .' She shook her head. 'You could easily have afforded me.' She felt the wobble to her bottom lip; it was hard trying to contain all that threatened to burst from her, not least of which the idea that it made her sound like a commodity to be bought and sold, a thing. A thing which Sarah had let slip through her fingers. And it hurt.

'Oh no, Vic . . . Victoria. Our initial separation had nothing to do with money and everything to do with the fact that neither Prim nor I expected me to *live*. I wanted heroin more than I wanted anything, even you.' Her face crumpled in tears at this truth. Her words were like rocks, which pounded Victoria, hitting her full in the chest, making breathing tough. 'And that's a hard thing for me to say, to admit, but it's the truth. The only way money came into it was that I knew I could afford to buy the stuff to put into my veins and end my life.'

'So what stopped you?' She looked at her squarely.

'Jens.'

'Jens?'

'Yes, ultimately. He was the reason I came to Oslo.' Sarah smiled. 'He is everything.'

'Jens,' Victoria repeated. *Who is everything. But me, your daughter, for eighteen years I have been nothing . . .* 'Do you . . .' She hesitated. 'Do you have any other children?' Victoria held her breath, wondering how it might feel to know that there were other people on the planet who Sarah got to mother and who were mothered by Sarah.

'To my mummy, Sarah, on Mother's Day . . .'

'Can my gran run the Mummy race?'

'No, my mum's not picking me up. I don't have a mum . . .'

Sarah shook her head. 'No. Just you. Just you.' She reached for a tissue to blot at her tears. Victoria exhaled, unable to hide her relief.

'Jens has worked with me, helped me, and he got me clean one day at a time, and we have been together for sixteen years and we are still keeping me clean and keeping life on track, one day at a time.'

So you loved the stranger who came into your life more than you loved me . . . you could do it for him, but not for me . . . Victoria hated the feeling in her gut that her self-worth, her value, was draining away.

'So when you stopped taking drugs sixteen years ago, I would have been, what? Two, nearly three – why didn't you come and find me then?' She hated the pleading tone to her question.

Sarah looked over her head, along the track towards the dark tunnel, and her brows knitted, as if to recall that time was not easy. 'I did write to Prim, but she was doubtful of my sobriety, said she would only risk giving you your mother back if there was a cast-iron guarantee that I wasn't going to disappear, relapse or kill myself, as she would not put you through that. But I told her there were no cast-iron guarantees, and she said it wasn't worth it as you were happy. And she was right.'

'God, you were as bad as her!' This news was monstrous. Sarah had asked for contact and Prim had denied them . . . a simple decision that had shaped her whole life.

'She wasn't bad.' Sarah let her eyes mist as they spoke of Prim, who they clearly both missed. 'She wasn't bad, not at all.'

And in that moment it felt like a connection, both of them, Victoria knew, picturing the woman who had mothered them and who she knew, deep down, had loved her so very much. Sarah took her time.

'She was just doing what she thought she had to. Figuring it out, like we all do, every day, working with what we have in front of us and hoping it all turns out all right in the end. It's so easy when you can look back and point out where bad decisions were made or where you went wrong, but at the time, in the thick of it, you just have to make a choice and go with it. That's what I did and that's what Prim did.'

'I see that, but I didn't get the chance to make a decision and go with it. I was told you had died, completely irreversible, no chance for me to take a second look or change my mind – dead, Sarah! That's for ever. And my grief has cut me to the bone. All that I missed, all that I longed for, it shaped the person I became. And the crazy thing is, I would have been an entirely *different* person if only you had both trusted me with the truth!'

'Do you think you would have been a *better* person?' Sarah asked.

Victoria shrugged. 'I don't know, but probably a happier one, certainly right now. Because it's having to deal with the dishonesty, the lies, that is the very worst part of all this.' Her voice was small.

'I think . . . I think it's important that you look at all the letters. I think it might explain, way better than I am able, what it was like for me, for her and for you.'

She took a deep breath; they were, after all, still on the platform, which was filling once again. 'How did you get the letters you had sent to Prim?'

'She sent them back to me when I moved to Oslo. I think she felt safer having them out of the house. And I had kept hers and' – she opened her palms as another train came and went and once again the crowd on the platform thinned – 'I guess I hoped one day to show them to you. I had never shown them to another soul, kept them locked away until a few weeks ago, when I gave them to Jens to read.'

'Oh, you did? What did he think?' She felt her jaw tense at the thought of another highly personal aspect of her life being shared with strangers before she was made aware; even this most precious correspondence was coming to her second-hand.

Sarah drew breath. 'He thought they were unbearably sad but honest, and I think it made him proud of how far I have come.'

Well, good for you and Jens! Victoria nodded.

Sarah tucked her hair behind her ears. 'I haven't looked at them. I can't. I vaguely know what's in them, but I guess I feel nervous because I can't truly remember what I wrote, the detail. Not only was it a long time ago, but also I don't think I was always in my right mind. In fact, I know I wasn't. Even the thought of them is painful.'

'Yes. I'll do that. I'll read the rest of them.'

Sarah turned to face her. 'I can tell by your tone that something is not right, and it's important that we discuss anything that's bothering you—'

'Jesus, Sarah, there is so much that's bothering me!' She cut her short.

'I know. I know.' Sarah closed her eyes.

'Actually, you don't know. You don't know at all—'

'No, and you don't know either!' It was the first time Sarah had raised her voice, interrupting, her gaze now steady. 'I get that things are messed up. And I know things haven't always been great for you, but you don't *know* my life, Victoria – you don't *know* what it's been like for me.'

Victoria hadn't meant to laugh, but the snort of derision left her nose nonetheless. 'Yes, poor you, Sarah! Jesus! Imagine if the boot was on the other foot and you had been told your child had died? Imagine that! Only for her to pop out of a cake – *surprise!*' She waved both hands. 'Yes, imagine if she just popped up, but only after you had grieved for her for the best part of eighteen years – and now think about the fact that you weren't misinformed of her death by accident, but by design; someone lied to you, Sarah! They *lied* to you, they chose to make you feel that way.'

'I can't imagine.'

'Well, lucky you!' Victoria folded her arms, desperately trying to stop her anger turning to more tears.

'But I do know what it was like to lose you. Because I lost you! And I know what it was like to wake each day and wonder what you were doing and who you were with and whether you were thinking about me, wondering if you were happy . . . I knew you were loved. I knew you were loved near and far, by Prim and by me, even if you weren't aware of it, and I knew you were safe and warm and comfortable and all the other things that every parent wishes for their child.'

Noble, but you didn't love me enough to choose me over drugs. That honour goes to Jens . . . 'So, what, I should be *thanking* you?'

Sarah shook her head. 'That's not what I'm saying.' She pinched the top of her nose, frustrated. 'I am trying to tell you that you are not the only one who has suffered.'

Victoria bit her lip and made a 'hmph' noise.

'You know, I thought – I have *always* thought – that the best life you could have would be one with me by your side.' Sarah paused. 'But I hear you talk about your hurt and how messed up you feel your life is and I don't know if I still think it. I know I made mistakes – Prim and I both did – and I thought I could make amends. But I guess you're right: I can't know what it was like for you, just like you can't know what it's been like for me.' She let this trail and wiped again at her eyes.

'I guess.' Victoria looked back towards the terminal, feeling the weight of emotion that was almost too heavy to bear. 'I am honestly thinking that, right now, it might be better if I just jump on a plane back to England.' She pictured the sofa in the drawing room with her on one end and Daksha on the other. This was already feeling like too much and they were yet to leave the airport terminal. If she could have clicked her heels . . .

Sarah shook her head and spoke with a note of panic. 'Don't do that! Please, please, don't do that. Talking like this, so openly and honestly, is tough, I know it is! But it's also necessary; it takes guts, and each time we do is a step we take across that long and precarious bridge that separates us. Please, don't go. Stay here in Oslo, just for the weekend, please. We have to keep taking these steps. We have to keep talking, and hopefully, one day, if we are *very* lucky, we will realise that we have come to the middle of the bridge and the place we meet is where the past gets left behind and from that point on we can go in any direction we choose! But we go together.'

'Okay.' Victoria felt seduced by the promise of a future like that. It sounded like the calm waters in which she wanted to swim, just as it had been when Prim was her guardian and she had been unaware that anything in her life was amiss. She stood and hitched her bag on to her shoulder as the next snub-nosed silver train pulled into the platform, sitting high on the tracks.

'Can we get this one?' She pointed to the open doors.

'Oh, we could have got any of them.'

'Well, why didn't you say?' She rushed and jumped on board, with Sarah following suit.

'I was enjoying our chat,' Sarah levelled.

Victoria couldn't help but laugh at this calm admission. Sarah had Prim's quirkiness about her, and it was one aspect of her character she knew she would like.

The two slotted into seats side by side and Victoria realised their legs were touching, her thigh now sitting alongside that of the body in which she had grown. She found it remarkable and emotional, looking out of the window now to hide the nose itch that was usually, for her, a forerunner to tears.

The train sped along through countryside, passing places whose names she tried to pronounce in her head: Kløfta, Lindeberg, Frogner and Lillestrøm. Every platform looked clean, graffiti- and litter-free; a bit different from the slightly tatty stations she passed when travelling into town at home, where a lick of paint and the quick strokes of a yard broom wouldn't have gone amiss. She watched, fascinated, the Norwegians who smiled and chatted in their native tongue, a sing-song language that sounded to her ear, happy. It made her think of Daksha's survey facts, and again she smiled, wondering what the homes might be like to which they returned and picturing the families possibly waiting for them.

How different my life would have been if I had moved here with my mum all those years ago. I might speak like you and might, right now, be sitting at home, waiting for you to alight from this train and come back . . . come back to me . . .

She particularly liked the little red barns that were dotted throughout the landscape, standing out among the beautiful blaze of autumn-bronzed leaves and reminding her of Monopoly hotels in both colour and design. The lights coming through the windows of the rural buildings illuminated the landscape in a honey-coloured arc. She could see from this one journey that this was a beautiful, beautiful place. Finally, the train pulled into the Nationaltheatret Stasjon and she and Sarah left the station, walking up the wide steps and emerging into the city.

Victoria's first impression was that there were more trees than she might have imagined in the middle of a city. Walking along the street, she took in the glorious, ornate stone buildings, the fancy spires and the lines of flag poles – each one bearing the striking red, white and blue Norwegian flag – that led the eye up to a grand park at the top of a hill. There were eye-catching sculptures; clean, cobbled streets; vast fountains; and everywhere she looked were tall, beautiful people. She had read how Norway only had eleven hours of daylight at this time of year, but she knew that any lack of light was the very last thing she would remember about this, her first visit to Oslo.

'This place is so beautiful!' She spoke her thoughts aloud.

Sarah nodded and looked around as if seeing it through new eyes. 'I never get sick of it.'

'I bet. Bit different to Epsom.'

'Just a bit. I would have followed Jens anywhere, but I'm glad it was to here. He is my reason, my anchor. He is the person in my life who listens, and I think we all need someone like that, that person to whom you can witter about everything and anything, from politics to bowel movements.'

Victoria felt her nose wrinkle in distaste. Sarah gave a wry smile. 'It's true. Everyone needs a listener.'

'So how did you guys meet?'

'We met in London; he was a law student on placement and I was a long-haired junkie working a couple of shifts in a coffee shop. I saw him. He saw me. And that was that.' She shrugged her shoulders, as if it were a fait accompli. 'All we had to do then was find a way and a place to be together.'

'And that place was Oslo,' Victoria guessed.

'That place was Oslo. Come on, we can walk along the water-front. I can't wait for you to meet him. And for him to meet you.'

Victoria nodded and walked alongside, feeling none of the excited anticipation Sarah clearly felt. For her, the overriding sensation was still that this whole situation was strange, surreal and a little fearful. She wondered if it would ever change; she wanted so much to get to that bridge Sarah had described, the one where they met in the middle and started afresh, but with her hurt raw and her grief still all-consuming, she doubted that was going to happen any time soon.

The air was crisp and clean and the dark sky clear. Lights from the restaurant frontages, on the masts of boats and the subdued deck lighting of the many docks, as well as those on the quayside, where people sat sipping cream-topped hot chocolate or nibbling crêpes, were reflected in the still, cold water of the fjord, giving every view an ethereal, reflective quality. It was one of the most scenic places she had ever been. She thought how much Prim would have loved it and her heart flexed at the thought that she never got to see it. This was instantly followed by a flash of anger that, had her gran been honest with her, they might have both been able to come here . . . *Such a bloody waste.*

'I love to see people in love,' Sarah said, nodding towards the many couples strolling hand in hand, wearing thick coats to ward off the chill. 'I think it is one of the most hopeful sights known to man. I think as long as people love one another, then there is hope.'

'Hope for what?' Victoria asked.

'For everything!' Sarah beamed at her. 'Do you have a boyfriend?'

'No.' She shook her head. 'I was hanging out with someone for a while, but . . .' She pictured Flynn sneaking along the hallway, hand in hand with Courtney. 'He was a bit of a turd.' She borrowed from Gerald. 'And it all went a bit wrong. Horribly wrong, in fact.'

'Well, his loss. You could have the pick, Victoria. My advice would be: stay away from turds.' She smiled, seeming pleased to have finally, finally spoken her name without any hesitation. 'Seriously, you could have the pick.'

'I don't know about that. Prim was always keen to remind me that the Cutter women looked like potatoes—'

'Aaah, but only until they evolved into a chip!' Sarah finished her sentence and they both laughed, spontaneously and without an edge, and it was nice, a hint maybe of how life might be if they could only reach that bridge . . . 'I think I reached full chip at about twenty.'

'Well, I've got that to look forward to then.' Victoria held her eyes for a second, again a moment when they let their guards down and optimism bound them. It was almost intoxicating.

'Many of my problems were of my own making, there's no denying it. I felt caged, antsy, not just at home but in general. If ever I had to sit in a room – I wanted to run.' Sarah kept her voice low. 'But I remember before my life veered so wildly off track, being about your age and feeling that life was crushing me, coming at me from all sides. Mum was very controlling.'

'You see, I just didn't experience that; I don't recognise that Prim! But then, what did I know?' she huffed.

Sarah sighed. 'Maybe age mellowed her? Plus, as I suggested, I think maybe she learned her lesson with me: that the more you hem someone in, the more likely they are to smash the lock and run. I couldn't seem to do anything right. I was being pushed out of my teenage years, where I had been quite carefree and happy, and being pulled into adulthood, which I was in no way ready to face. Everything felt like an enormous pressure. I had one foot in my childhood and another on the path to my future, and a lot of the time all I wanted to do was jump and not have a foot in either. I guess drugs were the springboard that helped me jump.'

This resonated; it was just as Victoria felt, and again the shared experience drew them a little closer. 'I don't . . .' she began, before remembering she was talking to Sarah, who she was still intent on keeping at arm's length, wary.

'You don't what?' Sarah urged, her smile encouraged, and her eyes crinkled at the edges in the way Prim's used to. It was hard to see the similarity and Victoria looked away.

'I don't want to mess my life up, but it feels that every single decision is fraught with pitfalls. This guy I was seeing, well, kind of seeing . . . I was scared to be myself and then, when I was myself, he cheated – it felt rubbish.' She pictured herself hiding in the larder and throwing up.

Sarah laughed. 'Welcome to the world! The secret is to just make a plan and go with it. You can always change your mind, nothing is for ever; I remember Dad telling me that once . . . Stagnation is bad for my mental health; I think it is for most people. And as for that guy, if something is right, if you are with the right person, you don't *have* to second guess or worry about getting stuff wrong because it feels so right you have absolute faith and just go for it, like me and Jens!'

There he was again, this guy who was never far from Sarah's thoughts, apparently. Victoria hated the thought that what she was feeling was good old-fashioned jealousy.

She nodded. 'I don't remember too much about Grandpa; he was quiet. Apart from him telling me stories about when he was at sea.'

'Oh, he was always very proud of his naval service, rightly so. I think of him often when I look out over the water; he came to Norway.'

'He did? He came to see you?' Her heart raced at the prospect of her and Prim on any other school night sitting in the kitchen, while Grandpa was here idling along the waterfront with her dead mother.

'No! No! More's the pity.' Sarah shook her head in lament. 'I mean, when he was on active service, he spent a lot of time in the North Sea.'

'I didn't know that.' Her pulse settled. 'I also remember him being fanatical about his roses, which are still beautiful, and I also remember the way he smelled – kind of woody.'

'Ah, his roses . . . Yes, the woody smell, that'll be his cigars. Mum used to go bonkers about him smoking secretly in the drawing room, but I always loved the smell. He was lovely.' Sarah suddenly caught her breath and cried. 'I miss him still. I miss Mum too, of course, but my daddy . . . I miss him,' she repeated in little more than a whisper, sniffing and wiping her nose on the sleeve of her jacket. This display made Victoria think again of just how the woman might have suffered too.

'Sorry,' Sarah sniffed. 'I keep a lot of my feelings at bay; a case of having to over the years, but seeing you . . .' She shook her head and took a deep breath. 'Come on, let's get home. Jens will be wondering where we've got to.' Putting her hands in her pockets, Sarah quickened her step and Victoria fell in beside her. Her heart thudded: supposing Jens didn't like her, didn't want her there? It was a terrifying prospect.

Sarah reached into the small handbag slung across her body for her door key.

'Here we are.'

The apartment block was fantastically central, practically on the water. It was built in an old warehouse and the developer had cleverly kept a lot of the old salt-weathered brickwork and supporting steel girders with their large dome-headed rivets, all painted black. The industrial feel, however, was somehow softened when paired with high-spec lighting and soft woods. Every gap in the building that wasn't original had been filled with smoked glass and shiny chrome. It was modern, fresh, very clean and could not have been more different to the house they had both grown up in. Victoria wondered if Sarah ever missed the honey-coloured carpet on the half landing where the sun came in through the ornate window and pooled shapes and colours on the floor.

Sarah ran up the open-tread stairs and stopped at a wooden door with a small porthole window on the upper floor.

'This is us!'

Before Jens appeared, a front door on the other side of the corridor opened and out walked a young man, a very tall young man. He was very blonde and smiley – not a lopsided smile, but an open one that invited her to smile back.

'Hallo, Sarah! *Litt kaldt i dag.*'

'Yes, too cold. This is Victoria, my . . . erm . . . my . . .'

'I am staying for the weekend,' she interjected, raising her hand in greeting, unable to stand the flustered nature of Sarah's response, which left them all feeling a little awkward.

'Oh cool! Well, have a good time – see you around. *Ha det.*'

'Yep, bye, Vidar!'

No sooner had they watched Vidar run down the stairs than the door opened and a tall man wearing jeans, a white shirt and with stockinged feet stood in front of her. He had short, fair hair and a wide smile, which showed off his large, neat teeth. He shook his head and briefly placed his hand over his mouth, his eyes misted with emotion. This, she had not expected. Her concerns over any potential lack of welcome disappeared.

'Oh my God! Oh my God!' He exhaled deeply. 'I'm Jens, and I don't need to ask who you are! I could have picked you out in any crowd!' he managed eventually, with laughter in his voice. He did something then that neither she nor Sarah had so far been able to do when he stepped forward and wrapped her in a hug. 'Oh my goodness, Victoria.' She was glad he got her name right. He set her free and stood back to stare at her, which was more than a little disconcerting. 'It is incredible and wonderful just how much you look like Sarah! You must be able to see it?' he asked with kindly enthusiasm.

'A little bit, I guess.' She glanced at Sarah and then back at him.

'Oh my God!' Again the hand over the mouth. 'You even have the same facial expressions!' He clapped. 'Wonderful, just wonderful! Come on, let's go sit somewhere comfortable and you can tell me all about it.'

'Tell you all about what?' She was a little confused.

'Your life! Your whole life! Everything!'

She followed the man through to the open-plan lounge/dining area, which was tastefully modern with the addition of tapestry cushions and faux fur rugs to soften all the hard edges. It was different to Rosebank in every possible way. It was also lovely and warm, homely, and not only because of the furnishings but because Jens made it feel that way. It seemed so neat and perfect; she wondered how a girl like her, a stranger to all intents and purposes, would fit without being intrusive.

'My whole life?' She drew breath. 'It might take a while.'

'*Skal jeg få litt vin,*' Sarah breathed.

Jens nodded at his wife. Victoria wondered what had been said and her eyebrows rose involuntarily.

'Sorry, we were just asking about wine,' he explained.

It was her turn to nod.

'Now.' Jens beamed at her and folded his tall frame into a chair, removing the cushion and gripping it to his chest. 'It doesn't matter how long it takes, we have all the time in the world.'

'And I thought I was only here for the weekend.'

'Ah! You might never want to leave.' He beamed.

'Well, I don't know about that.' She thought of how, over the last eighteen years, she would have loved to receive an invite like this.

'I have read letters that Sarah wrote to your erm . . . *bestemor* – what's the word in English?' He clicked his fingers. 'Grandmother! And oh! Wow! I feel so close to you, even though I have never met you because I know what you went through at the very beginning. Your mother is a remarkable person. Your grandmother too.' He looked over at Sarah, his eyes drinking her in, as if they were still a new couple. She felt a little embarrassed, unused to this. She barely remembered interactions between Prim and Grandpa, and with her gran and Gerald things had always seemed quite proper.

'Well, you are a few steps ahead of me.' She meant that she had yet to read all of the letters, but it sounded very much like she was yet to find something remarkable about Sarah. She looked over to the kitchen island, where Sarah, with both hands on the countertop, looked a little aghast. Victoria felt her stomach sink. This trip was going to be a little harder than any of them might have thought.

TWELVE

There was a brief moment when Victoria opened her eyes that she didn't know where she was, but the sound of Jens and Sarah chatting in the kitchen anchored her to the place and time. Pulling the fat duvet up to her chin in the small, white-walled bedroom which, judging by the desk and bookshelves, doubled as a study, she lay still, taking in the sounds that, to most, would have seemed quite unremarkable, annoying even if they had woken you from the deepest sleep, but for Victoria they were like music, a composition just for her. She listened to Sarah open and close cupboard doors, click switches, clatter crockery, and the metallic rattle of items ferreted from the dishwasher. She heard her hum and laugh softly, cough twice and chat in both English and Norwegian to her love. These were the sounds that countless people woke to every day of their lives, the sound of family, but for her it was the first time she had slept under the same roof as her mother, the first time she had lain in a bed with her mother on the other side of the door. It was an experience that was both mournful and joyous. Her thoughts flew to Prim, who would call up the stairs:

'Morning, sweetie! Breakfast is ready . . .'

'Your bus leaves in twenty!'

'Don't forget your PE kit!'

'Chop chop, Victoria, you are going to be late!'

She wondered if Sarah had lain in her turret bedroom and heard the same from Prim decades earlier; she felt the dull ache of missing her gran in her stomach and wondered if it would ever fade, despite now seeing her gran with the veil of deceit lifted.

Victoria reached for her phone on the desk and fired off a quick text to Daksha.

Morning! Arrived. Obvs. So far so good, bit odd, bit awkward, but a nice apartment and Jens seems great. A day of sightseeing, yay! (Just to clarify – this is a genuine yay and not a sarcastic one.) Hope you and Ananya are having a good time and haven't burnt the house down (bad) or had a party (worse) – right, loving you and leaving you. Speak later. V Xx

Daksha's reply came through.

Too early. Go away. (Just to clarify – this is a genuine go away and not a sarcastic one) D X

Victoria laughed out loud.

There was a knock on the door and Sarah poked her smiling face in.

'Morning, sweetie!' she called, and it made Victoria's heart lurch. 'Breakfast ready in about ten . . .'

'Thank you.'

'How did you sleep?'

'Good.'

Sarah hovered, as if she wanted more. It would have been a hard thing for Victoria to explain, how she might have been cosy and welcome under her mother's roof, but these people were to all

245

intents and purposes still strangers and she felt shy about pulling back the duvet and leaping up for the day.

'I thought . . . erm . . .' It was then that Victoria saw the paper bundle in her hands. 'The letters I scanned and sent to you. I thought you might like the actual letters, rather than reading them on a screen. I think it will help bring them to life. That's what Jens said.' She raised the stack of envelopes, tied with a wide, glossy red ribbon. And having met Jens, she felt none of the flicker of jealousy that he had been privy to her history before her, none at all.

'Oh.' She wasn't sure what to say. 'Okay. Thanks.'

Sarah walked forward tentatively and carefully placed them on the desk. 'I'll leave you to it, then. Ten minutes or so?'

Victoria nodded and Sarah closed the door behind her.

She peered at the neatly fastened bundle of correspondence. Taking the stack of letters into her hands, she felt the weight of it in her palm; mail considered so precious by its recipients it had been kept, stored and hidden for her whole life. She ran her fingers over the aged paper then put them back on the desk and stared at them for a bit longer, until, with her breathing calm and her head clear, she pulled the ribbon and shuffled the papers, finding the letter she was to read next and very carefully opening it. She could almost feel the weight of Sarah's hand on the sheet and her heart twisted at the words written.

June 2001
Sarah Jackson
Henbury House
West Sussex

Mum,
Can you please call me?

Please. I can't use the phone. They won't let me, it's part of the fucking programme! But you can call me. Please. Please.

Urgent.

S

July 2001
Sarah Jackson
Henbury House
West Sussex

Mum,

Your visit was unexpected.

It felt odd and good at the same time. Thank you for coming all this way.

I had forgotten just how guilty you make me feel. That permanent look of disappointment on your face that tells me what you are thinking: that if life had gone how you planned it, I would be taking my law degree and you would be telling everyone at the tennis club how marvellously I was doing. Instead, I am in this shitty facility, trying to quash the desire to put heroin into my body. It was getting easier, I felt a shift in my craving, my wants, but since Marcus's death I am folded in half with grief and I hate that this sadness, which flows through my blood, goes straight into the veins of my unborn child. She deserves better, I know she does, you are right. I hate that this is her start. I have to keep reminding myself that things for her would be a whole lot worse if I were using.

This I cling to.

I have just read this letter back, and to read that Marcus is dead – it's like I hear it for the first time every time and my tears are falling and I don't want to live without him. I don't. I can't care about anything. How can I live in a world where he is not? How could he leave us? My heart is in tatters. I am so broken. I am beaten. I want to go to sleep for ever . . .

S

'Oh my God . . .' Victoria whispered into the ether. Her dad died and her mum wanted to join him. The facts were as hard to digest as they were upsetting. Not that this information was new, but to see it written . . .

July 2001
Rosebank
Epsom
Surrey

Oh, Sarah, my love!
That was not disappointment on my face. It was pain: your pain, because if you hurt, I hurt. You are my child, my only child, and I love you. I will never forget how frail you seem, despite that glorious baby bump.

I have spoken to the counsellor to tell them of my worries that you might be in danger, and they tell me they are concerned too. You tried to hurt yourself? I wept when I found out. Sarah, my love, I urge you, please think of that little baby – cling to the idea of her and the thought of how your life will change.

I might not have liked Marcus, but I know you grieve for him and any grief that fills you up is so very hard for me to bear. I can see he had his demons and I feel sad for his family, sad for you, sad for that little baby who will never meet her dad. But I would be a hypocrite if I didn't also say that no matter how hard it feels right now, this is your chance to start over.

Don't give in to the pull of destruction. Don't you do that!

If I could take your sadness from you and wear it like a cloak for eternity, I would.

I only want for you to be happy, and I want this little baby to be happy. You are both my flesh and blood.

Please hang in there, darling. I asked the doctor if you would be better off coming home, but he said he feared for you if you were not under such close medical supervision. I want you home. I want you home healthy and safe. That is my wish.

I am afraid, Sarah, possibly more afraid than I have ever been. I fear I may lose you both. I fear that you might, weakened by your grief, do something unspeakable, and the thought of it stops the breath in my throat. Please, please, stay with us.

Keep fighting. Please, Sarah! Tell me how I can
help you . . .

I love you. Always, always, I love you.

Mum Xx

Victoria wiped her eyes, Sarah was right: there was something about
holding the actual letters, written with fingers no doubt gripping
pens that trembled with all the writer tried to contain and with
thoughts dictated by the situation in which they found themselves.
It was moving and draining in equal measure. She looked with
longing at the soft pillow and knew she could quite easily have
slipped back to sleep. But there was no time for that today; jumping
up, she raised the blind and looked out over the morning hustle and
bustle of Aker Brygge. People walked at pace with babies in bug-
gies, and others dawdled, engaged on their phones; some had cups
of coffee, the steam of which rose in tiny plumes into the morning
air. Opening the window wide, she drew in lungfuls of the fresh
breeze, cool and clean, blowing up from the fjord. Looking down
to the steps at the dock in front of their apartment block, she saw
the man who lived opposite, Vidar, fastening a bike helmet strap
under his chin, a shiny red mountain bike leaning against his thigh.
She liked the look of him and, as she studied him, he looked up and
smiled. Her wave was almost instinctive, and he waved back before
tapping his watch face and climbing on to the saddle. It felt like a
message which she was left to decipher as he cycled off towards the
centre of town, but what?

Gotta go, I'm late! or *See you later?* Ridiculously, she hoped it
was the latter.

Victoria pulled a hoodie over her pyjamas and took a deep
breath before opening the bedroom door, her nerves jangling.

'Good morning!' Jens threw his arms wide. With a dishcloth looped over his arm, he looked like the most exuberant of waiters, and her nerves settled. 'Come, sit!' He pulled out a chair at the table, which was sumptuously set with an array of food: cold meats, various cheeses, yoghurt in pots with indecipherable labels, jam, brown bread rolls and what looked suspiciously like waffles.

'This looks amazing!'

'Coffee or juice?' Sarah asked, a jug of each in her hands.

'Can I have both?'

'You can indeed!' Sarah bent forward eagerly to fill both her glass and her mug.

'So, we have a whole list of places we want to take you to.'

'That *Jens* wants to take you to,' Sarah interrupted him, giving her a subtle wink. 'I'd be happy to find good coffee and sit somewhere with a view, but . . .' She shrugged, as if she had no choice in the matter.

'She always does this, makes my suggestions sound like rubbish, and then if they *are* rubbish she can say, "I told you so!", and if we have a great day, she can act surprised.'

'Ignore him. I do not!' She laughed and Victoria noted the way she tilted her head . . . coy. She again felt like an interloper in this cosy set-up and wondered where her place might be in it.

'Tuck in!' Jens handed her a large white plate and the two of them watched her, like she was a foundling babe they were keen to see take food from a spoon, nodding and smiling as she reached for yoghurt and then slices of Jarlsberg. She half expected to hear a 'choo-choo' sound as a bread roll chugged in her direction. Sarah watched her every move and Victoria wondered if she had missed this most ordinary thing, feeding the child she had given birth to, as much as Victoria had missed being fed by her mum.

'Eat up!' Sarah nodded.

Victoria lifted her fork and, as instructed, tucked in.

The eagerness with which Jens marched her around the city was impressive, his enthusiasm contagious. By midday, they had toured the magnificent opera house, which seemed to rise like a ship coming up through ice, and now they were heading over to the Vigeland sculpture park.

It was a busy space and she noticed that Sarah took the opportunity to place her hand on her arm and guide her through the crowds, mothering her in a way she felt comfortable with or was allowed. It wasn't that Victoria disliked the contact, not exactly, but rather that she didn't know how she was supposed to respond. If Prim ever hugged her, she hugged her back, ditto Daksha, but the touch of Sarah's hand on her arm was an unknown thing and Victoria knew it was made all the more conspicuous by her awkward reaction. It was a reminder that they were still very much in the infancy of getting to know each other. Not that she thought about that now, too drawn by the surreal and wonderful exhibits that surrounded her.

'Wow!'

'Yes, wow!' Jens was clearly delighted by her reaction.

Victoria wandered, fascinated and a little overwhelmed by Vigeland's creations, where human life in all its forms was vividly and thought-provokingly captured in granite, bronze and cast iron. She ran her hands over the installations, which had been warmed by the sun, and it moved her that this warmth seemed to give them life. Victoria stood in front of one particular piece, a bronze sculpture of a woman with her arms crossed safely over her baby as she held him tight, her head bowed, their faces touching. It was a scene so perfect, so moving – the child held snugly in the woman's arms and her stance screaming, 'I will protect you, I will love you and I will keep you with me . . .'

Sarah came to a stop by her side and they both stared, its poignancy lost on neither of them. The two women looked from it to each other and back again, Victoria with a tightening in her throat and words skipping on her tongue, which she swallowed, pushing them down into the bottle where all her deepest, darkest and truest thoughts lived, the newness of their relationship still a barrier to her speaking openly about anything that might help them take steps across that bridge.

How could you have left me, Mummy . . .?

Why did you give me away . . .?

It was when I needed you the most . . .

How could you have lied to me?

You and Prim. I was only a baby, I had no choice but to trust you . . .

You made a deal and I had no choice . . .

These thoughts, a reminder of why she was here and why her excitement was still justifiably tinged with a little anger, diluted the emotion that threatened. Sarah shoved her hands in her pockets and looked at Victoria with eyes brimming.

'I find this piece very, erm . . .' She faltered.

'Me too,' Victoria agreed. It was hard to keep her tears at bay.

Jens had strolled up behind them. 'What are you two staring at?' He bent forward and, with natural ease, placed a hand on each of their shoulders, doing so with confidence as he peered through at the sculpture, the conduit connecting them. Victoria wondered if anyone looking might think they were a family.

And this is what my life could be like . . . me, Sarah and Jens. A little family . . . It's what I have always wanted, but I don't know how I would cope with losing you again . . . if things didn't work out . . . It might hurt too much.

'Ah, I see. It's a thought-provoking piece, for sure.'

'The mother looks so scared, and yet so proud, protective, as if, despite her best efforts, she knows something bad is around the corner.' Sarah reached up and held Jens's hand.

'Well, it's amazing what different people see.' Sarah's words had lit the kindling which, despite Victoria's best intentions, she felt was only ever a match-strike away from flaring. 'I think the mother looks afraid, complicit and wary.'

Jens straightened and rubbed his chin, his tone conciliatory. 'Well, maybe she's afraid because that child is the most precious thing to her and she is concerned for its welfare, knowing she is helpless to stop whatever is coming her way?'

Victoria began to walk away. 'Or maybe she's afraid because she knows she is going to get found out.' She could well imagine their expressions, so she chose not to look at them as she marched towards the exit, having had enough of sculpture for one day. Jens clapped his hands and marched too; seemingly, his good humour and enthusiasm could not be dented. She had to admit, he was nice to be around. He helped calm the maelstrom of confusion and anger in her young brain, a brain that with more years and more life added to it would see her able to voice rather than act out all that ailed her.

She had hoped spending time in Oslo might provide answers and insight to help calm her busy head. If anything, however, it only added another layer of questions. It was almost impossible to see how she and Sarah could ever walk across that bridge when Sarah was either fighting the urge to cry or the urge to physically hold her and Jens was busy working like a sweeper in a curling match, doing his level best to remove all and any bumps in the road to ensure day-to-day life for the woman he loved was as smooth as it could be.

It was easy, Victoria decided, to take her to see the sights, share a joke and whip up a cake. Not that she wasn't grateful, far from it, but it all felt very much like a bright, shiny distraction, getting her to look to the right so as not notice what was going on to the left.

Afterwards, the trio had continued to zip around the city, fuelled by good coffee, fresh pastries and Kvikk Lunsj, which Jens had insisted she try, as it was a Norwegian staple. She 'oohed' her enthusiasm, not wanting to offend and so deciding not to tell him it was, disappointingly, exactly the same as any old KitKat she could get at home. Despite keeping her guard up, wary of her muddled emotions run through with grief, which skewered even the most pleasant of experiences, Oslo had surprised and welcomed Victoria. Like the sculpture that had so touched her, the city and its people had wrapped their arms around her and she felt at home. Not that she would ever consider leaving Epsom, or Rosebank for that matter, but she could certainly understand how when a boy had come along and looked at Sarah and she had looked at him and they had fallen, Norway must have been an easy choice when all they had to do was find a place to be together.

Jens's enthusiasm for his place of birth could not be dampened by fatigue or the post-lunch dip and after eating he was still keen to show her the best of the stunning city. They packed in the sights: the understated cathedral, the accessible royal palace and the many beautiful parks, and each experience was a surprise.

Not before time, they took a rest stop at the Kafe Oslo, which looked to Victoria to be part café, part bookshop; people sat inside and out, either with books open in their palms or newspapers spread wide on the table, sipping at hot chocolates or stopping to take bites of fancy macaroons. It was a wonderful atmosphere with a great view over the park.

'So, no university for you?' Jens quizzed her.

She shook her head and sipped her hot chocolate. 'Nope.'

He drew breath. 'I think better to say, "Not right now", because who knows what is around the corner?' He spoke sincerely and she liked his interest.

Victoria made a 'tsk' noise. 'Trust me, *no one* knows what's around the corner – I mean, look at us' – she extended her index finger and drew a circle at chest height – 'who would have thought only weeks ago that this is where we'd be?'

'Not me!' Jens smiled his agreement while Sarah stayed quiet. 'But aren't you glad?' Jens enthused. 'I know I am! *Very* glad!'

She liked him *very* much and she liked the way the couple interacted with each other, taking note of how Sarah often looked to him for reassurance, as if he was her mentor, her protector, her good friend, as well as her husband. But it wasn't overly deferential: there was balance. Sarah made him laugh, teased him.

'Oh, hello, Mr Careers Advisor! How can you give her advice on university or studies? You were a nerd who wanted to be a law-yer since the age of five! Blinkered! There was no room for artistic expression, you were so focused.' Sarah shook her head at him mockingly. 'I bet you had a briefcase and a little suit when you were five too.'

'Well, actually, I did!' He laughed, and they all joined in. 'But as for having no room for artistic expression, I take offence at that. Do I have to remind you that I chose the cushions for our couch!'

'That's true, you did, you did.' Sarah wrapped her arm around his and rested her head briefly on his shoulder.

Victoria wished at some level that the woman could be as relaxed with her as she was with him, convinced it would make the whole walking on the bridge thing a lot easier. *Hello, pot . . .* Her interior monologue reminded her that this was a reciprocal thing. She knew Oslo had made its mark on her, but spending time with Sarah and Jens, this is where she had learned the most. Her grandpa had died when she was nine and, having spent the last ten or so years living alone with Prim, she was unschooled in what it was like to live in a house with a couple, a younger couple at that. It was very different to having Gerald pop in for a cup of tea and a shortbread petticoat. It gave a whole other dynamic to family life, and it was a life far closer to the one she had always dreamed of, where a mum and dad took her to the park and they ate together around a table. The trouble was, her spikiness made it hard to relax, and she still half expected someone to tell her this vignette of family life was not hers to enjoy.

'What are you thinking?' Jens asked as he drank his coffee. 'You look thoughtful.'

Victoria didn't know where to begin and, without overly censoring her thoughts, she spoke with an honesty that did not come easily. 'I was just thinking it's been nice to spend time in Oslo, and especially with the two of you.' Jens and Sarah beamed at each other, clearly liking the compliment. 'But' – Victoria looked towards the park and spoke her mind – 'I guess I feel wary, a little bit scared that someone is going to come along and shout, "That's it! Time up!" because I don't feel this is real, it's like . . . too much sometimes.' She sighed. 'I . . . I don't want to be abandoned again. I think it would be harder now because I'm older, less gullible and I don't have Prim to rely on.' It was then that she looked at the two people sitting opposite her, and the look on Sarah's face was one of horror.

'I won't . . . I couldn't . . . I mean . . .' Sarah shook her head, choking on her own sadness, and Jens put his coffee cup down and wriggled forward in the chair.

'Ah, I think what Victoria might have meant to say was . . . that this is so much a dream come true it feels unbelievable? Is that right, Victoria?' He looked at her imploringly.

'Kind of.' She again looked away, but not before seeing Jens reach his hand under the table and gather Sarah's hand on to his lap. He had done this throughout the day, acted a little bit like an energetic interpreter, a buffer, whipping out a verbal scythe greased with humour and platitude as he hacked away the brambles of awkwardness that tended to wrap any extended conversations between her and Sarah. He had a knack for it, knowing when to intervene or fill a silence with informed chat and kindly words of encouragement.

'We should . . . we should probably be getting back.' Sarah stood, and she and Jens followed suit. The walk back was sedate. Sarah, Victoria suspected, like her, was lost in thought about the fact that it felt very much like they took one step forward, two steps back, but what was she supposed to do? Sarah wanted honest, open conversation.

'Hey!' Vidar called from his balcony as the trio arrived at their apartment block.

'Hey, Vidar!' Jens waved.

'I am on my way down!' Vidar shouted, and before they had time to get to the top of the stairs he met them in the hallway. He was breathing hard and had clearly rushed.

'*Hvordan går det?*' Vidar asked casually.

'*Bra takk.*' Jens smiled.

'So you want to get a coffee?' He turned to face her, addressing her so openly, so publicly, that Victoria felt she had no option other than to agree – not that she minded, not at all, and in truth, she guessed that Sarah and Jens might be in need of a break from the intensity of their day, as was she.

'What, like, *now*?' She tucked her hair behind her ears, aware of her end-of-day state and wishing she could at least drag a comb through her curls.

'Why not?' He smiled.

'I'm not sure if . . .' She looked to Sarah for guidance.

'You go! Be back by six.' Sarah touched her fingers together, her manner excited. 'In fact, it's good you're going out. We're preparing a bit of a surprise!' She beamed.

'All right then!' Victoria turned on the stair to follow Vidar back out on to Acker Brygge.

'So, I'm Vidar – Vee-dar,' he enunciated.

'Yes, and I'm Victoria – Vic-taw-ree-aaah,' she offered, with only the smallest hint of sarcasm, holding his gaze, and they both smiled.

'You want to get coffee and sit on the bench?'

'Sure, bench-sitting sounds good.' She fell into step beside him, liking his sweet nature and the silences between them that didn't feel at all stilted or like she needed to fill them with idle banter. They walked to the food truck selling waffles and coffee further along the quayside and, each with a warm cup in their palms, made their way to the bench at the top of the stairs in front of the apartment block.

'Sometimes I just like to sit on a bench and watch the world go by.' He stretched out his long legs in front of him. 'Your weekend has been good so far?'

'Mm.' She nodded, taking a mouthful of good, hot coffee. 'How was your bike ride?'

'Oh, good, yes. I was going to see my mom. She lives in Grünerløkka.'

She nodded like she might know where this was.

'I pop in on a Saturday morning and we have breakfast.'

'That's nice.' She meant it, liking the ordinariness of his routine and the fact that he was happy to share it. It was interesting to her how other people spent time with their mothers.

'If I don't make it a regular appointment, time runs away with me, you know?'

'I do.' She thought of how time had slipped by since she had lost Prim; the day she'd found her in the chair felt simultaneously like days and months ago.

'So you've had a good weekend?'

She turned to face him on the bench, the pretence being to better consider his question, but in reality she wanted the chance to study him. His straight hair was naturally fair and his features strong. He smiled at her, as if taking the exact same opportunity to study her and her heart did a little rumba.

'Yes, it's been busy, you know, but good, cramming it all in.'

'So what have you seen?' He rested his elbows on his raised knees and she inhaled the vanilla scent of his aftershave.

'Oh, the cathedral, the royal palace, the opera house, Vigeland Park and I think just about every café within a ten-mile radius.'

He laughed, an easy, natural laugh, and she liked that he didn't need to fill the air with an immediate response, happy to just be . . . it made her relax.

'Did you get out to Ekebergparken?'

She shook her head.

'It's the best. You can get a tram from right here or you can drive around, of course, but that's not as much fun.'

'Well, no, why would anyone choose car over tram?'

'Exactly! Who would do that?' He smiled. 'It's a beautiful park, there's sculpture too, and good hiking – I have a favourite bench over there in the graveyard. It sounds weird, but it's beautiful. Death doesn't scare me. My dad died a couple of years ago.'

'Mine died too,' she whispered. 'When I was a baby. And then my gran, quite recently.'

'It sucks.' He stared out across the fjord.

'It does.' She liked how he didn't feel the need to give her advice or match her story or talk about feelings, just the simple statement of the truth, because yes, it did suck.

'Ekeberg has the best view of Oslo. You know how you can only really appreciate something when you are looking back at it, the whole picture from above, and when you're not in it.' He made a downward motion with his hands and she thought of Prim, wondering if she was now able to look back from above with the whole view, and what she might now think of the choices she made. She thought of the letter she had read earlier that day. The words burned into her mind and were just as powerful now in reflection.

> If I could take your sadness from you and wear it
> like a cloak for eternity, I would.
> I only want for you to be happy, and I want
> this little baby to be happy. You are both my flesh
> and blood.

That's all you wanted, isn't it, Prim? For us to be happy . . . for me to be safe . . .

'Yes, Ekeberg is special, and the only way to see the city, in my opinion.'

'I would like to see it.'

'Well, I would like to take you there.'

'Oh! Really?' The unexpected invitation made her gut leap with joy.

'Yes. If you are ever at a loose end in Oslo, just knock on my door. You know where I live, right?'

'I do.' She laughed, but it was a different laugh, a happy laugh, and not in the least bit doll-like and dumb.

'Victoria!' Jens yelled over the balcony, and she looked up. 'Five minutes! Are you warm enough?' he hollered, his hands either side of his mouth, as if she were much, much further away.

She nodded and waved her hand over her head, embarrassed to have had her name broadcast loudly over Aker Brygge and even more embarrassed that Vidar seemed to be enjoying the spectacle.

'Hang on!' Jens called, and despite her avowal to the contrary, he dangled a mustard-coloured wool blanket over the edge of the balcony, which he dropped when the coast was clear, watching it crumple on the cobbles of the pavement. Vidar jumped up to retrieve it. Victoria was a little bit delighted that Jens cared enough about her welfare to drop the blanket, delighted that Vidar had fetched it for her and grateful to slip it over her legs, realising in that moment that the air had indeed turned a little chilly. Vidar sat down hard, capturing the corner of her blanket under his bottom, not that she mentioned this.

'So, Vic-taw-ree-aaah,' he enunciated, speaking neither in statement nor question, but rather as a forerunner of more words to follow, as if they were already familiar to each other and not the strangers that they were. 'I was just going to say: Jens and Sarah are great people.'

'Yes.' She bit her lip, aware that this was straying into awkward territory and that this boy from across the hallway had probably spent more time with and exchanged more words with the woman who had given birth to her than she had. It was a sobering thought. 'Yes, they do seem great.'

'Oh, so you don't know them that well?' She saw his perplexed expression.

'Well, I do and I don't. It's complicated.' She looked out over the water. 'But it's been good. Oslo is such a great city. I've loved it. The parks, the sculpture – everything,' she babbled, changing the subject to spare having to give the detail she felt unready to share.

'It is.' He smiled dryly and seemed to take the hint. 'And where's home for you?'

'London. Well, I say London, because most people know that and not Surrey. But, Surrey. Home is Epsom in Surrey.' She coughed, knowing she sounded about as flustered as she felt and hoping that her foreign tongue might have disguised it slightly.

'Where the racecourse is? Home of the Epsom Derby!'

'Yes. Have you been?' She warmed to him even more, thinking there might be a link to her hometown.

'No.' He shook his head. 'But I know that in 1913 it was where Emily Davison died for the cause of the suffragettes, isn't that right? There's still debate, I think, over whether she jumped in front of a horse or simply had a terrible accident trying to grab its reins. Either way, she was a martyr to her cause and will always be remembered for it.'

'Yes, I think so.' She felt a little embarrassed that he knew detail she was lacking. 'I'm more of a maths fan than a history buff.'

'And in England you are only allowed to pick one?' He laughed.

'So you like history?' she deflected.

'I do, *and maths*.' He shifted in the seat and stretched out his legs once again. She pulled the freed blanket into her lap, liking his height and his easy manner.

'Well, there we go. You are clearly a better scholar than me, or just smarter. You are certainly taller,' she added, stretching out her own legs.

'I am taller.' He nodded. 'But I haven't been a scholar for a while. I graduated last year.'

'In what?' She was curious.

'Maths, history and tallness.'

She laughed loudly. He was smart. Smart and funny. She thought of Flynn, with a flash of indifference.

'So, what do you do now with all that cleverness and height?'

'I'm a web designer.'

'For spiders?' She matched his humour.

'Yes. Mainly for spiders, but also for silkworms and then, in the off-season, I switch to cocoons – not as pretty, but the money is good.'

'Nice.' She smiled at him, not in the least bit awkward for holding his gaze and no longer concerned about the blush that spread from her cheeks to her chest. She pointed towards the balcony. 'I am not supposed to know, but I have a terrible feeling they are planning a mini party, for my birthday.'

'Ah, happy birthday! *Gratulerer med dagen!*'

'Thank you, I think . . . but actually, it's all a bit premature. It's not my birthday for another couple of weeks, but obviously, I'll be back in Surrey by then.'

'Obviously.' He smiled at her, and she liked the way his mouth curved over his teeth and his eyes lifted at the corners. 'So, a party sounds good.' He put his coffee cup on the floor and his hands under his arms. She tried to figure out whether he thought he might be invited, which he most definitely was not! The thought of having to navigate an evening with three strangers who all knew each other was, she figured, more than she could handle.

'Oh, it's not really a party, just the three of us and a piece of cake, I expect – not a *party* party. Although I did have a party: a big one, quite recently. I hadn't planned on it, but it kind of happened and it all ended horribly.' She closed her eyes and breathed quickly at the memory. 'I had to call in a man with a gun and he threw everyone out and I had to leave the area for a bit. As I say, all horrible.'

'Are you a gangster?' he asked, his smile now a little more fixed.

She laughed loudly. 'A gangster? What? Oh! Oh, the gun thing, no.' She tutted, pulling the blanket around her shoulders. 'That was just Gerald with a pistol.' She giggled. 'To be honest, he's more used to wielding secateurs. He looks after the orchids and tomato plants for me.' This time, she was fully aware of her babbling and laughed at her giddiness.

'You are different and interesting, Victoria,' he surmised, and firecrackers of happiness exploded in her stomach.

'Thank you.' She meant it. 'And so are you, Vidar. What does Vidar mean?' She was curious.

'Vidar was the son of Odin, a god.'

'Wow! More of that history stuff.'

'Technically it's mythology, not history. And for the record, I wouldn't want to come to your party, even if I was invited. Either the mini one with cake upstairs or the one with the pistol-toting Gerald.'

'Well, good.' She smiled, thinking of the mild-mannered septuagenarian and how he would like this moniker. 'Because, technically, you *weren't* invited.'

Although I think pistol-toting Gerald might like you . . . Nothing little or turd-like about you at all.

'I'm glad we have established that.' Vidar nudged her with his elbow. 'And don't take it personally – I hate parties. I *really* hate parties; I would rather be over at Ekebergparken, walking and reading or just thinking.'

'Or sitting on your graveyard bench,' she cut in.

'Yes, that too. I'm not really the party type. Do you know what I mean?'

'I know exactly what you mean,' she whispered, ridiculously wishing that she had more time in Oslo.

'Victoria! You can come back up now! Come on!' Jens called again, louder this time, his tone almost urgent.

She stood, leaving Vidar on the bench. 'I guess I'll see you.' She cringed, not knowing how to end this exchange.

'Yeah, I guess I'll see you.' He smiled at her and again her heart did its little rumba.

Victoria climbed the stairs and smiled as the apartment door was flung open and Jens and Sarah stood side by side with matching grins. Sarah held a cake covered in lit candles and they were singing, badly and loudly:

'Happy birthday to you . . .'

Victoria threw her hands over her eyes in mock embarrassment, then suddenly, behind her cupped palms, she thought of all the years that this had been her wish, for her mum to be standing in front of her with a cake – it made her unbearably sad at all that she had missed, and through no fault of her own. She pictured her six-year-old self holding back tears as Prim wrapped her in a hug.

'You can't cry today, darling! Not on your birthday!'

'I wish my mummy was here . . . I wish . . . I wish I could see her!'

'I know, my love, I know . . . Shh . . . And I bet wherever she is, she wishes it too.'

Oslo. Victoria thought. That was where she was. *Not on a cloud somewhere, but Oslo.*

Jens put his hands on her back and guided her into the sitting room, where balloons littered the floor and couch and a 'Happy Birthday' banner had been strung across the pictures by the dining table. There was a bottle of champagne sitting in a nest of ice inside a silver bucket, smoked salmon on a platter and bowls of hummus, nuts, olives and other delightful snacks dotted around.

'This is lovely, thank you.' She meant it, but was unable to alter her subdued tone, finding the whole charade unbearably sad. She took a seat at the table, where Jens proceeded to pour three flutes of bubbles, oblivious.

'You need to blow out your candles and make a wish!' Sarah urged, holding the cake towards Victoria's face.

'I don't know what to wish for.' She closed her eyes briefly, before looking at the two people in front of her, both with expressions so eager, it felt a lot like pressure. Her tears bloomed and

266

she felt the heat of embarrassment as Jens and Sarah stared at her. 'I really don't know what to wish for,' she mused. 'This is really hard for me. Every birthday since I was a child I would send my wishes and thoughts up to heaven, hoping you might get them and know that I was thinking about you and missing you. And so this feels . . .' The words were not forthcoming. 'This feels a bit odd. I'm sorry.'

Sarah began to cry, loudly. The sound of her sobbing cracked open the party-themed veneer to reveal a dark inner core that was impossible to ignore. It was evident that a few balloons and bubbles were not enough to erase the awkwardness. Victoria felt horrendously ill at ease as Sarah tried to catch her breath and swallowed what sounded like a lump in her throat, and just like that, the jovial atmosphere and all the joy that had bounced from the walls suddenly evaporated. Sarah quickly blew out the candles and put the cake on the table next to a long silver knife, presumably there to make a ceremonial cut. Jens put the glasses down and handed his wife one of the gold napkins meant for cake with which to blot her tears.

'Th-thank you,' she stammered. 'Actually, would you just excuse me for a minute?' She gave a false smile and left the room, closing the bathroom door behind her. Jens sat in the chair next to Victoria, who felt the hot, swarmy feeling of embarrassment wash over her.

'I didn't mean to make her cry.' She swiped her eyes. 'I was just telling the truth. Sarah said we have to be able to say the hard stuff to move forward, that we should be honest.' She hated her own note of desperation, wanting to make it right.

'I know, I know.' He held her gaze and she could tell he was not mad, just sad. 'And the truth is important, honesty *is* important. But no matter what she says, it's hard for her too.'

Victoria looked towards the closed bathroom door and felt at a loss as to what to do or say next. Her response was slow in forming. There was an awkward beat or two of silence, which no canny words of distraction from Jens could halt.

'I have been dreading my birthday,' she began, rolling the edge of her paper napkin back and forth between her fingers. 'My first without Prim, and here I am. And all the things I have ever wished for and dreamed of came true . . . but it doesn't feel like I thought it would. I am feeling every emotion you can imagine. Sarah should be dead! But she's not. And it's amazing and weird to be in her house, but there's a small part of me that doesn't know how to stop mourning her. Every time I had to say, "*My mum died . . . my mum's dead . . .*", which I have done more times than I can remember, it erased a little bit of my self-confidence and it stole a little bit of my happiness. I wasn't like the other girls, who ran into their mum's arms after school. Yes, I had Prim and she was wonderful, and I can see that she only did what she thought was best, but it wasn't the same – how could it be? It took the shine off any occasion: birthdays, Christmas, parties, any celebration. "*Where's your mum, is she collecting you? Is your mum coming?*" And I'd look at the person asking, knowing that what came next would only make them and me feel like rubbish. "*No, my mum's not collecting me, I don't have a mum. She died . . .*" But all that time it was a lie. She wasn't dead; she was just hiding from me. How do I get past that?' She wiped her tears on the napkin she was fiddling with.

Jens too took his time and, when he did speak, his voice was calming. 'Sarah wasn't hiding from you. She was waiting for you, waiting for either the right moment or the sad loss of Prim or something, I don't know . . .' He bit down on his tucked-in lips. 'But I do know that she has waited your whole life, never giving up the idea that one day she would get to make you a birthday cake and start over.'

'It's not that simple.' *I wish it was . . .*

'Of course it's not that simple!' He took a deep breath and knitted his fingers. 'It is a delicate situation, I know. And I cannot begin to imagine what you are going through. There is no right or wrong way to do things, no blueprint for this, there is only what works for the two of you. But I can tell you, hand on heart, that Sarah told me about you on the first day I met her. She was working in a coffee shop in Soho and one of the first things she said was, *"I am a mum."* Like it was her proudest achievement, and then she cried and the whole story tumbled out, and not a day has gone by that she hasn't spoken about you in some way, even if it was just to wish you goodnight through the window before she drew the curtains. *"The same moon,"* she'd say. *"We look at the same moon."'*

Victoria pictured her doing just that and her tears came afresh.

'And I can tell you, Victoria, that despite what you might think or how hurt you might feel, you are still her proudest achievement. And she has a lot to feel proud about: her legal work, of course, which changes lives, and beating her addiction, which is tougher than you can know, but they pale into insignificance when she talks about you.'

'Thank you for saying that. It means a lot.'

'It's the truth.' He held her gaze.

'The trouble is, I have spent my whole life coming to terms with the fact that my mother took drugs and died. Despite me being just a tiny baby who really, really needed her. Have you any idea what that did to my self-esteem? I clung to my gran like a little bookish limpet. I never did anything! Scared the world would reject me, the way my mother had. I found it hard to understand how someone could make the decision to leave her three-month-old baby. I believed that she pushed the contents of a toxic syringe into her veins rather than hang around to see me grow up, and it has taken me my whole life to get it straight in my head and now? Pfft!' She made her fingers into star

269

shapes. 'I just have to forget all of that and blow out the candles as if nothing is amiss? And the way you talk about her sounds to me like you are talking about a stranger. I don't know her! And I can't help it!' She cursed her sadness, which now slipped down the back of her throat and nose. 'And now I have ruined the evening. After such a lovely day and all you have done for me, Jens.'

'No, you haven't.' He spoke kindly. 'There is plenty of evening yet. I'll go and see if she is okay.' He stood and smoothed the creases from the thighs of his jeans. 'I know it's *your* birthday, but I am going to tell you of my wishes: I wish one day that things might become clearer for you. I wish that one day you might call my wife Mum and not Sarah; I wish that one day you will refer to her as your mother; and I wish that one day, just once, you might acknowledge the name she gave you. A strong name: Victory. The name she gave her daughter. Because I know that this would all mean the world.'

'That's a lot of wishes,' she whispered, feeling the weight of pressure.

The bathroom door opened and in walked Sarah, her eyes red and puffy. She sat down and folded her hands on the tabletop. Jens squeezed her shoulder in solidarity before sitting back down. Victoria hated that she was the cause of this distress.

She felt the prickle of her own tears, wishing she had never come to Oslo; like Jens, wishing many things . . .

'Okay, okay.' Jens tried to calm the tense atmosphere. 'How about we all just—'

'Actually,' Sarah cut in, 'I want to talk to Victoria. Do you mind?' She smiled at her husband.

'Of course not!' He leaned over and kissed his wife on the forehead.

'Come on,' Sarah instructed. 'Let's go sit on my bed.'

Victoria left the table and wiped her eyes before walking into Sarah and Jens's bedroom, which was as sparse as hers, the furniture and walls white, but with a pretty quilted silk counterpane on the bed, the colour of a summer sky, embroidered in a variety of flowers that lifted the whole space.

'This quilt has always reminded me of the lake at home and the planting around the edge.' She ran her fingers over the irises and reeds that sat in a neat border.

'I can see why.' Victoria felt sad that this quilt was as close as Sarah had got in all these years to going home and again pictured her by the side of the lake on the day she first saw her.

'Get comfy. I shan't be a mo.'

Victoria sat back on the pillows and thought how many times she might have sat on her mum's bed if she had grown up with her – countless times, after bad dreams, before going out, Christmas morning . . .

Sarah came back into the room clutching the bundle of letters.

'We need to figure this out, Victoria. We need to go back to the beginning and figure this out, because I tell you now—' Sarah kicked off her shoes and climbed on to the bed, coming to rest right next to her, both of them now leaning against the headboard with their toes flexing inside their socks. 'I have waited too long and missed too much of your life to let you walk away. To not smash down the walls. We are going to figure this out, do you hear me?' Her tone was sharp and yet wavering as distress plucked her vocal cords.

'Yes.' Victoria kept her voice low, a new sensation taking root in her gut. This woman was not going to give her up, was not going to reject her again; her words echoed, and she had to agree: they had already missed too much . . .

'Right, I am going to be brave.' Sarah sniffed and opened the bundle. 'Give me the next letter you were about to read and I'll read it aloud.'

Victoria sorted through the stiff paper and handed her the next sheet. Sarah took it into her hands, drew breath and began to read.

'August 2001
Sarah Jackson
Henbury House
West Sussex

Yes, yes, you are right.
    You are right and I hate that you are.
    I want to use again, I want the pain to go away.
    I want the world to stop.
    I want Marcus back.'

Sarah stopped reading and took a moment to gather herself, dabbing at her eyes with her sleeve before continuing.

    'I want to die.
    I am numb.
    I am broken.
    I am lonely, so lonely, and the only person who can take away my loneliness is Marcus.
    How can I be lonely when I have this little baby curled inside me?
    How can I have a baby? How can I give her what she needs when all I seek is oblivion?
    I don't trust myself and it's a scary place to be.
    I am with the counsellor 24/7, because if I could score, or if I could hurt myself, I think I would. That's a lie. I don't think I would. I know I would. But please don't be angry, please, please, please, be proud that I have had the courage to admit this and to say it out loud.
    I am a mess, Mum, but it's not the real me. It's the hollow me. The broken me. And how I

loved him! I loved him. He was my sun, he was all I could see, and I will mourn the loss of him every single day I get to breathe.

Don't reply.

Because there is nothing you can say.

Nothing. I am clinging on, but I don't want to, Mum.

I don't want to be, and I know, I know that as soon as I can, baby or not . . . I will find a way to end this fucking pain. I am done.

Sarah'

Sarah folded the paper and looked at Victoria, barely able to contain her distress.

'I remember the way it felt, so much pain.' She faltered. 'It was like the end of the world. Everything was dark, everything was hopeless, like living in a black hole, and I couldn't see a way out.'

'Shall I read Prim's reply?' Victoria asked tentatively, liking the close proximity of Sarah across the mattress and the fact that she was holding her gran's words in her palm. Sarah nodded.

'August 2001
Rosebank
Epsom
Surrey

Please, Sarah, I am begging you. I am begging you not to do anything stupid.

I came to see you when I received your last letter, but they told me you have asked for no visitors and they wouldn't let me see you! They wouldn't let me see you, and I begged them and I sobbed and I would have crawled in the dirt, but it made no difference. Why, my love? Why did you not want me near you? Daddy said it was because you knew I would try and talk you out of doing something stupid, because you think I might nag you, and he is right. I would, I would, I would, because I feel like you are hanging on to life by a thread and I would do anything to try and keep you here.

Please, my darling girl, please do not listen to those negative voices, please don't hurt yourself again.

Please don't harm that unborn girl who has no part in any of this and no say in how her life unfolds.

I am at a loss. I feel like I am in free fall, thinking about you and fretting over you every single second, and I can only imagine what this must be like for you.

This is a very hard thing for me to write, but I need to say what is in my head.

I know I can't stop you from taking drugs. I know I can't choose the path you take, not any more. But I beg you, Sarah, think about the life of that little girl growing inside you. What is best for her? I want you both home. I want you both safe, but if that cannot be, then let me take her. Let me give her the start she might be denied if you go back to using drugs. Don't take her with you on that journey to hell. I beg you.

I know this is not an easy thing for you to consider, and it's not something I wanted to write – it is something I wanted to say to your face, had I been able to see you.

I would love her, and I would tell her all about her wonderful mother. Because you are wonderful, my Sarah. You are. I can hardly see the page for my tears.

Mum X

'Oh, Prim!' Victoria found it hard to read. Her gran was fighting for her, fighting hard, and she began to imagine what her life might have been like had Prim not fought so hard; where might she have ended up? Would she have even lived? It made her shudder. 'It must have been heartbreaking.' She raised the letter in her hand.

'It *is* heartbreaking!' Sarah managed through her tears.

'Knowing these were written at a time when everything was teetering on the brink, the despair – I can *feel* that.'

'Yes. I can feel it too,' Sarah agreed. 'I have always felt it.'

Sarah raised the next letter in her hand and cleared her throat.

'September 2001
Sarah Jackson
Henbury House
West Sussex

I have thought it over.

I guess you are right, and to write these words takes more strength than I knew I had left.

Take her.'

She paused and looked at Victoria, who could only replay the two words in her head: *take her . . . take her . . .*

'It will be easier in the long run for us all. I know where I am heading and I don't fear it. I am biding my time, but the truth is I don't even want to fight it, Mum; I can't. I am sick and the drug is like my medicine. My whole body is crying out for it, and losing Marcus has taken away the last of my strength to say no.

You are right, the thought of taking her with me on that journey to hell is more than I can stand and yes, I am using again, Mum. I am doing so in a controlled way, but as soon as I leave here that control goes.

Who knows what's around the corner?

None of us, that's who. None of us.

Maybe I'll make it out of the other side, maybe I can come for her then?

It's so hard! I don't expect you to understand, but it is so very hard.

I am an addict.

I will always be an addict.

I will die an addict.

I will also always be Victory's mother, no matter how far away I am or how much time passes.

Victory: that's what I will call her. A strong name.'

Again, Sarah broke her reading to gather herself and try to contain her distress. Victoria wondered if she should hold her hand but didn't have the courage.

'I shall keep the memory of her inside my head and the pulse of her little heart inside my womb, and I shall mark a calendar to enable me to picture her at every stage of her wonderful life, for however long I live.

Let her be free, Mum. Please, please, let her be free!

Don't try to shape her, just let her be.

And if she is anything like her daddy, she will be perfect, absolutely perfect.

Sarah'

Sarah let her head fall to her chest, overwhelmed by her sadness.

'Poor, poor Marcus,' Victoria whispered. 'You really, really loved him . . .'

'I really, really did.' Sarah smiled with her eyes closed, sitting so close that it felt like a safe space where they could speak freely.

'And Prim did what you asked. She let me be free, she let me be.' This an acknowledgment of the care she had received.

Sarah nodded and ran her fingers over the embroidered flowers of the counterpane.

'How did you get through it?' Victoria asked softly.

'Because I realised I had no choice,' Sarah offered dryly. 'Once I had decided to live, I had no choice but to cope.'

'I guess so.' She thought for the first time of the bravery of the two women, the two generations who had created her. 'I'm overwhelmed,' she admitted. 'It's like the two voices are either side of a ravine and both are screaming at the other about the best way to get across, but neither is really listening and therefore both are unaware the rock is crumbling beneath their feet until they have no option but to run in opposite directions.'

'I like that.' Sarah sniffed. 'Yes. It was exactly like that.'

Emotionally drained and physically tired, Victoria felt the pull of sleep and closed her eyes briefly.

She woke in an unfamiliar bed with the embroidered quilt thrown over her. She stretched and looked at the other side of the bed, which was empty. Gently opening the bedroom door, she peered at the sofa, where Jens slept with Sarah in his arms and the mustard-coloured blanket from the arm of the chair covering them.

Jens, as if aware of her scrutiny, opened his eyes. 'Hey, morning!'

Sarah too sat up. 'How did you sleep?'

'Better than you two, I'd say.' She took in their dishevelled hair and creased clothes. 'You should have kicked me out of your bed.'

'I couldn't bear to. You sank down on the mattress and spread out like a starfish, and you were so cosy.'

'Thank you.'

'You are welcome.' Sarah smiled. 'So that was quite some evening. I sat and read all of the letters after you had dropped off and I feel like I have run a marathon. What . . . what did you think?' She sounded nervous.

'I think I have a new perspective on things, for sure,' Victoria answered truthfully.

'A good perspective?'

'I would say so, yes. I can't imagine . . .' She paused, emotion drawing the words from her mouth.

'I thought we said no crying!' Sarah pointed out.

They both laughed.

'How about I get us some coffee?' Jens stood slowly and yawned.

'How about we go out for coffee?' Sarah suggested. 'All I ever really need is good coffee and a view.'

'Ah, you win!' Jens chuckled. 'You guys go without me. I need a shower.'

Aker Brygge was busy even at this hour on a Sunday morning. Vidar was again on the quayside, saddling up his bike. '*God Morgen!*'

'*God Morgen*, Vidar,' Victoria answered, and he chuckled. 'Where are you off to? It's not Saturday – you can't have another breakfast date?' she teased.

'Actually, I do. Saturday is with my mom and Sunday is with my dad.' He pointed over the water in the direction of Ekebergparken.

His sweetness was lovely, and she closed her eyes briefly to show him she understood.

'I'll see you.' He held her gaze as he fastened his helmet and jumped on his bike.

'Yes, I'll see you.'

'I like him,' Sarah stated as they walked along the cobbles towards town.

'I like him,' Victoria admitted, and they both laughed.

Espresso House was busy, but they nabbed a table with a view out over the fjord. The coffee was hot and strong and blew away the cobwebs of the night before.

'I feel . . . lighter.' Sarah took a deep breath.

'Yep, me too. It was really hard hearing you read your own words. It made it real for me. I can't imagine,' Victoria continued. 'I can't imagine what it must have been like for you, or for Prim, when I was born.'

'It was terrible, that's the truth, and it has been terrible for me every single day since.'

Victoria nodded. 'You said you were full of anger. Where did that come from?'

'Well, it was drug-fuelled mainly, or rather lack of drugs, but I think it was rooted in how Mum viewed Marcus. I loved him dearly, but to her he was the knife that pierced my breast, the bridge from which I might jump, the loaded gun that held the bullet aimed at my temple. Her hatred of him coloured her thoughts, and it never cooled, not once. If anything, it intensified. And that was hard for me and no doubt hard for her, as he was your dad.'

'Whether she liked it or not.' Victoria filled in the gaps.

'Not!' Sarah offered dryly. 'I know Mum wanted the best for me, and it was hard for her to give up the image she had of me in her mind; she wanted me to be a professional in neat clothes and with a steady life, not sharing needles on a dirty mattress in some rancid squat or constantly badgering my dad for money, which he gave me.'

'What parent *would* want that?' Victoria spoke her thoughts aloud.

'No sane ones, that's for sure. But I couldn't see that; I felt persecuted.'

'I bet Prim did too.' It felt good to be in her corner, loyal.

'Yes, I'm sure of it.'

'This is good, Sarah. It's this kind of detail I have been missing. I have never had anyone to ask because you weren't there and it never felt like Prim wanted to talk about it, and I understand why now. I can see how things broke down and you both just sort of went around in circles. You trying to get a foothold and her trying her best and not always understanding what you were going through.'

'That's about the sum of it. The day you were born feels like yesterday and a lifetime ago all at the same time.'

'October the twelfth.' Victoria looked up. 'Coming up.'

'October the twelfth,' Sarah repeated. 'Coming up soon. Nineteen? How is that even possible? I remember every minute of the day you were born. Every single minute. I was mourning Marcus, hurting so badly and beyond sad that he would never know you or you him. It was made harder because Mum wouldn't talk about him, wanted me to move on, like it was nothing, but my loss ran deep . . . I was still desperate for drugs: worn down by what was happening with Mum, and I knew my time with you was limited . . . It was the best and worst day of my life.'

'How was it?'

Sarah drew breath. 'Because I got you, because I held you in my arms and you clung to me, like you knew . . .'

'Maybe I did.' She felt a wave of sadness for the little baby who had clung to her mum, possibly able to sense that their time together was limited.

'And it was the very worst day because I knew I would never love anything more and I knew I was going to lose you. And I knew I was going to die. I had it planned, and I didn't fear it. I just wanted that hit.'

'But you didn't die.'

'No. No, I didn't.'

'Did you, erm . . . did you see Prim and Grandpa after you had left, after you had me?' She braced herself for the reply, quite unable to stand the thought of them organising clandestine get-togethers while she lay in bed sending nightly prayers up to her mum in heaven. It was unthinkable. And yet, a small, unselfish part of her wanted to know that Prim and Grandpa got to see their daughter before they passed away.

Sarah made no attempt to hide her distress, now obvious and still apparently lying very close to the surface. A question or mention such as this was seemingly enough to prick the skin and release the sadness.

'No. I never saw them, and I thought I had got used to the idea of it, until I heard that Mum had passed away and I felt my world crash. It was really hard when Dad died too, of course, but Prim . . . I thought she'd go on for ever. I thought there was always a chance that she'd pick up the phone or answer my letters.'

'You wrote to her?' *Jesus Christ! Did I unwittingly hand her the mail with your letters in it? Have I sat on the sofa with my nose in a book while she wrote you letters at the bureau, only feet away?*

'Not for many years. She asked me to stop. And I did. When I left the facility . . .' Sarah spoke plainly and with more than a hint of justification in her tone. 'Prim, despite our differences and being well into her sixties, stepped up to the plate and came and stayed close to where I was living, in a grotty shared house. She booked into a smart little B&B and she brought you to see me twice a day, no matter what my state. And often that state was not good. Not good . . .' She looked at the floor with knitted brows, as if even the memory was too painful. 'It was brave of her. I can see that now. Morning and night, she would come to that lousy bedsit so I could hold you and settle you, every day, twice a day for three months. I would kiss you sweetly on the forehead, trying to imprint myself on your memory – once when you arrived and once when you left. Do you remember anything of it at all? A smell? A thought?' She asked with such hope it was pitiful.

Victoria shook her head. *Nothing. Absolutely nothing. I wish I did.*

'I have survived on the thought that you might somehow have sensed me, remembered me in some way for all these years.'

'I didn't.' She spoke softly.

'I knew I had to give you up.' Sarah was crying now, and didn't bother to address her tears, as though the state was as natural to her as breathing. Victoria found it hard to hear. Sarah sniffed. 'I thought I would die. I *wanted* to die. And I knew you deserved more and so I kissed you twice a day, every visit until my time ran out. Prim let me hold you one last time and left me with some money, and she took you back to Rosebank and I went even further off the rails . . .' Sarah looked at her. 'That was all I got of you. Three months, twice a day. One hundred and eighty kisses. And I cherish each and every one. No one expected me to survive, especially not me.'

Victoria sat, stunned, watching mothers with small children walking or cycling along the quayside on this bright, bright morning. She tried to imagine the scenario, almost unable to equate the woman Sarah described with the neat, smart lawyer sitting opposite her. She tried to picture herself in Prim's arms, being carried up the stairs to a grotty bedsit where her junkie mother was behind a door, in what state, Prim could only have been able to guess. It *was* brave. It was unthinkable. Victoria took a sip of her coffee.

'I think losing your mum is one of the worst things imaginable. It doesn't feel right. And I thought I had gone through it, but I was thinking today that I am going to have to lose you again one day, when you really die, and I don't know if it will be easier or harder the second time around.' She was glad of this openness and the seemingly calm manner in which they were now talking. It felt real, and it felt a lot like progress.

'I hope it will be easier, because I don't want you to have a day of sadness, but I also hope it will be harder because I hope by then you might feel a bit more favourably towards me. I know you are angry at me, doubtful of me, which I understand, I do' – she put in the caveat – 'but I would like some of that anger to have gone.'

'I have been angry at Prim too, since I found out, and it has stopped me mourning her properly, I think. But today, I don't know. I think she tried her best.'

'She did,' Sarah acknowledged. 'She tried her best; I was not easy.'

'Things seem a bit clearer right now, and missing her not quite so painful. I found her, you know, on the day she died.'

'Oh!' Sarah sighed. 'I did not know that. That must have been terrible.'

'It was. Even though she was older, I still never expected her to die, not really.'

'I felt the same,' Sarah reminded her. 'I thought we would always have time to make things good. I shall regret it for the rest of my life. My consolation is that I know you would have brought her so much joy, so much joy . . .'

'Daksha and I went shopping and for a coffee, and Prim asked me to buy her a balaclava—'

'A balaclava?' Sarah interrupted with a note of surprise.

'Yes!' Victoria laughed. 'But she meant baklava, the Greek pastry!'

'Oh, makes more sense.' They both laughed.

'I came home, and there she was in the garden room . . .'

'Her favourite place.'

'Her favourite place,' Victoria concurred.

There was a moment or two of silence which felt a lot like peace as the two women, connected by blood and history, looked out over the water, where big ferry boats came and went, taking people out to the islands around Oslo. 'I wanted to ask you something, Sarah.'

'You can ask me anything.'

'Why did you decide to tell me you had died? Why that?' And there it was: the big question. The one that pained her the most. 'It was so final and so brutal.'

'I have avoided—' Sarah stopped abruptly.

'Avoided what?' Victoria sat forward in the chair.

Sarah's voice now sounded a little sticky, as if the words had to pass through a dry, nervous passage to reach her.

'I have avoided telling you this because I didn't want you to feel badly towards Prim. You are the most amazing human being, and that means she did it right! She did a good job. And I can't, hand on heart, say that I would have done the same, had you been in my care, and it's important to remember that.'

'Avoided telling me what?' Victoria pushed, her pulse now racing.

'I didn't know that Prim had decided to tell you that I had died. It was a dreadful, unbelievable shock to me. It still is.' She toyed with the handle of her coffee cup.

'You . . . you didn't know?' Victoria didn't know what to think. This information told her that Sarah had not been complicit in the deception, but that Prim . . . *her beloved, flawed Prim* had deliberately chosen this act . . . this lie to . . . *Oh, Prim!* She steeled herself for what might come next.

'I made contact with her when you were a toddler to say that I was trying to get myself straight, that I had met Jens and that things were looking up for me. And what I told you at the airport was the truth – Mum said she was doubtful of my sobriety, and I don't blame her! I can't blame her. All she had ever seen was me promising to get clean and then falling straight back into my old habits. She said she would only risk giving you back to me if there was a cast-iron guarantee that I wasn't going to disappear, relapse or kill myself, as she was not willing to put you through that, and that you deserved more. I told her the truth – there were no cast-iron guarantees – and she said it wasn't worth the risk, as you were happy, and she was right. And so I worked hard at getting back on my feet and then, when you were six, I contacted her again, and that's when she told me you thought I had died.'

'How did you feel?'

'How did I feel?' There was the unmistakable sound of a sob under her breath. 'Like I *had* died, or a part of me, at least. Like all the grief I had felt for Marcus came rushing to the top, but worse, deeper, harder to handle. Like the small window letting in light was barred shut and the future was just as dark and lonely as my present. But I had to tell myself that you were happy and that she had her reasons.'

'But she didn't give you a chance! She didn't give us a chance!' Victoria raised her voice.

'Because she had already given me so many chances and this was no longer about me. It was about you, the little girl who she wanted to protect and who she loved.'

'But . . .' Victoria felt the slip of tears over her cheeks. 'But why would she do that? Why would she do something so extreme? So irrevocable? Why would she do that?'

'To keep you safe.' Sarah's tears now matched her own. 'Because she didn't trust me and she knew there was no way back from what she had said without causing you the maximum of confusion and pain. Something neither of us wanted.'

'She took you away from me! And she kept me away from you!' Victoria sobbed.

'Yes, but she did what she thought she had to do to keep you safe . . . and when you are a mother, you'll be surprised what you would do to keep your child out of harm's way. You need to try and understand that!'

'But she wasn't my mother! You were!' Victoria's tears now clogged her nose and throat as her eyes streamed.

'Only in name, Victoria, only in name . . .'

The two cried together until their tears began to ebb, and they breathed deeply as calm returned. 'It's not easy for either of us.' Sarah spoke softly. 'And all we can do is keep talking about it, keep working things through until we reach an understanding. But this weekend feels like we have made a start. And never forget that Prim and I loved you as much as we loved each other, and that is how you and I will get through this: with love.'

'Yes, with love.' Victoria could only echo the beautiful senti- ment. She realised she was shivering. 'I'm getting a bit chilly. I think the temperature's dropped.'

'It does that. Do you want to get back? I know Jens will have prepared waffles, plus we have a birthday cake to eat!'

'Yes, we do.' Victoria stood, and the two walked back towards the apartment, side by side.

'I feel like we have taken a step on to that bridge, Victoria, do you?'

'I do.' She nodded, looking to the other side of the water, towards Ekebergparken. 'I do.'

THIRTEEN

The rain fell as Victoria boarded the plane and that suited her just fine. The plane began to taxi along the runway and her thoughts turned now to home – she was excited to see Daksha. As she soared higher into the sky, she looked down from the incredible vantage point at the city of Oslo below and thought of lovely Vidar. He was right: you could only really appreciate something when you were looking back at it, the whole picture from above, and what she appreciated was that Sarah had spoken the truth, and now she had the full story, the answers she had been looking for. Opening her laptop, Victoria read the last two letters, hearing Sarah and Prim's voices in her head as she did so, voices that were a little bit like her own.

> October 2001
> Rosebank
> Epsom
> Surrey
>
> Sarah,
> I have read your letter and I have cried an ocean.
> It seems like you have given up, and that makes me feel very afraid because, if you are not fighting, then the fight is over, and the thought

of losing you breaks my heart into pieces. You *are* my heart.

Please, please, I beg you, don't give up!

I want to make you a promise that I will love Victory and care for her as I have you, with every fibre of my being. It has been a privilege to be your mum, and to take care of your little girl will be the same.

The sadness your addiction has brought us is more than I thought I would be able to bear. I cannot think that this little girl might suffer in the same way.

If you choose the drug, Sarah, if you want to end your life that way, as you seem so set on doing, then you cannot contact her. You cannot let her love you and get close to you, only to lose you. That would be too much, and trust me when I tell you the pain of being so helpless, unable to intervene, is more than any person, mother or daughter, should have to go through.

I am praying you choose to stay clean. I am praying you choose to come home with Victory and live a life! A wonderful life! But if you can't do that – let your daughter have that wonderful life. A life not marred by drugs and the world that comes with that choice. A choice I will never fully understand.

I love you, Sarah, I will always love you, but I also love my granddaughter and I will fight to keep the world you seem insistent on inhabiting away from her door.

I will be there when you need me.

Keep me posted and know that my heart and spirit are broken, entirely broken. I don't know how we have got to this.

I don't and never will understand, but keeping Victory safe and secure means losing you, and that is something I will have to live with for the rest of my life.

I cannot think what I will tell her. I can't think what I might say to explain how we have arrived at this desperate, desperate crossroads.

I love you. I can only keep repeating, I love you, I love you, but I know that is not enough.

Mum Xx

October 2001
Sarah Jackson
Henbury House
West Sussex

October . . . any day now.

And I agree not to contact her. I hear what you are saying, and I don't want to confuse her or bring her a moment of sadness. I only want for her the best, the very best.

Tell her anything, Mum.

Tell her anything you think might make it easier for her in the long run. I don't care what.

You are right, she doesn't need to be part of this world I inhabit.

I am sorry I let her down.

I am sorry I let you down.

I have one thing to ask.

Please don't take her immediately.

Please let me see her.

I won't take her anywhere you can't get to.

You can be there, but please . . . let me hold her a few times.

Kiss her a few times.

To try and give her something to remember me by, that's all, just something to remember me by . . .

Please.

Sarah

'Something to remember me by . . .' Victoria whispered.

◆ ◆ ◆

Closing the cab door, Victoria was delighted by the sight of her friend.

'Welcome home! Welcome home!' Daksha yelled, and grabbed her as she walked up the front path. 'How was it? Did you miss me? What was Oslo like? Meet any nice Norwegian boys? Was it cold? How was Sarah? Did you guys talk? What was her fella like? Do you want a cup of tea? I'm afraid there's no cake left. We ate it all. I ate it all.'

Victoria stared at her. 'I had almost forgotten how much you say and how quickly.' They both laughed. 'I must invest in the very best ear plugs on the market – it's the only way I will ever get through our trip,' she levelled, only half joking. 'Right now, I can only respond to the last question: yes, please, to a very large cup of tea, and then I need to get changed. I have a double shift at the coffee shop this afternoon. I promised Stanislaw.'

'No! Not the coffee shop!' Daksha sulked. 'We have so much to catch up on; it's been a whole weekend, and I have to go home today. I'd stay longer, but Nani has cooked and Mum has summoned us. You're welcome to come too?'

'I can't, Daks, but thank you. I need to go to work and get laundry done and stuff.'

'Well, the offer's there. Ananya is just packing – you won't believe how much shit she brought just for a weekend. The girl's a klutz! And I've had some great ideas about our trip, and I've been looking up hostels and things in Vietnam and Cambodia – some amazing places! Oh, don't go to work, Vic – can't you phone in sick? You could come to ours and we could write a list or do a spreadsheet – you know how much you love a spreadsheet!'

'I do absolutely love a spreadsheet.' Victoria hitched up her carpetbag and looked at the wide frontage of Rosebank. It looked old and a little ramshackle, dated, and didn't really look like home, not now things were different, not now she was different. 'But, no. I absolutely cannot phone in sick.'

'In that case, I'll give you a call and come over later in the week.' Daksha smiled, happy, it seemed, to have her friend home.

'I'll look forward to it.'

'I love you, Vic.'

'Yep, I love you too.'

It had been a long and demanding day, on top of her flight, the busy weekend and the emotional rollercoaster of spending time with Sarah and Jens. By the time she put the key in the lock after her shift, as evening fell, Victoria was beyond tired. She went around the house, putting on lights and peeking into rooms, still cringing when she thought about the awful party that could have been so much worse, feeling thankful that there was no lasting damage and wishing, again, that she had not been so stupid. Her thoughts flew to Flynn, trying not to recall how nice it had been to have him around of an evening and the sheer joy she had felt at feeling his skin against hers. It was maddening how she had felt such attraction for the boy, who was both a liar and a cheat. Interestingly, she then conjured a picture of Vidar, the tall Norwegian she had flirted with on the bench, and she wondered if he had thought about her at all . . . she had certainly thought about him.

The house was quiet and felt huge with only the soft pad of her bed socks on the wooden floors to pepper the silence. She pictured Sarah and Jens's cosy flat and the warmth that emanated from wherever the two of them sat. She figured it must be nice to live like that; the image of them asleep on their sofa, snuggled together like dormice, was one that would stay with her.

With a hot cup of tea in her grip, she took up residence on the sofa, pulled up the soft blanket and once again opened up her laptop to look at the photograph Sarah had sent her, the only one she had, until this weekend, when many more had been snapped at just about every opportunity. But this was the one she wanted to look at right now. She stared at the woman who shared her blood and her heritage, the woman who was broken, thin and desperate. And the hand of Prim, her beloved Prim, cupping the baby's head, keeping her safe, protected, doing her very best to find a way through the mess, to figure out the best outcome for the baby Sarah was carrying. A steadying hand that was no doubt scared, and yet so proud, protective, because despite her best efforts, she knew something bad was around the corner . . .

Me . . . that's me . . . I am that little baby . . . It was a painful thing for her to grasp.

She pictured her gran, possibly sitting on this very sofa with a pen in her hand, writing the letters to Sarah – knowing that to give that baby the best chance, the stability Prim believed she needed, it meant sacrificing her own daughter.

'You did that for me . . . you did that for me . . .' She wept as she again went back to the beginning and read the letters through once more.

Victoria was unaware that sleep had claimed her, but clearly it had, as a knocking on the front door woke her mid-morning. She jumped up and rubbed her eyes into wakefulness, before putting the letters on the table and racing to the door, trying to look as fresh-faced as possible in case it was Gerald. The last thing she wanted was for him to think she had returned to her slatternly ways and had fallen asleep on the sofa in her clothes. Even though that was precisely what she had done.

As she pulled the front door wide, she felt the smile slip from her face and transform into a cold scowl.

'Hi, Victoria.'

Flynn. She noticed how he preferred to look at the toes of his grubby trainers than into her eyes. The coward.

'What do you want?' she snapped, walking forward to block the doorway and placing her folded arms across her chest, making it very clear that he would never set foot inside her home again.

'I just wanted to, erm . . . I just wanted to say . . .' He took a deep breath and swallowed. 'I just wanted to say that I'm sorry.'

'For what?'

'What?' He looked up at her now, perplexed.

'I am curious as to what it is exactly you are apologising for?'

'Erm . . .' Again he floundered.

'Let me help you out, Flynn. Are you saying sorry for lying to me? Making out to be interested in me? Taking my virginity, like it was nothing? Or that bloody party, perhaps? Or having sex with Courtney in my dead grandmother's bed after stealing the key I'd hidden in the plant pot? Or for just generally being a total prick? Or is it something else altogether? Like, did you forget to put your dirty mug in the dishwasher, or maybe leave one of your little drug sticks on the floor of the garden room for Gerald, "*the courgettes guy*", to find?'

Not only did it seem she had lost the inane desire to giggle in his presence, she had also apparently found her voice. And that voice was loud and assertive, that of a woman who was not going to be curtailed by sadness but had taken the reins of her life and was going to steer her future.

He looked up at her. 'All of it, I guess.' He kicked at the gravel. 'Can I come in?' He looked past her into the hallway and she gave a dry, genuine laugh.

'No. No, you can't come in. Jesus!' She tutted.

'I also wanted to say goodbye before I left for Newcastle.' He stared at her, seemingly waiting for a reply that never came. 'And I wanted to say that I don't really know what happened. I thought the party would be a good laugh, but it wasn't, was it?'

'No. It was not a "good laugh"!' She shook her head at his piti-ful explanation.

'And I didn't make out to like you. I *did* like you. I *do* like you. I really do, you are cool, you are different, and if I hadn't been drunk . . .'

'Oh, pur-lease!' She rolled her eyes. 'Don't you dare!'

'It's the truth! I never planned it! I never wanted to hurt you. I liked it when it was just you and me here, eating noodles . . . but I guess it doesn't matter now.'

'It doesn't.' She sighed, slightly irritated, if anything.

'You said it was just sex.' He swallowed.

'That's right, Flynn. Just sex.'

He looked up and took a deep breath. 'And I wanted to say thank you for letting me stay here with you for a few days. I was wrong. This isn't an old-lady house: it's a wonderful house. The nicest I have ever been in. Not the stuff in it, but the way it feels. I think it must have been a very nice house to grow up in and I think you're very lucky.'

She cursed the thickening of her throat and the tears that pricked the back of her eyes. Flynn wasn't quite finished.

'And I know you don't care what I think—'

'I don't,' she interjected.

'But I think your mum coming back from the dead is the most amazing thing I have ever heard. I lied to you about Michael junior. I do care. I think about him all the time. I wonder how it was possible that I got a whole life and he only got a couple of years. It's not fair, is it?'

'No, Flynn.' She gave him the beginning of a reserved smile, recognising that he, like her, was a passenger in a life where events unfurled that were way, way beyond your control. 'It's not fair.'

'And I know that if my mum and dad could have him back, they would jump at it. It would be all their dreams and wishes come true.'

All she could do was nod and bite down on her lips.

'Well,' she sniffed, 'good luck in Newcastle.'

'Thanks.' He gave her that lopsided smile that made her heart flex, just a little bit.

'And happy birthday for the eleventh.'

'How did you know my birthday was coming up?'

He looked surprised. 'I used to stalk you on Facebook. For years, in fact.'

This made him laugh cautiously, and he looked up into the bright morning sky, where birds flew overhead, possibly after refilling at the last bird service station before the motorway, stocking up on two different types of sweet, an out-of-date chicken salad sandwich and a compilation CD of crappy covers.

'I . . . I don't know what happened with Courtney,' he stammered. 'I regret it, I really do, and I am sorry, Victoria. I never wanted to hurt you. I think you are brilliant. You are cool. I was looking for you, I swear. I went upstairs, and there she was on the landing, and she just looked at me and . . .'

'Let me guess: your pants fell off?'

'Something like that!' He laughed, and raised his palms as if it had been quite beyond his control.

'Don't worry, Flynn. It's her superpower.'

Victoria spent the day cleaning the house and pottering in the garden with a new and profound sense of calm that was most welcome. She was, for the first time, able to walk into the garden room and see the beautiful display of orchids nestling along the back wall, rising up to give colour and form to the pale brickwork, and not the image of Prim slumped in the steamer chair with her head lolling to one side. She also felt lighter. Flynn's words might have been too little too late, but they did have an effect on her and, despite her best efforts, she knew she would be unable to hold a grudge against him. If anything, she felt sorry for him. Flynn McNamara, the boy of her dreams, who had turned out to be just a boy; a boy who, like her, had his secrets. Who didn't?

Her phone rang. It was Daksha.

'Just checkin' in, little miss.' Her tone was nonchalant.

'Hey, Daks!'

'I was thinking, do you want me to come and sit with you, Vic? I could bring some lunch? Or we could bake?'

'Daks, my lovely friend, today I want to be alone.'

'You . . . you want to be alone? Oh . . . I just thought . . .' It was rare for her to hear Daksha at a loss for words.

'I love you, Daksha, I really love you, but I need to pull up my big-girl pants and cook my own food and sleep in my house, alone. I need to be mature: an industrious coper, the very best kind of person!' She heard Prim's voice in her ear, '*That's my girl . . .*' and she smiled, *That's right, I am your girl . . .*

'Okay, doll, but you know where I am if you need me.'

'I do. Thanks, Daks. See you at the weekend?'

'You bet.'

As dusk fell on the day, Victoria sat on the veranda in one of Grandpa's old chairs with the double duvet wrapped around her. It sat snugly over her clothes and, with a red, moth-eaten woolly hat on her head, which she had found in Prim's gardening trug, she was, despite the chill of the October night, warm and cosy. The fact that she looked a little peculiar didn't bother her – it was, after all, highly unlikely anyone could see her here in the back garden of the detached house as she sat looking over the lake. She couldn't imagine what it must have been like for Prim to carry the burden of the secret her whole life, and it made her sad to think that behind the wonderful, outgoing, happy façade, the woman who had danced with her at Grandpa's funeral hid her own secret burden. Victoria would have liked to lighten it for her; it would have been the least she could do for the woman who saved her.

She fished for her phone in her pocket.

'A misdial?' Sarah answered casually.

'No! Are you ever going to let that go?'

'Not sure.' She laughed.

'I thought I'd call, as I'm sitting in one of Grandpa's old chairs by the lake.'

'Aren't you cold?'

She blew her warm breath in a plume out into the dark, inky pallet of the night sky. 'Says you, who lives in Norway!' She laughed. 'No, I have a coat on and an old hat of Prim's I found, and my duvet is wrapped around me for good measure.'

'Well, I'm stuffed on to the balcony in my pyjamas and Jens's ski socks and jacket. And I might or might not have a large glass of red wine in my other hand.'

'I'm picturing the lights on the water; I loved that view so much. I thought Oslo was beautiful.'

'And I'm picturing the big moon that hangs so low over Rosebank that on some nights it felt like I could reach up over the lake and touch it. I used to sit with Dad and gaze at it.'

'We look at the same moon . . .' Victoria whispered.

'We look at the same moon . . .' Sarah managed.

'What did we say about that crying thing?' Victoria smiled.

'I know, but it's going to take a bit of practice.' Sarah sniffed. 'Go inside, don't be cold.' Her words sounded a lot like maternal concern, and it felt nice. 'Yes, go inside and light a fire or have a warm bath. The deep bath in the bathroom on the second floor is the best, the one with a view of the oak tree. I used to spend hours lying in it.'

'I might just do that. This has been . . . nice.' She meant it, hating the inadequacy of her words. It was so much more than nice.

'It really has. And thank you, Victoria. Thank you for calling and thank you for talking to me. It means more to me than I can say. Can I call you on your birthday?' Sarah asked with a note of caution that was heartbreaking and unnecessary.

'That would be fine.'

'All right then.' Sarah sounded positively perky at the thought. 'Oh, before I forget, Vidar has been asking after you.'

'Oh yeah?' She tried to sound casual as her heart boomed in her chest. 'I like Vidar.'

'Yes, I told him as much.'

'You did not!'

'No, but I thought about it. He asked if I might give him your number. I said I would ask you first, of course.'

'I guess you could.' She tried to sound casual about it, hiding the whoop of delight in her gut at the prospect of him getting in touch.

'Okay, well, night night, Victoria.'

'Night night, Sarah.'

There was a second of silence after they stopped speaking, but the call was still connected, and it was in that moment of quiet that the most was said. It was no more than a crackle on the line, faint with their breathing, which spoke of hope, and of the future. Victoria ended the call and went inside, closing and locking the French doors behind her, expertly fixed by Bernard-the-handyman. She looked back through the glass up into the night sky.

'The same moon.' She spoke aloud and smiled.

Having clicked off the lights, she made her way up to the second-floor bathroom, where she decided to run a deep, hot bath. And as she sank under the bubbles she felt a sense of contentment that was alien to her, and with the contentment came clarity.

Victoria made a decision.

This was her one life, and she was not about to waste a second of it. She looked at the shadow of the vast oak tree outside the window and thought of her daddy's words, written by Sarah in a letter:

'. . . hate and recrimination are big things and if you let them fill you up it brings you the opposite of peace because if you hate it takes all of your energy – and that's such a waste; how can you live life weighed down like that?'

'You can't live like that, Dad, can you? You can't, and I won't.' Again, she spoke aloud, hoping her words went all the way up to heaven.

◆ ◆ ◆

It was mid-morning on October the twelfth as Victoria sat in the back of the taxi and saw the number flash up on her phone for the third time that morning.

It was Sarah. She pressed the little red icon denying the call as she sighed; to speak to her right now would be no good at all. In fact, it would ruin everything.

Messages from Daksha and Mrs Joshi had come in bright and early, along with the obligatory jokes about her age, and with birthday cake emojis tagged on for good measure. Even Gerald had popped a card in the post, which she opened, noting it was a scene of the Lake District, the same he had sent in sympathy when Prim had died. She set it on the kitchen table.

Victoria,
Rave on.
    Gerald X

It made her laugh far more than it should have. And Bernard-the-handyman had picked her a bunch of flaming orange dahlias and set them in a vase in the garden room. She liked to hear him pottering, going quietly about the chores that kept Rosebank ticking over, just as he always had.

Nineteen! She missed Prim today with an ache in her heart, knowing she would have come down the stairs to a smartly laid breakfast table and her favourite pancakes with lemon and sugar.

'I miss you, Prim.' She closed her eyes and pictured her glamorous gran.

The cab pulled over in the busy street and Victoria climbed out, hitching her carpetbag up on to her shoulder. She paid the driver before pushing on the door of the building and walking inside, where she trod the shiny marble floor and took the lift up to the fourth floor.

The first thing she noticed as she stepped out into the space was that the reception was busy. Two sofas pushed into a corner were crowded with people and a low table in front of them was home to stacks of magazines. Victoria waited for the man behind the front desk to finish his call. And she thought of Jens – the man with a list of wishes for the wife he so loved . . .

'Sorry to keep you waiting. How can I help you?'

'I am here to see Sarah Hansen.'

'Right, do you have an appointment?'

'I don't, but if you could tell her that I am here.'

The man picked up the phone, she assumed to make the call.

'Who shall I say is here?'

She looked up from the front desk and saw a glass-fronted room, and standing in it was Sarah, the shape of her so familiar, one she had known since before she was born. Sarah was busy with papers on a desk, but as if called by a sixth sense she looked up and stared through the glass. Victoria saw her reach for the edge of the desk, as if needing to steady herself.

The two held each other's gaze, and Victoria could not help the swell of tears that she did nothing to hide. Sarah, too, she noticed, although she was in her place of work, let her distress fall and yet smiled through the sadness, because she recognised what this was. It was the middle of the bridge, the place they met where the past was left behind, and from that point on they knew they would journey forward together.

Victoria's own words came back to her now, words uttered at a time when her head was spinning with confusion. *'I always thought that if it was ever possible to meet my mum, in heaven or whatever, I would run to her and fall into her arms and she would hold me tight and we'd never let each other go. And it would feel like coming home . . .'*

'Sorry, could I ask?' the man pushed. 'Who shall I say is here?'

'Can you tell her . . . tell her it's her daughter. Her daughter, Victory . . . and I'm here to see my mum.'

EPILOGUE

Victoria guessed that, for some people, the graveyard on the Ekeberg slope might be a strange destination for a family hike, but not for her. Not only was the view one of the most beautiful and worth making the climb for, but also, she had lived for so long with the lines between the living and the dead a little blurred that she felt quite at home here.

The three of them climbed the last of the incline and Victoria sat down hard on the wooden slatted bench, breathing in the clean, fresh air that invigorated. Her husband caught the edge of her coat under his bottom, trapping it against the seat. She let her eyes sweep the blue vista below, marvelling at the treeline, where the pointed green spires of the birch and spruce reached up into the sky as they stood like sentinels along the bank of the fjord. It was on a much grander scale, of course, but nonetheless reminded her of the lake at Rosebank, the family home they had sold some years ago. It had been cathartic moving on, and quite joyous selecting which pieces of art and furniture to hang and keep in their own wooden cottage with its wonderful parcel of untrained land.

'I like it up here.' Stina kicked her long legs, inherited from her pappa, against the side of the bench, sitting between her parents, who she knew liked to sit here and natter, and had been doing so since long before she was born.

'Why do you?' Victoria thought it was a strange choice for a six-year-old, who some might think would have an aversion to graveyards.

'I like the view and I like all the dead people.'

'You like all the dead people?' Victoria laughed and exchanged a look with Vidar, who raised his eyebrows.

'I think it's nice to chat to them,' her little girl explained. 'And tell them what's going on, because they can't read papers or see a computer when they are under the ground, can they?'

'No, they can't.' Vidar nodded earnestly. 'You are absolutely right. So, what would you like to tell them today? Anything in particular?'

Stina seemed to give this some thought. 'I would like to say we have nice weather.' She twirled the end of her long blonde braids, a habit that was beyond cute and something she did when she concentrated.

'Always a good talking point.' Vidar nodded his approval and Victoria felt a rush of love for the man who would never mock but always embraced his daughter's ideas and thoughts, giving her a wonderful confidence that Victoria, at the age of twenty-eight, would like a pinch of. It was just one of the reasons she loved the man she had fallen for on her nineteenth birthday, a day when she and her mum had rushed home from her office and he had been invited to a small party where four people had sat around the table in the flat across the hallway from his and eaten a very grand home-made chocolate cake as they sipped champagne. She had blown out the candles on the cake and made a wish, a wish that had come true. She twisted the gold band on the third finger of her left hand, taking comfort from it.

Vidar was a man who essentially liked her for her, *all* of her: warts and all. His love provided a kind of universal acceptance that was the greatest of comforts. And once she recognised it as love and knew she was loved in return, she stopped worrying about the future. In fact, she stopped worrying about most things, because she knew that with Vidar Larsen by her side everything would be just fine. In fact, so certain was she of that future that she had waved goodbye to him one cold, sunny day to travel the world with her best friend, Daksha. The time with her best friend, spent wandering the planet with a pack on their backs and sturdy boots on their feet, still provided some of her very best memories.

It was a great source of joy to everyone, other than Dr and Mrs Joshi, that Daksha had decided, after seeing the world, that university wasn't for her after all, puncturing their dreams of her medical career, and she now lived in the south of France, running a bakery school and patisserie with her wonderful wife, Margaux. Where cake was *always* on the menu, of course.

Stina leaned back against her and Victoria folded her form into hers like a warm and comfortable cushion. Proximity to her child made her heart beat a little faster and a smile form on her face. She might be a tutoring assistant in mathematics at Universitetet i Oslo, but being Stina's mamma was still her very best job.

'And I would also like to tell the dead people that it is not nice to make anyone eat vegetables they really don't like. And I would tell them that *Bestefar* Jens agrees with me.'

'Give it up, Stina. Firstly, *Bestefar* Jens is your grandfather and therefore agrees with whatever you say and do – you have him wrapped around your little finger; and secondly, we have talked about this – you *have* to eat vegetables!' She looked over her little girl's head and tried to stifle her laughter.

'Anyway' – Victoria reached along the back of the bench and held Vidar's hand – 'people aren't really dead if you still talk about them.' She looked down over the fjord that swept to the left. The wispy clouds seemed perfectly placed in the clear blue sky and birds, with wings stretched, hovered on the breeze, low on the water as they scanned for fish.

'Like you still talk to Prim?' Stina asked, quite matter-of-factly.

'How do you know I still talk to Prim?'

It made her laugh to hear her little girl talk so confidently about the woman she had never met, her great-grandma, who had shaped all of their lives in ways her little girl could only guess at.

'I hear you. You say things like, "*Prim, you should see Stina*" – that's me!' She touched her fingers to her chest. '"*She is so like you it's scary: a bossy little thing with her dad's beautiful blonde hair but Grandpa's twinkly eyes!*"' The funniest thing about the retelling was the way Stina put on her mum's very British accent, masking her own Scandinavian tones.

Vidar laughed. 'She's a mimic.'

'She's a horror is what she is!' Victoria leaned over and kissed her daughter on the cheek, each kiss a gift . . . It was quite unimaginable to her to think of their time being limited, knowing that one hundred and eighty kisses would never have been enough. Since becoming a mum herself, this fact had burned itself into her mind. The very idea was unthinkable, it was cruel, it was brave and it was crazy, and something she could not in a million years imagine; having to wave off her darling girl and play dead. She doubted she would ever fully understand Prim's motivation, but accepted that, as a mother herself now, she knew she would do whatever was necessary to keep Stina safe, out of harm's way.

She and Sarah had fallen in love over the years, and what they shared now was a deep friendship and a healthy respect for the journey the other had taken from the other side of the bridge. They talked daily, saw each other weekly, and she knew the novelty and joy of this contact would never wane.

Vidar squeezed her arm. '*Jeg elsker deg så mye.*' (I love you so much.)

'*Jeg elsker deg også.*' (I love you too.) 'Come on!' She stood up from the bench and yanked her coat free, wiping the damp residue from the seat of her jeans. 'We need to get home, *Mormor* Sarah has made lunch!' It was a regular occurrence, Sunday lunch with her mum and Jens, all swapping stories they had read in the weekend papers and laughing, laughing, and laughing some more, because life was so damn good!

'Sarah won't mind if we are a bit late,' Stina asserted, and again she and Vidar laughed.

A couple walked by, a boy and a girl, hand in hand, stopping only to kiss and then resume their stroll again.

'Yuck!' Stina said, without paying attention to her volume.

Vidar gave his now familiar eye roll and took her hand. 'Come on, you.'

Victoria watched her beautiful husband and her little girl start the descent to the main road, where they would jump on a tram. They always took the tram. I mean, who would ever choose a car over the tram?

'It's not yuck, baby girl!' she called after them. 'I love to see people in love. I think it is one of the most hopeful sights known to man. I think as long as people love one another, then there is hope.'

'Hope for what?' Stina asked, with that perfect little wrinkle to the top of her nose, this pretty little girl who was born full chip.

'For everything!' Victoria beamed. 'For absolutely everything.'

BOOK CLUB QUESTIONS

Discuss whether it is ever okay to tell a big lie in the way that Prim did.

How did you feel about Sarah coming back into Victoria's life? Do you think she had the right to do that?

Discuss the conflict that Victoria must have inevitably felt – how would you advise her?

This book made me lament the loss of letter-writing in this world of email and push-button communication. Have you kept any precious letters and, if so, why?

I know I would have really liked a friend like Daksha. Did you ever have friend like that and, if so, how did she help you through a hard time?

I think this book proves that home is not always a place; home can be a person too. Discuss.

Do you think Victory would have had a better life had Sarah not turned up and she had lived none the wiser? Which would you prefer?

I love the way that Stina's personality reflects that of the grandma she never knew. Has this happened in your family? Is there anyone who is the absolute embodiment of someone they never knew?

I love the way Sarah and Victoria both had such precious memories of Rosebank; I still find it hard to drive past our old family home and see someone else living in it – tell me I'm not the only one.

ABOUT THE AUTHOR

Photo © 2012 Paul Smith of Paul Smith Photography at
www.paulsmithphotography.info

Amanda Prowse likens her own life story to those she writes about
in her books. After self-publishing her debut novel *Poppy Day* in
2011, she has gone on to author twenty-five novels, six novellas
and a memoir about depression co-authored with her son, Josiah
Hartley. Her books have been translated into a dozen languages and
she regularly tops bestseller charts all over the world. Remaining
true to her ethos, Amanda writes stories of ordinary women and
their families who find their strength, courage and love tested in
ways they never imagined. The most prolific female contempo-
rary fiction writer in the UK, with a legion of loyal readers, she
goes from strength to strength. Being crowned 'queen of domestic

drama' by the *Daily Mail* was one of her finest moments. Amanda is a regular contributor on TV and radio but her first love is, and will always be, writing.

You can find her online at www.amandaprowse.com, on Twitter or Instagram @MrsAmandaProwse, and on Facebook at: www.facebook.com/AmandaProwseAuthor.